THE ASSASSINATION OF MOZART

A

THE ASSASSINATION OF MOZART

by

David Weiss

HODDER AND STOUGHTON

FOR
WOLFGANG AMADEUS MOZART

Contents

CONTENTS

Chapter		Page

A Letter

Dear Mozart
Do not judge us
Unless you know us

Dear Mozart
You cannot know us
Unless we trust you
And show ourselves
Show
Ourselves to you

Dear Mozart
We
Cannot trust you
You will blame us

Ours
Are strange ways
Imposed on us
By human instinct
And grow stranger
Grow
Stranger

Dear Mozart
Human instinct killed you
We did not
We are merely an instrument
Merely
Its
Instrument

Dear Mozart
Save yourself   Save
We cannot save you
Nor save ourselves
Nor save

A

Dear Mozart
This is
What truth was
And will become
And always be

Ever yours

        Ever   Ever
          yours

                                    Stymean Karlen

1

The Death of Mozart

O N December 5th, 1791, at five minutes to one upon a Monday
morning, Wolfgang Amadeus Mozart died.

Doctor Closset, who attended him, diagnosed his fatal illness as,
"without any doubt, a severe military fever."

The head of the General Hospital of Vienna, Doctor von Sallaba,
whom Doctor Closset called in for consultation, said positively,
"Mozart died of a deposit in his head."

The death register of St. Stephen's Cathedral, where Mozart just
had been appointed Deputy Kapellmeister, stated that his decease was
caused by *"a violent grippe with a high fever."*

A Doctor Guldern, who did not attend the dying man but who was a
friend of Doctor Closset, declared that the circumstances of the
musician's illness clearly proved that "Mozart died of a *rheumatic
inflammatory fever.*"

The court obituary announced that the third Royal and Imperial
Kapellmeister had died *"of a dropsy of the heart."*

But all the medical symptoms indicated that he had died *"of kidney
failure."*

Antonio Salieri, Vienna's most famous composer and the first Royal
Kapellmeister, was reported to have said upon hearing the news of his
rival's death, "Good riddance—otherwise we would all have been
breadless in a short time. The cause of death? Well, we all know he was
a libertine. Look at *Don Giovanni!*"

Mozart's wife, Constanze, denied this indignantly and said,
"Months before he died, he began to feel unwell and to be possessed
with the notion that he was dying. And when he was asked to write a

Requiem under the most mysterious circumstances, he came to believe that it was for himself."

A Viennese newspaper asked her: "There are rumors that your husband did not believe he was ill of natural causes?"

"That is true," she answered. "Many times those last few weeks he cried out in the darkness of the night that someone was trying to kill him."

"Who?"

"He had many relentless enemies who pursued him to his death."

Less than three months after Mozart's death, Emperor Leopold II died; and since it was known that he had relentless enemies, too, it was rumored that he, like Mozart, had not died a natural death.

Now the rumors spread. A musical newspaper wrote: "It is well known that Mozart returned home ill from the Prague production of his *La Clemenza di Tito* and grew steadily worse. It was thought that he had *the water sickness*; but when his corpse began to swell up after death, it was thought that he could have been poisoned."

But no autopsy could be taken, for the body had vanished.

There were whispers that Herr Mozart had fallen out of favor with the Court, that his devotion to Freemasonry had created much hostility, that his caustic criticism of his contemporaries had antagonized them, and that Antonio Salieri, in particular, had profited most from the death of Mozart. And now, without question, Salieri was first among all the musicians of Vienna.

Yet the rumors that Mozart had been poisoned increased.

Friends of Salieri, who had become the teacher of Beethoven and Schubert, denounced the rumors that Salieri had been involved in the death of Mozart as a gross injustice to a great man and a great musician—Salieri. They stated that poor little Mozart had died from poverty and overwork, and childhood illnesses and profligate living.

Defenders of Mozart replied that he had been too poor to afford dissipation, and that none of his childhood illnesses had revealed any sign of a kidney ailment. Further investigation found no evidence of a kidney condition or any chronic illness during the last years of Mozart's life.

But as the facts about his final sickness accumulated, the symptoms indicated that his kidneys had been affected. He had had fits of dizziness and fainting, but he had continued to compose until the last day of his life; his body had swelled, he had had boils, nausea, headaches, and hallucinations. He had had all the symptoms of a kidney damaged by poison.

And Mozart thought he had been poisoned.

2

The Death of Salieri

NEWSPAPER REPORT. VIENNA, 1823. AUTUMN: "Antonio Salieri, First Royal Kapellmeister in the Imperial Court, has confessed to having poisoned Mozart."

NEWSPAPER REPORT. VIENNA, 1823. SEVERAL DAYS LATER: "Salieri's mind has failed after his confession to his priest, and he has attempted to cut his throat."

NEWSPAPER REPORT. VIENNA, 1823. THE NEXT AFTERNOON: "The First Royal Kapellmeister's effort at suicide has failed, and, at the Imperial command, he has been committed to an asylum."

BEETHOVEN'S "KONVERSATIONSHEFTE." NOVEMBER, 1823: Johann Schickl, a friend of Beethoven's, informed the deaf composer of the latest news by writing in the latter's conversation book: "Salieri has admitted poisoning Mozart after all, and in his guilt he has cut his throat, but he is still alive."

BEETHOVEN ANSWERED: "I still, voluntarily, style myself *'Salieri's pupil'.*"

JOHANN SCHICKL REPLIED IN THE "KONVERSATIONSHEFTE": "Even so, the odds are a hundred to one that Salieri's conscience has spoken the truth. Virtually everybody in Vienna agrees with me. The manner of Mozart's death confirms Salieri's confession."

BEETHOVEN RESPONDED ANGRILY: "Gossip! Salieri taught me more than anyone else."

JOHANN SCHICKL WROTE IN THE "KONVERSATIONSHEFTE": "More than Mozart?"

BEETHOVEN SAID: "Mozart was dead when I needed him."

AN IMPERIAL ANNOUNCEMENT MONTHS LATER—JUNE 14, 1824: "After

fifty years of faithful service to the Crown, His Majesty is pleased to allow Antonio Salieri to retire on his full salary."

BEETHOVEN TRIUMPHANTLY TOLD HIS NEPHEW THE NEXT DAY: "I am right. Salieri is vindicated. He is simply unwell."

KARL VAN BEETHOVEN ANSWERED IN HIS UNCLE'S "KONVERSATION-SHEFTE": "Quite unwell, no doubt. The Emperor supports Salieri to conceal any injustice a Hapsburg may have done to Mozart, but all the reports say that Salieri still maintains that he poisoned Mozart."

BEETHOVEN REPLIED WITH A BURST OF RAGE, BUT A FEW MINUTES LATER HE ASKED HIS FRIEND ANTON SCHINDLER, HOW SALIERI WAS.

ANTON SCHINDLER WROTE IN BEETHOVEN'S "KONVERSATIONSHEFTE": "Salieri is very ill again. He is quite deranged. In his ravings he keeps claiming that he is guilty of Mozart's death. That is the truth, for he wants to confess it. And so everything has its reward."

THE ALLEGEMEINE MUSIKALISCHE ZEITUNG. AUTUMN, 1824: "No one can see Salieri; two keepers are with him day and night."

BEETHOVEN'S "KONVERSATIONSHEFTE." THE SAME DAY: Asked to write something for Mozart's anniversary, he wanted to know about Salieri's condition.

KARL VAN BEETHOVEN WROTE IN HIS UNCLE'S "KONVERSATIONSHEFTE": "Even more people claim very forcefully that Salieri was Mozart's murderer."

HIS UNCLE SHOUTED: "Fool, what about my teacher's health?"

ANTON SCHINDLER ADDED IN THE "KONVERSATIONSHEFTE": "He is mad. All he talks about is Mozart. He is full of despair."

THE ALLEGEMEINE MUSIKALISCHE ZEITUNG. APRIL, 1825: "Our worthy Salieri, sadly, just can't die. His body suffers all the pains of infirm old age, and his mind is gone. In the frenzy of his imagination he is even said to accuse himself of complicity in Mozart's early death: a rambling of the mind believed in truth by no other than the poor deluded old man himself. To Mozart's contemporaries it is unfortunately all too well known that only overexertion at his work, and fast living in ill-chosen company, shortened his precious days!"

NEWSPAPER REPORT. VIENNA. MAY 1, 1825: "It is said that Antonio Salieri's confession is in a Vienna church archive."

NEWSPAPER REPORT. VIENNA. THE NEXT DAY: "The church denies that any such confession exists."

NEWSPAPER REPORT. VIENNA. MAY 7, 1825: "Salieri has died. The Emperor has decreed that all the Royal musical establishments be closed in tribute to Maestro Salieri's services to the Crown."

3

The Question

"I Wolfgang Amadeus Mozart, sometimes known as the Wunderkind and sometimes as a performer and as a composer, believe that I have been poisoned. Ever since I returned to Vienna from Prague in September after the opening of my opera La Clemenza di Tito, for the Emperor, I have been ill. Then after I was Antonio Salieri's guest for dinner, my pains were so severe I could hardly breathe. And now I am dizzy all the time, I have fainted twice today, and my body has begun to swell. My fingers are so sore that I cannot play, but whoever I speak to about this matter regards my fears that I have been poisoned as hallucinations.

Sussmayer, my pupil and assistant, says I am worried because I am having trouble finishing my Requiem; my wife, Constanze, says it is because I am apprehensive about my debts; my doctor laughs at me. Only my dear sister-in-law Sophie seems to believe me, and even she does not seem sure. To whom can I turn? I am a rational man, but no one takes me seriously. Yet I am having such dreadful dreams and pains. I can only interpret that something terrible is happening to me.

Have I been abandoned by everybody?"

Jason Otis finished saying that to himself, and suddenly these words were as real as if Mozart had written them and as if they were not a product of his own imagination. And Mozart could have inscribed them, he was certain of that. Yet when Jason stared at the mahogany desk where he had been trying to compose a new hymn, there were no notes in front of him, nor were there any words either. Perhaps it was *he* who was having the hallucinations. The only objects on his writing desk and its shiny surface were the two letters that had been awaiting him when he had returned to his home in Boston.

Yet the words "*I, Wolfgang Amadeus Mozart*" and what had followed remained vividly in his mind. His friend and music teacher, elderly Otto Muller, who had known both Mozart and Salieri intimately, had told him much about the two men since he had become acquainted with Mozart's music the past year. The Viennese musician, who had been their contemporary, was sceptical about the official account of Mozart's death. "Some of us," Muller had told Jason, "cannot forget that no one knows where the grave is, that the body vanished in spite of Mozart's prominence. I keep asking myself: To what extent was a murderous mind responsible? In Vienna I was told that this question was unanswerable. But is it, Herr Jason? If I were younger . . ."

I am, thought Jason. I have the wish, the energy, but do I have the will? Yet every time he reviewed the chain of events which had led to the death of Mozart, he had the urge to investigate. Or did he perceive more than was visible? Was the intensity of his own emotions merely a desperate need to be *a Mozart*?

Abruptly, as if he could not endure where his reflections were leading him, Jason itemized his surroundings as if that would return him to reality. He lived in a small brick house and this chamber was drawing room, living room, and music room all in one and was dominated by his pianoforte, writing desk, and fireplace.

But he was still stirred by discontent. Ever since he had become involved in the question, his imagination had been inhabited by different presences and he had desired to go back to an existence that no longer was. Was there something supernatural near him? A communication from beyond the grave? A need to be revenged?

Jason walked to the window to remove this past that was seeking to drug him and stared at the city of Boston. Fifty years ago, during the lifetime of Mozart, a revolution had begun here. Yet no one seemed to care about that any more. Boston was prouder of its newly paved streets and sewerage system, and the fact that now only the poor neighborhoods littered their gutters with garbage. Another virtuous civic improvement was the numbers marking the houses, but Vienna had possessed that for many years. Jason was pleased that Boston recently had acquired a pianoforte manufacturer, Joseph Chickering, and he no longer had to order the instrument from abroad or New York. He stared at the churches which showed the influence of the Englishman Christopher Wren, but then, he thought cynically, everything in Boston was molded by old men who remembered lovingly when England had been the mother country and were forgetful of parturition, as if that had never occurred. It was only the young men like himself who believed in separation from the Old World.

Except for Mozart. Ever since Jason had heard Mozart's music and had compared it to his own, he had been deeply dissatisfied with himself and he had had to disinter the man. He turned back to the two letters that had been awaiting him and reread them. The first had delighted him; the second had appalled him.

The Handel and Haydn Society of Boston, the most important musical organization in America—by its own admission, he thought wryly—had written:

Jason Otis, Esquire:
    We are offering Herr Ludwig van Beethoven a commission to compose an oratorio for our Society, which should please Herr

Beethoven, since it is a great honor to be performed by the Handel and Haydn Society of Boston. Hitherto, we have only performed oratorios by Mr. Handel and Herr Haydn, both dead. And if you are proceeding with your plans to visit Vienna, the Society has graciously allowed you to present this commission to Herr Beethoven in person, in recognition for the services you have rendered the Society.

Considering the self-importance of the Society, this was a compliment, he realized, and yet it was depressing. Otto Muller had played the pianoforte sonatas of Beethoven for him, in addition to sonatas by Mozart, and although he had been most stirred by Mozart's music, he had been impressed with Beethoven's power and originality.

But the musical fathers of Boston had no true awareness of either composer; they were interested in Beethoven because *he* would bring publicity to their organization. They had no ear; they could not even tell when Jason borrowed from other composers, a common custom. Yet if they paid part of his fare to Vienna, that, at least, would be useful.

The letter from Otto Muller was a different matter. He reread it aloud, as if that would ease its terrible import.

Dear Herr Otis:

What we have talked about many times seems to have come true. My brother in Vienna has written me the following:

"There are many reports in the city that Salieri has admitted to poisoning Mozart, that he confessed this to a priest, and afterwards, shocked by the enormity of what he had done, his mind cracked, he sought to cut his throat, and he has been committed to an asylum.

"Thus, this confirms what we had suspected for many years. You remember, dear brother, how we, at the time of our beloved Mozart's death, wondered about the circumstances, the suddenness of it, the coming just when his future and financial success were assured with the public's enthusiasm for *The Magic Flute,* and above all, that no one was at the cemetery and the way the body vanished without a trace, as if the evidence had to be destroyed.

"It was very strange. But none of us dared speak, for fear of offending the authorities, and even today, in spite of Salieri's confession, it is said that it could be dangerous to discuss the affair publicly. Everyone seems to prefer that matters stay as they are, for Mozart, now that he is dead, is the idol of the Viennese.

"They say, 'Isn't that enough!' But if I were not so old and tired, I would look into it."

Otto Muller had concluded, "So you see, my dear Herr Otis, we are not alone in our doubts."

It was eleven-thirty in the morning. If he hurried he could talk to Muller before the latter took his afternoon nap. They had left Mozart sprawled in a ditch, he thought bitterly, but he could not leave him where they had thrown him. He was certain now that the words that he had imagined a few minutes ago were true.

The carriage that bore him to Beacon Hill seemed much too slow this winter day and he wondered where the coachman's eyes were, for several times they almost went into the gutter. Muller expected him, for the elderly musician had put off his nap.

His house was an oasis to Jason. Although it was in the heart of Boston, Muller's spacious music salon was a summons back to Vienna. Whenever Jason was within its walls, it drew him inexorably to the one city that was—for him—Mozartian.

Each day he came it was his pilgrimage. He loved the landscape: the clavichord, harpsichord, pianoforte, and organ placed about the chamber like sweet-sounding gods. In Boston, he reflected, it was assumed that the greater the elegance the less the virtue—luxury was regarded as kingly and austerity as democratic—but he was always excited by Muller's heavy drapes and tapestries, which were a royal red to match the upholstered chairs, a reminder of the Hofburg Palace where Muller had played, and of the past he was so deeply involved in.

Muller lit a brace of candles, for the sky had become gray, and he put them on his graceful and elaborately carved oak table, and said, "We have much to discuss. Do you want to read my brother's letter?"

"No, Herr Muller, I trust what you quoted."

"You shouldn't." He pulled out a silver snuffbox, took a pinch, and handed him his brother's letter. "Trust no one in such affairs."

This was a tone that Muller loved. Jason wondered whether the old musician liked intrigue for intrigue's sake. Muller wore an ancient gray wig and a long waistcoat with silver buckles, as if he could not discard the past, although these clothes were out of fashion now. He was almost seventy-four, but still full of life. It gave him joy to say, "I was born the year old Sebastian Bach died, seventeen hundred and fifty." For Otto Muller considered himself a music historian as well as a teacher, composer, conductor, and performer. He was proud that he could play the pianoforte, violin, organ, harpsichord, clavichord, clarinet, and oboe. He was the only oboist in North America, he enjoyed reminding Jason, and in his own opinion the only truly professional musician in Boston.

Consequently Jason accepted Muller's pendulous cheeks and deeply indented wrinkles as scars honorably earned, and while his short, heavy body was very round-shouldered now and each year it seemed to be returning more and more to the foetal position, when he sat at his pianoforte he was erect and vital, his blue eyes shining.

But now, as Jason read his brother's letter, Muller looked sad and worn. Jason was grateful that he could read German and he agreed with the way Muller had translated his brother's words. Yet he could not tell him how intensely Mozart had penetrated his self, of his desperate need to put himself in the *Wunderkind's* place. He had been a *Wunderkind* himself, playing the pianoforte at the age of five and composing his first hymn when he had been fifteen.

When he finished the letter, he felt full of monstrous half answers. He had the sudden feeling that Salieri, in his sickness, was crying out *in extremis,* crying out for help. Was that the truth of it, he wondered. But already, he had assumed that Salieri had the soul of a pig. He hesitated.

Muller said, "I cannot answer your questions. You will have to find out elsewhere, in Vienna probably, or in New York or in England."

Would that bring him contentment?

Muller asked suddenly, "What music would you like to hear?"

This was a ritual they always followed when Jason came to study composition, and he replied, as he always had since he had become acquainted with Mozart, "A piano sonata. By Mozart." The ritual had become almost as precious as the music itself. Then as Muller hobbled toward the pianoforte, unable to walk properly without his cane, it occurred to Jason that if Mozart were alive today he might be hobbling also. And his mind dwelled on the moment he had first felt love for him.

It had begun with a chain of circumstances, which in their own way had startled Jason as much as the unfolding events that had led him to believe that Mozart could have been poisoned.

One Sunday in church a year ago, as Jason was trying to decide whether it was sensible to continue to compose religious music when no one seemed to want to play it, although only sacred music was played publicly in Boston, he was accosted by Professor Elisha Whitney, the Handel and Haydn Society's director of music.

Professor Whitney led Jason out of the spacious new red-brick church so they could talk privately. The music director was like a small old tortoise, moving laboriously, and when he stepped into the bright sun he blinked, as if it were too much for eyes worn out from poring over ancient scores. He had some animation, however, as he asked, "You pursue music, I believe, as an avocation?"

"Yes, sir."

"You are wise. To depend on music to support oneself is dangerous. But I am happy to see that you have not been idle. The collection of sacred music that you have compiled and submitted to the Society reveals that you have been industrious."

Jason wondered whether Deborah would be angry over his failure to meet her, as he did every Sunday. She had a quick, sharp temper. And he could not say he was ill, for she had seen him.

The wizened professor was too pleased with himself to notice his listener's disquiet. "You have given expression to deeply devout feelings. Your hymns speak harmoniously of the glory of God."

"Thank you, sir."

"You have also skilfully avoided novelty and an excess of innovation. You are conversant with public taste."

"Then you approve of my work, Professor Whitney?"

"Indeed. It is neither frivolous nor familiar."

Nor should it be, Jason thought triumphantly. When he had entered the field of original composition with his compilation of church music, he had gone to the best sources for his melodies. He had used the sacred music of Handel and Haydn for his foundations, and thus, he was confident that he had constructed hymns of genuine worth. Yet no one should recognize their origin, since secular music was never played in public in Boston.

Elisha Whitney declared, "I am a very good judge of character. You have composed as a gentleman as well as a musician."

"I am honored by your good opinion of me, sir."

"And of your music. We must not forget your music, young man."

"Are you going to play one of my hymns, sir?"

Elisha Whitney took Jason by the arm, as if, suddenly, they were old friends, and maneuvered him until they were behind the church and out of sight and hearing. Then he exclaimed, "I have better use for your music than that! I am recommending that your compilation of sacred melodies be published and issued as *The Boston Handel and Haydn Society Collection of Church Music*."

"All of the hymns I submitted to you?" Jason was astonished.

"Yes. But we will not put your name on the Collection. Then our members will have the opportunity to be unbiased."

Jason saw Deborah driving away in her carriage and pair. He looked at the director with pained, searching eyes, and said, "I won't be paid either?"

"Oh, indeed! If we sell the Collection of Church Music to all the members of our three churches, you could realize as much as five hundred dollars a year."

"Whose name will go on the Collection, sir?"

"The Society's. After all, as a bank officer, you would not wish to be known as a musical man."

He was a teller, actually, but perhaps Elisha Whitney was right.

"You must not be emotional, young man. If the music has the Society's name on it our members will purchase it, but if it has yours on it no one will want it. You must prove yourself first."

"Do I have to keep it secret from everyone, Professor?"

Elisha Whitney smiled. "Do not worry. Deborah Pickering's father, the vice-president of our Society, has been informed of our interest in your music. You are fortunate to have such a gentleman as a possible father-in-law. Many young men must envy your prospects. You could become one of our leading bankers."

It was bitterly cold outside the Pickering mansion and it was starting to snow, yet Jason hesitated, feeling that Deborah would never understand his desire to be a composer—he would have to pretend it was a superficial interest. Then, overcome with a sudden longing to be near her, he climbed the double flight of marble steps.

At this point he felt resolute and brave, but he did not admire her father's efforts to imitate an English manor house. He was surprised to see Quincy Pickering waiting for him in the drawing room, too, as if they had assumed his visit was inevitable, for her father was not one to waste time.

Unable to disentangle Deborah from her father in this instant, he saw them as opposite sides of the same coin. Deborah was tall, dark, and finely proportioned, but her Elizabethan white collar and her severity gave her lovely face her father's arrogant reserve.

Quincy Pickering, who was even taller than his daughter, had the tightest mouth Jason had ever seen. It looked like a purse that never opened, yet he seemed to care only for money. It was the only feature that was not attractive. Quincy Pickering was considered a handsome man, for his other features were regular and he possessed an impressive Roman nose and a strong, sharp chin and deep gray eyes that were regarding Jason sternly now. Apparently he had been lecturing Deborah but now he waited for Jason to speak.

Jason wondered how to begin. He remembered her father's declaration, "If I had the power I would forever banish from America all gold, silver, precious stones, silk, and velvet." Yet Pickering was proud of the muslins he imported from England and Deborah had all the frocks a young lady could desire. And the Pickering drawing room was one of the most luxurious in Boston, with fine woodwork, a superb crystal chandelier, and new furniture in the latest English style.

"I am sorry I am late." Jason began, "but . . ."

"We know," interrupted Pickering. "You had business with Elisha Whitney. He informed me."

Jason sensed criticism in both of them; yet Pickering stood under a portrait of Handel and between busts of Julius Caesar and the Duke of Wellington, and perhaps, as vice-president of the Society, he was more sympathetic than he appeared.

"I thought you would both be pleased by my good news. It is an honor, isn't it?" ventured Jason.

Deborah said, "That is no excuse to break our appointment."

Her father said, "I had no idea you were serious about music."

"I was trained for it, sir. My father was a musician as well as a schoolmaster, and I attended singing school, and he taught me to play the pianoforte and the harpsichord and to compose."

"I know about your ability to perform," said Pickering. "You do that agreeably. But Deborah never told me that you *wrote* music."

"Father, you said that no one could trust a banker who could not control his interest in music."

"It has no value in Boston."

"Sir, you are vice-president of the Handel and Haydn Society."

"I have been given many honors. And they need one practical man to keep their accounts straight."

And it was good business, Jason decided. Now he realized that his composing had become a very serious matter indeed.

Pickering said abruptly, "Deborah, you should cancel your engagement!"

"Father, Jason and I love each other!"

"Because he taught you how to play the pianoforte. What rubbish! It simply provided you with something to do."

But Deborah had never looked more beautiful, and now, provoked by the passion of her statement, Jason felt that he truly loved her.

She said, "I am positive that Jason realizes how impossible it is to be both a banker and a musician."

"I am just a teller, dear."

"You could be much more if you put your mind to it."

That was unfair, Jason thought. He was not being stupid. He needed no reminder of her father's ability to promote him or to dismiss him.

"Father, he knows that he cannot make a living from his music."

"I doubt that he agrees with you. But when I began—as an errand boy and not as a teller, mind you—I devoted myself to nothing else. I would never have been able to found my own bank and become its president if I had devoted myself to other pursuits, especially such trivial ones."

"He will listen to reason. He knows where his duty is."

Deborah clasped Jason by the hand, but he felt no gentleness in her. She liked to assume the guise of a delicate creature, he thought, as if she were as defenseless as a butterfly, when actually she had the strength of a hawk, with a proud and imperious will. Sometimes he wondered what she saw in him.

It was a question she often asked herself. She sensed what he was thinking; it was one of the bonds between them, although occasionally it proved embarrassing, when they were being critical of each other.

Perhaps it was that Jason was so attractive, she assured herself. Not tall enough—she was taller by several inches—but his fair skin, blond hair, mobile face and hands, his musical speaking voice, and blue eyes, which were the brightest she knew, had a peculiar influence on her. They stirred her sensually. There were moments she yearned to give herself to him heart and soul. Then, his breath was always clean—a rarity: he was not a tobacco chewer or a whiskey drinker. He walked well, he stood well, he danced well, he was not round-shouldered like many of the young men she met, but firmly built. What was of considerable importance, his lips were not thin and compressed like her father's but full, red, and sensual. And since she had wealth and was unwed and the proper age, twenty-two, while he was appealing and promising and twenty-three, why shouldn't she marry him? With Jason, she was positive that she could have her own way, yet she also believed there was a spark in him that in an amorous embrace would be fiery, perhaps even ferocious, an idea she relished. Her father assumed that the creating of children was the only proper function of the conjugal bed; but she could not endure the thought of being a virgin much longer, and for a girl of her background and breeding there was no alternative to marriage. They did attract each other intensely; she could tell by the way he reacted to her touch. Such indiscretions were rare. Dancing with him, she sometimes wished that they would slip and he would fall squarely on top of her. She dreamt of this frequently. Only she was not certain of one thing—whether Jason loved her.

"Just imagine," she said suddenly, "having a grandson, Father."

"You are not a little girl who works below stairs," he replied. "Much has to be considered before your marriage can be arranged."

She replied, "I am sure Jason will never allow Handel and Haydn to interfere with his responsibilities at the bank."

A terrible weariness overcame Jason. Deborah had not penetrated his defenses by her charm or beauty, but by her will. He could not endure being deflated, not after Elisha Whitney had raised his hopes so high. He retorted, "I will do my job at the bank. But I will also continue to compose music."

Pickering smiled. It was the first time he had done so since Jason had entered the drawing room. He said, "I warned you, Deborah, that this young man was unreliable. It is a pity he could not do something useful. Pursuing music, he will become notorious, penniless, and have to live on the charity of friends."

"I am being dismissed for composing music in my spare time?"

"Father, Jason has done his work properly."

"I did not dismiss him. I merely pointed out what he faces. If he appears tomorrow morning promptly, he will be allowed to work."

Jason recalled Elisha Whitney's warning. He turned to both father and daughter, imploring now. "Professor Whitney said that the members of the Society must not know that it was I who composed the new hymn book, or they will not buy it. You will keep it a secret? You will not say anything about it, sir?"

Pickering said, "I would be ashamed to."

Deborah said, "So would I. Where are you going, Jason?"

"I don't know." He wondered how much his dread of poverty had influenced him to court Deborah. "I will be at the bank tomorrow."

"I won't," she said, with all the haughtiness at her command. "How on earth you can prefer music to . . .? Impossible!"

Never had Boston looked so distasteful. The harsh north-east wind from the ocean was like the slap of an enemy. The red-brick houses were dreary in their monotony. Suddenly there was only one way to turn. He felt dizzy, ill, on the verge of fainting.

To his great relief Otto Muller was home. Muller was delighted to hear that the Society was going to use Jason's music. He said, "Elisha Whitney is a pedant who is tone deaf to style, but the doctors and lawyers who are the foundation of the Society will like your tunes. They are less ponderous than what they have been listening to. Your craft is competent and you borrow skilfully."

"I . . ."

Muller halted him. "Don't apologize. No one in Boston is clever enough to detect the influence of Handel and Haydn, and I will not tell them. Do not be disconsolate. You are a workman. You compose music for the greater glory of God and to support yourself."

"Do you have any new music? That will lift my spirits?"

"The Pickerings have been critical, Herr Otis?"

"They say that music is a vain, foolish pursuit and that I am an idiot to care about it. Dear Herr Muller, am I going the wrong way?"

"Listen. Listen carefully."

Jason listened in silent wonder, for this fantasia that Muller was performing on the pianoforte was music of such surpassing beauty it made Deborah's prettiness seem like a faded pastel. It was also music that shook him, for into this fantasia came a feeling of sadness so compelling it caused him to weep. Yet however sombre the music, there was always the exquisite beauty. Long after the fantasia ended he asked himself: What kind of a human being could have composed music with such an extraordinary skill and feeling?

Muller did not utter a word, as if that would profane the moment.

"Fantastic! Unforgettable!" Jason finally exclaimed, as if he were about to burst with the emotions that had been evoked in him.

"It was by Mozart," said Muller.

Jason had never heard of Mozart.

Muller said, "He is not known in America." Then he muttered angrily, "The only music that matters in America is religious music."

Jason longed to ask many questions. He cried out, "Is he alive? Where was he born? What has he written?"

Without another word, Muller played another fantasia.

The two pieces were the most poignant moments of Jason's life. This discovery of Mozart made Columbus' discovery of America seem like a small thing. It was a revelation that he could not resist, that he did not wish to resist. As Muller played these fantasias over, Jason realized that these pieces were sustenances that he would return to time and time again for nourishment in days of darkness. The Pickerings might sneer at them, but they could not spoil them. This music was something to build a life upon! Muller had gone on to play several sonatas by the same composer, and they sang with a sweetness that had the perfection of God, of an order and a clarity that was always controlled and yet had a marvelous healing existence, with a grace that surpassed anything he had ever heard. Mozart produced melodies that impregnated him with musical sensibilities hitherto undreamt of. This was a language he could not live without. How glad he was he could hear! This was music that possessed him and that would live in him perpetually. Yet he sensed that such an attraction could be far more perilous than a love embedded in sexual appeal.

Realizing how much Jason was loving Mozart, and loving him so much himself, Muller spent the rest of the day telling his pupil about this composer. He confessed that he had intended to write a book about Mozart. He had actually begun one years ago; but there had been no interest in this musician in America, for no one knew anything about him or his music, and thus he had given up the book.

Of all the things that involved Jason, he could not free himself of his shock over the manner of Mozart's death. That such a human being could have been thrown into a common grave seemed the ultimate humiliation. He could not accept this as accidental or as an act of carelessness. And when Muller told him that Mozart had died under suspicious and contradictory circumstances and that the composer himself had thought he had been poisoned, Jason was inclined to believe him. He asked, "Did he suspect anyone in particular?"

"Yes. Antonio Salieri, his chief rival in Vienna when he was alive, and now, over thirty years after Mozart's death, still first Royal Kapellmeister to the Imperial Court of the Hapsburgs."

"What do you think, Herr Muller?"

"I have many suspicions, and I saw evidence of Salieri's hostility to Mozart; but poisoning . . . there never has been enough proof."

Jason divided the months that followed into hearing as much music by Mozart as was available, and finding out what he could about the musician's personal life, especially the circumstances of his death.

Deborah did not break off their engagement, and she continued to see him every Sunday, but there was no talk of marriage.

He still occupied his teller's cage at the bank, where her father treated him with the utmost formality. He sensed that Quincy Pickering assumed that their engagement was a thing of the past, and was willing to wait, rather than to precipitate a possible quarrel with his strong-willed daughter.

Jason did seek to instill a love of Mozart in Deborah by playing his discovery's music for her, saying, "Whatever anyone else did in music, Mozart did it better"; but he felt that the interest she displayed was artificial, for she replied, "His music is pleasant, but tinkly. You would do better to devote your time to religious music. Friends of mine inform me that the Society's new book of sacred music is in good taste and that the congregation likes it. You should persuade the Society to state that you are the author."

Shortly after she suggested this, his authorship of the Society's new collection of church music was revealed. He doubted this was because of Deborah or Quincy Pickering.

His compilation of sacred melodies—"the first that are easy to listen to as well as to sing, and very sensible of you," Elisha Whitney informed him—was popular from the moment it was published. Even churches that did not belong to the Society wanted the collection, then congregations as far away as New York, Philadelphia, and Charlestown. When it became necessary to publish a second edition, Elisha Whitney decided to put Jason Otis' name on it. The name had become useful. The professor was proud of himself; he was given credit for the discovery of this composer.

The news that a bank teller had composed such popular sacred music added to the interest in it and to its success.

Quincy Pickering never said a word about this, and Deborah assumed that it was her doing and was almost affectionate again.

A year after the Society had issued Jason's sacred music, the book had been published in seven editions, it had earned two thousand dollars for him, and it had given the Society financial stability.

On a Sunday after services, a day much like the one on which Elisha Whitney had first approached Jason, the professor asked him for a new collection of sacred music. He seemed startled when Jason hesitated.

Elisha Whitney, looking even more like a little aged tortoise, his skin resembling a dried-out shell, exclaimed, "My dear young man, we are prepared to increase your fees. Within reason."

"It is not a question of money, sir."

The professor thought, No industrious son of New England is heedless of the blessings of money, and this young man has displayed much industry in his music, but he said, "What is the difficulty?"

It was impossible to tell him that the more he heard Mozart, the more he was dissatisfied with his own work, and that he was beginning to feel that he had to visit the source of this music. He had played several sonatas of Mozart for Elisha Whitney, but the latter had been bored, declaring that they did not compare with Handel's sacred music. And he could not use Mozart's melodies for his hymns. It would be a profanation. Searching for an excuse, he blurted out, "I was thinking of a journey to the Old World. To visit various musicians in Europe." He recalled that the Society was considering asking Herr Beethoven for an oratorio.

"Do the Pickerings know of your plans to go abroad?"

"I wanted to speak to you first."

"Why?"

"I have even thought of visiting Herr Beethoven. If you could give a letter of introduction, it would be very helpful."

"He would ignore it. We have had no personal communication."

"He would not ignore a commission from the Society, sir."

But Elisha Whitney did not pursue that matter, saying, "If you should decide to visit the Old World, I would ask Quincy Pickering for a leave of absence. Many a vigorous, promising young man has sacrificed his best interests to the persistence of an illusion."

"What about the Beethoven commission?"

Jason came out of his reverie with a start. Muller had virtually shouted that in his ear, and abruptly he was back in the present. In his excitement over the news about Salieri, he had forgotten to discuss the letter from the Society. Elisha Whitney, in his own devious way, had been helpful. He said, "I may have to make some concessions."

"Once you are in Vienna, you will be able to talk to other people."

"Salieri?"

"Salieri is as good as dead. Take my word for it, no one will ever see him again."

"Then what purpose will I serve in Vienna?"

Muller took a pinch of snuff, adjusted his old-fashioned wig, fondled his silver buckles, then returned to Jason. "Herr Beethoven knew Salieri very well. Salieri was his favorite teacher. If I know his temper, he will defend his teacher vehemently."

"You are assuming that I intend to investigate Mozart's death?"

"You will never have a more favorable time. Vienna, with Salieri's confession and attempted suicide, will be full of rumors and stories. At this moment you may very well learn things hitherto hidden."

"Travelling will be hard."

"It was harder for Mozart. And the new coaches are no longer draughty and are well sprung. You will have no cause to complain."

It was silly to pretend that he was not interested. Yet . . .?

Muller said, "You may regret it if you do not go now. Many people are still alive who knew Mozart and Salieri. They may not be alive next year or the year after. My brother, Ernst, writes me that Herr Beethoven is ailing. And Ernst himself, who can tell you much about Mozart and Salieri and help you meet Herr Beethoven, is old and failing. Then there are the Weber women, the three sisters who dominated Mozart's personal life; his wife, Constanze, her older sister, Aloysia, whom he loved first—everyone knew about that—and her younger sister, Sophie, in whose arms he died. They are no longer young. Soon their memories will be dulled by age and sickness, or obliterated by death. Mozart's own sister, Nannerl, is very ill, and it is said that she will not live much longer. Yet what a fountain of information she must be! If you are truly interested in speaking to those who knew Mozart and Salieri best, you cannot afford to wait. For instance, Lorenzo da Ponte, who was close to both of them, who wrote librettos for both of them, must be almost eighty."

"Was da Ponte a countryman of Salieri's?"

"Salieri introduced him to Vienna. Da Ponte was a master of intrigue. He would know as much about Salieri and Mozart as anyone I can think of. He is living in America now, in New York."

"Would he talk to me, Herr Muller?"

"He would talk to anyone who would listen to him."

"Do you know him?"

"Everyone who was in the musical world of Vienna did. It was a small world, emotionally, marked on one side by St. Stephen's Cathedral, on the second by the Danube Canal, on the third by the Hapsburgs and their Hofburg Palace, and on the last by the Burgtheater, where most of the operas were performed."

"Did you ever see Mozart and Salieri with da Ponte?"

"Yes. But then we all see things so differently. The truth is God's rarest blessing." Muller leaned back in his red upholstered chair, which was a replica of those he had seen in the Hofburg, so silent and inert Jason was certain he had fallen asleep. Or was he having a long colloquy with himself and the past? Then suddenly he cried out, "Otis, come here!"

"Herr Muller—I am here."

"Closer. I remember during a rehearsal of *Così fan tutte* an argument about poisoning between Salieri and da Ponte."

"What were they saying?"

"They were interrupted by Mozart. He was afraid that Salieri was persuading da Ponte to leave him. Then Salieri said that *Don Giovanni* was an opera that encouraged the Devil. Mozart was quite angry, which was unusual. It took place before the orchestra."

"Who invited Salieri to the rehearsal?"

"Da Ponte, probably. They were good friends. Da Ponte was friendly with every important composer in Vienna. It used to make Mozart sad. He said that no human being could like everybody, that it was against human nature."

"How did this argument over poison end?"

"I will introduce you to the Mozart I knew. Listen."

Suddenly Jason was apprehensive. What if the illusion was greater than the reality? He wanted to shout Stop! but he was paralyzed, half expecting a nasty surprise, yet compelled beyond reason. The sky had grown very gray, and it had begun to rain heavily, the water beating on the windows like an ominous drum. Muller closed the curtains, and the only light was the brace of candles upon the carved oak table next to his harpsichord.

And as Muller ransacked his memory to snatch Mozart from the darkness, Jason listened intently. In his mind's eye he was back in the world of Mozart.

4

Otto Muller's Vienna

"HERR OTIS, January, 1790, was a difficult time in Vienna. Some months before the French had stormed the Bastille and had imprisoned our Emperor's sister, Marie Antoinette, and Vienna was filled with rumors that our Emperor, Joseph, intended to attack the new revolutionary regime in France to rescue his sister. These rumors became ominous as young men were forced into the army. It was said that the opera would be closed for the duration of this crisis. I wondered how Mozart could compose when there were so many oppressive rumors about.

"Yet when Mozart and da Ponte were given an Imperial commission to compose a new opera and I was hired to play in the orchestra, it cheered me. By now I had played Mozart's music so much, I felt I had it in me to my fingertips.

"Mozart, da Ponte, Salieri . . . I thought of each of them as I walked to the Burgtheater for the first orchestral rehearsal of *Così fan tutte*. They dominated the opera in Vienna, and if you pleased them you were employed. I felt essential, and I tried to dismiss the fresh rumors now infecting conversation in Vienna: '*Joseph has aged so. . . . He is bitterly disappointed by his subjects' distaste for his reforms . . . Everyone knows that his brother, Leopold, who will succeed him, despises him and intends to put down any new uprisings with an iron hand. . . .*'

"I did not know what to think, Herr Otis. There could be a simple explanation for the Emperor's failing health, and yet I wondered.

"Infamous schemes were the fashion those days. Ever since the reign of the Borgias, it was said in Vienna that with the Italians, '*Poison was king*'; and Leopold was reputed to be, after twenty-five years in Tuscany, more Italian than German.

"I could imagine many reasons for Joseph having been poisoned. He had lessened the influence of the Italians at Court; his attempted reforms had created many enemies among the nobility; there were sudden, frequent, mysterious deaths those days.

"At the end of the Michaelplatz I reached the Burgtheater. The gray stone of the Hofburg nearby—the Burgtheater had been built close to the Hapsburg palace for their convenience—was massive in the midday sun, as if every knee must bow before it.

"Seeing two workmen from the Burgtheater arguing over the placing of the poster announcing the opening of *Così fan tutte*, I had more doubts. Usually the first rehearsal with the orchestra was an exciting time, one of discovery and hopes realized; but I recalled the new rumors I had heard this morning that Joseph had fallen ill suddenly, that his priest had been called, and that the opera would be canceled because of this, and because the score was not ready, and because the composer had fought with his poet and was ill, also.

"Yet, curious as to why the two workmen looked secretive, I hid in the shadows of the Burgtheater and heard the older workman grumble, 'Fritz, we are supposed to put this up so that it will not come off, but no one knows if the opera will go on.'

" 'Leave it in the gutter. It will be worth a gulden if we do.'

"They were about to do so when I stepped out of the shadows and said, 'Put that poster up, or I will report you to the authorities.'

"Fritz spit as he answered me, 'You musicians act as if you have been bred like the nobility!'

"Yet when I started to hang the announcement myself, Fritz took it from me and hung it properly, sneering, 'One has to know how, fiddler. Do you really think this opera will be done?'

"I hid my fears, replying, 'All is going properly.'

" 'In this wilderness of spite? Where have you been living, gypsy?'

"Long ago I had learned that musicians were regarded as gypsies. I did not reply, for I saw Mozart approaching. I was surprised by the sadness of his countenance. I had not seen him for several months and he looked older, tired. But as he greeted me, his face brightened. He was quite a small man, slight and pale, but now he seemed to spread in size as he smiled. His blue eyes gleamed and he unconsciously adjusted his fair hair, of which he was proud—he had not bothered to wear a wig for the rehearsal—and he wanted to know what was wrong.

"I told him, but he was not surprised to hear that the two workmen, who had retreated backstage with his appearance, had not wanted to hang the announcement of the opening of *Così fan tutte*.

"I asked, 'Who do you think is responsible, Herr Kapellmeister?'

"Mozart answered, 'Ever since I arrived in Vienna, as far back as 1781, Salieri has been hostile. Oh, he is polite to my face, he shouts *Bravo* at my operas and calls me his dear friend, but behind my back he does all he can to harm me.'

"Mozart added, 'Even years ago, when I first came to Vienna and was not a rival of anyone's, he injured me. When everything indicated that the Princess of Wurttemberg wanted to be my pupil on the clavier, Salieri spoiled it for me with his malice.'

" 'Yet you are polite to him, Herr Kapellmeister.'

" 'As he is to me. Herr Muller, I cannot challenge him to a duel, for he is too clever to offend me openly.'

" 'Can you not silence him in some way?' I suggested.

" 'It is impossible. Vienna is a vast cabal. Intrigue is the rule. The city is such a mixture of Germans, Bavarians, Hungarians, Poles, Slovaks, Bohemians, and Italians that even Joseph suffers from malice.'

"I said, 'They say that he is very ill, that he will not live much longer. There are even whispers that he has been poisoned.'

"Mozart replied, 'It is the disease of our time. It is called the *Italian disease,* and it is said that it is almost as prevalent as the pox.' He sighed, and asked me, in a sudden change of mood, 'How is your brother? I heard that he has been quite ill.'

" 'He is much better. It is good of you to ask, sir.'

" 'He is a fine musician. Will you please give him my regards.'

" 'Ernst will be honored, Herr Kapellmeister.'

"Mozart smiled wryly then, but he also looked pensive. His red waistcoat and white silk stockings and square-toed black shoes with their shiny silver buckles reminded me of when I had first seen him as he said reflectively, 'I have known the Emperor most of my life. Vienna will be strange without Joseph. I played for him when I was six.'

" 'I know!' I blurted out. 'I heard you at that time!'

"Mozart was startled. He exclaimed, 'But I am older than you!'

"He did appear older, Herr Otis, for his high forehead had become lined and there were deep pouches under his eyes, although I knew he was only in his early thirties, but I said, 'Begging your pardon, Herr Kapellmeister, but I am older. I was born in 1750.'

" 'I feel older. I have had so many illnesses in my life.'

" 'I heard that you have not been well yourself, sir.'

"A shadow came upon Mozart's features as if he could not afford to be ill, and he hurried to say, 'A passing indisposition. Today I feel much better. Where did you hear me play when I was six? I have performed so often, I forget myself where I played. Music I recall, but performances—they are like the sand in the hourglass.'

"I told him, 'I never forgot the occasion, sir. It was at Prince Kaunitz's palace. My father warned me that he was Chancellor and second only to Maria Theresa in power. We were not supposed to attend—only the nobility were permitted—but my father, who was also a fine musician, like your father, had done several favors for Kaunitz, so we were allowed, if we stood in the rear, behind everybody else. Standing, it indicated our humble position. Yet it was difficult for me to see. I was only twelve, and not very tall. But I heard.'

"Mozart replied with a vehemence rare for him, as if I had touched a vital nerve. 'They say I am too small to conduct properly, that my legs are too short, that the orchestra cannot see enough of me; but Haydn is not much taller than I am. What did you hear me play?'

" 'Scarlatti. The Younger. My father took me to hear you in the hope that I would want to become another Wolfgang Amadeus Mozart.'

" 'I am not sure it was worth it.'

" 'Why, Herr Kapellmeister?'

" 'There has been so much suffering, illness, and always, intrigue.' "

Muller's voice broke and Jason, greatly moved, also, cried out, "Are you sure he said that?" After all, old men's memories were notoriously fallible, yet Muller's voice had become decisive and precise. "Do you really believe that he was that bitter?"

"Or pessimistic. Instead of Mozart looking happy at the sight of the announcement of his new opera, he stared at the poster of *Così fan tutte* with a sadness that I shall never forget. Herr Otis, I am simply trying to tell you of my experiences with Mozart that were significant for me. He had his reputation; I believe he knew his own genius, but I think that, somehow, he felt that he did not fit in here. And my next question aroused Mozart even more."

Jason moved closer. He had no heart for anything but what Muller was telling him. Yet none of this was making him peaceful.

"Herr Otis, after I recovered from my shock—actually the silence had been only a few moments as I stood impotently—I asked Mozart, 'You resented being dragged around Europe by your father?'

" 'Dragged? Resented?' Mozart repeated angrily. 'I loved it! We were such a close family, my father, mother, and sister, that it stimulated me. I was playing for them. It was one of my great pleasures. I was very, very happy. In some ways it was the happiest time of my life. Resent my father? Incredible!' The blood drained from his face. He was astonished by the charge. 'People are stupid!'

" 'Your music was greatly applauded, Herr Kapellmeister, even then.' I hoped that would mollify him, and it was true. 'As it still is.'

" 'Herr Muller, the public is an indifferent beast. They are interested in the creation, not the creator. They enjoy using what I produce, but the creator is in the way, like a glove to be tossed aside when it wears out or has lived past its usefulness.'

"He is depressed, I thought, because he is afflicted with the exhaustion that possesses the creator after he has completed his work, but I knew I would never forget our first meeting.

"It was many years before, 1762. I remember the date because I was twelve, and the music chamber of the Palace Kaunitz was in red in imitation of the Red Room of the Hofburg, with tapestries by Boucher and a grandiose chandelier that dwarfed even the jewels of the nobles. But all I cared about was the little boy in silk breeches and a vivid scarlet waistcoat and a small sword by his side like an Austrian archduke sitting at the harpsichord. How young he looked, even with powder on his face and a grown man's wig! His mamma must have taken great care with his clothes. I was positive that this six-year-old child, half my own age, must be terrified. Instead, Herr Otis, although he looked pale under the brilliant lights, he played with amazing composure. What the results would be for him I could not conjecture, but as I pressed my father's hand tightly, I was very agitated. Inside, I cried with anguish. I realized that I would never be able to equal such a performance.

"Mozart brought me out of my reverie by saying, 'Kaunitz never really helped me, although he pretended to. I was a puppydog to the Hapsburgs, to be petted when they were young and then forgotten. We must start the rehearsal. If I am not there, they will make many mistakes.' He took me by the arm and led me inside affectionately.

"We both knew there was not much time to spare. *Così fan tutte* was scheduled to open in two weeks, and today was supposed to be the first performance of the score by the orchestra, but no singers were to rehearse for some of the libretto was still not finished, and I realized, as Mozart must have, that drastic measures would have to be taken to get the opera produced on the day scheduled. And when we reached the orchestra, I sensed a frightening anxiety. A violinist from the pit informed Mozart, 'The Konzertmeister has fallen ill, Maestro. The *Italian disease*, perhaps. He was healthy yesterday.'

"As if it had been prearranged, Count Orsini-Rosenberg, Director of the Court Theaters, who had been sitting in the rear of the Burg-theater, strode down the aisle and told Mozart, 'The rehearsal will have to be canceled. We cannot proceed without a Konzertmeister.'

"Mozart cried out, 'We cannot afford any further delays. One more will ruin the production, Herr Director.'

"The Count replied sternly, 'We cannot afford an inefficient production. Mozart, you will have to get a new Konzertmeister.'

" 'Yes,' said Mozart. He wanted da Ponte; da Ponte had hired this Konzertmeister, but no one knew where the librettist was.

"Orsini-Rosenberg said, 'It is your responsibility. I am sorry.'

"But I thought the Director of the Court Theaters, who ruled the opera in Vienna with an iron hand except for the rare occasions when he was overruled by the Emperor, was not sorry at all. I knew the Count did not approve of Mozart; the fact had become evident during the production of *Le Nozze di Figaro*, which had been saved only by the craftiness of da Ponte.

"Orsini-Rosenberg repeated, 'No Konzertmeister, no rehearsal.'

"As the Count dismissed the orchestra and Mozart looked desperate, I suggested, 'I could fill in. I know the Konzertmeister's duties.'

"The Director said contemptuously, 'Muller is a second-rate musician. He is not a suitable match for the music. It is impossible!'

"Orsini-Rosenberg looked very pleased with himself, but Mozart replied, 'Muller was one of the first violins in *Le Nozze di Figaro* and in *Don Giovanni*. You did not complain about him then, Herr Count.'

" 'We could not get rid of him.'

"Mozart retorted, 'Sir, I will appeal to the Emperor.'

" 'Which one? I doubt that Joseph will live another week.'

"Mozart said insistently, 'Muller is a good sight reader, his tone is clear and agreeable, he has taste, and he plays like oil. Take the Konzertmeister's place, Herr Muller; we will manage.'

"Herr Otis, it is difficult to describe my emotions then. For years I had prepared for this moment. But not in such imperfect conditions. Yet it is a moment I will preserve forever in my memory. For as I sat down at the first desk, the rest of the orchestra followed me. I could not tell whether it was a vote of confidence, or their own form of rebellion, or an impulse, without premeditation. But as I tapped my violin for order, there was utter silence.

"Mozart smiled at the Director and said quietly, 'Herr Count, I am always at the Emperor's service.' Orsini-Rosenberg stood speechless with astonishment, and Mozart began conducting.

"At first I was unnerved by the strangeness of my situation, but gradually, as there was much in the score of *Così fan tutte* that was similar to other music of Mozart's I had played, I gained assurance. Then Mozart superimposed upon me the firm conviction that I was transformed. His incredible face with its many shades of sensibility was more revealing than words. His blue eyes gleamed and his small hands were extraordinarily flexible and plastic. His music was delightful, melodic, and as always, beautiful.

"What helped me the most was something Mozart had said during a rehearsal of *Figaro* years before: 'There is more to conducting than knowing the parts of a score. I do not think of a page of notes. I hear the score as a whole, its architecture, its sweep. I want a clean and clear performance, with exact tone and phrasing.'

"When we finished the first full performance of the orchestral music of *Così*, I could not tell how efficient we had been, but I knew we had played with great care. The entire orchestra applauded.

"Mozart turned to the Director, who had slumped into a seat, and bowed low and said, 'Your honor, I am no great lover of difficulties, but I am sure our improvisation was satisfactory.'

"Orsini-Rosenberg rose abruptly, and walked rudely away.

"Mozart was motionless a moment, then as the men in the orchestra applauded him again, he seized me in his arms and embraced me.

"His wonderfully expressive eyes glistened with tears, and I was deeply moved. Then awkwardly, I found myself going in a contrary direction. From the darkness of a box near the orchestra pit, I heard da Ponte whispering like a conspirator, 'Salieri, you see, the time for equivocation is past. I am very pleased.'

"I realized, as Mozart must have, with shock and dismay that da Ponte and Salieri had been sitting close to us without revealing their presence. I heard Mozart mutter, 'What are they up to? Is da Ponte

allowing Salieri to seduce him? At this late date?' He whispered to me,
'If the poet is in league with Salieri, I shall never get anything more out
of him.' He told the orchestra to rest, and hurried into the box. I
followed him. I wanted to know if I was to remain Konzertmeister, and
everyone knew Salieri and Mozart did not like each other, whatever
they pretended.

"Mozart said, 'Da Ponte, why didn't you help me with Rosenberg?'

" 'I was busy, Wolfgang.'

" 'Is that why the Konzertmeister you hired vanished?'

" 'Wolfgang, nothing was lost. Muller was adequate.'

"But I was sure, Herr Otis, that Mozart felt Salieri was persuading
da Ponte to leave him. The poet sat with an assurance that indicated
that if Mozart did not listen to him, Salieri would.

"Yet Salieri bowed almost to the floor as he greeted Mozart, and
exclaimed, 'Bravo! The music is bellissimo! Where did you get it?'

"I thought, Salieri was never convinced that Mozart's music came
from himself, but somehow was stolen from someone else, and if he
could only find out from whom, it would solve his problems, too.

"The vain fellow was wearing his Sunday best, and his hair was
elaborately dressed, and he was animated. But actually, Salieri was a
plump little man, with a large, long nose, dark eyes that were almost as
bright as a cat's and features that were soft, with a wide mouth that
curved up petulantly, and a sharp chin that was in contradiction to the
rest of his face, suggesting a bird of prey.

"Da Ponte, although he was just a year older than Salieri, looked
much older. The poet considered himself a handsome man with his tall,
lean figure, his aquiline nose, his black hair, and his brilliant eyes. Yet
in the last few years his long face had seemed to stretch, his cheeks had
become gaunt, and his Roman nose, always prominent, now vied with
his piercing eyes for dominance.

"He informed Mozart, 'I have decided that in the scene where
Ferrando and Guglielmo, disguised as two Albanians, persuade
Fiordiligi and Dorabella to consider their suit, they pretend to take
poison.'

"Mozart said, 'Is that what you and Salieri were arguing about?'

"Da Ponte assumed a conspiratorial attitude, it increased his sense
of theater, and said, 'It will lead to a splendid first-act finale.'

"Salieri said, 'I am quite in love with your music, Mozart. As you
know, I am quite devoted to our dear friend da Ponte.'

" 'An honest fellow,' declared da Ponte. 'Maestro Salieri introduced
me to Vienna and the Emperor. I owe him much.'

"And, Herr Otis, they would cut each other's throat, I thought, if
either stood in the other's way, but I said nothing.

"Mozart said, 'But Maestro Salieri stated that *Don Giovanni* was an
opera that encouraged the Devil. It was somewhat irritating.'

"Salieri said, 'Mozart, such remarks should amuse you. It shows truly that you have become the envy of all of us. And everyone says things in haste that later they regret.'

"Da Ponte added, 'Look at the aid the Maestro has given us. He is an authority on poisons. He is indeed our friend. He has just told me how I can use poison without any ill effect on my plot.'

"Mozart said, 'I do not believe we should use poison in our plot, even as a pretence. It is too unpleasant.'

" 'Wolfgang, it is Venetian. And *Così fan tutte* is Venetian.'

" 'It will work, Mozart,' volunteered Salieri, 'Believe me.'

"Mozart asked, 'Then why were you quarrelling?'

"Da Ponte replied, 'I am a Venetian. When I disagree, I do it openly. But now, Maestro Salieri has convinced me. He has even told me what poison the two lovers should pretend to use. Acqua toffana.'

"Salieri said proudly, 'And it is very efficient, too. It contains arsenic and lead oxide, and yet, given in small doses, it works slowly and cannot be detected. I may use it myself in my next opera. I do have a gift for situations, if I say so myself.'

"Mozart asked, 'Da Ponte, does that mean you have promised to write the libretto of Salieri's next opera in return for his advice?'

"Da Ponte shrugged. 'One has to be enterprising.'

"Mozart said, 'They say that the Emperor will be dead before we open. If that happens, this production will be cancelled.'

"Da Ponte said pontifically, 'I saw Joseph yesterday. He is ill, there is no doubt about that, but he did look better. The Emperor is not going to die before our opera opens. Trust me.'

"Mozart said, 'He has not been poisoned?'

"Da Ponte cried out, 'Where did you get that impression?'

"Mozart retorted, 'Where everybody else has. And what about the difficulties in France? They, too, could halt *Così fan tutte*.'

"Da Ponte said, 'I heard that Joseph is negotiating with the French for the safety of his sister. The French will only be too glad to get rid of Marie Antoinette. But she is not our worry.'

"Mozart said, 'If her death should lead to war, it is.'

"Da Ponte said, 'You must be tired, Wolfgang, everything worries you. Now that we have decided to use the pretended poisoning, suitable music will have to be written. We would be mad not to use the poison idea. It is the fashionable thing today.'

" 'What about the Konzertmeister and our Herr Director, da Ponte?'

" 'Wolfgang, I will take care of Rosenberg and you take care of the music. That is all you have to be concerned about.'

"Thereupon, Mozart appointed me Konzertmeister. I felt he could not find a more appropriate conclusion; but before the rehearsal could resume, I saw the three Weber women approaching from the rear of the Burgtheater: his wife, Constanze; her older sister, the prima donna Aloysia Lange, whom Mozart had loved before his wife; and the youngest sister, Sophie Weber, who was often in his house.

"I could guess why Aloysia had come. She had been considered for the role of Fiordiligi until da Ponte had maneuvered his mistress, La Ferrarese, into it, and there was always the possibility a new soprano might be needed. La Ferrarese was notoriously unreliable and Mozart was not infatuated with her singing, and he did trust Aloysia's voice, if nothing else. But his wife rarely attended rehearsals. Something must be wrong, I thought, for she was also agitated."

As Muller paused in his narration, Jason was troubled by recurring questions. How much was Muller's ego fattening on these memories? Had the old musician held on to them because he had so little else? Even as Jason felt drawn back inexorably to Vienna, the one city that seemed worth living in musically, he wondered how many of Muller's reflections were illusory. Reflections, he told himself, which could have been falsified by purposes not even recognized by Muller. Yet whatever his doubts, Jason knew he must hear more. The very act of listening had in itself brought him an unforeseen, exhilarating involvement. A fine, wonderful thing was happening. He loved Mozart very much, and in this loving he was entering a musical world of great beauty.

Yet he was not entering heaven, or a state of bliss. Until he found out how Mozart had really died, he sensed he would have no peace. Mozart had shown him the loveliest music man was capable of creating but there was still much he had to learn. What Muller was telling him was only whetting his interest, not satisfying it. He asked, "Did you know the three Weber women well?"

"I knew all of them. There was a fourth sister, too, and a mother. I played in Mozart's house with him on numerous occasions."

"Did you like the Webers, Herr Muller?"

Muller did not answer.

"Did you . . .?"

Muller said abruptly, "What I remember has nothing to do with liking or disliking. I simply want to see justice done."

"And Mozart revenged."

"No, no, no. He has had his revenge. If Salieri is remembered, it will be only because he assassinated Mozart."

"You do not want to see Salieri punished?"

"If he has gone insane, he has been punished enough."

"Then why do you want me to pursue this investigation?"

"There are some things it would be useful to know."

"You are not sure he is mad? You think it could be a ruse?"

"Sometimes, Herr Otis, just when we think we understand everything, we understand nothing. I remember what I remember. In Vienna you will hear other versions."

"You assume that I am going?"

"Isn't that why you are listening to me so intently?"

"Many things would have to be arranged. I haven't decided yet."

Muller said thoughtfully, "You should talk to the Weber women. They knew him in a way that no one else did. Think of the memories they must possess. Three sisters: the oldest, who discarded his love; the middle one who became his second-choice wife; and the youngest, his adoring sister-in-law. Do you think they agree about him?"

Jason's imagination expanded at the thought of speaking to them. They were inherently involved; their memories could be significant. He could hardly bear to part with the three sisters as he exclaimed, "Why did they come to the Burgtheater?"

"I don't wholly remember, but some things remain vivid."

"Mozart, the instant he saw his wife, ran to her and kissed her and cried out, 'Stanzi, you should not have come, you are just out of bed, you have not recovered your strength yet'; and I recalled that she had lost a child several months before. But before she could reply, Aloysia kissed Mozart right on the lips, not as a sister-in-law, I thought, but as a charmer. And then he asked Sophie, 'What is wrong, dear?' They had marched in like one, and I was distressed that everyone could hear what was happening, even Salieri.

"None of the sisters was especially attractive. Aloysia, who had been a handsome girl, a beauty in Mozart's eyes, had hardened, and her sharp features had become severe and cold. Constanze, never particularly pretty, had become plain after her last illness. Sophie had remained boyish.

"Constanze said, 'Wolfgang, I have been exposed to such a dreadful embarrassment and unpleasantness. The tailor informs me that if his account is not paid at once, he will seize the new waistcoats you obtained from him and you will have nothing to wear for the opening.'

"He whispered, 'How much do I owe?' and she replied, 'Twenty-five gulden.' Everyone was waiting for the rehearsal to resume and that appeared impossible, and I asked myself, Could Salieri have put the tailor up to such a nasty trick at this precise moment? It had upset Mozart; he had slumped into a chair by the harpsichord where he conducted. I sensed that what stunned him was not the debt but the humiliation, and I blurted out, 'I have a waistcoat that might fit you, Herr Kapellmeister,' and da Ponte added, 'Admirable, we cannot allow anything to halt *Così*, can we, Maestro Salieri?' And Salieri smiled weakly and said, 'I am sorry my clothes are too large for Herr Mozart,' although they were almost the same size.

"Then Aloysia started to say, 'If I sang Fiordiligi, Wolfgang,' only to be cut short by da Ponte, who snapped, 'That is impossible! I will speak to the tailor. How much is it, Constanze?'

" 'Twenty-five gulden,' she said. 'You will help us, Lorenzo?'

"Da Ponte took Mozart by the arm, ignoring the sudden expression of resentment that came across Aloysia's face and Salieri's gesture of annoyance, and said, 'It is a lovely score, Wolfgang. It will do us both honor. If my suspicions are correct . . .'

"A loud crash backstage obliterated the rest of what da Ponte was saying, and knowing da Ponte's devious ways, I was not surprised when he changed the subject and convinced Mozart to continue the rehearsal.

"After it ended Sophie came up to me and whispered, so no one else could hear, 'Watch him, will you please, Herr Muller. He is reaching the final stages of exhaustion. He fainted several times last week. But when I tried to caution him, he said it was a temporary illness, a heavy cold, a touch of diarrhea. 'There is so much dysentery,' Wolfgang says, 'our sewerage systems are overwhelmed these days.'

"I said, 'You do not believe him?'

"Sophie said, 'I don't know what to believe. But he is not well.'

"Yet, Herr Otis, when I mentioned this to Herr Mozart the next day, he laughed and said, 'Sophie is a little foolish sometimes. She fears too many things.' He was in a better, spirited humor, for da Ponte had appeased the tailor and the new poison scene that da Ponte had interpolated had become an effective musical moment.

"I asked, 'What about Salieri?'

"Mozart laughed. 'All men lie or lessen the truth or add to it as it suits their purpose. If *Così fan tutte* continues to improve, I will feel fine, and all of Salieri's plots will come to nothing. Herr Muller, I must recapture the ear of Vienna!' "

The old man finished buoyantly, determined to match Mozart's mood, but Jason felt there were many unanswered questions. He asked, "What did Salieri do?"

"I did not see him at any more rehearsals, as if he realized that he could no longer damage or destroy *Così fan tutte.*"

"Did Mozart recapture the ear of Vienna?"

"By the time of the dress rehearsal he was so pleased with the way the opera was going he invited Haydn to hear it, and the Emperor was able to attend the premiere and he stated that *Così fan tutte* was the best of Mozart's operas. Mozart was jubilant. He told me that he should have commissions regularly now. But the Emperor died a few weeks later and *Così fan tutte* was withdrawn because of a period of national mourning, and when it resumed, there was a new Emperor, Leopold, who did not like music. Soon after, there was no opera at all."

"Was the Emperor Joseph poisoned?"

"No one knew. Everyone in Vienna was distracted, disturbed by the events occurring in France. Now, as I look back, I realize that the French Revolution was a watershed, when the world altered, never truly to return to its past. But then we did not know that. We were concerned that we would be dragged into war over Marie Antoinette. That in itself was quite unpleasant. I doubt the nobility or the new

Emperor, worried about the revolution in France, thought much, if anything, about their third Court composer, Herr Mozart."

"Did Mozart look ill during the premiere of *Cosi fan tutte*?"

"Indeed, not!" Muller was positive. "I sat there, looking into his face, and he was transfigured with joy. I realized that his music was his reality, and that the beauty and enchantment and happiness of his music was his way of speaking against his fears."

5

The Decision

_____

WHEN Muller finished, the figure of Mozart did not dissipate as Jason had expected, but grew larger and lodged in his mind. Yet what he had been told tantalized him instead of enlightened him. Muller had not told him enough. Constanze, Aloysia, Sophie . . . Who had been the best loved? Or had Mozart cared for someone else? Mozart had written sensuously of love.

Jason asked. "Is Vienna as it was in Mozart's time?"

"I believe so," Muller answered, "but you must remember, I have not been in Vienna for many years. I left when Napoleon came."

Nothing remained constant, thought Jason. Even more than before, he was certain that he could not assume that everything Muller had said was true. He wavered, not sure what he should do. Yet when the old musician said, "Less than two years after the opening of _Così fan tutte_, Mozart was dead under the most suspicious circumstances," once again he felt drawn inexorably to Vienna. By now he was unable to tell whether he was pursuing or being pursued, but he blurted out, "Could you obtain an introduction to the Weber women for me?"

"My brother could."

Which of the three really had given Mozart her heart? Had Constanze actually been a good wife? But how could Muller judge? Muller, as a musician, might understand Mozart, and that was a fine thing; but the old man was misanthropic on the subject of women.

"Ernst knows almost everyone who knew Mozart in Vienna. They were part of the same circle, as I was. But if you wait," Muller repeated, "who knows who will be still alive?"

"One of them could be gone soon, then others," said Jason.

"And now that you have the Beethoven assignment, your reasons for going to Vienna will seem straightforward. Elisha Whitney assumes you are going, or he would not have asked you to approach Herr Beethoven."

"But when I asked him for aid, he ignored the subject of money."

"Ask him to pay part of your fare. You expect that, don't you?"

"Yes. Do you think anyone will recognize why I want to go?"

"If, in visiting Herr Beethoven, you should come upon new facts about Mozart, no one has to be aware of your real reason. Then no one should threaten you. There will be nothing to be afraid of."

Jason carried the letter about Beethoven as if it were a precious scroll, and when church services ended the following Sunday, he handed it to Elisha Whitney, whose wizened face was beaming with pride. The choir had sung one of Jason's hymns with devotion, and he was receiving many compliments on the noble state of music in Boston. It was one of his finest hours in his years of tenure as Director of the Handel and Haydn Society, and he had no intention of sharing it with anyone else. Thus, he was taken aback by this intrusion. Elisha Whitney thought angrily, Otis is being irresponsible. He exclaimed, "What are you showing me this letter for?"

"You wrote it, didn't you, sir?"

"The Society did. I am merely their spokesman."

"You have used many of my hymns, sir."

"As many as have been suitable, Otis."

"I will be honored to present your commission to Herr Beethoven."

Elisha Whitney allowed himself the luxury of a slight smirk.

"But it will be an expensive journey, Professor."

"It is, indeed. It is too bad that we cannot afford to pay you."

"Then why did you ask me to present this commission?"

"To be a representative of the Handel and Haydn Society of Boston is a privilege. A letter from us is a great thing. It should open many doors for you, particularly Beethoven's. It should please him, having the request for an oratorio presented to him in person, for I hear that he is dyspeptic. You do wish to visit him, don't you?"

"Yes, yes, of course!" Jason added for emphasis.

Elisha Whitney's countenance was so satisfied then, Jason thought he would burst with self-love. He declared, "Nowhere else will you find such industry and intelligence as Heaven has bestowed on Boston. But if you insist on pursuing your dream of becoming a composer, I will be generous and indulge you. Beethoven is well known in Vienna. So present our letter. All we will expect in return will be whatever hymns you compose as a result of this journey."

The next few days Jason walked slowly and reflectively across the Common, along the Charles River; he studied the high-gabled houses of weathered spruce and pine, and the red-brick houses which were increasing rapidly. He was especially attracted by the wharfs. They were crowded in spite of the fierce winds that blew in from the ocean, and he learned that a new kind of a boat was travelling from New York City to England, a sailing packet with a steam engine that crossed the Atlantic in twenty-six to thirty-one days, depending on the weather, and which was a tremendous improvement on previous voyages, which had taken several months. He also found out that he had saved enough money from what he had received for the editions of the Collection to pay for his passage to Europe, but that he did not have the funds to bring himself back. Yet it was becoming inevitable that he risk this journey. He was tired of the "practical goodness" that the inhabitants of Boston prated was characteristic of their town. He felt it was a pity that no one in the community took pride in a bit of sin occasionally. After he examined the town thoroughly, his mind was made up. He sensed that the moment he told Deborah of his plans, she would suspect his motives and ask, "How much will it cost?" But she might be able to help him with a plan that was formulating in his mind—if he was clever.

His optimism faded however, as he approached Deborah the following morning. The Pickering home looked gloomy this gray day, as did the other mansions around it. The banker called his place "Great House," in the English fashion, but Jason saw it as "Gaunt House," for the Puritan strain in Pickering kept off all adornments from the exterior even as he exhibited his wealth within. Suddenly Jason was apprehensive. He expected Deborah to exclaim, "Why aren't you at the bank?" No employee was ever absent unless he was seriously ill. He thought bitterly, The assumption that she could help him was an illusion.

But it was too late to retreat. As he stood in the drawing room, after informing the maid that he wanted to speak to Miss Deborah, he yearned to tell her that he must take the journey from the child's clavichord in Salzburg to the common grave in Vienna, that already in debt to him as a composer, he must know more about him as a man. If Mozart had been murdered, how could quiet ever remain!

When Pickering heard that Otis was not at work, he felt that this was providential, that he had been correct to assume that the teller had been profligate with his time and was not to be trusted and that this would open Deborah's eyes to the true nature of her suitor. He appeared in the drawing room unannounced, determined not to spare anyone's feelings.

Jason was startled. Pickering's chin was even more sharp and pointed than before, his lips were thinner, and his mouth was a straight, harsh line. The banker proudly fondled his gold watch fob, an essential part of a gentleman's dress, and declared, "You should be at the bank."

"Sir, I want to speak to Deborah."

"During hours?"

Jason took a deep breath, wishing he was not so nervous, and blurted out, "Mr. Pickering, I am resigning."

"Resigning . . .!"

But that came not from Pickering, but from Deborah, who had just entered the drawing room.

"Yes." Now that it was out, it was a little easier.

Pickering said, "You are a very confused young man."

"You don't accept my resignation?"

"What is there to accept?"

Pickering turned away with obvious disgust. Jason realized that Deborah's father not only disliked him, there were moments when Pickering despised him, perhaps even hated him. He sensed that Pickering blamed him for Deborah's love of romantic novels, her passionate speeches about the rights of women, and her assertion that no one was truly educated until he took the Grand Tour, as the English gentry did. He noticed that Deborah was leaning heavily on the sideboard, which was unlike her. This was a room of which she was proud. She had papered it in pink and had given it the air of an English lady's drawing room, very much the mistress of the house since her mother had died. Jason knew its design by heart; it prevailed in so many wealthy Boston homes: oak for wainscoting, cedar for doors, mahogany for furniture, and the woodwork in gilt. He said, "Deborah, I wanted you to know first."

"It is Mozart, isn't it," she said suddenly.

"And the opportunity to meet Beethoven. The Society has honored me by asking me to present a commission to him."

Pickering interrupted, "I was informed about it. There is no money in it. And honor, without money, is empty." He had to struggle to hide his contempt. Otis was lazy, improvident, and with his interest in music effeminate. He could not endure this interest, yet the thought of losing his daughter's affection, the only person's affection for which he cared, appalled him. It went against his nature to say, Let her marry whom she likes. His daughter would demean herself in a marriage with a musician, yet all she seemed to desire was a proposal from this fellow.

Jason tried to ignore Pickering as he asked her, "Would you help me?"

"How?"

"If you could loan me . . ." After all, Deborah was an heiress in her own right, from her mother's estate; yet it was embarrassing to ask for money, and so he equivocated. ". . . and then we could marry when I return."

Pickering declared angrily, "He is interested only in your fortune. Deborah, you must break off the engagement."

She said, "We are not discussing that."

Jason wondered if she had to outdo her father.

"Loan you what, Jason? My china? My white cashmere shawl?"

"You know what I mean. I have enough to reach Vienna, but not enough to return. You do want me to return to Boston, don't you?"

"Is that why you wish to investigate the death of Mozart?"

"Who told you that? Muller?" Jason was very upset.

Pickering stated, "Muller asked me for a loan from the bank so he could go to Vienna. He said he wanted to go there to obtain new oratorios for the Society, but I turned him down. He has no collateral: a few concerts he plays for gentlemen amateurs such as John Adams and John Quincy Adams, several music students like yourself, and a rundown music shop on Franklin Street. Deborah, why did you see him?"

"I had to find out what Jason was up to. Did you really think Muller desired the money for himself?"

Jason asked sharply, "What did Muller tell you?"

"I don't believe that your idol was poisoned. I don't."

"What is this about poisoning?" demanded Pickering.

"It's a theory," said Jason, "just a theory of Muller's. It is not why I wish to visit Vienna." He could not tell them how he was haunted.

Pickering said, "It is to be expected that a young man will be restless, but you are pursuing the Devil in you."

Jason said, "Sir, the Devil went out of fashion a hundred years ago."

"Mozart and Beethoven," she mused. "What a strange pair to love!"

"I love you! But I must go to Europe!" Jason was aware that he was doing this wrong, not in the least as he had planned it; but her father should not be here—it was not fair; it was not what he had expected.

"I would love to see Europe," she said abruptly.

"Then you understand how important it is to me."

"Of course. One should finish his education on the Continent."

Jason sensed a trap, but it was too late to retreat. "You are very well educated as it is, Deborah. You do not need a European education."

This was the last compliment she desired. She could have wept genuine tears. She took his hand in hers, calculating that this was not the time for humility, and said with an air of innocence, "In good conscience, I cannot allow you to go alone, Jason. It is too difficult."

"But he has not proposed to you!" her father exploded.

"He would if you were not here, wouldn't you, Jason?"

Jason stared at her in astonishment, speechless.

"Do you think he has no heart, Father? With his love for Mozart?"

"Mozart be damned! Don't you have any self-respect? In decent society it is the custom for the young man to propose."

"He has."

"When?"

"You heard him say he loves me."

Pickering was outraged. Otis stood there like a stick of wood, but his daughter was saying, "I can finish my education on the Continent." It is the fault of modern learning, he thought. When he had been her age no respectable young lady was encouraged toward knowledge—it corrupted her abilities as a mother. Born in 1770, Pickering was grateful that he had been too young to fight in the Revolution, which he considered an odious excess, and too old to serve in the War of 1812, which he regarded as foolish and a waste. She was saying now, "I will love Vienna," and he retorted, "That is romantic nonsense. I hear that there is cholera in central Europe."

"My German is almost perfect. Think of how much I can help him."

Pickering was not deceived. "Suppose I disinherit you?"

"You can't. Mother left half of her fortune to me."

"They will say he married you for your money."

"Didn't they say that about you?"

That was ridiculous, Pickering assured himself. His wife's wealth had been a convenience that he had utilized by loaning it on high terms of interest. He could not forgive anyone who referred to his wife as an heiress, for that put a slight upon his vision of himself as a self-made man. If she continued to behave this way, he would not like her any more than Otis. He exclaimed, "I will not give my permission."

"I don't need it."

Jason felt her hand pushing him down, but he had never intended to get down on his knees, even if he did propose someday. Yet, although he resisted her physical pressure, he found himself saying, "Will you marry me, Deborah dear?" as if hypnotized by the urgency of her feeling, even as a part of him remained unwilling.

She said, "I shall cherish your proposal all my life. We must not be separated any longer. I will go with you to Europe, a devoted wife."

Pickering thought bitterly, Why did I allow her to study music? What a grievous mistake it was! Perhaps she is possessed by the Devil, too.

She said, "So you see, Father, if you do not want to give your permission, we will arrange it at the church without you."

"My own church? You wouldn't dare!"

Her smile said, Try me.

He glared at her, but her gaze did not waver. Character cut both ways, he realized: the strength she had inherited from him had become his cross. In his rage he wanted to smash her pianoforte, but she would only laugh. She was, indeed, his daughter.

"Think of all the gossip, Father, if you are not at my wedding."

He could not endure that. It would be humiliating. However, to show that he still had some control over her, he said, "You must marry in this house. Where you were born. Where I married your mother. I insist."

"If it will make you happy."

Very little about this marriage would make him happy, he reflected resentfully, and he added, "Jason, you are a confused young man. You cannot resign from the bank and live on what you will earn from music. I suggest that you take a leave of absence, and then, after your year in Europe, you can come back to the bank."

"Yes," said Deborah. "That will give you time to pursue your dream, Jason, and afterwards we can return to Boston and a sound occupation."

"That's settled," said Pickering, with an inward sigh of relief. At least he still possessed a portion of her.

Jason recoiled instinctively. Did they believe that he would accept their decisions without question? He looked at her, but she was not looking at him. He longed to attack her father, to state that his answer was no, but Pickering had hurried out of the drawing room. He remembered how severely Mozart had suffered from poverty, and that he must never allow this to happen to him. Fatalistically, perhaps the situation had developed for the best. Yet as he said goodbye to Deborah, her father reappeared and declared, "If you had written something clever like 'Home, Sweet Home,' I could see some chance of popularity for your music, but your compositions will be out of fashion soon, like your Mozart and Beethoven."

Twenty-four hours before the wedding Jason became panic-stricken. Once again he was not certain he really loved Deborah. She derived such satisfaction planning their European journey, he felt she was arranging this expedition for her benefit and not his own. And while she had never looked more attractive and desirable, if she could outwit a strong-willed person like her father, she would surely dominate him.

Jason had not seen Muller since the day of the proposal, as if Muller's revelation of the reason for travelling to Vienna had been a betrayal, but in his sudden need for advice he put his scruples aside.

Full of anxiety, he knocked on Muller's door. Muller seemed to be waiting for him. He blurted out, "You were expecting me?"

"You would not have departed without saying goodbye, would you?"

For a moment Jason did not recognize the mentor he had known. There was a note of entreaty in Muller's voice that was new. In the time that had intervened since they had seen each other, Muller's bodily ailments had multiplied and now he could no longer conceal that he was old and feeble. Muller wore a cape, although there was a brisk blaze in his fireplace, and as he hobbled back to his chair, bent over like a distorted tree, he held his back to ease his pain.

And when, to lessen the strain between them, Jason suggested that Muller play a Mozart sonata, Muller said, "I am troubled by the gout. Even in my fingers. The last few days I have been unable to play a single note. My hands, which were once powerful, are dead."

Jason sought to console him, saying, "It must be just a temporary affliction," and Muller cut him short. "It is too late. Even when I sit by the fire, this Boston cold penetrates my bones. You play."

Jason turned to the pianoforte, but Mozart's music, usually their refuge, was no consolation now. Muller sat brooding, looking more mournful than Jason had ever seen him, his furrowed face, his waxen skin like a death mask. Jason hit so many wrong notes he was ashamed.

Muller cried out with asperity, "Is that why you came? To show me how little you have learned? You should practice scales."

"Have you been sick?" Jason asked.

"Old age is a sickness," Muller said irritably. "You do not have to play so loudly. I am not a Beethoven. I am not deaf."

"He is deaf?"

"Only an American wouldn't know that. When are you leaving?"

"I am not sure I should marry her."

"She will make it possible for you to visit Vienna."

"Is that why you asked her father for a loan?"

"I was able to give John Adams and Thomas Jefferson as references. The one thing these gentlemen amateurs share is a love of music. They have bought much from me. Two ex-Presidents. I did not know that Pickering was a Tory at heart, and hated them."

Jason was still suspicious. "You did not have to tell Deborah about Mozart's death. Unless you wanted her to marry me?"

"She would have found out sooner or later. And if her father had loaned me the money, you would not have had to marry her."

Jason was confused.

"Don't be so thoughtful. Use your intuition. As Mozart did."

"You said he could have married better."

"Constanze Weber was penniless. But you have an heiress within your grasp, who is also beautiful, intelligent, and . . ."

"Domineering."

"That depends on you. She does love you."

"She loves the idea of being married. And I please her physically."

"Many husbands begin with far fewer advantages and are very happy."

"You never married!"

"Who said that?"

"You have never talked about it."

"Herr Otis, you must not destroy everything in a moment of fear. You will have many more important things to be afraid of in Vienna. What should I write my brother? That you are not coming after all?"

"Deborah does not believe that Mozart was poisoned."

"Convince her. Succeed with her, you will succeed with others."

But how much of himself would she possess? Yet while he furiously resented the manner in which she had manipulated him into proposing and he felt he must thwart her, if only to show her that she could not always have her own way, she had kissed him so eagerly after the proposal that he sensed a sudden concentration of emotion. And he was attracted by her beauty, and her body suggested a voluptuous richness. Whenever he had touched her, she had responded with a subtle yet instinctive intensity. It was as if each of them gave the other a powerful presence which could sweep everything else away.

Muller stood up. It took great effort. But for this instant, despite the pain shooting through him, he was determined to stand straight. "My brother writes that Herr Beethoven still has some hearing in his left ear. I wish I had your opportunity, Herr Otis. Deborah Pickering might well become a gracious wife. And it is the only way you will find out what you want to know."

"Yes, yes. I wish you felt better."

"Mozart made many compromises. Often he had to hire inferior singers in order to gain Royal patronage, and then rewrite his arias to suit the singers' voices. Go, Go! While I can still stand!"

"I will write you, Herr Muller. I promise."

"Of course. Remember, you must not be reverential."

"I will look only for the truth."

"Hmm? And you must not assume that you are Mozart. It is one thing to identify with him; it is dangerous to think *you are him.*"

"I will never make that mistake."

"I hope not. Inevitably, you will make many enemies."

"Goodbye, Maestro". Jason embraced Muller fervently. He could feel the old man quiver under his touch, then recoil.

"People only hear what they want to hear," Muller whispered.

He pushed Jason out of the music chamber before he lost control of himself and the parting became even more painful.

Deborah moved into Jason's small brick house after their marriage, although she regarded it as too humble and plain for a permanent residence. She assumed this was a temporary expedient, until a new home could be built to her specifications, but Jason said that such plans were premature, that he preferred to wait until they returned from Europe. He was not certain he would return. However, he did not give that as his reason, just that it was too soon, too hasty, such a vital matter demanded deliberation.

Deborah was determined to be a good wife, and she did not pursue the matter. She was surprised by the elegance of his bedroom. The four-poster bed was large, with a lute at its head; there was a spacious, efficient fireplace to heat the room, and a lacquered walnut screen for her to undress behind.

As Jason expected, she used the screen with becoming modesty, very much the lady. Then, when he put out the lamp at her request and the bedroom was in darkness except for the glow of the embers in the fireplace and the reflection of the moonlight on the window, she came to bed. But she was not protected by a heavy flannel nightgown as he had assumed, but naked. And the instant he put his arms around her, she sank into them, pulling him down on top of her as she had so long dreamed, as if his body was hers also. His entry came easier than he had anticipated, although he was positive she was a virgin, for she was uncertain in her aid, while very willing. She was as eager for sexual satisfaction as he was. Once they were joined, she responded with a passion that heightened his own.

She gave him a feeling of godlike power; and yet, as they lay together and felt complete, he also felt that his had to be a performance, and only as long as he maintained their love at its present pitch would their marriage endure.

The second time, she was even better, sustaining her emotion slowly, then rapidly, and with an excitement that matched his. Where had she learned her sexual skill, he wondered. Perhaps it was intuitive, he thought, like music.

They went to say goodbye to her father before departing for New York, where they were to visit Lorenzo da Ponte and then sail for England; and Pickering said to his daughter, although quite grudgingly, "Deborah, you do look exceedingly well."

Jason was very pleased. It was as if he had won a great victory. He wondered if this was the way Mozart had felt when the musician had married Constanze.

6

Lorenzo da Ponte

NEW YORK was dirtier and noisier than Boston. Deborah viewed the city with apprehension and wondered if Jason's determination to visit Mozart's librettist was wise. Jason replied that he was stimulated by the brisk April wind, the crowded wharves along the Hudson River with the many square-riggers docked there. As they walked toward Greenwich Street, where da Ponte resided, he pointed out that Broadway, on which they were strolling now, was a street that even the natives of Boston might esteem. Broadway was lined with properly shaded houses and fine shops, most of them built in the English style of which she was so fond.

But as they reached Greenwich Street and Deborah saw the ugly side streets, she was disgusted by the many pigs wandering in the mud, drawn by the garbage in the gutters. A passerby from whom they asked directions said that the distant towns of Flatbush and Brooklyn were cleaner, that the part of New York that was expanding northward was neatly constructed and possessed many pleasant red-brick houses like Boston, but her distaste for New York grew. A pig was nibbling at her feet; another was rooting around Jason.

Deborah said that the sooner they left New York the better. She was troubled about Jason. He had awakened hours before the dawn and he had tossed fitfully, evidently disturbed, although they had made love earlier and he had seemed happy then. It could not be money, she had decided; she had taken care of that. Was it that Jason had come to realize that he expected the wrong things from this venture? Deborah could not accept the reasons he gave for this expedition. She did not believe that Salieri had poisoned Mozart. She assumed that Jason must have other motives for this journey. Perhaps he felt that the genius he attributed to Mozart would touch him upon closer contact. Perhaps he was restless and needed an excuse to get away from Boston—she could sympathize with that. Or possibly he yearned to study music with the masters, to learn whether he had any genuine ability. But da Ponte would only discourage him. This was what Jason feared, she concluded; this was what had kept him awake the rest of the night.

Jason refused to reply to her expressions of distaste for New York. He was relieved to be free of Boston and its stifling atmosphere, where many people knew him and thus took it upon themselves to criticize him. Yet ever since they had arrived in New York, he had been concerned about meeting Mozart's librettist. Even as he was excited at the prospect of speaking to a person who had known Mozart intimately, he feared that da Ponte would ridicule him, or corrupt his image of Mozart, or, worse, would not talk to him at all.

These last fears seemed borne out when, at the address Otto Muller had given him as da Ponte's, no one answered his knock.

Deborah said, "It must be the wrong address."

Yet the polished nameplate said: ANN DA PONTE'S BOARDING HOUSE.

Jason knocked more boldly this time, although it was not the way he felt; and this time he saw a face peering at him from behind heavily drawn curtains. Then, a minute later, the door was opened carefully.

The elderly man who stood in the doorway was taller and straighter than Jason had expected. He was surprised by da Ponte's erect posture. Otto Muller had told him that the librettist must be at least seventy-five, yet da Ponte stood without the suggestion of a stoop. He thought the poet's long, large features intriguing, and he was attracted by the brilliant, penetrating eyes and the lengthy, white wavy hair that fell below the shoulders, but he was surprised by the sunken jaws and the lack of teeth. Then, da Ponte's attitude was a mixture of suspicion and eagerness, and it was impossible to tell which prevailed.

But when da Ponte saw that one of his visitors was a beautiful young lady, he bowed flamboyantly and led them into his drawing room.

How poor yet pompous he is, thought Deborah. His drawing room was small and shabby, the carpet was patched and stained, the curtains were old and yellow, the furniture was seedy and second-hand, and the ivory ornaments were imitation.

Jason liked the fact that the walls were lined with books, but he was shocked that there was nothing of music in this room, which, to judge from da Ponte's manner, was the heart of the librettist's life.

Da Ponte stated proudly, not waiting for them to declare their business, "I am a master of Rhetoric, a master of the Humanities, a master of Italian Grammar, a scholar expert in Dante and Petrarch, a professor of Latin and Italian literature; I have translated Lord Byron into Italian, and Dante, Petrarch, Tasso, Ariosto, and many others into English; I, more than any other man alive or dead, have made known the glories and passion of Italian literature to the New World; I have imported over a thousand Italian books to America; I possess the finest library of Italian classics in the New World. Now what would a charming, handsome young couple like yourselves desire? A room facing the street, or one at the rear? It is quieter at the rear. My wife serves a magnificent European cuisine, and you can study Italian while you live here. I also teach French and German, but Italian is my specialty. Our charges are reasonable, and we have many noble evenings during which the very best of European culture is brought to you free of any expense. I am well known in this great city of New York."

"That is one of the reasons we are here," Jason said politely.

"We have many students from that splendid institution Columbia College in my residence as roomers and boarders. Most of them study with me. I have been invited to teach at Columbia College. Next year. In 1825. Would you like my wife to show you what rooms are available?"

"I am sorry, sir, but that is not why we came!" Jason blurted out.

Da Ponte regarded them with a sudden, almost overwhelming suspicion, and cried out, "What slander has been uttered about me now? I thought I had experienced them all, but there are many liars who are willing—no, anxious—to spread calumnies. We have an utterly respectable boarding house, and my books are the best in America."

"But you have no musical instruments," said Deborah. "Why?"

"Why should I have musical instruments?"

Jason said, "You were Mozart's librettist."

"A dear, dear friend. A hundred years would not wipe from my memory my recollections of my beloved colleague Mozart." Da Ponte wiped away an imaginary tear from his eye. "I was his poet, not his librettist. I was poet for all the great Vienna composers; Salieri, Martin y Solar, and Weigl. Salieri and Martin had many successes thanks to my efforts. If they were alive today, much would be different."

"Salieri is still alive," Jason volunteered.

Da Ponte looked startled, then said hurriedly, "I have not spoken to him for many years. We drifted apart. After Mozart died. These days I devote myself to Italian literature; it is a more worthy pursuit." He added contemptuously, "There is no opera in America."

Jason said, "Did you know that Salieri tried to commit suicide, and it is reported reliably from Vienna that he confessed to poisoning Mozart?"

"Nothing is reported reliably in Vienna. Even though I was the Emperor's favorite, there were many slanders spread about me."

Deborah asked directly, "You don't think that Salieri poisoned Mozart?"

"Of course not! There were rumors about that ever since my dear friend Mozart died years ago. There were always rumors in Vienna when someone died suddenly, unexpectedly. Is that why you are here?" Da Ponte's suspicions turned to annoyance. "You don't desire rooms?"

"Later, perhaps," Jason said quickly. "About Mozart . . ."

"No!" Da Ponte cut him short abruptly. "I will not endure any slanders against my good friend Salieri. What you suggest is inconceivable."

"Even his suicide?"

"Salieri would never try to kill himself. He was not one to feel guilt."

Deborah said, "But how do we know that you were Mozart's librettist? There is no sign of music in your house."

"Words are my concern, Madam, not notes. Who sent you?"

Jason replied, "Otto Muller."

"Who?"

Deborah said, "An old musician in Boston, who came from Vienna. He claimed that he knew you and Mozart years ago in Vienna."

"Many people claimed to know me, and the important ones did. I was the most famous poet in Europe. Casanova knew me intimately, Mozart, and the Emperor, and Salieri. But this Muller sounds like an impostor."

Deborah smiled knowingly, indicating that she agreed with him, but Jason declared, "Otto Muller told me that he was appointed Konzertmeister during a rehearsal of *Così fan tutte*, and I believe him."

"Oh, that Muller!"

"Muller insisted that Salieri hated Mozart."

"Muller hated Salieri because Salieri never hired him. Salieri said that Muller was a second-rate musician. Which he was."

"Mozart trusted him."

"Mozart had a kind heart."

"Not about music or musicians."

"And, of course, Muller is the authority for that, too, Mister . . ."

"Jason Otis. This is my wife, Deborah. We were just married."

"I could tell. Mrs. Otis' beauty has a radiance that befits a lady newly wed. Now who would you believe, Mrs. Otis: Muller, who knew Mozart only as an inferior, or Lorenzo da Ponte, who was Mozart's equal, and in some respects his superior? It was I who obtained the commissions for the operas he wrote. The Emperor heeded me, not Mozart, who was a great musician, but poorly regarded by Joseph. Joseph did not like it that Mozart was often in debt. It was as if that placed a burden upon him."

"About his debts, Signor . . ."

"We all had debts occasionally." Da Ponte shrugged that off.

"What about his wife and the other Weber women?" asked Jason.

"Morals have always been more elastic in Europe. Mozart never said one thing ugly. With him, everything was expressed beautifully. His form and content were always one and the same thing."

"But Muller told me that Salieri created many difficulties before you could get *Così fan tutte* produced."

"We had no difficulties with *Così*. I solved them all. Everything went smoothly once I was aware of the intrigues against us. It was *Figaro* that was difficult. Most of the nobility resented the story. Do you know *Le Nozze di Figaro*?"

"Only what Muller told me about it. I have never heard it."

"I forgot," da Ponte said scornfully, "that nothing of da Ponte and Mozart is known in America. *Le Nozze di Figaro* is a beautiful opera."

"Muller said—"

Da Ponte interrupted Jason, "You must not heed anything he said. Muller is an old man; his memories are faulty."

Jason did not remind da Ponte that he was a year older than Muller.

Deborah stated, "My husband is convinced that Salieri poisoned Mozart."

"I am not convinced," said Jason, "but I believe that it is possible. That is why I am here, why I desire your opinion, Signor da Ponte."

"Salieri was my best friend. Until we quarreled. He introduced me to Vienna and to the Emperor. I wrote the librettos for his best operas. But he would never have poisoned Mozart. It would have been too obvious."

"Salieri is said to have confessed to poisoning Mozart."

"Salieri would never have confessed to anything. It was not his nature."

Jason asked desperately, stricken with the possibility that his entire venture was in vain, and now what would he have to look forward to? "You are sure, Signor, that Salieri did not intrigue against Mozart?"

"Everybody in Vienna intrigued against somebody."

"Even Mozart?"

"Why should he be different?"

"Yet the suddenness with which he died? The way his body vanished mysteriously? And now Salieri's confession? How can you help but wonder?"

"I have had to endure worse things. Weep no more for Mozart. He has been at peace for many years, but I have had to go on with my memories."

Da Ponte began to talk about himself, but now Jason was not interested, for there was not one word about Mozart.

Lean, venerable, arrogant, da Ponte was bound by his own vanity, Jason reflected. He saw Deborah smile triumphantly. He broke in on da Ponte, for if he didn't, the poet would talk incessantly, "Thank you, sir, for your opinion. But we must go now." Suddenly Jason was afraid that this was just the first of many disappointments.

Da Ponte halted him at the door. "I will go with you, Mr. Otis."

"With us? Where?"

"To a coffee house. Where we can talk freely. You never know who is spying on you. Mozart and I often went to a coffee house when we wanted to discuss something important. It was safer."

"But you said, Signor, that Salieri did not conspire against Mozart."

"I do not believe that Salieri had anything to do with Mozart's death. But Salieri was not his friend. Nor mine either," he said, almost spitefully, "toward the end." He took Deborah's arm as if she were a queen and escorted her to the door." I am sure Mrs. Otis is tired and would enjoy a genuine coffee house. You must hear how Salieri fought to halt *Figaro*. And would have succeeded, if not for my valiant efforts."

Jason asked, "Was that opera your greatest success?"

"Many connoisseurs preferred *Don Giovanni*. While the Emperor liked best the opera I wrote for Martin y Solar, *La Cosa Rara*. It was the first opera to have a waltz in it." Da Ponte hailed a carriage. And as he helped them in, playing the host graciously, he said reflectively, "Mozart has been dead almost thirty-three years—it was 1791 when he died—and yet none of his operas has been produced in the New World. Even so, I suspect that now he is a legend in Vienna."

"Then I am not the only one who thinks he may have been poisoned?"

"That is not the question, Mr. Otis. You are too eager to prove it."

7

Le Nozze di Figaro

D A PONTE told the driver where to go, and a few minutes later they reached the coffee house. He assumed that Jason would pay for the carriage, and he helped Deborah step down while Jason paid the driver.

The coffee house was attractive, with a ladies' entrance, and as they entered, da Ponte's voice dropped to a whisper. "This establishment is run by an Italian compatriot of mine. I don't trust him—he is always trying to steal my students and boarders for his brother, who fancies himself an Italian scholar—but his food and wine are the best in New York." Da Ponte was acting the conspirator now. As he led them into a small, empty room in the rear, he glanced over his shoulder to make sure that no one was following them. He proudly pointed out that this room was illuminated with gas lights, and smiled with gratification when Jason insisted that he must be their guest. He said, "It is wonderful to meet such charming Americans. You must be an artist too, Mr. Otis."

"I am a musician," said Jason.

"In his free time," added Deborah. "My husband supports himself with his position in my father's bank."

Deborah would never change, Jason thought angrily. She had to poison the atmosphere whenever he considered himself a musician. But he said, more quietly than he felt, "I have taken a leave of absence from the bank to pursue the study of music in Europe."

"Are you a composer, too, Mr. Otis?"

"Yes. I composed the *Boston Handel and Haydn Society Collection of Church Music*. You may have heard about it. It is used in churches here."

"Indeed. The substance of your work is found in the sacred melodies of Handel and Haydn. Mrs. Otis, you are fortunate to have wed such an industrious young man. It takes skill to know whom to borrow from."

Deborah said, "I do not find that gratifying. You know what happened to Mozart. He died impoverished. He was thrown into an unknown grave."

Jason shouted, "I am not Mozart!"

"Sometimes you think you are."

"Never!" Didn't she understand that if he was seeking to breathe fresh life into Mozart, it was because Mozart had been deprived of many years of a productive existence. Only she was so sure of her own views. He said to himself, I will make her pay for her skepticism! The very manner of Mozart's burial was a perversion of what Mozart's work was. "Signor da Ponte, the Society is also offering Beethoven a commission to compose an oratorio, and I have been given the honor of presenting this to him."

"I never met Beethoven. He was a boy when I was Imperial Court Poet."

Jason's feeling of distrust toward Deborah did not vanish, although she was smiling at him now to express her affection.

Da Ponte said, "In Vienna all the coffee houses had billiard tables. Did you know that Mozart loved billiards and was skilful? He claimed it kept his fingers limber. He was a fine pianist, too. We are at Park Row and Broadway, the center of New York. Now we can talk with candor."

A waiter brought water, and da Ponte ignored it.

"You cannot trust the water," da Ponte told them. He requested wine.

But he asked the waiter to sip the wine first.

Then he said, "It is absurd, assuming that one composer poisoned another, especially when the first composer was more renowned at the time than the second."

Jason asked, "Was Salieri better known in Vienna than Mozart?"

"Of course. Salieri became the First Kapellmeister at the Imperial Court, while Mozart never rose above the post of Third." Da Ponte ordered an Italian meal for the three of them, hushing their protests, and when the food came, Jason and Deborah agreed that it was tasty. Da Ponte was quiet while he ate, except for the sound of his toothless jaws chewing.

When da Ponte finished, he said abruptly, "All my teeth were destroyed by an enemy in Vienna, who tried to poison me. He thought I was making a cuckold out of him. Many assassinations were attempted in Vienna."

Deborah had been engrossed by his courtliness to her. There was a limpid sensuality in da Ponte's eyes when he gazed at her, despite his age, and they sparkled as he addressed her. She had never experienced this in an old man, and she did not know how to respond to it. Even while she felt she should regard him with contempt, she enjoyed his attentions. But then his knee pressed against hers under the table and she was sickened. With a sudden revulsion for the world this elderly lecher and would-be charmer represented, and a fear that she and Jason were about to enter waters too deep and difficult for them to navigate, she stood up, saying, "We must go. We have another appointment and . . ."

It was Jason who yanked her down with a harshness that was frightening and stated, "My wife gets confused about the time. The appointment she spoke of . . . is tomorrow."

She sat motionless, too proud to indicate any pain, although inside she seethed. How dare he after the way she had helped him? He would not be sitting here if not for her money! He would suffer for this.

Da Ponte said, "I am sorry, madam, if I have created any misunderstandings. But there was a conspiracy against *Figaro.*"

Deborah said slowly, "My husband is obsessed with Mozart. And this obsession could poison him as he thinks Mozart was poisoned."

Jason spoke as if he had not heard her. "Signor da Ponte, you were going to tell us about *Le Nozze di Figaro*. And Mozart and Salieri."

Da Ponte shut his eyes and slipped into a reverie. Now there was only the sound of the horses on the cobblestones outside the coffee house, and occasional laughter and the clink of glasses from the patrons.

So Salieri was virtually dead, reflected the poet, as was his great rival, Mozart. Was it the fact that Mozart's work far exceeded Salieri's in the public estimation in Vienna, now that Mozart was dead, although Salieri had remained the First Royal Kapellmeister in Vienna, that had brought on the would-be suicide? Had a sick mind, long tormented by Mozart's superiority, used an attempt at suicide to seize attention?

Some things he remembered so clearly it was as if they had happened a few minutes ago, but others were very vague. He shook his head in perplexity, and in irritation. But this young American wanted to know exactly what he recalled, and now his own curiosity, whetted by Salieri's reported attack on himself, yearned to be satisfied also.

Many things had occurred in Vienna that had caused him to wonder. Had it been almost forty years since he had met Mozart? They had been friends and collaborators, but intimates—hardly! He had never been sure that Mozart had even liked him. The composer, for all of his naïveté, had used him. Despite everyone in Vienna who mattered being aware that he, Lorenzo da Ponte, was the *master* of intrigue, while Mozart had no talent for it, it had been the composer who had profited the most from his persuading the Emperor to permit *Le Nozze di Figaro*. Whoever had heard the opera had praised the music and had taken the libretto for granted.

Was Salieri, actually, a scapegoat for someone else's misdeeds, da Ponte asked himself; a composer who should be remembered because of his passion for sweets and success? Did it matter that there was no trace of Mozart's ashes? He found himself dreaming of the many women he had known sensually. He had far exceeded Mozart in this; he doubted that Mozart had known any female but his wife, Constanze.

His just-published memoirs would reveal that he had been second only to Casanova and Don Giovanni in this respect. He gloated over his triumphs with the Emperor—such a few, brief years. When was the last time he had been treated as a great man? 1794? 1804?

Yet little Wolfgang Amadeus Mozart, shorter than average, sensitive about his lack of height and vain about his blond hair, was the one that people wanted to talk about. Didn't they realize that he had had a great career, too? If Mozart had been buried respectfully, like Joseph Haydn, would his death have aroused such sympathy? Was there a divine logic in this?

But obviously this young, intense, athletic American believed there was an explanation which was foul and terrifying. What did old Otto Muller really know of his colleague? That second-rate violinist had not lifted a finger to help Mozart. But he, Lorenzo da Ponte, had tried.

His eyes became dark and brilliant again as he returned to his waiting listeners.

In this moment Jason thought that da Ponte's appearance had become remarkably exciting, almost handsome, and certainly appealing in spite of the loss of his teeth and the erosions of old age. And Deborah, although she still felt that Jason had asked a monstrous question and that she must doubt whatever da Ponte said, had to hear what the poet remembered. For while she expected anything he said to be extravagant, there was an intensity about him that was convincing, and he was saying, "I will resurrect Mozart for you," and part of her believed him.

"I had assured Mozart that I would convince the Emperor that *Le Nozze di Figaro* should be produced by the Imperial Court Theater, but as I strode toward his rooms on the Grosse Schulerstrasse with the completed first act of the proposed opera, I sensed that he still did not believe me. We had met only recently—although I had heard about him for many years, for he had been famous throughout Europe because of his precocity—and the comedy we intended to base our work on, Beaumarchais' *Le Mariage de Figaro,* had been banned from the Vienna theater by the Emperor because of its caustic comments about the nobility, and I was sure that Mozart did not believe I could excise the political references and yet have an effective libretto. But I was pleased with my first act. The question in my mind was: Would Mozart's music be equal to my vivacity and skill?

"As befitted my position as Court Poet, I lived in a far better and more accessible neighborhood than Mozart, in luxurious rooms on the wide, spacious Kohlmarkt, next door to where the most famous poet of the century, Metastasio, had lived, and near my dear patron, the Emperor, and his favorite theater, the Burgtheater. Salieri was my neighbor, and Gluck, and most of the important musicians in Vienna.

"But Mozart was pleased with his rooms on the Grosse Schulerstrasse, so I resolved to praise them too. They were behind St. Stephen's, the most famous cathedral in the Empire, where Mozart hoped to be the first Kapellmeister some day, and as I entered his house, I was appalled by the chill in his hallway, and the tiny bit of sky many floors above. However, he greeted me warmly at the top of the first landing.

"He apologized for the steps. 'Twenty-three in all,' he said.

"I never forgot the number, for it was strange that with all the music in his mind, he would remember that, and he informed me proudly, 'We have the livers of geese for dinner, it is a great delicacy, signor, and you must be our guest for dinner,' and I could tell that he loved this barbaric German food and in his enthusiasm I was supposed to also.

"Since I believe in being a good guest, I nodded, although his food did not compare with what we have just eaten here. It is strange what one remembers; but it was my first visit to his quarters, and I was eager to observe how he lived and to judge whether I could trust him to fulfil his obligations, for I did like his ability to create melodies. Many a composer writes correctly, but to have heart, that is very difficult.

"He proudly showed me his four-room apartment, and I knew it was considered desirable, for it was on the first floor, had fine bay windows on the Grosse Schulerstrasse, and a splendid stucco ceiling in his study with a lovely, sensuous Venus in the center panel, and pretty, voluptuous nymphs and cupids about her, and enough space for his pianoforte, harpsichord, and clavichord. But his quarters did not compare with my own, although I did not tell him so.

"I said, 'It is quite gracious of you, Maestro, to invite me to your home. I am honored. Everything here has the mark of excellence.'

"The maid served the three of us: Mozart, his wife, Constanze, and myself. It was early evening and after his wife—who had spoken very little and who I thought rather plain, considering that my mistress was one of the leading prima donnas in Europe—put their son to bed with Mozart expressing lavish affection toward the child, he read my first act and accepted it without question as a libretto. But as I expected, he did not think that the Emperor would allow it.

"He said, 'Even with the political references eliminated, the servant, Figaro, outwits his master, Count Almaviva.'

"I assured him, 'The Emperor will permit it. After I speak to him.'

"He answered, 'Moreover, our contemporaries could not endure a success by me.'

" 'What do you mean?'

" 'Salieri, Gluck, Orsini-Rosenberg consider that I am dangerous.'

"I asked, 'They believe that you threaten their lives, Mozart?'

" 'Worse, that I threaten their careers. Thus, they will do anything to stop me.' He said this with the utmost seriousness.

" 'Incredible!' I exclaimed, but I did not feel that it was incredible.

"Mr. and Mrs. Otis, what you Americans do not understand is that in Europe one always fought the battle of life with personal weapons such as gossip, slander, blackmail, and treachery, and anyone who was vulnerable, like Mozart, could be damaged. You did not attack his music; you attacked his character. It had happened to me often by the time I met Mozart. I had been even accused of murder. Unjustly."

Jason interrupted, "You said that Mozart was vulnerable. Why?"

"He was a public figure. In Vienna that was enough."

Deborah said, "Jason, you must not distract him. Signor da Ponte, do you really think that Mozart had as much talent as my husband claims?"

Jason snapped, "My wife doesn't always know what she is talking about. She, forgive her, doesn't understand music."

Deborah glared at him furiously and declared, "I despise people who spend their life in speculation. It is such a waste."

"Children!" Da Ponte was very upset. "Don't you want me to continue?"

"Of course!" They said that as one.

"Mozart sat quietly as he spoke to me, but he had a strong sense of ridicule and he could be pitiless with other musicians. He was not much of a dissembler, even with the Emperor, while I had the talent to be an ambassador, as the Emperor himself told me many times, and Mozart said I reminded him of his father, I was such a shrewd diplomat. And our joint interest in *Figaro* had made Salieri an enemy of both of us.

"When Mozart repeated his doubts that my version of *Figaro* would be acceptable, I assured him again, 'I will obtain an audience with Joseph.'

" 'When?'

" 'At once. Tomorrow, if necessary. I can always get his ear.'

"I could tell by the slight smile on his pale features that he did not believe me. I asked, 'Have you written any music for *Figaro*?'

" 'Why?'

"I said, 'So we can play it for Joseph if he should desire to hear it. To prove the worth of our venture, Maestro.'

"Mozart answered, 'I have composed several arias, and now that I possess the first act I will write more. They will be ready, if that should be necessary.' He was positive of that.

" 'Even if Joseph should want to hear them tomorrow, or the next day?'

" 'Whenever you need them. I have much of the score in my mind.'

"As he played two of his arias on his harpsichord, to express their delicacy, I was much moved. I did not tell him this, for I did not want him to feel that I could not do without him. I was correct in this, for later I was to write for Salieri again, and Martin y Solar and others, with great success. I agreed that these arias were suitable, if we could find someone to sing them. What surprised me was that Mozart had played the two arias without a single note before him.

"Mozart said with a shrug, 'From memory. It is no great trick.'

"But I had never known any composer quite like him, and I replied, 'You must put the notes on paper. For the singers.'

" 'I will. As soon as you are gone.'

"I pointed out, 'The evening is almost over. It is time for bed.'

"He replied, 'But since it is necessary, as you say, it will be done.'

"I wondered if Mozart was mocking me. The slight smile had reappeared on his face, and I had a feeling that he would insist on having his own way. I was not sure that would be tolerable. But suddenly, apparently sensing my misgivings, as he bid me goodbye he threw his arms around me with a genuinely warm embrace, surprising for a German, and I realized that he was two men: a musician who was fanatically critical and a human being who was full of human affection.

"I promised, 'I will do my best to bring honor to the names of Lorenzo da Ponte and Wolfgang Amadeus Mozart.'

"He said, 'I am sure you will. But you must remember, as my father always warns me, nothing in this world is wholly free of self-interest.'

"Supported by Mozart's confidence in me, I arranged for an audience with the Emperor the next afternoon. I was surprised to learn that he was in residence at the Schönbrunn Palace, for Joseph preferred the Hofburg Palace, which he considered his own. He felt that Schönbrunn was his mother's, Maria Theresa's, although she was dead now and he was the sole ruler. At first I was annoyed, for Schönbrunn was outside of Vienna and I had to hire a carriage, while I could have walked to the Hofburg from my rooms. But it was a fine, clear day, and as I rode along the Mariahilfestrasse and through the woods before Schönbrunn, my hopes rose. Here, I, alone, should have the ear of the Emperor.

"Beautiful, beautiful Schönbrunn. I have been in many palaces, but none as magnificent as Schönbrunn. While I waited outside the Mirror Room for my audience, I wondered why Joseph was here. Was it for some vital State business? Or that he wished to impress some visiting ruler? Or was he tired of the plainness of the Hofburg and needed the change? To my amazement, Salieri emerged from the Emperor's audience chamber.

"All my life I will remember that moment.

"For an instant, Salieri looked as astonished as I was. Then he recovered his composure, as I did, and bowing graciously, said, 'It is good to see you looking so well, Lorenzo. What brings you so far to speak to the Emperor? A new opera, no doubt?'

"I bowed just as graciously, not to be outdone in civility, and retorted, 'My dear Antonio, perhaps the same reason that brings you.'

"He said, 'You share my concern for our noble Emperor's health?'

" 'Of course! Of course!' I exclaimed. I thought, Salieri also has his stupid side, particularly when his vanity is concerned. 'We are fortunate to have a ruler with such an exquisite taste in music. Even if he hasn't always appreciated your brilliant efforts.'

" 'What do you mean, Lorenzo?'

"Salieri stood there, like many of the famous men in Vienna decidedly below middle height, while I, quite tall, towered over him. But Salieri was always neatly dressed, with a carefully coiffured wig, and although his stature was slight and his face was pale, his cheeks were rouged in the French fashion—he had just returned from the French Court with Gluck—and his eyebrows were painted and enlarged to give his features vividness. But they caused his large nose to look even larger, and I thought that his long features inclined to be flabby, except for his dark eyes, which were wide and glittering.

"I said, 'The Emperor was distressed with *Il Ricco d'un Giorno.*' If I provoked Salieri, in his vanity he might reveal why he was really seeing the Emperor. I had a feeling that it concerned myself and Mozart, and our wish to create an opera out of *Le Mariage de Figaro.*

" 'Distressed!' snarled Salieri. 'Lorenzo, much as it pains me to say so, it was your libretto that gave the Emperor indigestion.'

" 'Ah, a wit,' I replied. 'Perhaps you should have written the words.'

" 'Indeed, I could not have done worse,' he answered angrily.

"I was startled by the vehemence of his emotion. I knew that after our unhappy collaboration on *Il Ricco d'un Giorno* Salieri had sworn never to work with me again, adding a comment that had become known throughout Vienna: 'I would rather cut off my fingers than ever put words of da Ponte's to music again.' I had assumed that he had said this in a momentary fit of temper and vanity, but now I was not certain.

"Salieri added—I felt spitefully and reproachfully—'I hear that you are considering Beaumarchais' revolutionary work.'

" 'Revolutionary?' I cried out. Salieri was not even being subtle.

" '*Le Mariage de Figaro* has been forbidden in Vienna.'

" 'As a theater piece. And, as Beaumarchais wrote it.'

" 'And are you going to write it in that barbarous German language?'

"We were speaking Italian, for although Salieri had lived in Vienna for almost twenty years, since 1766, he rarely spoke anything but Italian. He hated German and didn't care for French and insisted that only Italian was fit for music, sentiments I was inclined to agree with.

" 'Lorenzo, if you are not careful, you will be regarded as a revolutionary.' I could not tell whether he was saying this with malice or whether he was warning me. 'I thought you had better taste.'

" 'Is that what you have been discussing with the Emperor?'

"Salieri grinned with a private satisfaction, displaying his white teeth, which, I knew, he considered magnificent, especially since I had lost mine in the past few months. His handkerchief smelled strongly of perfume, and he preened himself like a peacock, but he didn't answer my question, saying instead, 'You would still be eking out a miserable existence if I had not introduced you to the Emperor.'

" 'I appreciated your help. But now you criticize me often.'

" 'Never—except when it is deserved.'

" 'I deserve it now, Antonio?'

" 'Lorenzo, I respect your talent, but not your judgment. If you insist on working with composers of inferior standing with the Emperor, you will never amount to anything in Vienna.'

" 'Are you referring to Mozart?'

" 'Oh, no! I admire Mozart's instrumental music. But when it comes to opera, he has written only one piece in Vienna, *The Abduction from the Seraglio*; and there is nothing remarkable about that opera.'

" 'I am not going to quarrel with you today,' I said. 'I have to see the Emperor, and I must not keep him waiting.' So Salieri did resent my working with Mozart, I thought—I, the greatest poet in Vienna and the favorite of the Emperor. 'But I am sorry that you are jealous of Mozart.'

" 'Jealous?' He glared at me with such an air of denial I was sure I was right. 'As I said, I am his friend. But *Figaro* is such an attack on established authority, such an opera could have sad consequences.'

" 'Is that what the Emperor thinks?' I asked.

"Salieri smiled knowingly, but he did not say anything.

"I said, 'It is kind of you to warn me, Antonio. I appreciate it.'

" 'You know that you were banished from Venice for activities against the State. One more difficulty and you could be in grave trouble here.'

" 'My activities were not against the State, but against certain people.'

" 'What was the difference? They were the rulers of Venice.'

" 'Is that why you oppose *Le Mariage de Figaro*?'

" 'Exactly! For your sake! When you are free, Lorenzo, I have an idea for an opera I would like to discuss with you.'

" 'Despite our quarrel over *Il Ricco d'un Giorno*?'

" 'All of us say harsh, unthinking things about each other. It is our Italian nature. But *basta!* We are *simpatico!* Not like these German composers. They don't understand that opera is in our blood, not theirs.'

"I agreed. There was no question in my mind that my beloved Italy had contributed more to the growth of opera than any other country.

"Salieri grew confidential, as I desired. He pointed to the exquisite chandeliers, the gilded stucco ceilings, and whispered, 'This is our culture, not theirs. Even Mozart himself admitted to me that he had serious doubts about *Figaro*. I met him at a musical party for Joseph Haydn, and he confessed to me that he had received a letter from his father that had upset him very much. You know that he is very much influenced by what the old man says, many people think too much.'

" 'What did Leopold Mozart write?' I asked. I had heard numerous tales about the older Mozart and how he had manipulated his son as a child. But Joseph Haydn respected his musical judgment, and so did other able musicians. 'He is against *Figaro*, Antonio?'

" 'Absolutely. Mozart told me that his father wrote him that *Figaro* is a tiresome play and that it will require a genius to create an effective opera text out of such tedious discussions and running abouts.'

" 'He told you that?' I knew that Mozart could be tactless, and that he never suffered fools easily, but Salieri was not always trustworthy.

" 'Would I deceive you, my fellow countryman? I who introduced you to Joseph? I have always respected your taste. And *Figaro* is in bad taste. It offends the Emperor and many of the nobles. An overwhelming majority of the Court are against it. Most of them have told me.'

"There was no question that Salieri had touched on a sore spot, and he was more likely to remain in public favor than Mozart with his skill as an intriguer, yet I felt that Mozart's music was superior. I said, 'Thanks, Antonio, I will keep everything you have told me in mind when I speak to the Emperor.'

"He said passionately, 'Opera is an Italian prerogative. If we want to keep the opera Italian, we must keep it in the hands of Italians.'

" 'Of course.' As I walked in to my audience with the Emperor, I saw that Salieri's dark face was unable to disentangle itself from Italy. But much as I adored my native land, I said to myself, 'Not I.' Lorenzo da Ponte would do whatever his Emperor wished."

Da Ponte paused in his narration to rest and to regain his breath. He had become passionate, he realized, recalling the glory of his past, and he was too old for passion. He hoped that he was accurate; most of what he remembered seemed true, but somehow in the recollection he wondered if he and Salieri had ever truly liked each other or simply used each other. Yet he had worked with him even after *Figaro*.

Like all egoists, thought Jason, da Ponte could not bear to take second place. In a way the poet was lifting himself up to superiority over Mozart, even over his corpse. Yet some of what he was telling him appeared possible, and could explain part of Salieri's enmity to Mozart. Da Ponte had much knowledge, but how much understanding?

Deborah had been determined not to be responsive, but the poet had penetrated her defenses, not by charm, intelligence, or wit, but by the persuasiveness of his personality. In spite of his threadbare clothes, his flamboyant gestures, his occasional contradictions, there was an eloquence about him that was intriguing. She felt that Jason was disappointed that there had not been any startling revelations, but she liked da Ponte's vitality and she was fascinated by his view of Salieri.

Breath and energy regained, da Ponte resumed. This time a note of love, which had not existed before, entered his voice. "The Emperor received me with urbanity and grace. Joseph was alone, except for his Court Chamberlain and the Director of the Imperial Theaters, Count Orsini-Rosenberg, and as soon as the formalities were observed—the Count had ushered me in—Joseph indicated to Orsini-Rosenberg that he wished to be alone with me. I could understand why; it would be easier for me to be candid without an intimidating witness.

"The Emperor sat in the Mirror Room surrounded by seven of the finest ceiling-high mirrors in the Palace, a slight man in a huge chamber, his high, slanting forehead the most distinguished feature of his face, although I also admired his strong nose and clear, interested eyes.

"I noticed to my surprise, however—for Joseph had a reputation for dressing plainly—that this afternoon he wore his Order of Merit and several other Royal decorations and that he held in his hand the gold baton which was the symbol of his Imperial authority; and although he seemed accessible, I sensed that there were more things on his mind than the fate of his opera company. Yet he greeted me warmly and smiled—he liked that I amused him—and he asked me why I had requested an audience.

" 'For your pleasure, Your Majesty.'

" 'That was what Signor Salieri was telling me.'

"I said, 'Signor Salieri is a splendid artist, Sire. I will always be grateful to him for introducing me to Your Majesty.'

" 'And now you wish to put *Le Mariage de Figaro* to music?'

" 'You know, Sire?' I pretended surprise.

" 'It is common knowledge, Signore. Particularly since I banned the play. I am amazed that you should want to convert it into an opera, considering these circumstances. Unless you intend to do it *sub rosa.*'

" 'Never, Your Majesty. I want to do it for your pleasure.'

" 'I have a tremendous responsibility, Signor Poet. I cannot allow my people to be infected with the play's unpleasant, revolutionary ideas.'

" 'Sire, that is precisely the way I feel. That is why I have removed all the vulgar political references, and anything else that could offend the public taste and decency. I brought the first act for you to read.'

" 'And to approve?'

" 'Without your approval, Sire, I would not write another word.'

" 'Not even for Paris or London, where such sentiments are applauded?'

" 'Of course not, Your Majesty.' I sensed that Joseph was regarding me with humorous indulgence, a condescension that he was bestowing upon me out of his affection for my taste, but that he did not believe that I could satisfy the needs of the moment. 'Although London and Milan have said that they would do the opera. But if you do not approve of what I have written, I will destroy it, Sire.'

"I started to tear up the act I had intended to submit to him, but he halted me—as I had prayed that he would—and said, 'I will read it.'

" 'Thank you, Your Majesty. I am deeply honored.'

" 'I haven't said I would accept it. Who is writing the music?'

"I was sure that he knew, and I was surprised by his duplicity; but then I realized that as a ruler he had to dissemble and intrigue—otherwise he could never rule. I said, 'Sire, the music is by Mozart.'

"He said, 'His instrumental music is charming, but when it comes to opera, he has written only one piece in Vienna, *The Abduction from the Seraglio,* and there is certainly nothing unusual about that.'

"I could hear Salieri speaking now, but I replied, 'Gracious Sire, without your generosity I would not have been heard in Vienna.'

"He nodded, but added, 'And *Figaro* is such an attack on established authority, its views could not be tolerated.'

"I could still hear Salieri talking and I replied, 'Your Majesty, I will make *Figaro* a comedy of love and intrigue, but not politics. One that we can all enjoy. Even Maestro Salieri.'

" 'Kapellmeister Salieri admires your talent, Signor Poet. Moreover, I understand that Mozart himself thinks the play tiresome.'

"I was furious at Salieri. He had done his work skillfully; he had even used Mozart's own words to damage him. But I could not allow Salieri to triumph; it would have been too humiliating. I explained hurriedly, 'Sire, Mozart was speaking only of the political comments. His music is lovely. If he could play it for you, with your exquisite musical taste, I believe that you would like it. And approve of it.'

" 'But suppose I don't care for your first act?'

" 'Sire, I stake my reputation that you will like it.'

"Count Orsini-Rosenberg appeared at the door—I was certain that as a close friend of Salieri's he had appeared at this moment so that the Emperor could not commit himself. The Court Chamberlain informed Joseph that the Privy Council had assembled in the anteroom and were waiting to see His Majesty when he was ready. Joseph motioned to show them in, and then, in an unexpected gesture of generosity, he rose and escorted me to the door, putting his hand on my shoulder. I will never forget his touch as long as I live . . . gentle . . . kind."

Da Ponte's eyes filled with tears, and for a minute he could not go on.

"Then he said to me quietly, as if he were confiding in me rather than telling me from above, 'Signore, the great majority of the nobility want me to keep the people in ignorance. They say it is utter foolishness to provide an opportunity for education for everybody. They claim that it is the natural lot of the masses to be illiterate. And now they want me to turn my back on my people.' He sounded very tired.

" 'Sire, you have done more for the opera than any ruler in the world.'

" 'You exaggerate somewhat, da Ponte, but I have tried.' He led me out of the hearing of the Privy Council, who were filing in behind

Orsini-Rosenberg. 'Now the nobles want me to impose total censorship.'

" 'Even on the theater, Your Majesty?'

" 'Even on the opera,' he answered gravely. 'And to have our poets use only mythological subjects for their librettos. Orsini-Rosenberg, as Director of the Imperial Theaters, says there is no need to search for original subjects when there are six thousand volumes in the Imperial Library for a poet to find a subject in. What do you think, Signor?'

" 'Whatever Your Majesty desires. When will you read my first act?'

" 'Tonight. If this meeting of the Privy Council does not take all afternoon. My reforms are making the nobility restive. They have asked to meet with me, in the hope they can convince me to revoke them.'

"Out of the corner of my eye I could see that this was a vital session, that the nobles gathered on the other side of the Mirror Room included the most powerful in the Empire. This was clearly a matter of the gravest importance. I had a sudden chill then; perhaps this was the wrong time to ask Joseph to consider my treatment of *Figaro*. But it was too late to do anything about that, for he had placed the first act on his desk, with the title, which I had written in vivid red ink, *Le Nozze di Figaro*, across the cover and my name, Lorenzo da Ponte, Court Poet, on top and Wolfgang Amadeus Mozart on the bottom. I saw an expression on Prince Kaunitz's face, staring at the manuscript, saying What the Devil is this? He was Chancellor, and second only to the Emperor in power.

"Joseph suddenly asked me, 'Isn't this a beautiful chamber?'

" 'Yes, Your Majesty, even more striking than anything in Venice.'

" 'I heard Mozart play here. When he was six. It was strange. I think I was more nervous than he was. My mother liked him, as a child.'

" 'Did you, Sire?' If I only knew which composer he preferred!

" 'He was so small. I had never heard anyone so small play so well.'

" 'Your Majesty, he is even more skillful now.'

" 'But he is no longer a miracle of nature, and so, less interesting.'

" 'You don't like him, Sire?' I was upset. Had I chosen the wrong composer after all? 'I thought that Mozart was one of your favorites.'

"Joseph smiled cryptically, but he did not answer my question.

"The nobles were becoming restless; and since I did not want their hostility to turn against me, I bowed low and said, 'Your Majesty, if my opera of *Figaro* will cause you any trouble, I will withdraw it.'

" 'No, no!' Joseph exclaimed. 'You have aroused my curiosity, and now I must read your first act. Perhaps it will divert us from our present difficulties, as you say.' Then he said something which, in view of what occurred after he died, I never forgot. 'However, I must warn you, as a friend, Signor da Ponte, that the nobles who already resent my reforms could resent an opera of *Figaro* even more, particularly if the character of Figaro triumphs over the Count, as he does in the comedy.' "

As da Ponte paused again, to refresh his energy and his memory, Jason blurted out, "Is that truly the way it happened, Signore?"

"Word for word," da Ponte said firmly.

"After all these years?" Jason was skeptical.

"I have a remarkable memory, and I never forgot Joseph's interest."

"Did Mozart know what happened?"

"I told him. But I minimized the difficulties, and stressed how successful I had been with the Emperor. As I was."

"Was he afraid of what the nobles might think?"

"Certainly he sought to please them with his music, but he never hesitated to criticize them if he felt they were injuring his music. You must realize that although Mozart had a mild demeanor, not like myself, who could cower people with my presence, he had a caustic tongue which he did not spare the use of when provoked and which did him much damage."

"Did you allow Figaro to triumph over the Count?"

"I had to. Mozart would not write the music until I allowed that."

"Did he comprehend the risk he might be taking?"

"Yes. But he said that without Figaro's triumph the story would be emasculated. And he was right."

Deborah interrupted, "Jason, you must allow Signor da Ponte to finish. It is growing late, there may be no carriage available."

Da Ponte said, "I will get you a conveyance, dear lady."

Jason asked. "Is that all that happened that was dangerous?"

Da Ponte sighed. "Not quite. But at the time I thought so. I made sure that Figaro succeeded charmingly and entertainingly so that no one should be offended. And certainly Mozart's music was pleasing."

"Was anyone offended?" Jason asked.

"That is the finish of my tale."

"As I expected, Joseph read my act after his meeting with the Privy Council, approved it, and ordered Mozart to appear at the Hofburg the next night with several singers to perform the complete arias. Mozart complied. He had enough music finished to satisfy the Emperor, although I had doubted he could have it ready in such a short time.

"Soon after, we were given permission to proceed with the opera. There were some difficulties and delays, but nothing that seemed to involve Salieri directly until a few days before the dress rehearsal.

"Apparently Salieri and his accomplices were waiting for the opera to fail, but when, at the first complete rehearsal *Figaro* was performed brilliantly, especially the first act and the aria '*Non più andrai,*' Orsini-Rosenberg suddenly and abruptly ordered us to eliminate the dancing in the opera. As Director of the Imperial Theaters he had this power, and only the Emperor could revoke his edicts. Herr Director's excuse was that Joseph had prohibited all dancing in the Imperial Theaters. Mozart was sure that Salieri had persuaded Orsini-

Rosenberg to do this, and I was inclined to agree with him. Mozart was in despair, but I convinced Joseph to view a complete rehearsal of the opera, except for the dancing. Then I substituted pantomime for the ballet, which caused the story to be incomprehensible.

"As I had expected, the Emperor had been enjoying *Le Nozze di Figaro*, and so, when the story became ridiculous—the need for the dancing was obvious—he was furious. He demanded to know what had happened, and after I told him, he commanded Orsini-Rosenberg to put the dancing back and to restore the opera as it had been conceived. To make his point, Joseph insisted that Herr Director obtain the dancers himself.

"Orsini-Rosenberg did so, but I had a feeling that he would never forgive me or Mozart for this public humiliation.

"However, I put these fears aside when I was asked by Martin y Solar to write a libretto for his new opera, *La Cosa Rara*, and Salieri also requested a libretto from me. Both of these commissions had Imperial approval, and so I was positive I had nothing to fear.

"For while *Le Nozze di Figaro* was received indifferently, *La Cosa Rara* was the sensation of the season. Every opera composer in Vienna desired my services, and now it was evident, even to Mozart, that I, the Court Poet, was more vital to the success of an opera than the composer. But that was not the end of *Figaro*, or the difficulties that it brought down upon our heads, like a terrible landslide."

Da Ponte paused. Even now the memory of what had occurred was still too painful to recollect, and yet, somehow, he had to continue. If he could only hear one of his operas once more! It had been so many years since he had heard voices singing his words! *Le Nozze di Figaro* had been enchanting. It must have been, he assured himself. His memories of it were. He shut his eyes, but all he heard were fragments. Disgusted with his errant memory, he resumed talking about what he did remember.

"In 1790, when Joseph died and his brother Leopold succeeded him on the throne, I was expelled from Vienna, and a year later Mozart was dead. But years later Salieri was still Kapellmeister. Now I am convinced"—and the more da Ponte thought about it now, the more he was convinced—"that we were never forgiven by the nobility for the creation of *Le Nozze di Figaro*. To have the servant, Figaro, constantly outwit and best his master, Count Almaviva, was regarded as unforgivable."

Jason interrupted, "What is your proof?"

"Wait until the police search your rooms in Vienna, as they searched mine," said da Ponte.

Jason asked, "When was that?"

C *

"After my dear and enlightened friend Emperor Joseph died and his brother Leopold succeeded him on the throne."

"What was their excuse?"

"They didn't need an excuse, but I heard that they were looking for what they called seditious material. Anything that was critical of the Hapsburgs was considered seditious. The assumption that *Figaro* was an attack on the nobility was reasonable enough cause to search my rooms."

"Did they search Mozart's?"

"I don't know."

"Why don't you know, Signor da Ponte?"

"I was out of Vienna by then."

"Why didn't they arrest you?"

Da Ponte said vehemently, "They tried. I had to flee for my life, to Trieste, when I heard that I was to be banished from Vienna. The official charge was that I had said unflattering things about the new Emperor."

Jason, who was searching for the vital fact which would fit Mozart's death into the pattern he had decided upon, was disturbed. Da Ponte was suggesting a new line of inquiry. Yet he could not halt him, for Deborah, usually quite sceptical, appeared almost convinced.

Da Ponte added, "Vienna, with the triumph of the revolution in France, had become a cesspool of accusations. Anyone who had a connection with a play like *Le Mariage de Figaro*, which many said had helped bring on the revolution in France with its criticism of the nobility, was automatically suspected of treasonable sentiments."

Deborah asked, "Signor, had you said anything critical of Leopold?"

"Mozart had. He had been free with his criticism of the new Emperor. He never forgave Leopold for rejecting him years before in Tuscany, where the younger brother of Joseph had been ruler for a long time."

"What about the accusations against you?" asked Deborah.

"If they were not sufficient, they found others. If the Hapsburgs wanted you to be guilty, you were guilty, or they made you guilty."

Jason said, "Without evidence?"

"As I told you, our creation of *Figaro* was evidence enough. With the revolution in France, anyone showing the slightest sign of democratic sentiments was suspect. And Mozart was also a Freemason."

"That made him guilty of treason?" Jason was shocked.

"That made him guilty of democracy," Da Ponte replied emphatically. "I advised him to leave Vienna without delay."

Jason asked, "How did he respond?"

"I received a most melancholy letter from him."

"Did he accept your advice?"

"No."

"What happened then?"

"A few weeks after I heard from him, Signor Otis, he was dead."

Perhaps he had been right after all, Jason thought with relief. Then he felt guilty, as if, somehow, he had caused Mozart's sudden death to happen. The gas lights had burned low and da Ponte was smiling sadly, while Deborah had a sardonic expression on her face. He felt trapped by conflicting emotions. Was he so committed to the belief that Mozart had been poisoned that he could not trust any other evidence? He asked, "Do you have this letter?"

"Yes."

"What did Mozart write?"

Da Ponte did not answer at first. He was thinking, He had had enough experiences for five men, and some of his memories were superbly satisfying, and yet, inevitably, those that remained most vividly with him were self-consuming and sometimes so painful that they were almost unendurable. Yet even as they tormented him, he returned to them. He had had virtually every gratification a man could seek, but with the passage of time it had become the bitter memories that had become dominant. He wondered, Was gall the natural condition of old age. He said suddenly, "I wrote Mozart from Trieste, asking him to join me in England. I said that we would find many friends in London—Joseph Haydn was there and a great success, and the Storaces, whom he had taught in Vienna and loved—and that we would be far more esteemed there than in the Emperor Leopold's Vienna. I was deeply shaken by his reply."

He pulled out a faded letter and read:

"My dear da Ponte:

"I would love to heed your advice, but it is impossible. My head spins so I cannot see a straight path ahead, but see only darkness and the grave. I cannot rid my mind of the spectre of death. I view him constantly these days: he begs me to join him, he persuades me, he says I must labor only for him. I go on working because composing exhausts me less than doing nothing. Moreover, there is little left to fear. There is such a heaviness in me that I know my hour is striking. I am near death. I am finished before I have had time to enjoy my ability. And yet life has been so beautiful, and my career started with such fortunate circumstances. But no one can alter his fate. No one can measure his days. One has to resign oneself. What Providence wills, will be done. So I have to finish my funeral song, which I cannot leave incomplete."

Jason exclaimed, "Was that letter from Mozart himself?"

Da Ponte showed him the signature. The yellowing letter paper, which was on the verge of crumpling under his touch, was signed: "W. A. Mozart."

Da Ponte said, "The letter is in Italian. You couldn't understand it." He took it out of Jason's hands as if it were a hot coal. "Mozart was as fluent in

Italian as he was in German. And it showed in *Figaro.*" He added scornfully, "Anyone who thinks *Figaro* is a German opera is crazy."

Listening avidly, Deborah felt confused. It was as if she were being sucked into a maelstrom against her wishes and better judgment. Da Ponte's memories struck her as such a strange mixture of bad drama and provocative testimony, she didn't know which to believe. If she could only find out what were da Ponte's reasons for what he was revealing. There were many more questions she longed to ask, but she was drained emotionally.

Jason asked impatiently, "Despite this letter, you still deny the charges that Salieri had anything to do with Mozart's death?"

"I do not believe that Salieri poisoned him, as you insist."

"I said, I am not sure."

"In your mind you are sure. But if anyone in Vienna was guilty of Mozart's death, it was the nobility. After Joseph died, there was deliberate neglect by the nobility and the Hapsburgs. In this, Salieri may not have been innocent. Perhaps Salieri encouraged this neglect."

The waiter was at Jason's side, suggesting that since they were closing, it would be appropriate that the bill be paid now. Jason asked for the bill, only to be interrupted by da Ponte, who said, "Be kind enough to give it to me," and snatched it out of Jason's hands.

Da Ponte went over the account with the utmost care, figuring out the exact total to the penny, and then he handed back the bill to Jason, saying triumphantly, "See how much I saved you! If I had not examined the bill, they would have overcharged you several dollars. I wanted to be sure that my dear friends, Mr. and Mrs. Otis, would not be cheated."

Jason paid it without another word, but da Ponte was not finished.

Suddenly he was compelled to tell them that they must defer their departure to Europe. He explained, "Stay at my wife's boarding house. Her cuisine is superb, even better than this coffee house. You will have charming, comfortable rooms, and you will find out far more about Mozart. What I have told you is just a beginning."

Jason said, "But if you don't think he was poisoned . . .?"

Da Ponte shrugged. "One does not have to be moralistic about it. If you think he was poisoned, perhaps I can help you find something that will advance your theory."

For a moment Deborah was afraid that Jason would succumb to da Ponte's blandishments, and she was about to refuse to pay for any room or board at the Ann da Ponte Boarding House, when Jason said, "Sorry, signor, I appreciate the help you have given me, but our passage is booked."

After da Ponte hailed a carriage, he drew Jason aside and asked, "I really did help you, Mr. Otis?"

"Indeed," replied Jason, not to be outdone in politeness, although he was not certain how helpful da Ponte had been—much of what the poet had told him had contradicted Muller—and he said, "I listened to everything you told me with the utmost attention."

"Fine! Thus, I am sure a small loan would not be amiss. For my services. Ten, twenty, thirty dollars. Otherwise, I will have to walk home. Improvidently, I was so excited by your interest in my work that I ran out of my house without my purse. Thoughtless of me, but. . . "

Jason, not knowing whether to be grateful or angry, but ashamed to appear stingy, handed da Ponte a compromise, twenty dollars.

"Thank you, sir, thank you." As da Ponte assisted them into their carriage, he said, "I would consider it most gracious if you could visit me tomorrow. Oh, just briefly," he hurried to add, as he saw Deborah give Jason a warning glance. "And I will give you something that will tell you even more about Mozart than the letter I read you."

Deborah was against accepting this invitation. She believed that da Ponte was using this merely as a ruse to borrow more money or to inveigle them into becoming boarders, but Jason disagreed. He could not sleep and he was too distracted to respond to Deborah's suggestions that they make love. It was very disturbing, she thought. When he was preoccupied with Mozart he was virtually impotent. Even when she lay beside him naked, which usually aroused him passionately, he was without desire.

She did not pursue the matter, but she could not sleep either. She felt as if his will and sensuality were being burned away by the quicklime of Mozart's grave. How could she compete with an idol? Or an obsession?

As soon as the hour was reasonable the next morning, Jason arranged to visit da Ponte.

The poet was expecting them. Deborah started to say, "We can only stay a minute." Da Ponte said, "I know," and bowing before Jason as if the latter were the Emperor Joseph himself, he handed him a book.

"About Mozart?" Jason asked.

"About Lorenzo da Ponte," the poet said proudly. "And Mozart. This is my memoirs. This will tell you what you want to know about Mozart. This first volume goes up to the day I sailed for America, in 1805. I hope you have a more comfortable voyage. When I left from England, it took an endless time. Eighty-six days."

"Eighty-six days?" Deborah was skeptical. "My husband, to get my consent to voyage to England, assured me that he knew of a new kind of a boat, a sailing packet with a steam engine that can cross the ocean in twenty-six to thirty-one days, but positively no more."

Actually, reflected da Ponte, the voyage across the Atlantic ocean had lasted fifty-seven days, but perhaps now, realizing how long it could take, they would become boarders. With all he knew about Mozart, Jason should pay him plenty.

Jason asked, "How much is this book?"

"Nothing. This is an expression of my interest in your search. You are sure you don't want to stay here and learn more? We have some very intelligent college students as boarders, about your own age."

"Thank you, but no!"

As Jason turned away, da Ponte grabbed his memoirs from Jason's hand. As the youthful composer looked startled, the poet said, "You do want me to inscribe it, don't you?" Jason and Deborah agreed, and he wrote on the fly leaf. And when they didn't read what he had written, he cried out, "Aren't you interested in what I said?" They were halfway to their carriage, which Deborah had ordered to wait for them, afraid that if they didn't leave now, they would be delayed for hours.

The poet appeared so aged, woebegotten, and imploring that Jason read it aloud:

"To Jason and Deborah Otis, my dear friends, who love Mozart as much as I do. Lorenzo da Ponte."

Even Deborah was touched, although she told herself that the inscription was not true. She put out her hand as he desired, and he kissed it with a gallantry that pleased her in spite of her determination not to care.

Da Ponte asked Jason, "You are going to London before Vienna?"

"Yes. My wife wants to see that city very much."

"Good. While you are there you must visit Ann Storace, the first Susanna in *Figaro*. This famous soprano is the one woman I know of that Mozart might have had an affair with. He liked her very much. She was extremely skilful at singing Italian opera. You might also visit her friend, Thomas Attwood, a well-known English composer who studied composition with Mozart. Both of them knew Salieri."

"Thank you. Do you have their addresses, signor?"

Da Ponte shook his head regretfully. "No, I have been out of touch with them for many years. Ever since I left England in 1805. But they are so well known, you should be able to locate them. Ann Storace sang many times at the Italian Opera in the Haymarket. Tell them that I sent you."

As they waved goodbye to da Ponte and he waved back, he looked like the scholarly old gentleman he was to his students, the master of the arts who knew so much and had experienced so much, a relic of another age.

Then suddenly, he ran after them, ordering their carriage to stop.

Jason cried out, "What is wrong, Signor da Ponte?"

"You must be very careful when you reach Vienna. You must not tell anyone that you think the authorities could have had something to do with Mozart's death. That could have serious consequences."

Deborah assured him, "We won't tell a soul. No one will find out. I will make sure that Jason will be careful." But now she was afraid.

Da Ponte added, "There are still people alive in Vienna who could be damaged if your husband's suspicions prove correct. You could find yourselves in a dangerous situation."

8

London

"ISN'T London elegant?" Deborah asked Jason, but it was more of an answer than a question. "I feel so much a part of it already, and yet . . . you are not." Now that the horrible ocean voyage was over, and da Ponte's warnings were far away, and they were comfortably located in a fine hotel suite, she felt high-spirited again and she was distressed that he wasn't.

For Jason didn't reply, looking reflective instead, almost hostile.

"You can only think of Vienna, as if, once you are there, you will find Mozart as you feel he was actually. Despite what da Ponte said and wrote."

Jason shrugged.

"London is much more my kind of a city."

Jason glanced away.

He had been preoccupied ever since they had arrived yesterday, she thought angrily; she doubted that what she felt mattered to him. To return herself to her affirmative mood of a few moments before, she sat down before her dressing-room mirror to prepare herself for the day ahead. For over a month she had been unable to do this. The steam packet had tossed so much, even in mild seas, that it had been impossible to dress properly. But this morning, thanks to her father's foresight, she was living once more in style and luxury and comfort.

Pickering had arranged for a banking associate in the city of London, Arthur Tothill, to rent the best hotel suite available for his daughter, and this had been done. They were residing in Pall Mall, where the dandies strolled, and within view of Green Park, where she could catch a glimpse of the greatest dandy of them all, George the Fourth. And the suite was furnished in such a costly and handsome manner, she decided it had been done for people with a certainty of their own importance.

Yet Jason still sat absently, staring out the windows at the vividly green park, apparently melancholy and uneasy, although the sun was shining brightly and the rain, which had followed them across the Atlantic, was gone. What possessed him now, she wondered.

Nonetheless, Deborah did not pause in her efforts to confront the day cheerfully. She peered into the mirror and relentlessly began the morning as if she were home in Boston. She was determined not to allow a single blemish to mar her beauty. She slapped her neck to avoid the perils of a double chin. She smiled over and over to keep her mouth from becoming stern and taut like her father's. Next she pressed her fingers against her forehead to assure herself that this part of her beauty was not neglected either, and to remove the danger of wrinkles.

Today, she told herself, no one could deny that she was beautiful, not even Jason. Finished with her toilette, she leaned back in her dressing-room chair with satisfaction. Only Jason seemed oblivious to what she had done for him. Suddenly she bent over and kissed him, to signify that now that they were in London, all past quarrels were forgiven.

She said, "If we could stay here a few months and rest from the rigors of the voyage, it would make me very happy. London is full of grace and fashion. I have heard of a fine, well-appointed house on Park Lane that we could rent. With a garden, court, servants. I am well provided for such a contingency and . . ." She halted. Damnation! He was not listening. Yet she was being utterly reasonable. She was furious, but determined not to give him the gratification of knowing that he had provoked her, she returned to her dressing-room mirror and began to comb her hair.

As Deborah spoke, Jason thought of how ill-prepared he had been for the hardships of the Atlantic voyage, and he wondered if this would be typical of the entire expedition?

He was startled by the immensity of London, by the tremendous number of people living in this vast sprawl of a city. Boston and New York were small by comparison. In the past twenty years London's population had increased from a million to more than a million and a half. At the desk the hotel clerk had warned him, as the clerk warned all visitors to London, to stay out of certain sections of the city, particularly at night, when assault and robbery were frequent. Yet he felt that the clerk had overcharged him, on the assumption that being an American who could afford to travel to England he was rich and naïve.

This feeling of being taken advantage of had begun when the master of the steam packet had assured Jason that his boat was the fastest on the Atlantic, that it would require only twenty-five days to reach England, or at the worst, should the weather turn bad, no more than thirty days.

Instead, although they purposely had sailed in May, when the weather was supposed to be at its best, the voyage had been miserably wet, foggy, and chilly, and had dragged on for thirty-six days, forcing them to spend entire days in their cabin.

That had been another reason for his discontent. He had been told that he had the best quarters on the packet, and he had paid the highest rate for them, but the cabin had been just one room actually and too

small and confining for either of them to have privacy. Yet the captain
had insisted that none of the other fifty passengers had so large a room.

Then the extra days had cost him extra money. And now they were
staying at one of the most expensive hotels in London. His purse could
not stand such strains much longer. Yet when Deborah had handed
him a draft for two hundred pounds, which had been waiting at the
hotel desk for her, he had given it back to her. Without a word, he
thought gleefully, which must have irritated her; he had not even
uttered a thank you. He could not endure indebtedness, least of all to
her—it would give her such an advantage. And while one of the reasons
he had married her was to use her money to accomplish his mission, he
was resolved to accept her money only at his own convenience, not
hers.

What had caused the voyage to begin on an especially tiresome note
had been her determination to deny him sexually as punishment for
finding fault with her in the presence of da Ponte.

Jason had assumed that the reading of the poet's memoirs would be
an effective substitute, helping the time to pass interestingly and
swiftly. But they had been grievously disappointing. Instead of revealing information, the memoirs were confusing. When they mentioned
Mozart, it was rarely and briefly. There was nothing in them that
suggested that Salieri had poisoned Mozart, or even hurt him very
much. It were as if da Ponte's mentions of Mozart were an after-
thought, a belated recognition years later so that this association might
reflect favorably on da Ponte. And most of what the poet wrote about
Mozart contradicted what he had told Jason in New York, and implied
that in every situation da Ponte had been the leader and Mozart the
follower. The intrigues that the poet revealed were about himself. The
more Jason read da Ponte's memoirs, the more they became a confused
mixture of illusion, fantasy, and occasional reality, and a loud, piteous
cry of self-justification. Da Ponte's constant need to explain how often
he had been wronged exhausted Jason, and the enormous number of
the poet's intrigues stupefied him.

Yet in spite of how Jason differed with what da Ponte had written,
he could not dismiss the poet's personality. And he believed what the
poet had told him about the nobility damaging Mozart. Now if he could
only prove that. But first, he must convince Deborah.

Once she was out of the reach of da Ponte's vivid temperament, she
disparaged everything that he had told them. She refused to read the
memoirs, saying that they were full of lies, as da Ponte was.

Gradually, however, when there was nothing for her to do in the
evenings, she became enticing. The sea, even when it soaked them to
the skin, stimulated their senses to a sexuality they had not
experienced before. Many nights Deborah resolved to refuse him, and
Jason swore not to make the first move, to give her any advantage or
satisfaction, but neither of them could resist the surge of the sea, the

vigor of the air, the memories of the joys they had relished already. And the sway of the ship, its dip and rise, and the booming of the wind all contributed to the sexual provender being offered them. Often, toward the end of the voyage, they responded to each other's flesh with agitation. As if, Jason thought sometimes, they must grasp this pleasure before it was too late.

Deborah stood up suddenly, tired with combing her hair, and blurted out, "What should I do if I don't want to go to Vienna?"

"Don't go," Jason said curtly.

"You mean that?" She was surprised by his curtness.

"What else can I say? You knew when we married that I was going to Vienna. Nothing has changed that."

"Even after what da Ponte said?"

Jason stressed, "Da Ponte did not tell me I should *not* go to Vienna."

"He warned you that it could be dangerous," Deborah retorted even more emphatically. "He made quite a point of that."

"Da Ponte is just one person. And not always trustworthy."

"Yet you believed some of the things he told you. Especially about the nobility. And Salieri's involvement with them."

"Didn't you believe him, Deborah? You acted like you did."

"He is an excellent storyteller. Fascinating at times."

"And he did admit that Salieri was no friend of Mozart's."

"Was da Ponte, Jason?"

"That is a matter of opinion. In any event, it is not relevant."

"Jason, I love you, but do you really care what I think about Mozart?"

"I care what you think about me. And our marriage."

"You don't look happy about it now."

"I don't like the extravagant way we are living."

"I can afford it, Jason."

"Deborah, I can't."

"It is not my father's money that troubles you. It is mine."

"That doesn't make it any easier to depend on someone else."

"What do you want me to do? Disregard it? Ignore it? Not use it?"

Jason paused, then said slowly and carefully, "Not unless it is essential. And we might not need your money, at least not for the next few months, if we would travel sensibly. But everything we do has to be the best, the most expensive. Like this suite. I wager it is one of the costliest in London." He shook his head. "It is very disturbing."

She replied in justification, "This hotel is close to the Italian Opera, to almost any place in London you might wish to visit."

"But you just announced that you do not care to go to Vienna."

"You could change my mind, if you discovered something here that would cause such a trip to be significant. But so far what have you learned? That da Ponte was involved in intrigues? Da Ponte could not have existed without intrigues." A note of concern crept into her voice. "Stop, Jason, before it is too late, before what is just an obsession now becomes an hallucination and destroys you even as you say that Mozart was destroyed."

"Then you do believe what da Ponte said about danger?"

"I believe that if you insist on pursuing this search you are in grave danger. From many things. Some of which you may never recognize."

Deborah put her arm affectionately through his, and smiled at him with such tenderness that everything about her became beautiful. And he liked her protective expression. But he could not stop. Even if he was utterly wrong, that was impossible. He sensed that with all of her studied tenderness, she still thought he was being foolish. Yet now his life had direction. Da Ponte had convinced him of a vital fact: that Salieri had been Mozart's enemy. If he could find proof that the nobility had conspired against Mozart, he would be much closer to his goal. He said, however, "Deborah, will you do me a favor? Please?"

"What?" Her arm tightened in his.

"Don't tell anyone why I am going to Vienna."

"Why not?"

"It could be misunderstood. Even used against me. Keep it a secret, will you, Deborah, dear?"

"Because of da Ponte's warnings?"

"For many reasons."

"What should I say, Jason?"

"That I have come to Europe to finish my musical education. That should be excuse enough to ask questions about Mozart."

"Despite what I said, you are still assuming that I am going with you to Vienna?"

"You must. You will see things that I miss."

"Even though you think I am too sceptical? Too critical of you?"

He moved out of her grasp. She was unusually intelligent, he thought, yet she wanted him to be a dilettante. She despised clumsy behavior, but she was willing to place him in a subservient position. She assumed that money took care of every imaginable need, and disagreed with her father.

Deborah sighed, then asked suddenly, "Jason, why did you marry me?"

He hesitated.

"Because you love me? You never say it. Or because of my money?"

He shrugged.

"Oh, I know it was an important factor in your proposal, only you don't want to admit it or show it. You want to know that the money is there if you should need it, but you don't want to acknowledge that fact."

"Is that why you don't want to go to Vienna?"

This time she didn't answer. This moment she longed to settle in

London; she felt comfortable here, happy, but Vienna was an alien world, and she was afraid of what she would encounter there. And while it was easy to express concern because of da Ponte's warnings, it was impossible to tell him that she feared that their marriage would not survive the difficulties of his quest. He would accuse her of being irrational, and worse, he would feel superior.

He repeated, upset by her unexpected silence, "You will not tell anyone that I think Mozart might have been poisoned? Unless I do? Please?"

"That depends." Deborah did not say on what.

They had been sitting quite a while without saying another word when there was a knock on their door. Arthur Tothill was calling on them.

Jason was startled by the banker's foppish appearance. The stout, puffy-faced, middle-aged dandy was prodigiously scented and wore conspicuous diamond studs, a red velvet waistcoat whose padded shoulders rose almost to his ears, and a curled toupee that was an exact copy of the wig favored by George the Fourth. His complexion was florid, and his heavy, droopy cheeks reminded Jason of those of a bulldog.

Tothill bowed before Deborah like a dancing master, although his large stomach made him an awkward figure, presented his card, which was engraved in gold, and exclaimed, "Your father did not exaggerate in his communication to me, Mrs. Otis. You are a beautiful young lady!"

Jason felt that Pickering must have discussed him, also; for Tothill, while he pretended to be polite, was regarding him with barely concealed disdain. And his diamonds must have cost a fortune!

Tothill saw Jason staring at them, and he said, "They are the fashion. The King and all his friends wear them. As an expression of our devotion to him. Mrs. Otis, are you comfortable?"

"The suite is lovely."

"Good. Mr. Otis, I hear that you are interested in music. By God!"

Jason asked, "Are you, sir?"

"I am devoted to the Italian Opera. All the best people go."

"Do you know a soprano named Ann Storace?"

"Is she a friend of yours?"

"She was a friend of Mozart's."

"Who?" Tothill looked confused, and thus, irritated.

"The composer."

"Oh! Yes! They play his operas occasionally. No, I don't know of any Ann Storace. I don't like operas—deadly stuff, actually—but everybody fashionable goes at least several times a season. The Italian Opera is the one entertainment in London where it is obligatory to dress. Even the pittites—the lower orders who sit in the pit"—he explained to a bewildered Deborah—"have to appear in full dress. And the boxes are crowded with statesmen, ministers, lords."

Deborah asked, "Are musicians treated honorably in England?"

"Not really. Only the musicians who are recognized by the King are permitted in our clubs. Unreliable fellows. Most of them are little better than vagabonds. I hope your husband is not serious about music. Very unfashionable. One must stand for something, like your father does."

Jason inquired, "Have you been in banking long, Mr. Tothill?"

"My dear fellow! Really!" Tothill was indignant. "My grandfather created our establishment. He did George the Second a great favor. He lent that King a large sum of money without charging interest. Our family has been famous ever since."

Deborah said, "My husband is a banker, primarily."

Tothill's expression altered, as if suddenly Jason had become a man of spotless virtue, and as he marched toward the door, saying proudly, "I was at Waterloo, we showed Bonaparte a thing or two," Deborah cut in abruptly, "Mr. Tothill, I think you have something you want to discuss with my husband," and hurried into the bedroom so they could be alone.

The banker was startled for an instant, then remembered. "Mr. Otis, you are fortunate to be married to a beautiful heiress."

Jason cut him short. "That is a private matter, sir."

"Naturally. And as her steward in England, she has many guineas on deposit with me. She transferred a thousand guineas here without her father's consent. Quincy Pickering was quite angry when he found out. But he could do nothing. She is of age. Why must you look so gloomy? This draft should take you to Vienna and back comfortably."

"You know about Vienna?"

"Quincy Pickering wrote me that you are going to visit some musicians." Tothill became jovial. "Where have you put your own money, young man?"

"It is on my person."

"In cutthroat, thieving London?"

"I had planned to go only to the opera."

Tothill laughed as if that was a great joke. "The opera is full of pickpockets. By God! It is their favorite hunting ground. The grand ladies wear their jewels, the important nobles try to outdo them, and somebody stumbles against them, begs their pardon, and their purse or jewels are gone. You should put your money where it will be safe. Tothill and Tothill is a banking house of considerable taste."

"Is that what my wife wanted you to discuss with me?"

"Anything that concerns a client of mine is of importance."

"But I have no money deposited with you."

"Mrs. Otis gave me strict instructions that the one thousand guineas she put in our bank should be in both your names. So you can draw upon it whenever you wish. Freely. Without any restrictions at all."

"Thank you, sir. I will consider it. Good day."

When Jason returned to the bedroom, Deborah asked, "What is wrong?"

"Nothing. Why?"

"You look upset. As if you had just seen my father. Is that what he talked about? He was supposed to . . ." She blushed, unable to continue.

"He is hardly my idea of a charming or brilliant man."

"Tothill is a man of influence."

"Perhaps. Thanks for not telling him about my feeling about Mozart."

"Did he talk about us?"

"He talked about my beautiful wife." Jason was surprised and pleased by her generosity, but he could not acknowledge it, not until he was certain there was no guile in her offer or a devious effort to secure another advantage over him. "He admires your cleverness."

"Was that all?" She could not hide her disappointment.

"That was all."

Deborah did not believe him, but she did not pursue the matter, for he was dressing for his trip to the Italian Opera. And Jason insisted on going by himself, and suddenly, with all of her self-sufficiency, the thought of being left alone in London gave her a desolate feeling. She was too proud to admit that to him; but when it came time for him to depart, she kissed him passionately and begged him to be careful.

9

The Italian Opera

JASON hired a coach to drive him to the Italian Opera. He was excited; he had been anticipating this moment ever since da Ponte had told him about Ann Storace. He ordered the driver to hurry.

As the poet had said, the Italian Opera was located in the Haymarket, and Jason was amazed by its grandeur. He had never seen any theater in America given such importance, and now he was sure that his decision to come to London had been wise.

He saw opera bills pasted on the side of the theater, and when he found *Le Nozze di Figaro* listed, he shouted with joy. He scanned the list of principals, but there was no mention of Ann Storace. WOLFGANG AMADEUS MOZART was in large letters over the name of the opera, and at the bottom, in much smaller print, LORENZO DA PONTE. But they should know about Ann Storace in the opera house, and Jason hurried through the stage door.

An opera was being rehearsed on stage, and he paused in wonderment and pleasure: the aria the soprano was singing was exquisite. Could this be Ann Storace? The singer was middle-aged, dark, and had a lovely musical voice, warm and velvety. And the music had a familiar ring, yet he had never heard it before. Jason edged closer to the stage to hear better, and was accosted by a burly stagehand who ordered him to leave, stating, "No strangers are allowed backstage."

Jason cried out, "I knew Mozart!"

"You couldn't! You're too young!"

But this got Jason the attention he desired, and he declared, "I was sent here by an old friend of Mozart's, Lorenzo da Ponte, the . . ."

He was cut short by shouts of "Hush! How dare you!"

A tall, thin young assistant stage manager rushed over to Jason and pulled him outside. But when Jason handed him two shillings, as he had been advised by da Ponte, the assistant asked, "Who do you want to see?"

"I am looking for Ann Storace."

"Who?"

"She sang for Mozart. And later, da Ponte told me, she became a prima donna with the Italian Opera Company."

"Da Ponte hasn't been here for over twenty years."

"Isn't Ann Storace singing with your company?"

"No! No! I don't know the name."

"But she is a famous Mozartian singer. And you are going to do *Figaro*."

The red-haired, sharp-featured assistant stage manager laughed.

"It is no joke," Jason said indignantly. "Ann Storace sang in the first production of *Figaro*, in Vienna."

"You are an American, aren't you?"

"Yes. But I know about Mozart."

"What do you think we are rehearsing now?" The assistant put his fingers to his lips to indicate that they must not make a sound, and led Jason inside where he could hear the music.

Suddenly Jason stopped feeling unhappy. This music was passionately interesting, a world unique in itself. He knew it must be Mozart. No one else could have created such sheer melody, such genuine emotion, and such a lyrical purity of expression. Yet there was also gaiety and joy, and clarity and brilliance, and an eloquence and grace that removed all melancholy. Listening intently, he thought, Every note draws me closer to Mozart, yet drives me further from Deborah. But oddly, this brought no sadness or pain. This music possessed him with a need to know more.

When he inched forward, subtly, he hoped, so that he would not be noticed, the assistant dragged him back and whispered, "I have allowed you to hear too much as it is. The prima donna would have my head if she knew that I had permitted a stranger to hear her rehearsing." He pushed Jason outside.

But Jason looked so stricken, as if he had been cruelly deprived of a glimpse of heaven, that the assistant relented a little and said, "We will be doing this opera in a few days. And it will be a far more suitable way to hear *Figaro*."

He could hear a martial air starting. He longed to march himself. What a marvellous rhythm! He sang after the bass, chord for chord.

"*Non più andrai*," the assistant said softly. "It always brings the house down. It is difficult to believe that such a little man composed such powerful music." He closed the stage door before he weakened and allowed this passionate young man to go inside again.

"What about Ann Storace?" Desperation crept into Jason's voice. "I have come all the way to London from Boston to find out things about Mozart from her. Did anyone in your company know Mozart?"

"Michael Kelly did."

"Who is he?"

"He used to be manager of the Opera, and one of our principal singers and composers. He claimed he sang for Mozart in the first *Figaro*. Michael Kelly is always talking about Mozart."

"Good!" Jason's spirits rose.

"But he retired years ago, when his voice disappeared."

"Oh!" Jason was so disappointed he could have screamed, but thinking there would be many such difficulties, or worse, before he finished his search, he asked quietly, "Do you know where I can find Michael Kelly?"

The assistant stage manager regarded Jason questioningly.

Jason, without another word, handed him a pound. He knew that Deborah would consider this extravagant and scold him if she found out, but he had travelled too far and with too much discomfort to be halted now.

The assistant took him through a private passage that led from The King's Theater to a small bookshop over which there was a large sign: MICHAEL KELLY, IMPORTER OF BOOKS AND COMPOSER OF MUSIC. He said, "This passage was built so that the lords and ladies who wish to depart quickly from the opera can avail themselves of this privilege, for two guineas. When Kelly was manager of the opera, he built this passage so that it led to his shop. He no longer owns the shop, although it is still in his name, for he is well known as a composer of popular airs. But he likes to sit in the shop as if he still does own it and reminisce about Mozart and make notes on a book he says he is writing about the composer. Kelly was in Vienna at the time of *Figaro*, and when he returned to England he was manager of the Italian Opera for many years."

No one was in the shop, and the assistant shouted, "Ochelli!" Then he explained, "That is what they called Kelly in Vienna, and it is our signal that the business has to do with Mozart. It will bring him if he is in."

A stocky, ruddy-faced, white-haired elderly man appeared abruptly from the rear of the shop, holding a bottle of port, and without waiting for an introduction, greeted Jason with a roar. "You want to know about Mozart?" He waved to the assistant to go. "Many people do."

Jason was upset. Were others engaged in his mission? It was his, alone, and he felt possessive, resentful, and worried.

"What do you want to know? You are not writing a book, too?" Kelly stared at Jason suspiciously. "Do you like port? It clears the head."

"First I want to inquire about Ann Storace. Do you know her?"

"A dear, dear friend." Kelly started to cry. "She is dead."

"Dead? Don't cry, please. Da Ponte said . . ."

"Da Ponte said!" Kelly's tears stopped and so did his brogue, and he did an exact parody of da Ponte as he asked, "Is that rogue still alive?"

"Very much so. In New York. Teaching Italian and talking about himself."

"That is da Ponte. Did he mention me?"

"No. He talked about Ann Storace, Mozart, Attwood, and Salieri."

"Salieri." Kelly's grin faded. "Are you a friend of Salieri's?"

"Was Mozart?"

"Mozart was a dear, sweet, noble man."

Kelly's eyes filled with tears, and this time Jason felt that they were genuine and perhaps he could trust this man.

"Mozart loved to introduce me to everybody as his excellent friend, Michaele Ochelli. He was amused that the Italian Opera in Vienna had to Italianize my name to make me acceptable. He told me that when he had been in Italy as a child he had been called Amadeo Wolfgango Mozarto."

"Yet da Ponte said that Mozart had many enemies."

"Everybody with ability did, and he had more ability than anyone."

"Do you think that had anything to do with his sudden, early death?"

"I wasn't there at the time. Is Salieri still alive?"

"Yes . . . but quite ill."

"Why are you investigating this situation?"

"What situation?"

"Faith, Mozart's death. It is behind every syllable you utter."

"I want to study his music. I am a composer, too."

"You are unusually well dressed for a musician. Why are you so involved in Mozart?"

"I love his music and so I have fallen in love with the man."

"That is easy to understand. But your interest in his death is more than love. What is the real reason you have come to London?"

Jason introduced himself, and said that he wanted to learn about Mozart and his music in the hope that this would help him as a musician, that this was the reason he was seeking out those who had known Mozart. He did not tell Kelly of his growing belief that Salieri had poisoned Mozart. He felt that Kelly would say such a premise was incredible.

Kelly asked suddenly, "Where are you staying?" Jason told him, and Kelly said, "It is one of the most fashionable hotels in London. I must introduce you to Attwood, he studied composition with Mozart and was his favorite pupil. Have you ever heard *Le Nozze di Figaro?*"

"No. Mozart's operas are unknown in America."

"I sang in the first *Figaro*. In England we have been doing his operas for years." He enumerated proudly, *"Le Nozze di Figaro, Don Giovanni, Così fan tutte, Die Zauberflöte.* Do you want to hear *Figaro?*"

"That would be a great privilege."

"I will get a box." Then Kelly sighed. "But that will be costly."

From habit now, Jason asked, "How much?"

"A box for four, properly located—we must include your wife and Attwood—will cost at least twenty pounds. Attwood is George the Fourth's composer. He wrote the music for his coronation. Attwood will not accept my invitation unless he is seated prominently."

Jason gave Kelly twenty pounds, and the latter's eyes widened at the amount of money the American was carrying.

He suggested suddenly, "Perhaps you would like to study composition with Attwood. He was indeed Mozart's favorite pupil."

"How many years did you and Attwood know Mozart?"

"Four. Five. But it was like a lifetime, it was at the height of his career. I can still see his agreeable, good-natured countenance."

"When did Ann Storace die?"

"Almost ten years ago. Mozart was quite fond of her. I must introduce you to the man who lived with her after she came back to England, John Braham, now our most renowned male singer."

"Is there anyone else in England who knew Mozart?"

"No, no, not as Attwood and I did. You should like Attwood. He is a bit stiff these days, what with age and advancement, but once he knows of your interest in Mozart, he should unbend. I will get a lovely box." He held the twenty pounds as if it were two hundred.

Kelly kept his word. A week later he arranged for Jason, Deborah, and Attwood to be his guests at a performance by the Italian Opera Company of *Figaro* at The King's Theater. It was a gala occasion, for members of the Royal family were to be present, and Kelly was proud that he had obtained one of the choicest boxes in the house. While they waited for Attwood to arrive, Kelly explained, "Attwood always comes at the last moment, to make a suitable entrance, for in music he is next in importance to the King."

He showed Jason and Deborah the wonders of the theater. "My box is on the second tier, an ideal place to be seen. We have to be looked up to, yet there are many seated above us. This is the finest opera house in the world. All foreign opera in England is done here. The original house was built in 1705 by Vanbrugh and Congreve, but after a fire in 1789, which I saw—the smoke was visible for miles—it was rebuilt on a much grander scale. A few years ago, in 1818, it was remodeled, and now it possibly may be the largest theater in the world. It is bigger than Drury Lane and Covent Garden, and it is the first theater in England to have a stage shaped like a horseshoe. Notice how the stage curves, a wonderful innovation, and our gas chandeliers are the marvel of the age. Mrs. Otis, have you ever seen anything like them?"

Deborah had to admit that she had not. The King's Theater was lit with a grandiose chandelier that held a double circle of gas, which shone like a crystal sun in the middle of the ceiling. She thought it was too bright for most complexions, but not her own. She was pleased with the location; Kelly was right, it commanded a superb view of the audience, although it was impossible to see the entire stage despite its new horseshoe shape. She wondered how much Jason had paid for this box, for there was no reason for Michael Kelly to be treating them.

"Everyone dresses here," Kelly said. "Our box is usually reserved for a lord."

Deborah, although she sought to be reserved, liked Kelly's animation and gallantry. His energy never flagged, he treated her as if he were about to present her to his Sovereign, and he was filled with happiness waiting for *Figaro* to begin. She wished she could tell what Jason was thinking; Jason had said hardly a word since they had entered the box.

Then, just as the Royal family arrived, Attwood did also. He bowed as Kelly introduced him, but Deborah felt that he had come at the overture to avoid any conversation, while Jason continued to look preoccupied.

She liked Attwood's appearance. He was a tall, fine-featured man of about sixty with a smooth skin and attractive eyes and wavy grayish-white hair, and he wore his black dress clothes with an assured air.

Jason sat through the first act of *Figaro* in mute wonder. The opera was even more melodic and enchanting than he had expected. But while he exulted in the glory of the music, he was sad at the possibility—which grew with the development of the opera—that he would never approach Mozart in skill and feeling.

As the principals appeared for their curtain calls, Attwood stood up so that he could be seen by the brilliant audience. He grumbled that the performers were the usual London mediocrities, but his face gleamed when the Royal family nodded to him. Suddenly the composer decided to join the notables assembling in the waiting room of the opera house to pay homage to the Royal family. Kelly motioned to Jason and Deborah to come along, although Attwood had not suggested that they do so. They stepped out of the box and bumped into Tothill standing in the corridor.

Tothill looked surprised, but Jason thought this meeting was no accident. The banker had placed himself in such a position that they had to acknowledge him, and he was scented as if this were an affair of state.

Jason assumed that Attwood would be annoyed by this interruption; but when Tothill introduced himself, Attwood was surprisingly attentive.

Attwood inquired, "Of Tothill and Tothill of Lombard Street?"

"I am the senior partner," said the banker. "And you are, sir . . .?"

Kelly said, "Thomas Attwood, Composer to the King."

"Ah, yes, and the organist at St. Paul's. I attend the services there."

Kelly added, "And my good friends, Mr. and Mrs. Otis of Boston."

Tothill said, "I have had the pleasure. Mrs. Otis' father is a valued business associate of mine. One of the leading bankers in America."

"Indeed," said Attwood. "And you represent Mr. Otis' interests here?"

"In a way. My attractive American friends can reside in London with considerable elegance if they should so desire."

Jason, curious about Attwood's changed attitude, bowed modestly.

Tothill was proud of himself. When he had learned from the clerk at the hotel that the Otises were going to the opera, he had attended in the hope that this would help him become Jason's banker in England. He knew who Attwood was: Attwood resided in Mayfair with a splendor that must require large sums of money, even for a King's musician. He expected Attwood to be attentive. He had learned that once these artist chaps became involved with society, they could become avidly dependent on him.

Attwood made no effort to move on. Tothill and Tothill was one of the influential banking houses in England and close to the Throne. Kelly had said that Otis was rich and possessed a devotion to Mozart that could make him a profitable pupil, but Attwood had not believed Kelly. Kelly was too optimistic about money matters; it was why the singer had failed as an opera manager and bookshop owner. But now Kelly's suggestion seemed sensible. He loved Mozart as much as anyone. He could prove it. Attwood wondered how much Tothill's diamonds cost. They were magnificent.

Jason asked, "Mr. Attwood, aren't we going to the waiting room?"

"It is too late now. The crush will be impossible. I understand that you are interested in Mozart. Do you like *Figaro*?"

"It is magical, sir. Did you know Mozart well?"

"Quite well. But this is no place to discuss such serious matters. Mr. Otis, I would be honored if you and Mrs. Otis would be my guests for dinner, and then we can have a heart-to-heart talk about Mozart. You can play some of your own compositions for me, and possibly I can offer you some useful advice."

"Thank you, sir, but what about Mr. Kelly?"

"Michael will come. And Mr. Tothill, I trust?"

"It will be a privilege," said the banker.

Attwood said, "I will also invite Braham, who lived with Storace for years. He should have interesting views on Mozart, whom she knew well."

Tothill said, "Won't so many guests put a strain on your household?"

Attwood declared proudly, "My dining room can seat twelve comfortably."

Kelly added, as he saw Jason hesitate, "Mr. Otis, there are families in London who would sacrifice much to receive such an honor."

Jason watched Attwood's face during the remainder of *Figaro*, but it was expressionless and told him nothing. The charm and beauty of the music came at Jason now like a long colloquy from the grave. He recalled, too, da Ponte saying how much this opera had offended the nobility. The assumption was that Mozart was dead, but he longed to shout that Mozart was not dead, he could feel *his* blood in the arteries of his arias. If God was anybody, Jason decided, He was an art such as *Figaro*'s. The music was so alive Mozart could not be dead. Anything else was unthinkable.

10

Mozart's English Friends

THE Attwood home on Curzon Street was elegant, as Jason expected. "But it is a rather obvious elegance," he told Deborah as they stepped out of the carriage he had hired and approached the front door. "While it is attractive and in good taste, Attwood has made certain that his house suggests wealth and position and excites attention."

Deborah thought Jason was being too critical. She replied, "His residence reflects good breeding and fashion, as I knew it would."

Everything indeed did, she felt, as the impeccable footman led them to their host, who was waiting for them in his drawing room. Attwood greeted them warmly and said that the other guests had arrived and were waiting in his music room. He was dressed as if it were a grand occasion, in a handsome long blue frock coat with a thick red collar, perfectly tailored red trousers, a stunning white cravat, and two Royal decorations.

When he saw Deborah admiring his furniture, he said "My chairs are original Sheraton. I bought them from the cabinet maker before he died."

A gas chandelier hung from the ceiling in the style of the one in The King's Theater, and as she admired that, too, Attwood added, "A recent invention. There are very few houses in London that are lit by gas." There were busts of Handel, Wellington, and Mozart on the mantel, and above them an etching of St. Paul's. He said, "Some people believe it is an original sketch by Christopher Wren. But I have never been able to prove that." He sighed. "It would be worth a fortune if it were."

Attwood took Deborah and Jason by the arm and led them into the music room. Tothill, Kelly, and John Braham were standing by the fireplace discussing the advisability of investing in the India trade. The singer bowed as he saw a lady entering, and said, "I am honored."

Braham was middle-aged and middle-sized and unusually dark for an Englishman, with a long, lean face, a large, slightly curved nose, and a complexion that reminded Jason of a young da Ponte.

Braham turned to him and said, "Mr. Otis, it is kind of you to consider me a friend of Mozart's. I only knew him through my dear departed Ann."

Jason asked, "Did she know him well, sir?"

"Very well. She told me that she was his favorite soprano."

"She was deeply sympathetic to his work," said Kelly. "She could not endure any criticism of him. Some people thought they were in love."

"What did you think?" asked Jason.

"It was difficult to say. I never saw them in any compromising situations, but it was taken for granted in Vienna that an opera composer had affairs with his prima donnas. Only Mozart was not an ordinary man. He was devoted to his wife, and a person of infinite sensibility."

"You hear it in his music."

"It was evident in many ways. He loved to laugh, dance, eat, drink. Most of all, I think, he loved beauty. Like this music room. Isn't it beautiful? I am certain it would have pleased Mozart very much."

Attwood said, "I would like to believe so. It is patterned after his."

The music room was spacious, comfortable, and dominated by an organ, harpsichord, and pianoforte. The compositions within view were by Attwood, Mozart, and Handel. There were silhouettes on the wall of Mozart, Haydn, and Gluck, each autographed, and engravings of a spinet and lyre.

Braham said suddenly, "Attwood, I can think of no more felicitous composer than your Viennese friend, Mozart, to grace your hospitable home. It would be a privilege to hear his music in your hands."

Attwood said, "Perhaps Mr. Otis will play it for us."

Jason was frightened. The part of him that clung to Mozart was making him less sure of his own musical ability. He replied, "Afterwards, perhaps." He was relieved that Attwood did not pursue his suggestion, but took them into dinner.

Deborah found the dining room the most attractive part of the house. It was, indeed, elegant like Attwood himself. She had to admit that it was an obvious elegance from the huge mahogany dining table to the sparkling plates, the spotless linen, the wine glasses brilliantly reflected in the polished mahogany; but this was the kind of a room she was used to, and now she felt at home.

Wine came first, and Attwood insisted that everyone's glass be filled to the brim. Then there was a salad, a choice of beef or minced chicken, fresh strawberries of which their host was especially proud, and at the end, coffee and brandy. There was very little conversation; and as they were on the last course, Braham said, "Mr. Otis, would you play for us?"

Attwood repeated, "Would you, sir? I am sure it would a delight."

Jason changed the subject. "Did any of you ever have dinner with Mozart?"

"Many times," said Kelly. "He relished a good table as much as anyone, but he had to be careful. Some foods upset his digestion."

"What foods?"

"It depended."

"On what?"

"How hard he was working. How his music was received."

"Did Salieri know this?"

Attwood glanced at Kelly as if to say, Let us keep this to ourselves, but Kelly was enjoying his recollections too much to be halted. He said, "Of course." He turned to his host. "Remember, Attwood, when da Ponte invited us to dinner, and Mozart and Salieri, too."

Attwood's expression said, Do we have to talk about that?

Braham said, "Ann told me that Mozart had to be careful what he ate."

Kelly said, "She was at the dinner when the question of diet occurred. She must have remembered it. Some of the discussion was strange."

Attwood shrugged. "It was simply a discussion of food and drink and how it affected the body. Salieri was proud of his knowledge of cooking."

"He certainly was. He considered himself an expert on the subject."

Jason asked, "Did he talk at all about poisons? I understand that Salieri regarded himself as an expert on that subject, also."

Kelly was silent. How odd that this young American had divined what he had feared. He had never quite accepted the medical reasons given for Mozart's death, but he had been far away when that had happened, and deeply involved in other matters. Then the French Revolution had erupted and Europe had been at war for many years, and it had become too difficult to investigate. Yet now, stronger than ever, the doubts returned.

Jason prodded, "Was there any dispute between Mozart and Salieri?"

Kelly said, "They rarely agreed about anything."

"But you must not guess," said Attwood. "We have no proof that Salieri harmed Mozart. He disliked Mozart, but that is no reason to convict a man of murder. We all dislike people, but that does not mean we kill them."

Kelly said, "I remember when Salieri hurt Mozart."

Attwood said, "A particular incident? I do not recall any."

"Salieri tried to get me out of *Figaro*. At the last moment. It would have disrupted the opening. Attwood, remember how disturbed we were?"

"I forgot. But actually, it was Orsini-Rosenberg who tried to do that."

"Whatever Rosenberg did, he did for Salieri."

Deborah asked, "Mr. Kelly, did you really know Mozart well?"

Kelly was offended. He declared, "Mrs. Otis, I am the only one of the cast of the original *Figaro* who survives. The reason Mozart is so

D

well known here is because I introduced him to England, with Attwood and the Storaces. I was manager of the Italian Opera for ten years."

Deborah asked, "What did happen at da Ponte's dinner?"

Kelly said, "Even now, it makes my hair stand on end."

Everybody was attentive then, as he had hoped.

Kelly glanced at the fair-skinned American, whose complexion and clear blue eyes reminded him of the Mozart he had known, and as he remembered the days with Mozart he felt blessedly young again, prepared to try, and try, and try still again. Attwood's dinner party was like so many Mozart had given. He had been welcome always in Mozart's home, but this was the first time he had been invited by Attwood in years. Tothill must have told Attwood that the Otises were rich. But now that didn't matter. Bursting with emotion, he no longer felt sixty-two, a failure after great expectations, and living on the pittances that friends gave him and aware that if he would be remembered—if he would be remembered at all—it would be because he had known Mozart, although his career had been varied and prominent. He had been a leading character singer in Vienna, and first tenor at Drury Lane when he had returned to England, until he had lost his voice. Then he had been manager of The King's Theater and the Italian Opera for ten years, only to be pushed out because he had done too much Mozart, yet now Mozart's operas were done often and profitably. Next, to keep close to the world of the opera, he had opened his book and music shop, selling wine on the side, and had lost possession of it after he had drunk away the earnings. What hurt most was that while he had composed music for over sixty dramatic pieces, all of which had been presented on the stage, and he had written many English, French, and Italian songs, including several for the King, a year after their performance they had been forgotten. What people remembered about him now was what his friend Richard Brinsley Sheridan had said about him, "*Michael Kelly, Composer of Wines and Importer of Music.*" But not everyone could be a Mozart; when he had borrowed, he had borrowed only from the best, Handel, Haydn, and Mozart. And no one could accuse him of borrowing his memories of Mozart. The composer had been his friend, his good friend, a better friend than Sheridan or Attwood. That made him feel young again. He was determined to remember accurately.

He settled back in his chair, and his lilting tenor voice gathered an extraordinary sweetness as he started to speak.

"*Le Nozze di Figaro* opened in Vienna on May 1, 1786, and a few days later da Ponte invited me, Attwood, Ann Storace, Mozart and his wife, and Salieri and his mistress, Catherina Cavalieri, to dinner. Salieri was married to a wealthy merchant's daughter, and it was said that her money had been very helpful to him; however, he never took his wife anywhere but displayed Catherina Cavalieri as his mistress. She was a buxom, handsome prima donna, actually German, who had assumed an Italian name to aid her career, and she had sung Constanze in *The Abduction from the Seraglio*. But Mozart's wife did not come, nor did Ann's brother, Stephen Storace."

Deborah interrupted, "Why didn't Constanze Mozart come?"

"Mozart told me that she was pregnant and that the sight of Salieri would upset her too much. But I must admit that could have been an excuse, to make it easier for him to devote himself to Ann Storace."

Deborah continued, "Was she Mozart's mistress?"

"I said before that I doubted it."

Deborah said, "Mr. Braham, what do you think?"

"Ann was wise. She never talked about the men in her life before we met. But she did say that Mozart had an intense loyalty to his wife."

Jason asked, "What about her brother? Is he in England now?"

Kelly said sadly, "Stephen Storace is dead. I don't know why da Ponte didn't invite him. Mozart was very fond of Stephen. So many who knew Mozart are dead. It is odd. Often I have wondered about that."

Jason shivered, while the others pondered what Kelly had said.

Kelly resumed, "Da Ponte told us that he was giving his dinner party to celebrate the opening of *Figaro* and his new commission for Salieri, but I felt that the poet desired a truce between the two composers, since he needed both of them, and he fancied himself in the peacemaking role.

"I was not surprised that Salieri came. In public he pretended to be Mozart's friend, and he liked to display Cavalieri as a precious jewel.

"While we were invited because we were a bribe for Mozart, especially Ann. He liked that we were young, attractive, enthusiastic, and English. Mozart was fond of England, where he had been acclaimed as a child, and he hoped to return there. Ann, already renowned in Europe for her art, was his favorite soprano, and I think that he too was curious about how Salieri would behave, especially after the opening of *Figaro*.

"Da Ponte's rooms on the Kohlmarkt were much more luxurious than Mozart's on the Grosse Schulerstrasse; but as the poet's house-keeper and her pretty sixteen-year-old daughter, who da Ponte made obvious was his mistress, waited on us, I did not feel at home as I did in Mozart's quarters. And at first the conversation was just polite trivialities while we waited for the wine to be poured, but when da Ponte took out a brilliant jeweled gold snuffbox and used it, Salieri's eyes widened and I felt something envious occurring within him. Salieri, who had been waiting for da Ponte to taste the wine before he drank any, a common custom among the Italians in Vienna, asked, 'Lorenzo, is the snuffbox new?'

" 'Quite new, Antonio,' da Ponte replied proudly.

" 'I didn't know that you cared for snuff.'

" 'I don't usually. But in this instance I cannot slight the donor.'

" 'Who?'

" 'The Emperor. It is a present from Joseph.'

"Salieri indicated that he did not believe da Ponte.

"Da Ponte boasted, 'And Joseph filled it with ducats.'

" 'For what?' Salieri could hardly conceal his annoyance.

" 'For services to the State. And for *Figaro*, perhaps.'

" 'Perhaps!' Salieri sneered. Clearly he did not believe his friend.

" 'You don't agree?' Now it was da Ponte's turn to be annoyed.

" 'For *Figaro*?' The doubt in Salieri's voice increased. 'Oh, I grant, Lorenzo, that the music is pleasant and that it has been sung competently by our young friends Storace and Ochelli, but the choice of a subject could be a grave error. It serves no useful purpose.'

"Mozart said, 'I thought we settled all that when Joseph gave us permission to perform the opera and encouraged us with his presence.'

"Salieri said, 'The controversy remains. I tried to warn Lorenzo that it was dangerous to read works forbidden in the Austrian States, but he did not heed me. Those French revolutionary works are better ignored.'

" 'Such as Beaumarchais?' Mozart inquired.

" 'Isn't that obvious?' retorted Salieri.

"Mozart said with dignity, 'I should know what I put to music.'

" 'But you think what cannot be said can, however, be sung.'

" 'I doubt many people *heard* the words.'

" 'The words were heard. By many people who didn't like them. You and Lorenzo are wading into dangerous waters. You could be investigated.'

"Mozart said softly as he saw da Ponte imploring him to make peace, 'I appreciate your concern, Maestro Salieri. What do you suggest we do?'

" 'Remove *Figaro* from the stage.'

"No one spoke for a moment. Da Ponte, who an instant before had been the peacemaker, now looked ready to explode with fury; I could see that Ann was appalled; even Attwood, who was more diplomatic than I was, seemed shocked. I wanted to cry out in protest. What had given Salieri the audacity or the arrogance to make such a suggestion? Only Mozart appeared calm. He said, 'Maestro, that might be difficult.'

" 'Impossible!' exclaimed da Ponte. 'Why. . . !' He sputtered with rage.

"Mozart said, even more quietly than before, 'Wait, Lorenzo. Maestro Salieri, why do you think we ought to halt the production of *Figaro*?'

" 'For your own good.'

" 'Naturally.'

"I could not tell whether Mozart was being sarcastic or serious.

"Mozart went on, asking, 'But why, Maestro?'

"Watching them in this moment, I reflected that they faced each other like two fencers, both quick of movement, with the rapidity of gesture often characteristic of small men, each normally pale, except that Salieri was heavily rouged in the French fashion. Yet in essentials they had no resemblance to each other. Salieri insisted always that he was telling you the truth and you rarely believed him; Mozart seldom used the word and you always believed him. Salieri embellished his music with the fashionable ornamentation of the day and you felt nothing; Mozart disdained tricks and effects and he reached your heart. No wonder the loveliness of his music frightened Salieri. Mozart's quality was impossible to achieve by anyone else, and Salieri knew it. In this instant I felt sorry for him. But that did not last.

"For Salieri said, 'As your friend, Mozart, it is my duty to warn you that many of the nobility are offended by *Figaro*. They resent that Count Almaviva is outwitted always and at the end so strongly and humiliatingly. They feel that if you have done an opera as scandalous as *Figaro*, someday you will do one even more scandalous, and Joseph may not be Emperor much longer. His health is poor, he has no children, and his brother Leopold, who will succeed him, is a much sterner ruler.'

" 'Is that why you are so concerned, Maestro?'

" 'Yes. I hear that the Privy Council is asking Joseph to impose total censorship because of *Figaro*. It could destroy the opera. All of us!'

"Mozart seemed to be considering Salieri's suggestion, and I could not contain myself any longer. My two roles in *Figaro*, while not leads, were effective, and permitted me to act as well as sing, and as I saw Ann start to protest, and Attwood, usually restrained, looking upset, and da Ponte for once at a loss for words, I cried out, 'Herr Mozart, everyone admires your music except those whose vanity will not allow them to find merit in anything not composed by themselves. We have had so many requests for encores that Joseph has been forced to restrict them so that *Figaro* will not last all night.'

"Salieri said, 'That is not the only reason for the Emperor's edict.'

" 'What is?' asked Mozart.

" 'Many things! Remember, I speak as a friend,' Salieri insisted.

"I exclaimed, 'Herr Kapellmeister, you are not going to halt *Figaro*!'"

"Apparently there was such entreaty in my voice that a smile of rare beauty appeared on Mozart's face, and he said, 'Did you think I would?'

"I said, 'Maestro Salieri is persuasive.'

" 'Very persuasive. But your appreciation is even more persuasive.' Mozart glanced at Ann, whose expression implored him not to listen to Salieri; then he looked at Attwood, whose attitude agreed with ours, and he said, 'Maestro Salieri, there is always the possibility that you might be right, but I cannot betray my friends, or myself.'

"I breathed a sigh of relief, and so did Ann and Attwood. Da Ponte, upset with the way the conversation was going, decided to start the meal and tasted the wine, and we followed his example. I was surprised that Mozart did not touch his wine. His wife had told me that he loved good food and drink. I wondered whether another dispute was brewing. Da Ponte glared irritably at Mozart.

"Mozart said, 'I am sorry, but at the moment I cannot drink any wine.'

"Da Ponte said accusingly, 'You do not trust it?'

" 'I am sure it is of the best vintage. But it has to do with my kidneys. They have been behaving poorly of late.'

"Salieri declared, 'Wine should be good for them.'

" 'Possibly,' answered Mozart, 'but I cannot take the chance.'

" 'Since when?' asked Salieri.

"Da Ponte said, 'I didn't know you were interested in Mozart's health.'

" 'All of us are.' I saw Salieri nudge Cavalieri, who nodded assent.

" 'Besides,' said Mozart, 'my health is no secret.'

"Salieri said, 'I trust nothing I have discussed has upset you.'

"Mozart laughed. 'I am not upset. I have had kidney attacks before and I have recovered from them. I just must watch what I eat and drink.'

"When da Ponte's housekeeper served livers of geese, which I knew Mozart liked very much, he frowned, started to eat them, then halted.

"Da Ponte was even more distressed than before, and he said, 'Wolfgang, I arranged this course because you like it so much.'

" 'Thanks, Lorenzo,' Mozart answered. 'I appreciate your concern. But the last time I ate them, when you were my guest, I got sick. Apparently I have had a recurrence of my kidney ailment.'

" 'Apparently?' Salieri asked. I was surprised by the intensity of his interest. 'Haven't you consulted an apothecary or a doctor?'

"Mozart sighed, 'I wish I had more faith in apothecaries and doctors.'

" 'Yet,' persisted Salieri, 'you believe the fault lies in your kidneys?'

" 'Whoever I have consulted has said so. And the symptoms indicate that. But please, enough of illness,' Mozart said, as he saw the serious expressions on our faces. 'This is supposed to be a festive occasion.'

"Salieri however, was not finished. He asked, 'What can you eat?'

" 'Fruits, vegetables, meats without spice, tartness, or fats.'

"Da Ponte ordered his housekeeper to bring Herr Mozart whatever he wanted. Then he started to discuss *Figaro*, saying, 'Joseph stayed for the entire opera, applauded and shouted *Bravo*, looked very pleased, and gave us a special audience afterward.' Salieri did not listen to him but came back to the subject of food as if it were a matter of first importance, stating, 'Mozart, you should have consulted me. I have learned that there are many foods that can poison us under certain circumstances.'

" 'Poison us!' Da Ponte was alarmed, then irate. 'Are you imply-ing . . .?'

" 'Of course not, Lorenzo. You have one of the best tables in Vienna,' Salieri said soothingly. 'But as you are aware, I know much about foods and how they can affect us. I have given the subject long study. Poison is a relative thing. A food that might be eaten by one person with impunity can injure or kill another. All illnesses start in the stomach. Signor Mozart, you say there are foods you cannot eat. What are they?'

"Mozart hesitated—I sensed that he didn't like his weakness exposed—but when he saw that his English friends were interested, he said, 'I cannot stand a spicy diet anymore. My palate adores it, but my wretched kidneys and stomach rebel against it.'

" 'So I am right,' said Salieri. 'Some foods can hurt you.'

"Da Ponte said suddenly, 'Antonio, You talk like a Venetian.'

" 'You know I am not a Venetian!' Salieri was exasperated.

" 'Anyone who is an expert on poison is by nature a Venetian.'

" 'I am not discussing poisons!' shouted Salieri.

" 'You are not discussing anything else,' insisted da Ponte.

"I thought they would come to blows; then I recalled that my Italian colleagues were least dangerous when they screamed the most.

"Then Mozart said, 'I am sure Maestro Salieri meant well.'

"Salieri hurried to add, 'Of course! Signor Mozart, I only wanted to know what foods were harmful so I could give you proper advice.'

" 'But do be careful,' Ann Storace said suddenly to Mozart, and with a gesture of anxiety she put her arm through his.

"He brightened. When he smiled, which was often in our company, his face, which was pale, almost plain, was like the sunlight on an early spring morning, bringing hope, freshness, and beauty.

"After we had eaten, Mozart danced happily with Ann while Attwood played the music that had been written in *Figaro* for dancing. There was genuine affection between them, and he danced gracefully. When they finished, he said, 'Can your conscience allow you to sing a little tune?'

"Ann nodded, and she sang while he accompanied her. It was delightful, and I listened in wonder, for I had never heard this music before.

"I asked him when he had written it, and he said, 'When we were dancing.'

"Salieri did not believe him, so Mozart improvised another song, lyrical and enchanting. Then he suggested that Salieri do the same.

"Salieri didn't want to, but when Cavalieri urged him, his vanity overcame his caution, and he tried. But whatever came forth from the pianoforte had a familiar sound, and suddenly he banged on the keys in irritation and cried, 'A genuine composer needs solitude, and this instrument is not tuned properly.'

"Mozart returned to the pianoforte and played a variation on 'Non più andrai' that had the same magnificent rhythm and yet some of the delicacy and sweetness he had written into Ann's arias in *Figaro*.

" 'Beautiful!' she exclaimed. 'A miracle accomplished without appearing to. The truest kind. When did you compose it, Wolfgang?'

" 'While you were rehearsing *Figaro*.'

"He asked Attwood to play 'Non più andrai' itself, while he marched up and down as he would have acted and sung it. His movements were animated and inspired, and I was sure it was for the benefit of Ann, but I heard Salieri, sitting next to Cavalieri, mutter disdainfully to her, 'A cavalry march. It will be forgotten in a year.'

"No one else seemed to hear him, and I was too happy to retort.

"Da Ponte apologized for serving the wrong menu, and Mozart replied, 'Lorenzo, you have a fine table, you are a gracious host. I have always considered the dining room next in importance to the music room, although I have always had a high regard for the bed chamber, too.'

"Mozart was in such high spirits it seemed inconceivable that he had been ill a few days ago, and I was caught by his vitality. As long as he had that, I thought, nothing could destroy him prematurely.

"He joked that Madame de Pompadour had refused to kiss him because he had been too young—seven, and that Maria Theresa had kissed him because he had been just young enough. I saw Salieri look alert again—perhaps this could be used against Mozart, for Maria Theresa was a sacred subject in the Empire now that she was dead—and da Ponte seemed concerned.

"Salieri asked, 'Mozart, do you feel that royalty is heartless?'

"Mozart glanced at the flowers blooming in the window boxes and bent down and gently picked up three bees that lay dead. He said, 'Could they have lived longer? Did they partake of the wrong foods? Yesterday they were so quick with life. Today they are nothing. When I was fourteen I saw two thieves hanged. Then I thought it was done efficiently. Now I have seen death come too soon to too many. To my own mother, my own children, good friends. Does that mean that life is heartless?'

"Salieri repeated, 'Signor Mozart, do you think royalty is heartless?'

" 'No more than anybody else.'

" 'Did you like Maria Theresa?'

" 'Did Joseph?'

"Salieri said sharply, 'But Joseph was her son!'

" 'And we were supposed to be her children. I liked her. At six.'

" 'Afterwards?'

"Mozart replied, 'At least Joseph is musical.'

" 'And nothing else?' suggested Salieri.

"Mozart grinned like a mischievous little boy, and I had a vision of him walking on the edge of a precipitous cliff. One slip and . . . But then, as he saw the anxiety on my face, he laughed and said, 'Don't worry, Michael, they will have to assassinate me to get rid of me.' "

Jason was startled by Kelly's final words. Mozart's comment about assassination ran through his head like a refrain. Kelly, instead of appearing self-satisfied as Jason expected, was sad; Attwood seemed far away, brooding; Braham was biting his lips, possibly to keep from saying something he might regret later; Tothill had a bewildered, uncomfortable look on his face; Jason could not tell what Deborah was thinking.

Suddenly Attwood said, "Now that Mr. Otis has found out what he wanted to know, I trust he will reward us with some of his own compositions."

How could Attwood be so fatuous! *Found out what he wanted to know!* Jason thought of the people he had to talk to now, Constanze Mozart and her sisters, Ernst Muller, Beethoven, and Salieri, whether or not he was insane. Jason asked, "Mr. Attwood, do you think Mozart was assassinated?"

There was a hushed silence. Braham appeared stunned; there was disbelief on Tothill's face; Deborah's features were still expressionless; and there was a gleam in Kelly's eyes that could be assent.

Attwood answered, "I wouldn't interfere. No good comes from interference in other people's affairs."

"But you do agree with what Mr. Kelly just told us?"

"Word for word?" Attwood laughed dryly. "Of course not."

"Are the facts wrong?"

"I remember that Mozart did complain about his kidneys and that he could not eat some things, and that Salieri was interested, but then Salieri was proud of his knowledge of food. That does not make him an assassin."

"I didn't say he was."

"It is what you are implying."

Jason denied that, thinking Attwood didn't want to jeopardize his position while Kelly no longer had a position to jeopardize, and said, "If you have a different view, sir, you should enlighten me."

"I know very little beyond what Michael told you. I am not an eavesdropper." But when he saw Jason's scepticism, Attwood added, "So I recall Salieri suggesting that Mozart should stress teaching the pianoforte, which many amateur ladies, some of them noble and most of them rich, practised and played. Salieri assured Mozart that would provide him with a good, safe living. Possibly Salieri was right. If I had been in Salieri's situation I might have suggested the same thing, for who could compete with *Le Nozze di Figaro* and *Don Giovanni*?"

D*

"But you were not his enemy, were you?"

"Indeed not! The last letter I received from Mozart, shortly before he died, when he had given up the hope of joining us in England and apparently was beginning to have premonitions that he was dying, concluded, 'Do not forget me, Thomas, your true and faithful friend, W. A. Mozart.' "

Tears came into Attwood's eyes, and Jason said, quietly now, "Sir, I didn't intend to upset you."

"Soon after, he was dead. Suddenly. Unexpectedly."

"That is why I am so interested in Mozart and anything about him."

Attwood said, "It is natural. I was, too, when I met him."

"And later, sir?"

Attwood's reserve had returned, and he said coldly, "It is dangerous to lean on anybody else too much. It doesn't allow you to express your own abilities. And if you are so sure that Salieri was hostile to Mozart, why did Mozart invite Salieri and Cavalieri to a performance of *The Magic Flute* and afterwards come as Salieri's guest at a supper in Salieri's rooms? If Salieri was such a threat to Mozart, why did my dear friend do this?"

Jason was confused. He could not reply. There was an icy silence. He did not dare look at Deborah.

But Braham, who had been listening to Attwood with a sudden passionate intentness, blurted out, "Ann Storace told me of a letter she received from Cavalieri about that supper. Cavalieri and Ann were friends."

Attwood said, "That doesn't prove anything." He was annoyed.

Braham said, "Cavalieri wrote it in December, 1791."

"I don't see the connection."

"Cavalieri's letter was written just after Mozart died. Ostensibly, since she knew how fond Ann was of Mozart, she was writing her condolences. But that was not why Ann was troubled by the letter."

"Why was she?" Jason asked urgently.

"Cavalieri told Ann that she and Salieri had supper with Mozart just two weeks before he died, and that Mozart had seemed in good health. Thus, wrote Cavalieri, she was shocked to hear of his sudden death."

Attwood said, "Mr. Otis, that is what I told you. I don't see where Cavalieri's letter changes anything. Actually, it confirms what I said."

Braham added, "Cavalieri also wrote that Mozart fell ill the day after the supper. And that he never recovered from that illness."

Jason asked excitedly, "You're positive?"

"Yes. Ann said that Cavalieri seemed agitated by this coincidence. Cavalieri repeated several times that Mozart had been pleased with the way his stomach and kidneys were behaving, that they were much better, and that he had eaten heartily."

"Mr. Braham, do you think Cavalieri suspected anything?"

"No. And I doubt that Ann did either. Ann never did say to me that she thought Mozart had been poisoned. Yet somehow, she couldn't regard the supper and his subsequent illness as just a coincidence. It were as if Cavalieri's letter was an effort to exorcise her own feelings of guilt."

"Perfect," Attwood said sarcastically, "Ann Storace receives a letter written in 1791, and thirty-three years later it is suggested that she suspected murder. Braham, why didn't she talk about it then?"

"Perhaps because you don't want to talk about it now."

Attwood was indignant. "There is nothing to talk about."

"I thought so, too, when I came here tonight. But after what Michael told us and the news of Salieri's attempted suicide, it makes one wonder."

Jason inquired, "Mr. Braham, is Cavalieri still alive?"

"She died many years ago. And Michael was wrong about her. She was an Austrian, not a German. Ann told me."

"What is the difference?" said Kelly. "Are you sure about the letter?"

"Yes. Ann remembered it clearly. She was astonished that Mozart had eaten with Salieri, for she said that Mozart did not trust him."

Jason asked, "Do you have the letter?"

"No. Ann and I parted some years before she died. But she was certain about the contents. One night Mozart ate with Salieri, the next day he was ill, two weeks later he was dead. She thought it was very strange."

"Very strange," Jason reflected aloud. "Now if I can only find proof that this sequence of events actually took place."

Kelly said, "Mozart's wife, Constanze, might know, or her sister Sophie, who was with him when he died."

Deborah asked, "How do you know that his sister-in-law was with him at that time?" She was so mixed up her head had begun to ache.

"When I heard the terrible news that Mozart had died, I wrote Constanze and Sophie answered me. She said that Constanze was still prostrate with grief, and that she had attended Mozart during his last twenty-four hours. She told me that she would never forget his final moments, his swollen body, his protuberant belly, his staring eyes, and his convulsive movements."

"What did Sophie think was the nature of his illness?"

"Kidneys, Mrs. Otis. But now, I realize, it could have been poison."

Attwood said, "And like Braham, you conveniently think of that now."

"Things come back to you that at the time they occurred did not seem significant. If Salieri had wanted to get rid of Mozart, why not an attack on his kidneys? Not necessarily with poison, but with the wrong food."

While the others pondered what Kelly had said, Attwood rose with a gesture of impatience and announced, "I think Mr. Otis is afraid to play for us. Perhaps he is not a musician at all. At least Salieri was."

Jason was startled by Attwood's challenge. He wanted to refuse, but he felt he had no choice. The pianoforte was unfamiliar, and he sensed that he was playing for a hostile audience, but gradually, as he entered the world of Mozart—Attwood had placed a Mozart sonata in front of him—and the music took possession of him, some confidence returned. After he finished the sonata, Attwood put another Mozart piece before him. It was a fantasia that Otto Muller had introduced him to, but Jason pretended that he was playing it at sight. His performance gathered assurance and power, and the music, dramatic and intense, ironically fitted what he had just learned. He was glad that Attwood had chosen this fantasia.

Tothill applauded automatically, but Jason saw surprise on his florid face, while Kelly's eyes shone with delight. He could not tell what Braham or Attwood was thinking, and neither of them uttered any comment.

Jason asked Attwood, "You didn't like my playing, sir?"

Attwood assumed a pedantic air. "You performed some of the notes accurately. And you were better in the fantasia, although it is the more difficult piece. But you should study more. May I hear your own music?"

Jason played several of his hymns, but he felt they were cold and colorless by comparison with the Mozart he had performed. When he ended he saw Attwood and Tothill exchange a sly, cynical smile.

Yet Tothill seemed to feel called upon to say, "They are pleasing."

Jason turned to Attwood again. "What do you think, sir?"

"They are variations of Handel. You should study composition. I am very busy these days with my duties as organist at St. Paul's Cathedral and my compositions for the King, but I could fit you in somewhere. Mozart told me that I possessed more of his style than any pupil he ever had."

"I don't want to be another Mozart!" Jason cried desperately.

"Naturally not. That would be impossible. But you do want to know as much as is available about his music. When could you start your studies?"

"I am going to Vienna soon."

"But Mr. Tothill said that Mrs. Otis . . ." Attwood halted. Tothill was embarrassed and Jason was angry. "Aren't you staying here?"

"What did Mr. Tothill say?" asked Jason.

Tothill caressed his stout stomach as he assumed an air of grave importance and stated, "Attwood informs me that many pianoforte concerts are given in London for the nobility and the gentry and that occasionally they even enjoy royal patronage. And you do seem to have a good hand upon the instrument, and in your situation you can afford to indulge yourself."

But Deborah's headache had grown worse. Tothill, who sat next to her, was so scented and curled and proud of his toupee that it sickened her. His teeth were false; she could tell by the way they clicked when he ate and whistled when he talked. She found herself recalling da Ponte's open and unashamed admission that he lacked teeth with affection. Tothill should not have mentioned her name. Da Ponte would have been more clever.

Tothill went on, encouraged by everybody's attention, "Moreover, you have a lively mind, Mr. Otis, with all that you imagined about Mozart."

"You don't believe me?"

"Mr. Otis, in England we allow the gentry some eccentricity. It often makes them more interesting." Tothill thought that if *his* wife had been capable of settling an independent income on him for life on the condition that he give up a musical career to become a gentleman, he would have accepted her generosity with magnanimity. "Why don't you pursue your musical studies with Attwood? He is a gentleman of superior quality."

"Is that why you came tonight, Mr. Tothill?"

"I came as your friend. I could rent a fine town house like Attwood's for you. One could be found for fifty to a hundred pounds a year."

Attwood added as Jason hesitated, "You are an attractive young man. Good looks are not essential to a composer, but they are quite useful if you wish to play in public or teach. If you study with me, you will be allowed into many of the most fashionable houses in London."

"It is a rare opportunity," said Tothill. "I understand Attwood rarely teaches any more. And you can learn much more about Mozart."

Attwood declared pontifically, "I teach only advanced students."

"But you haven't said whether I have the ability to perform and compose professionally," Jason cried, growing desperate again.

"Your work is sung professionally, isn't it?"

"Yes."

"Then the rest will take care of itself. With the proper instruction."

Jason glanced at the others. Kelly was interested; Tothill wore a fixed smile; Braham was preoccupied. It was Deborah's expression that troubled him. It fluctuated between resignation and despair. He thought bitterly that she would not heed him; she did not hear his music, she never did, actually; she would conspire with Tothill and Attwood to keep him here.

Suddenly she said, "When I came here tonight I had no idea it would be so difficult to know what to do."

Tothill said, "You gave me reason to believe that you preferred London to Vienna. Mrs. Otis, you could live very well here."

"Oh, I love London. And I want to live here. But now I see that there is so much to know about Mozart."

"You think he was poisoned?" Attwood asked her incredulously.

"Not really. And yet after what Michael Kelly and John Braham told us, I am not sure what to think."

"If I were younger," Kelly said with sudden intensity, "I would go to Vienna. I would talk to Constanze, Sophie, anyone who knew Mozart well."

Jason saw Attwood give Kelly an irate glance, as if Kelly had betrayed him; but the former tenor was not to be halted now.

He added, "Mr. Otis, if I were you, I would go as soon as possible. I am convinced now that what Braham told us about Cavalieri is significant."

"But I can teach you much more about Mozart," Attwood assured him.

"Thank you. But I must go to Vienna."

"You believe Kelly and Braham?" Attwood asked skeptically.

"I believe them."

Attwood shook his head critically, while a look of surprise, almost disgust, appeared on Tothill's florid face. As if goaded by a sudden disagreeable task, he clicked his teeth and said self-importantly, "I have a letter for you, Mr. Otis. It was sent to me by your father-in-law."

Jason regarded the letter reluctantly until he saw that it was not from Quincy Pickering, but from Otto Muller. Then he was angry at the delay, asking Tothill, "Why didn't you give it to me sooner?"

"I forgot, the conversation was so absorbing."

Jason didn't believe him, for the flap of the envelope looked as if it had been tampered with, but before he could question that, Deborah urged him to read it, suggesting that perhaps new facts had come to light, perhaps Salieri had died, and the others were waiting for him to proceed. He read silently.

"Dear Herr Otis:

I can only pray that this letter reaches you. Not knowing your London address, I will have to send it through the Honorable Quincy Pickering, but perhaps God will be good to me and you will receive it.

I have not been well, but that is not why I wrote you. My brother informs me that he has heard that Salieri is failing and may not live much longer. Thus, I beg you, do not delay. London is an attractive city and you are young, but Salieri is old, in his seventies, and you will not have this opportunity again. Ernst himself is not in good health, and he writes me that Mozart's wife has been feeling poorly and that his sister has become bedridden and may not live much longer. One of the sad things about our mission is that so many who knew Mozart and Salieri are gone, and with the passing of each day another vital source of information may leave us.

I urge you to travel to Vienna as quickly as possible. I only wish I could give this letter and yourself wings to speed matters.

By now you must have learned much that is valuable, and eventually, after all these years, perhaps justice will be done. My brother has found out where Salieri is confined, he knows an attendant at the asylum, and if you get to Vienna in time, you may be able to see Salieri himself.

Your aging and affectionate friend,

Otto Muller."

Deborah asked impatiently, "What does the letter say?"

"Salieri is failing. And Mozart's wife is not well."

"Is that all?"

"What else should there be?" He was not going to tell anybody, not even Deborah, about the possibility of visiting Salieri; they would discourage him, but now that had become the most exciting prospect of all.

Tothill said, "You are sure that is all?"

"Why?" Jason stood up erect, straight. "Did you read it first?"

"Sir!" Tothill was horrified at that suggestion. "The letter arrived in this condition. But I confess, I had hoped you and Mrs. Otis would grace our city with your presence. Your wife seems happy in London."

She said, "I am. But some things should be answered. Mr. Braham, did Cavalieri's letter give any idea of how Salieri acted after Mozart fell ill?"

Braham replied, "No. I am surprised that I remember as much as I do."

"So am I," Attwood said wryly.

"But what I do recall," Braham insisted, "I recall accurately."

Tothill asked, "Mrs. Otis, what changed your mind?"

"Sir, I cannot desert my husband. My place is by his side."

As Jason and Deborah prepared to depart, Kelly stated, "Remember, if you do find somebody who knows about Mozart's last meal with Salieri and Cavalieri, such as Sophie or Constanze, or perhaps even Salieri himself, you must learn what Mozart ate and drank, and most important, what effect it had on his body."

"We will visit Mozart's wife and sister-in-law," Deborah replied, as if it were her idea, although Jason had intended to do that ever since he had decided to go to Vienna. In an ironic way Mozart no longer seemed dead and buried, she thought. The dead Mozart had no relation to the real man they were meeting wherever they went; he was not just a historic figure anymore. When all the words were said, what kind of a man had he been? What would his wife say? His sister-in-law? Would they be candid? Or protective? Jason was a better musician than Attwood had admitted; she had enjoyed the way he had played Mozart, particularly the second piece. Was she changing, too, she wondered. She was not sure, but perhaps Jason was on to something significant after all.

At the door she put her arm through his affectionately and smiled at him tenderly and said, "I still doubt that we will find proof that Mozart was poisoned, but I do believe my husband has reason to suspect foul play. Considerable reasons."

"I agree, Mrs. Otis," said Kelly. "But if your husband's suspicions should prove correct, matters could become difficult, even dangerous. There is much intrigue in Vienna. Even today."

Jason asked, "What do you suggest?"

"Be quick. Alert. Be sure of every step you take. And trust no one!"

11

The Journey Outward

YET while Jason and Deborah assumed that all the goodbyes had been said, Michael Kelly was waiting for them where the coach departed for the Dover boat and the crossing of the English Channel. He had brought them a parting gift, a biography of Mozart. Jason was disappointed that it was written in German; but Deborah said that this was fine, it would give them an opportunity to improve their German.

Jason asked, "Can I trust this biography?"

"Not completely," Kelly replied. "Some of the facts are wrong, and the author's views of Mozart are colored by what others told him. All that he learned he seems to have learned from somebody else—Mozart's friends, his widow, his sister—but it will give you a sense of Mozart's life. How he traveled, especially as a child. What he composed, and for whom. The author wrote me asking what I knew, but I have kept the best facts for myself, for the book I am writing—there is nothing about Mozart in English—but I have told you what I know."

Then the coach was leaving; and in the clatter of the hoofs of the horses on the cobblestones they could not hear what Kelly was shouting, although for an instant Deborah thought their friend was going to cry, and the expression on his face seemed to utter another warning. London was gray and misty this morning, and while Jason's face was eager with anticipation, she felt that their English visit had been just an interesting interlude and now the real difficulties were starting.

The coach ride to Dover was too bumpy to read the biography as Jason had hoped to do. The crossing was extremely rough, and it was no comfort to a seasick Jason to have Deborah inform him in Calais—she had been able to read the first few chapters of the biography—that the Mozarts had been seasick also when they had crossed the Channel. He was dizzy and nauseous the entire voyage. The boat was small, and many times he felt the water would engulf them. Every wave jarred him. Nothing was flat—not the sea, not the sky, not the deck certainly. He could not find anything stationary to focus on; yet Deborah kept reading. If he could only halt his suffering. He was possessed with a nightmarish fear of drowning—he had been afflicted with this terror all his life, for he could not swim, not a stroke—and he was afraid that he would slip on the wet, slippery deck and fall overboard. That increased his nausea, and he hated Deborah for reading while he could not even see straight. There were moments during the voyage when he thought he was going to die. Not even during the miserable journey across the Atlantic had he felt so awful. He was astonished that they reached Calais without anybody being swept overboard. He resolved that from now on he must travel only on land, except when he had to cross the Atlantic or the Channel. All during the voyage to France he felt that Deborah was regarding him with contempt.

Not until they were bedded down for the night in Calais was Jason able to turn to the biography, and only Deborah's common-sense choice of an inn with a cheerful room overlooking a green park speeded his recovery.

Deborah had been worried by the severity of his seasickness, but she hid her fears to avoid upsetting him, and pretended that his nausea had been of no consequence, more mental than physical.

Reading the biography, Jason was intrigued to learn that Mozart's mother had died in Paris and had been buried in a church there, Saint Eustace.

But in Paris he could not find the church with his scanty French, and Deborah, whose French was better, did not want to visit any graveyards.

She said that his interest was macabre, that they would not discover anything they needed to know. Yet Jason believed that he had to do this for Mozart as a friend, as Mozart would have done himself. There were times now that he felt he was Mozart's best, closest friend; he was beginning to feel possessive about this. Only he did not dare tell Deborah about these views. It was enough that he knew he was moving into a deeper appreciation of what Mozart was. He told Deborah that the visit to Saint Eustace would help him see the world of Mozart through the latter's eyes. She was still sceptical, but when she used her French, they were able to find the church, although he disliked feeling dependent upon her, while she was glad that she had this advantage over him.

Saint Eustace was a bleak, gloomy church, a massive pile of stone, looking denuded of human feeling, as if picked clean of emotion by the erosions of time. The garbage in front of the entrance shocked Jason, and he stared grimly at the once-white Grecian pillars which were gray from years of encrusted dirt. There were also yellow stains on the outside wall as if a child had urinated on it a long time ago, perhaps even in Mozart's time, and no one had bothered ever to clean that off.

No one inside knew anything about Mozart or his mother. Everything was oppressively cold: the marble floor, the stone walls, the noble tombs, the ancient armor of warriors long dead. There were windows, but no light came through them; there were stone angels, but they stood without feeling.

Jason was about to depart when Deborah found an old priest who was the keeper of the records. Father Pierre's eyes were wrinkled, he tottered when he walked, his hands had a perpetual tremble, but he kept talking about how lucky he had been to fight for Bonaparte.

Deborah replied that they were Americans and handed him two francs.

Father Pierre's eyes lit up and he led them into a little room and dragged out a huge book, explaining that this was the church register.

Deborah told him that according to her information, Madame Mozart had died in July, 1778, and he opened the register of deaths so that its pages covered the entire table. He mumbled that generals were buried here, and Rameau, a musician, but no Mozart that he remembered, and he had been at Saint Eustace a lifetime. Pages crumpled as Father Pierre turned them over. Jason thought the crucial page was lost, they were in the wrong church, the biographer had made another error.

He had turned to go when Deborah said abruptly, "Wait! This entry is blurred, but I can read it." She translated it for Jason.

Saturday—4 July 1778.

On the said day, Marie-Anne Pertil, aged 57 years, wife of Leopold Mozart, maître de chapelle at Salzburg, Bavaria, who died yesterday at Rue du Gros Chenet, has been interred in the cemetery in the presence of Wolfgang Amadée Mozart, her son, and François Heina, trumpeter in the light cavalry in the Royal guard, a friend.

(Signed) Mozart. F. Heina. Irisson, Vicar.

Jason was filled with a sadness so profound he could hardly bear it.

Father Pierre shouted harshly, "You are blotting the church register!"

Tears from Jason's eyes had fallen on the dusty, yellow page, and he knew what the priest meant, although he didn't understand a word.

Father Pierre glared at him as if he had committed a heinous crime.

Deborah asked, "Do you know where Madame Mozart is buried?"

"It is impossible to say. Many have been buried since 1778. And much of the cemetery is gone. In the Revolution many things disappeared."

Back in their inn, Deborah asked Jason, "Are you satisfied now?"

"Not in the least. I wonder how much Mozart was affected by the death of his mother, if I was moved so much many years later."

"You are sentimental. On reflection, it strikes you as very sad."

"No. We do not have the facts about her death. Or its effect upon Mozart." Jason was emphatic.

"I know the facts we have in our possession."

Jason insisted on spending the next few days reading the biography despite his urgency to reach Vienna. When Deborah reminded him of his skepticism about its facts, he replied that, even so, it would give him a better view of Mozart's life. She would have preferred to have toured Paris, but he refused. They sat in the living room of their suite in the inn and she translated when he came to a word or phrase he didn't know. She assured him that she was giving him the exact meaning, but he wasn't sure that she was telling him the truth, for he was surprised and disappointed that the biographer never mentioned the possibility that Salieri might have killed Mozart. And he was upset by the many illnesses Mozart had had, particularly as a child. He wondered if the smallpox, scarlet fever, and other ailments Mozart had suffered from had been the actual cause of his death.

Deborah paused in her translating—they had been rereading an account of Mozart's first visit to Paris at the age of seven—to say, "You must consider the illnesses. And the many journeys he took, especially as a child. They must have weakened him and made him vulnerable to the ailment that eventually killed him."

What she was suggesting was intolerable. Was his entire quest in vain? Was he deceiving himself? Was he, in his own way, as mad as Salieri?

"Overwork, poverty, and the many illnesses could have killed him."

He was unable to answer her. He had a premonition that if she took away his belief that Salieri had assassinated Mozart he would hate her.

"It is a possibility you must consider, Jason."

She was determined to deprive him of his mission, he thought angrily, but he hid that, retorting, "Salieri confessed."

"Did you hear him confess?"

He almost blurted out, *I will*, but no one must spoil this prospect, and she could. He said, "In England you agreed that I had reason to suspect foul play. Nothing has happened to change that view."

"I didn't know then that Mozart had had so many illnesses, or had worked so hard and had been so impoverished the last year of his life."

"I still don't think the biographer told the whole truth."

"Who does, Jason? Do you?"

"Mozart thought he was poisoned."

"Does that make it true?"

But he loved Mozart so. If he could only hear some of his music now. He looked out of the window. Paris was a Royal city again, much as it had been when Mozart had seen it last, many years ago, but in some ways it was as if Mozart had never been there. All the French wanted to talk about was Napoleon, and now that Napoleon was no longer

Emperor, about his glorious rule. Nowhere was Mozart to be heard. Gluck was being played, and Beethoven, but no Mozart. It was mortifying. He could have wept with rage.

"Jason you must recognize that you could be wrong."

He had to go through with it. Even if she did not believe that he was wise enough to find the truth, or strong enough. He said abruptly, "We have spent too much time in Paris. We must hurry on to Vienna, as Otto Muller suggested. We will follow Mozart's travels. In reverse. We will take the route he used in his grand tour."

"You said that you didn't trust the biography's account."

"Oh, that part of the book should be right." Jason began to pack.

Deborah, realizing that she could not alter his opinions, was afflicted by a terrible melancholy.

At the prospect of visiting Vienna he was smiling. He declared, "Paris has been a bore. We haven't learned anything here of importance, but in Vienna we will be given a warm welcome."

Only he had not touched her luggage. In anger and desperation she blurted out, "You don't want me to go with you?"

"I don't want you to be put under any nervous strain."

She felt superfluous and ridiculous. He was regarding her, she thought, derisively, and he was not in the least grateful for her help. Yet for a few moments in England they had had rapport. Suddenly, abruptly, she closed the biography with a bang. Swaying like a drunkard, she hurried to the water closet, where she was violently sick in the basin. And when she emerged she had to lie down, she had such an awful headache.

Jason was aghast. Her face was so pale it was like a death mask. She was intimidating him with her sudden illness. He stopped packing. He sat down beside her, put his hand on her arm to reassure her. She gave a little shudder and moved away from him, sobbing. "Go. Go. You are so anxious to leave me. Go."

"You don't understand."

"I understand very well. You are interested only in establishing that Mozart was assassinated, and nothing else matters."

"A week ago you agreed that this trip to Vienna was essential. Then you read one book, which is probably inaccurate, and change your mind."

"I did not change my mind. But I do think you must consider other possibilities. Many things could have contributed to Mozart's death."

"I wish I had a pianoforte," he muttered. "I miss his music so."

"I do, too!" she said with unexpected intensity.

"You do, Deborah, you do?"

"Of course."

"But originally . . ."

"His music was too new." Please God, she prayed, Forgive this lie, but nothing else seemed able to hold him. Yet, even as part of her was relieved that he was putting his arms around her and this time she did not pull away, she had a sudden feeling of resentment.

Now, as if by common consent, they sat facing each other in many conveyances—mail coach and stagecoach, cabriolet and diligence, but never in a boat, although sometimes it would have been easier, for after the trip across the Channel Jason had vowed to avoid water journeys.

Jason mapped their itinerary carefully: everywhere Mozart had performed on his grand tour of Europe that was on the route to Vienna. He loved the sound of their names; they sounded like a great adventure: Tirlemont, Liège, Aachen, Cologne, Bonn, Coblenz, Frankfurt, Mannheim, Heidelberg, Schwetzingen, Bruchsal, Ludwigsburg, Ulm, Augsburg, Munich, Salzburg, and Vienna. After the first few days Deborah couldn't even think about the difficulties that still lay ahead; but when Jason noticed her agitation, she said, "Just nervousness, and a little fatigue."

She tried to be useful, to read maps and road signs and to translate when Jason's German was inadequate. But by the time they reached the German towns she marvelled that any child could have survived such an arduous journey. When the sun shone, the roads were as hard as rock and they bounced so violently she thought her insides would come apart; when it rained, which was frequently, the dirt became mud and they swayed precariously. To make up for the time lost by the bad weather, the drivers would whip their horses frantically. A number of times they went off the road and into a hedge or a road bank, and once, quite dangerously, into a field, nearly turning over.

Even Jason was frightened. But he did not alter their journey.

When they reached Mannheim, he said it was halfway—to lift Deborah's spirits, she was sick of the travelling. Many of the inns had only two feather beds to sleep between. When she asked for sheets and a blanket, they regarded her as a lunatic. Most of the stoves in the bedrooms could not be used because of the threat of suffocation. Flies, fleas, bugs, and rats were everywhere, drains were stopped up, linen was filthy, and garbage was all about. Food was usually so bad that Deborah thought it was no wonder that Mozart had fallen ill so much while travelling.

She was surprised when Jason asked her to choose the inn at Mannheim, and that he did not object to her selecting the best, which was also the most costly. He was exhausted and depressed by the harsh travelling conditions, but he could not admit that to her. Instead he said that they should stay in Mannheim a few days to hear Mozart's music.

But nothing of Mozart was being played at the moment.

So after one night in Mannheim, Jason decided that they must move on. He informed Deborah, "We have accomplished nothing here."

"We rested. Don't you think Mozart ever did?" She was irritated by his sudden decision to move; she was just starting to feel human again.

He wanted to cry out that she was unfair, but he restrained himself. She would only accuse him of self-righteousness.

She said, "We ought to hire our own coach."

But as she expected, he retorted, "It will be an unnecessary expense."

To his surprise, she replied, "Perhaps you are right. The more we experience the hardships Mozart suffered as a child, the more I am convinced that these journeys, which he took many times, must have taken a fearful toll of his strength, and eventually sapped it, leaving him vulnerable to numerous illnesses. The way this journey is going," she said with growing assurance, "by the time we reach Vienna, I will be convinced that his travels killed him. It is no wonder he died young."

Her assumption was obscene; it violated *his* cherished assumptions. Yet he realized that she could be right. When he had planned this journey, he had had no idea that it would be so arduous and painful. Only this was not a conclusion he could admit to her. To apologize, to confess that he was wrong was too humiliating; it was unthinkable.

She said, "When I complain about traveling conditions, I am told that things have changed very little in the last hundred years."

"We will hire our own coach," he said suddenly, "as Mozart did."

After Jason did, Deborah was so grateful she came to him that night with a passion she had never expressed before. She insisted on squatting over him, as if she had imagined this position for a long time. And this unknown self crashed down from a great height, and he responded again and again and quicker and quicker until it was impossible to tell who pumped and who responded. Yet even as Jason felt propelled into a vortex of ecstasy, he felt also that she was pushing him down, and he was frantic with a determination to disprove this, to overthrow her dominance. With intense violence he straightened her out above him. Then as he pushed upward she seemed transfixed. But as he reached up and clutched her shoulders with all his strength and pulled her down against him with a convulsive motion, she quivered powerfully and recoiled so that their passion became one and she cried to go on and on. But there was no need to prod Jason. Deborah was sobbing and laughing at each lunge. And then like a spout giving expression to life, there was the flow of the orgasm.

Tears trickled down her cheeks. He was pouring with sweat and semen. Deborah still sat upon him. Then the paroxysm of her emotion was over, and she said self-consciously, "I had better get off."

"No! No!" It was frightening. He never wanted her to get off. He felt so vital. How had she known?

When she pulled away from him, the hurt was almost unbearable. He lay there a long time while she washed herself. He could still feel the touch of her breasts upon him. They were beautiful, and he longed to decorate them with flowers. But she would say that was foolish. And suddenly he felt trapped. To relive this experience he would do almost anything.

The next day, when Jason had to pay for the coach, he was dismayed by what it was costing him. Their innkeeper, Karl Linder, who was acting as the agent for the previous owner of the coach, delivered it to them at the inn for their inspection. As Linder had promised, it was a sturdy, handsome vehicle with an elegant yet comfortable interior. The upholstery was a royal red and the seats were softly cushioned, and there was space enough for four. There were glass windows to keep out the elements and a small canvas roof to cover the driver. There was a coat of arms on both doors, and Linder said, "Herr Otis, this is ideal for your needs. You can use it as a coach on the road and as a carriage in Vienna."

Deborah agreed and was delighted with it, but as they stood outside the inn and the young man who had delivered the vehicle had to quiet the horses, Jason felt crushed by the responsibility he had incurred. When he had decided to visit Vienna, he had never expected such difficulties.

Now, more than ever, he craved Mozart's music. It was the one thing, he thought, that could keep him going through all the hardships.

The surroundings were pleasant outside the inn, which was on a wide, straight road lined on each side with evenly arranged trees. The weather was clear, sunny, mild, typical of autumn in these parts, Linder assured them, but Jason felt that he was betraying Mozart by all the delays. He was behind his schedule, and at the rate they were travelling, Salieri could be dead by the time they arrived in Vienna.

Linder, who had learned about his interest in music and Mozart, was proud that people said he resembled Ludwig van Beethoven, who was making a name for himself in Vienna. But Jason didn't tell him that he intended to visit that composer. It was inconceivable that this florid-faced man with his broad, ugly features could have any similarity to Beethoven. He had neglected the proposed oratorio for Beethoven, but suddenly this commission was important again.

Linder was saying to Deborah, "You are getting a bargain, Frau Otis, with this coach. Two hundred gulden. What, I believe, your friend Kapellmeister Mozart received for his Singspiel *Die Hochzeit des Figaro*."

Two hundred gulden, Jason calculated, would leave him with very little money when they reached Vienna. Then there was also the cost of the driver, the upkeep.

Deborah drew him aside where no one else could see them, pushed two hundred gulden into his hand, and whispered. "I know this is wicked of me, dear, to have so much money with me without telling you, but I took this along to spend on the journey for anything that might be useful." And as he protested, she added, "This will be my expression of confidence in your mission. From now on, I am sure it will go quite well."

But after Jason had paid Linder—Deborah insisted on a receipt, which Linder had ignored until she mentioned it—there was the problem of the driver. The innkeeper suggested the young man who had delivered the coach, but Deborah, noticing his inexperience, said that was impossible.

Linder replied, "It is very difficult to find anyone experienced to drive all the way to Vienna. But Hans Denke, unlike most of the natives of Mannheim, wants to go to Vienna. Only it is too far to travel by himself, and too expensive for a person without means."

Jason asked, "Why does he want to go?"

"He says he will have more opportunities there."

"Do you agree?"

"I have never been to Vienna. Very few of us have."

"What are his other qualifications?"

"He speaks English," said Karl Linder. "Ask him, Herr Otis."

Jason did, and to his surprise Hans replied in excellent English, "Sir, I worked for an English nobleman who lived in Mannheim."

"As a secretary?" questioned Deborah. Hans worried her; he seemed much too slight and young to drive the heavy coach and the restive horses.

"No, Frau Otis, as a stableboy. But I can also read and write."

"Did you go to school?"

"No, Frau Otis, my father taught me. He knew English and French."

"What does your father do?"

"He was the English nobleman's gardener. He's dead, Frau Otis."

Jason inquired, seeing the tears in Hans's eyes and feeling sorry for him, "Is that one of the reasons you wish to leave Mannheim?"

"Yes, sir. I have no family here."

"And in Vienna?"

"I have an uncle, I believe, and cousins, sir."

After Jason's preconceived notion that German was a guttural tongue, he was intrigued that Hans's voice was pleasant and soft. And sensing Deborah's resistance, he thought she should like this, and his appearance. Hans was short, dark, with carefully trimmed black hair. His eyes were brown with tinges of green. And he had powerful forearms.

Aware of her objections, Hans said, "Frau Otis, I am strong enough to handle the horses. I have worked for a blacksmith, too."

"You have done many things," she said, "haven't you?"

"A few, lady."

"Music, too?" She couldn't keep the sarcasm out of her voice.

"I play the violin a little."

Jason asked, "Do you know who Mozart is?"

"Of course, sir!"

"Do you like his music?"

"Yes, sir! Indeed! Indeed!"

Jason was pleased, but Deborah was suspicious. She thought, This young man is too enthusiastic about Mozart and too eager to please. She asked, "Where did you learn about Mozart? From your father, no doubt?"

"That's right, Frau Otis. And Mozart is played in Mannheim. Often."

"Yet you are a stableboy?"

"Begging your pardon, lady, but one has to eat."

Hans was a bewildering collection of fragments, reflected Deborah, but what was the real person? There were things about him that she didn't trust. She could tell that Jason had taken a fancy to him, especially after he had expressed enthusiasm for Mozart, but she felt that was a ruse.

Linder, sensing Deborah's doubts, suggested, "Let Hans drive."

Hans was able to control the horses, but more from strength than skill, Deborah decided. She whispered to Jason, "This could be dangerous," and he replied, "You heard that it will be difficult to find anyone else." And he liked Hans's awareness of Mozart. That was a good omen, he thought.

He asked Hans, "What wages do you want?"

"Board, sir. And four gulden a day so I can enter Vienna."

Deborah asked, "They won't admit you if you have no money?"

"Indeed, not, Frau Otis. And perhaps you can use me in Vienna."

Jason asked, "Is your German as good as your English?"

"I think so, sir. Don't you, Herr Linder?"

"It is better. Herr Otis, the boy can translate for you, too."

That was what Jason was thinking, but seeing Deborah frown, he did not pursue this subject, but asked who had owned the coach. He was curious about the coat of arms and the luxury of the appointments.

Linder explained, "A baron who lives outside of Mannheim. The coat of arms shows that he was in the Hapsburg service. But unexpectedly and unfortunately he contracted the French disease, and now he is so badly afflicted that, sadly, sitting is most difficult and uncomfortable. And he needs the gulden. Yet there is nothing to worry about, the upholstery and the entire coach have been cleaned thoroughly."

Then, just as Jason was assuming that everything had been settled and Deborah was wondering why Linder had been so eager for them to hire Hans, the innkeeper insisted on being paid ten gulden for Hans's services and said, when Jason protested, that he could not go through with the sale of the coach unless he received the ten gulden.

Jason was furious, feeling this was extortion, but Linder was adamant, and the thought of having to start all over to find a coach and driver was so enervating that Jason gave in, although quite reluctantly.

They set off early the next day. Jason was still very angry at Linder, but Deborah had such an *I-told-you-so* look on her face he could not admit that he had made a mistake. Hans's driving was uncertain, as she had feared. He had trouble starting the horses and he halted them awkwardly, but with his strong arms he was able to keep the coach on the road. They were relieved to be free of the prospect of sitting across from total strangers in the public coaches. And they were heartened by the news that they could reach Vienna with two weeks of steady driving.

At first the weather was fine. They journeyed through Heidelberg, Bruchsal, Ludwigsburg, and Augsburg as Mozart had done. Jason reread the biography and learned that on the grand tour of Europe Mozart's father had bought his own coach and had been born in Augsburg.

But Jason was in too much of a hurry to pause at Augsburg. He had read also that Mozart had had trouble with his food when he travelled. He could comprehend this better now that he had experienced some of the hardships that Mozart had undergone. And now the urgency to investigate what John Braham had told him about Salieri dominated him again.

Past Munich and on their way to Salzburg the skies grew dark. Jason had looked forward to this part of the journey with anticipation—this was Mozart's country—yet the portents were unmistakable. While he had been examining the scenery with affection, an ominous storm had been building up in the mountains. It was too late to halt, there was no habitation within view—only trees, shrubs, and rocks—they were going through a mountain pass, and it was raining heavily and the air was becoming colder. The rain turned to sleet and then to snow. They struggled on for hours. Finally, however, when they went downhill, the snow stopped and became a steady, persistent rain.

At dusk they found a small town, Wasserburg. Deborah was so grateful for any kind of shelter that she pretended that the ramshackle inn, the only inn in this tiny German village, was fine, when she actually felt in a dark depression as she lay on top of the harsh straw mattress. She could not sleep between the mattresses, although that was the only way to keep warm. She fought with herself to keep from vomiting; the preserved veal they had had for dinner made her very sick.

It was no consolation when Jason said, "Now we know what Mozart endured." She could have killed him. The veal was almost petrified.

Hans was sleeping in the stable with the horses and the coach. He said that was the only way to be sure that nothing would be stolen.

The next day, as they approached Salzburg, the rain resumed. By the time they reached the town itself, the downpour was so hard and thick, so charged with a torrential force, it was as if they were riding through a vast sea. Jason had heard that Salzburg was one of the most beautiful places in the world, but there was nothing to see. Everything was blotted out. The clouds over the mountains around Salzburg had turned into waterfalls. The raindrops thumped upon the coach violently.

It was impossible to visit Mozart's birthplace as they huddled in another inn for comfort. Even inside it was cold and damp, and when it was still pouring the next day, Jason decided to move on. He could not believe that such a torrential downpour could be falling for many miles. He said, "If we go on, we will drive out of the rain."

Deborah didn't agree, but she didn't argue. This time the storm lasted all day and never abated for a moment. Hans assured them that he was not blinded—Hans could see eight or nine feet ahead—but the rain and wind chopped at them and shook the coach viciously. They had been assured that there were frequent shelters between Salzburg and Vienna, but most of the time they rode in isolation, seeing no one else.

At the end of the fourth day—the storm had subsided to a steady downpour—they reached Linz. They found a good inn, and Jason grew cheerful. He had been oppressed with a horrible premonition that their coach would break down, but now the weather was improving. He told Deborah, "We are not far from Vienna. A few days more, and we will be there."

They were sitting in the dining room of the inn, although she had no appetite, and she replied, "The innkeeper tells me that it would be easier to go to Vienna by water ordinary down the Danube."

"By water?" Jason was horrified at the suggestion.

"He says it will be more comfortable. And I read that this is the way Mozart went the first time he visited Vienna."

"What will I do with the coach?"

"Sell it. It has served its purpose."

"And Hans? He was promised that he would get to Vienna."

"You say that it is not very far now. He will manage."

"No." Jason was decisive. "We will need the coach in Vienna."

The next morning, when it was dry and sunny, Jason was sure that he had been right. But an hour out of Linz the wind changed suddenly and blew cold and damp upon them. A darkness even darker than before descended upon them, and Deborah was shaken by the sound of rocks hitting the coach. She shouted, "Someone must be throwing stones at us!"

Jason put out his head, then drew it back quickly. He said, "Hail, as big as my fist. It could kill you if it hit you on the head."

But Hans kept driving, for there was nowhere to halt. Once again there was no shelter in sight, and he was afraid that if he stopped, they would return to Linz and go to Vienna by boat and leave him behind. He huddled under the small canvas roof which was supposed to protect him and prayed that the elements would spare him, but as the hail rushed upon him with a loud crash and gashed the wood of the coach, he was terrified. The horses were hysterical, and it took all of his strength to keep them from bolting. The air was full of clamor and peril. The hail seemed to beat at him directly, personally. The wind raged and swirled, and he felt in a vortex. Yet it seemed better to move on, as if, somehow, that made him a less obvious target. And he must get to Vienna. Linder had assured him that once the rich Americans arrived in Vienna, they would find him indispensable and he could earn much money from them. But it was such a battle to keep the coach on the road.

Then, as swiftly as the storm had swept upon them, it ceased. The terrible wind vanished, the sun appeared. They had been travelling for hours without incident, and they were all sighing with relief when the coach lurched grotesquely and went over on one side.

"A wheel is broken," announced Hans like the voice of doom. He had no idea how to repair it, staring at the shattered spokes.

"What are we to do?" implored Deborah. "You're sure you can't fix it?"

"I'm afraid not, Frau Otis. But perhaps if I unhitch the horses and ride into the nearest village, I can find a wheel."

"And leave us alone?" Deborah was shocked.

Hans turned to Jason. "Sir, what do you suggest?"

Jason yearned to quit the whole absurd business. What had ever possessed him to set out on such an impossible journey? He said, "It is a very tricky situation."

"It always is," Deborah said pessimistically. But where was Hans going? Deserting them, as she had expected. He had run up the road waving his hands frantically.

A minute later he returned leading a mail coach which had been going across a crossroad beyond and behind a hill. The driver of the mail coach, which also carried passengers, regarded them as lunatics when he heard that they did not possess a spare wheel. He said, "The person who sold you the coach, didn't he warn you that this could happen, and usually does, on the road from Munich to Vienna?"

"No," answered Jason, avoiding Deborah's accusing gaze. "Hans, weren't you aware of this possibility? You should have been."

"I am not a coachman, sir. But the mail coach has an extra wheel."

The driver insisted that he could not spare it, until Deborah, anticipating the situation now from practice, offered him twenty gulden. Hard bargaining followed, but finally the driver agreed, out of the generosity of his heart, to give the wheel to them for thirty gulden.

If it fitted. Hans's experience as a blacksmith's helper was useful now, for he did know how to change a wheel. The driver of the mail coach said he was not allowed to touch another person's coach.

The new wheel didn't fit exactly—there was a lean and bump to the coach now—but the mail coach driver assured them that they could reach Vienna. If they rode slowly, carefully, and were lucky. He had to leave, for his passengers were making a scene, irate at the delay.

Deborah was desolate as she saw the mail coach disappear over the horizon, but Hans, attaching the broken wheel to the rear of the coach just in case it could be repaired, assured her they would be in Vienna soon. He was so positive, she almost believed him.

And several days later, standing on the hill beside the Belvedere Palace just outside Vienna—Hans had taken this route on the advice of Karl Linder, who had told him that the Americans should be much impressed with the view, and his wisdom in choosing it—Deborah thought that maybe her suspicions of Hans had been too harsh. The entire city seemed to lie before them, a compact cluster of buildings within a crumbling fortress wall, smaller than she had expected, much smaller than London, yet it was a superb view, as Hans said. The range of mountains behind Vienna appeared to palpitate in the distance and framed the city into a clear contour of palaces, churches, and houses. The visibility was remarkable, and the sky rested over the city and the surrounding countryside like a soft blue blanket. Only the spires of St. Stephen's Cathedral and several other churches rose above the horizon.

"Vienna is beautiful!" exclaimed Jason, holding Deborah affectionately. So many people who had known Mozart lived there.

"Quite beautiful," responded Deborah, "at least, from here. Hans, how much longer should it take us to reach the gates of the city?"

"A few minutes, I believe, Frau Otis. Perhaps, once you are settled in Vienna, you and Herr Otis will be able to use my services?"

"Perhaps," Jason said sharply, wondering what he was getting into. He had agreed to use Hans only until they reached Vienna, no longer.

Deborah was surprised that Hans suddenly and abruptly started the horses with his whip. Even during the most perilous days he had not done that. He must be anxious indeed about his arrival in Vienna, she thought: Was his tale about his relatives a lie?

But the shadows were gone from Jason. Now he felt philosophical about the hardships, discomforts, and exhaustion of the journey. Yet he said with much emotion, "Deborah, you must be very tired. But you did take the travelling bravely." His face lit up with a radiant smile. "And tonight, we will be rewarded. Tonight, dear, we will be with Mozart."

12

The Examination

AT THE gates of Vienna there were so many soldiers on duty Jason felt that he was trying to enter a closely guarded castle. He was surprised; he had not come such a long way for this. Vienna had been at peace for nearly ten years, and Napoleon, the great enemy of the Hapsburgs, had been dead for almost three. Yet wherever he glanced, there were soldiers, and they watched everybody. Hans halted the coach at a sentry's command, but suddenly and rudely the sentry motioned for them to get off on the side of the road. When Hans was too slow for the sentry, he pulled the coach off the road, almost turning it over in his haste to clear the way. A moment later a Royal carriage rushed through the gates at a breakneck gallop. The sentry sighed with relief, pleased that he had done his duty, but Jason thought, What a squashed thing we should have been if the Royal carriage had run over us.

After a long, anxious time they were ordered into a line of coaches for examination. While they waited again, Jason's thoughts were confusing. So much continued to be different than he had expected. Up to now they had arrived without much delay or inconvenience from officials, but here officials were everywhere and checking everything conceivable. He wondered if this was deliberate, to frighten. To ease his anxiety and Deborah's, he drew her attention to the courtyard inside the gates where they were waiting. It was crowded with market women, priests, travellers in other coaches, and peasants from the provinces.

But Deborah was not diverted. She disliked the delay, and the extraordinary number of people who seemed to have nothing to do but to lounge about the courtyard and stare at them. Jason was exultant again as he perceived the spire of St. Stephen's Cathedral above the heads of the crowd, but she thought, This scene doesn't fit the gracious sky overhead. She was appalled by the number of soldiers and officials pressing about them, and never before had she met such rude, insolent stares from hangers-on. She had an awful feeling that she could not move a step without someone intrusively prying. She was full of misgivings. Vienna, outwardly at peace, was not as peaceful as it was supposed to be.

Jason heard itinerant musicians playing nearby and he leaned out of the coach to listen carefully, but they performed so poorly, a waltz of the most obvious kind, he shuddered with distaste. Depressed, he remembered that except for Linder and Hans, not once had Mozart's name been mentioned, nor had he heard one note of any of his compositions.

Deborah nudged him and said, "A customs official is examining the passengers in the public coach ahead of us. We are probably next."

"What is he saying? That is a long document he is reading."

"He is enumerating a list of books forbidden in Vienna."

"But the Hapsburgs are not at war now. No one is in Europe. It is one of the main reasons I assumed it was safe to travel."

"He says Molière, Voltaire, Beaumarchais are not to be read here."

"Beaumarchais?" Jason had been reading *Figaro* in its original play version to comprehend what da Ponte and Mozart had altered and omitted. "He was not censored in France or England."

"This is Vienna. Apparently anything French that criticizes the nobility is feared by the authorities."

But then, unexpectedly and conspicuously, the hitherto severe looking customs official roared with laughter. He was staring at a pamphlet he had found on a wrinkled old priest and he was about to read it aloud.

Jason asked, "What is it?"

"Listen. His German is clear and he is speaking quite slowly."

And everybody within hearing was listening. For it was very embarrassing. While the wizened priest cringed against the coach as inconspicuously as possible, the other passengers were enjoying this.

The customs official read the title with gloating: *"The Remarkable History of a Violated Nun, or Twenty Years in a Viennese Brothel."*

The priest whispered, "I think, sir, that you have made an error."

"This isn't yours? I found it on your person."

"It was given me."

"By whom?"

The priest didn't answer.

Another passenger volunteered, "I saw him buy it. From an inn-keeper in Linz. I was curious why he was so interested in it."

"Did you see how much he paid?"

"Yes." The passenger sounded like a professional spy. "Five gulden."

The customs official turned to the priest. "You were cheated. You can buy this pamphlet in Vienna for three gulden."

Crestfallen and embarrassed, the priest declared, "I felt it was my duty to know what people are reading." The customs official gave him back the pamphlet and said, "Your amusements are modest. Would you like to buy a more useful pamphlet? Viennese brothels. Only two gulden."

The priest declined too fast, Deborah decided, to be credible, but a minute later she saw a passenger give the customs official two gulden for his pamphlet. But when he saw Deborah smile, he was stern. He waved for the public coach to go through, and as he noticed the coat of arms on their vehicle, he called a police officer over to examine them.

The police officer, who had been distracted from what could have been a profitable situation, irritably wanted to know why he was needed.

The customs man said, "This coach? Do you think it was stolen?"

Deborah said angrily. "How dare you insinuate . . . !"

"As I thought," interrupted the customs man. "Your accent is English."

"American," she said.

"Worse. What would Americans be doing with a coach of the nobility?"

"We bought it."

He turned to the police officer. "Herr Jacknel, you see what I mean."

Jacknel was undersized, excessively ugly, his face heavily pitted with smallpox marks, and several of his front teeth were missing.

Deborah cried. "We do have a bill of sale!"

Jason couldn't find it. He didn't recall where he had put it, not considering it as important as Deborah. She found herself raising her voice as soldiers were ordered over, possibly to arrest them. The police officer took their passports, but he didn't even glance at them. Then she recalled that Jason had a habit of hiding valuable papers in books for safety. She burrowed frantically into a bundle of books he had been carrying from London and Paris, although he tried to halt her. They contained books by Molière and Beaumarchais, but her attitude was, the officials can think what they want about us, a bill of sale is a bill of sale. When she found it between the first and second acts of *Figaro*, where Jason had paused in his reading, she waved it triumphantly.

However, the customs man, noticing the title of the book, gave her the feeling she was depraved as he stated, "I must examine all your luggage."

The soldiers stood motionless while the police officer indicated that he would start his part of the examination after Herr Schwine finished.

By now Schwine, thinking this affair could be of value to him—he had found Shakespeare's *Julius Caesar*, which also dealt with assassination, and he had confiscated that, too—called over his superior, Herr Puttlin.

The senior customs official was the fattest man Jason had ever seen. He was so heavy he had to pause for breath with each step, yet he decided to investigate the interior of the coach himself, a mountain of flesh with a sly expression that implied he believed nothing he was told. But his vast stomach caught in the doorway of the coach and he could not enter.

E

A titanic struggle followed to extricate him from the doorway. And his curses, thought Jason, were not calculated to soothe. Finally, although the coach tilted dangerously and it looked as if the new wheel would collapse, Puttlin was freed and Schwine entered the coach as Jason apologized for any annoyance he might have caused.

This was ignored as other prohibited books were discovered. Schwine gleefully held up copies of Rousseau and Molière, and they were seized, too.

Jason had a dreadful sense of despair. Why hadn't Otto Muller forewarned him of this? Then he realized that his friend hadn't known—Muller had left Vienna many years ago—and yet, somehow, he couldn't forgive the man who had put him on the trail. He asked that the books be returned to him, and he was told that this was impossible.

Puttlin declared, "These French revolutionary works are forbidden."

"Molière? Shakespeare? Revolutionary? How?" Jason was puzzled.

"They are objectionable," said Puttlin.

"In what way?"

"In . . ." Puttlin stopped suddenly. "No explanation is necessary. As it is, I have been too polite. With the books we have found in your possession already, we could forbid you to enter Vienna."

"But *Figaro* is played in Vienna, isn't it?"

"A mediocre opera. I prefer Strauss, as everybody else does."

It was as if Vienna was crumbling down upon Jason, but he managed to mutter, "Our passports are in order."

Puttlin grinned unctuously, "The police will decide that."

Deborah said, "We have a large sum of money on deposit in Vienna."

"Where?" Jacknel asked abruptly.

"With a banker, Anton Grob. And we have friends in the city."

"Who?"

She started to say Ernst Muller, but Jason halted her. He had a feeling that if he mentioned Otto's brother, the latter could be harmed.

Jacknel snapped, "I repeat, who are your friends in Vienna."

"What gives you the authority to ask such questions?" Jason retorted.

Jacknel said, "I will get the internal security officer."

Huber wore the insignia of the Hapsburgs on his sleeves and lapel, to show that he was in the personal service of the Crown, with power over both the police and the military. Otherwise, he was in civilian clothes, a middle-aged official inquisitor, answerable only to Prince Metternich, the Imperial Chancellor and Foreign Secretary. His sharp chin, lean jaw, thin lips, and pale gray eyes exuded coolness. He spoke English and French as well as German, and he listened to the results of the examination without expression. Then he asked in impeccable English, after glancing casually at their passports, which however, he did not return, "Otis, do you have any books about Bonaparte?"

"No."

"Do not lie," warned Jacknel. "We will find out in any case."

"I said, No. What would I want with books about Napoleon?"

Huber remarked, "Now that Bonaparte is dead, he is a martyr and a hero. Young people are easily inflamed. And you are reading Beaumarchais, a favorite of Bonaparte's. You read one act."

"How can you tell I read one act?"

"Look how the book folds."

"I am an American. I am not interested in Napoleon."

"You are reading *La Folie Journée ou Le Mariage de Figaro,* a play that is prohibited in the Hapsburg dominions."

"But the opera is allowed."

"Some of us have thought that a mistake. But the play never has been allowed. Even in the time of Joseph it was forbidden."

Jason was indignant. "Sir, the music is beautiful."

"That is a matter of opinion. But not Figaro himself. The character is a provocation. Perhaps clever, subtle, even amusing, but underneath, sly and malicious, always outwitting his superiors."

"Yet the opera is played often in Vienna, isn't it, sir?"

"Prince Metternich says the masses need some appeasement. But I am not as sure as some that Mozart was as innocent as he seemed."

And if Jesus Christ came to Vienna today, Jason thought bitterly, He would be prohibited as an undesirable visitor.

"Otis, what are you interested in, if not politics?"

"Music. I have come to Vienna to study music."

"All the way from America?" Huber was skeptical.

"You possess the greatest composers in the world. Gluck, Haydn, Salieri, Mozart, Schubert, and Beethoven."

"Beethoven accepts no pupils and Schubert is not a teacher."

"Salieri is!" It was out before Jason realized what he was saying.

"Why are you concerned with Salieri?" Huber's tone sharpened.

Jason was frightened, but he tried to sound innocent. "I heard that he is a famous teacher, the teacher of Beethoven and Schubert."

"He is ill."

"But still alive!" Jason blurted out in his relief.

"How did you know that he is ill?" Everybody else was quiet.

"I . . . well . . . you said so, sir."

"But you knew before I said so, didn't you, Otis?"

"I knew that he was an old man and old men are usually ill. Aren't they, sir?" Jason said with more confidence than he felt.

"And why are you interested in *Figaro*?"

"As I said, I like the music. I thought it was a great favorite here."

"What is the real reason you have come to Vienna?"

Jacknel added venomously, "If you lie, you could be arrested."

Jason was nervous, and his anger at himself for mentioning Salieri only made that worse. Fearful that he would utter the wrong thing again, his mouth began to tremble, and in his anxiety he stuttered. In his desperation he motioned to Deborah to explain.

She said, "My husband's German is so bad."

Huber said, "But we are speaking English, Mrs. Otis."

"I know, but he was confused earlier, speaking to the others."

"I can't wait much longer. If your presence here is not explained, I will have to confiscate your passports and you will be imprisoned."

"For Heaven's sake!" Jason cried out, "Tell him about Beethoven!"

"Oh, yes," she said, although she was on the verge of panic, too. "My husband has come to Vienna to see Beethoven. On a mission."

"Political? Beethoven is notorious for his republican sentiments."

"Oh, no! Our Handel and Haydn Society in Boston has asked my husband to offer Beethoven a commission for an oratorio."

Huber acted as if he did not understand, although Jason was sure that he did. However, this time Jason knew where his papers were. He had carried the letter from the Society on his person, next to his money. As he pulled it out of his pocket, with a thick wad of bank notes, even Huber's eyes widened at the large amount of money that Jason was carrying.

After the internal security officer read the letter, he asked, "What services did you render your Society in Boston?"

"I composed music for it."

Deborah volunteered, "It is sung in many churches in America."

Huber stared at Jason's clean-shaven, smooth, fair-complexioned face, and his trim figure, slim and elegant in an expensive blue coat. The American looked like a typical gentleman, reflected Huber, yet so much money and to be carrying it on his person—that was not characteristic of musicians. And then these books? There was much that he didn't understand. But he would, he thought, he always had. He had the patience. Even for the sly bastards.

Deborah said, "Of course, you like Beethoven."

"Like?" Huber's voice was tinged with sarcasm. "He is allowed, but not necessarily approved of. In many ways he is politically unreliable. But he has powerful friends at court. The Archduke Rudolf, the Emperor's brother, is his patron. That doesn't stop us from keeping a close watch on his activities." He turned to the other officials who had stood at attention all during his questioning. "Has everything been examined?"

"Everything, sir," they said in unison.

"And nothing else was found?"

"Nothing else, sir," said Jacknel.

"Go over it again!" ordered Huber. "More carefully!"

Jason and Deborah stood in silent humiliation. Hans, who had not uttered a word and who had been ignored, longed to flee, but that would be even more incriminating. So he held the horses, to make it easier for everyone. Their luggage was ransacked again, even their night bags which contained their personal things. Nothing else was found, but Huber didn't apologize or return their passports.

He said coldly, "Other things will have to be verified."

Jason asked, "Can't we enter Vienna?"

"Where did you plan to stay?"

"At an inn in the center of the city."

"If I were you, I would stay at the White Ox Inn on the Platz Am Hof."

"Why?"

"It is said that Mozart did."

Oh, why did Jason have to look like that, Deborah cried to herself.

Huber added, "And the White Ox Inn is close to Police Headquarters."

Jason asked, "We are not getting our passports back?"

"Not now. Not if you wish to enter Vienna."

"Suppose we go elsewhere. Say, south to Italy, or back to Mannheim?"

"I will return them to you as a present."

Jason hovered between apprehension and desire, feeling that he was facing one of the major decisions of his life. But how could he retreat on the edge of the promised land? He would never forgive himself. He asked, "What happens if we go to the inn you recommend?"

"I will give you a temporary visa which will explain your presence in Vienna until tomorrow. Then you will report to Police Headquarters, which is on the Graben—the innkeeper will know where it is—and if you answer all of their questions satisfactorily, your passports will be returned to you, after you register with the police for as long as you are in Vienna. Nobody is free and innocent of ideas, or unbiased, even if they come on a purely musical pilgrimage."

As Huber held out the address of the White Ox Inn and the temporary visas and Jason hesitated, Deborah's longing to be back in Boston was intense. She hated these officials, Huber more than any of the others, for he sounded more dangerous. She felt close to the breaking point, but she knew that if she didn't support Jason now, she would lose him. She took his hand to indicate that whatever he decided, she would do also, whatever the consequences, and waited.

"Thanks," said Jason, "for the address of the inn." He took that and the temporary visas and started to enter the coach, when Huber halted him.

"What about your postilion? Is he in your permanent employ? His papers state that he is a native of Mannheim."

Deborah said, "We hired him just to drive us to Vienna."

"You will be responsible for him if you employ him."

Jason said, "We will decide tomorrow."

"You must. Police Headquarters will want an answer." Huber motioned to the soldiers and to the three officials to return to their posts, then asked, his tone almost friendly, "How much did you pay for this coach?"

"Two hundred gulden."

"You were overcharged. Cheated. Oh, these French diligences are not draughty and they are well sprung, but you shouldn't have paid more than a hundred gulden. After all, this is not a new vehicle."

"It is French?" Jason was upset. "I bought it in Mannheim. The man I purchased it from said it belonged to a German baron. Didn't he, Hans?"

"Yes, sir. He did," said Hans. He wondered if he was getting into terrible hot water, remaining with these Americans.

Huber said, "You will be lucky if you get seventy gulden for it in Vienna. But I would keep it. Renting a carriage in Vienna can be difficult." And after all, he thought, this coach, with its coat of arms, was easy to identify and trace.

"Thank you," said Jason. "May we go, sir?"

"Yes." Then, as Hans picked up the reins, Huber said, "At the White Ox Inn you will not be far from your mission, Beethoven. Of course, we know where he lives. We know where everybody lives." And just as Jason sighed with relief that, at least now, they were free of the internal security officer, Huber added, "I expect to see you at Police Headquarters tomorrow. Promptly. In the morning."

Even after they were in Vienna itself, Deborah sobbed intensely, greatly shaken by this awful day. While Jason thought the more they travelled into the unknown, the more unknown it was. He kept thinking also about Huber's remark, "You are not in America now." He almost wished he were as he saw soldiers everywhere in Vienna.

13

A Path, Not An End

THE White Ox Inn on the Platz Am Hof was comfortable and much as it had been in Mozart's time, and the innkeeper proudly said that Mozart had stayed here on his first visit to Vienna as a child of six. And it was located conveniently, as Huber had stated, close to Police Headquarters.

The next morning was clear, pleasant, with an autumn crispness that usually delighted Jason, but he could not free himself from a feeling of oppression. The encounter at the gates was a perversion of what he believed in. And he was too shaken by the censorship to celebrate the fact that he was living where Mozart had lived, as he would have done a few days ago.

It was a short ride down the Bognerstrasse and across the Kohlmarkt and into the Graben and then on to Police Headquarters, past many places that Mozart must have known, and he could not dispel his gloom. Mozart had resided on the Graben and the Kohlmarkt, and Mozart had loved Vienna, and Jason was filled with rage. It was as if he were being deprived of what he desired the most, and just when he was about to savor it. For such a long time he had anticipated his first full day in Vienna. Normally he would have absorbed each detail of the city; today instead, he had to concentrate on preparing himself to say the proper things at Police Headquarters. How he hated those officials!

Deborah sat silently as they rode through historic Vienna. She could not look at a world that was so threatening. She was grateful that he had agreed to avoid the subject of Salieri, but dismayed by the prospects ahead, and she wished he would dismiss Hans.

Last night Hans had said he would sleep in the stable with the horses to save money and to prevent them from being stolen. But instead of impressing her, as she felt he intended, it only irritated her more.

Hans's view of the situation was shifting continually in obedience to the exigencies of the moment. Even as he was still afraid of any involvement with the Vienna police, by reputation the harshest in Europe, he kept recalling all the money that Herr Otis carried. So, in spite of his fears, he sought to please them. He had risen early and he had learned that Mozart had spent much of his life nearby.

As they entered the coach to go to Police Headquarters, he rattled off, "Directly across from the White Ox Inn, on the Platz Am Hof, is the palace of Count Collalto where Mozart played in Vienna for the first time as a child of six. And next door to the palace is the Jesuit church where he also played. And I have been told that he lived just around the corner, on the Judenplatz, Kohlmarkt, and the Graben, and many other places close by, and in this inn too." Hans was proud of his initiative. He expected to be rewarded with at least five gulden, and he was disappointed when Herr Otis, preoccupied with his preparations for Police Headquarters, ignored his efforts, and did not even give him a kreutzer. He wondered if he had taken this hard, risky trip for nothing.

Police Headquarters was a formidable gray stone building. The windows were shuttered, with bars on them, and the massive baroque doors were difficult to open. Jason, without having come to a decision about Hans, left him outside to watch the coach. Inside a guard directed them into a badly lit waiting room without a word of explanation.

They stood stiff and awkward, for there was no place to sit. There were a hundred human bodies crowded tightly together on rows of rough benches, which were more boards than anything else, and the stench was frightful. Most of those waiting were peasants in Vienna to obtain work permits, eating fruit, vegetables, raw potatoes, and dropping their leavings on the floor, and even Deborah could hardly comprehend their German, it was so guttural and provincial.

Finally, Deborah got the ear of a guard and asked him in her best German, "How long will we have to wait?"

"All day. Maybe longer. Some people have been here a week."

"But we have an appointment!"

He smiled derisively.

Appalled, she offered him two gulden. He refused the money, but when Jason held out four gulden and she said, "We have an appointment with Herr Huber," he grabbed the gulden and led them into a private office.

Jason was speechless. This room, as elegant as the waiting room was primitive, said, Look how clever I am. The windows were decorated with lovely red velvet drapes, the chairs were trimmed with gilt, there was a huge white stove in a corner, and Huber sat behind a handsome marble-topped desk. Apparently he expected them, for he did not appear surprised. This morning he was discreetly elegant. He wore no insignia, and his well-cut gray suit and silk cravat were in the height of fashion. However, there was one ominous note. He did not ask them to sit, and he said in English, "How much did you give the guard?"

Deborah answered, "Why should we do that?"

"To see me. Otherwise, you would have waited all day."

Jason said, "But we wouldn't have seen you, in any event, if you hadn't allowed it, would we?"

"You are learning," Huber said with a smile of self-satisfaction. He repeated, "How much did you give the guard?"

"Why do you want to know?"

"Otis, you must not corrupt them."

"I gave him four gulden."

Huber sighed. "Too much. Far too much. You must not be so wasteful, inefficient. Especially with servants. You will spoil them."

"He wouldn't have admitted us otherwise."

"The guard was testing you. Haven't you learned that yet?"

"Sir, my interest is music."

"With all the money you are carrying?" He noticed Deborah staring at a life-sized nude statue. "My Venus, Mrs. Otis. She lightens my day when I have unpleasant things to do. What do you think of her?"

"May we have our passports, Herr Huber?"

"You don't approve of my taste?"

"We haven't travelled from Boston to Vienna to study art."

"So I thought."

There was a sickening silence and Jason hurried to say, "Sir, you assured us yesterday that our passports would be returned to us today."

"I assured you that you must report here and answer some questions."

"More questions?" Deborah was horrified.

"As long as you are within our authority, that will be necessary."

Jason asked, "What do you want to know, sir?" He tried to sound resigned, when in actuality, he was furious.

"Anton Grob says you come well recommended."

"By whom?" Jason asked.

"Your wife's father. Grob tells us that he is an influential banker in Boston. That he has put a thousand gulden in your name with Grob."

"It's my money!" Deborah cried defiantly, but Jason was shocked. Did she believe that she could really buy him, he thought angrily.

Huber asked, "What do you intend to do with this money?"

Deborah said sharply, "That is a private matter."

"You would be well advised to answer."

"But this is not your affair."

"Mrs. Otis, everything that occurs in Vienna is our affair."

"When will we get our passports back?"

"How long do you intend to remain in Vienna?"

She longed to say not one day more, but she replied carefully, "That depends on my husband. And his meetings with Herr Beethoven."

"We have to know precisely. How long, Otis?"

Jason estimated hurriedly, "About three months, sir."

"And where do you plan to stay?"

"Vienna."

E *

"Nowhere else?"

"Salzburg, perhaps."

"Why?"

"They say it is a beautiful city. Lovely to visit."

"And where Mozart was born." Jason started to say that this was a matter of indifference to him, and Huber halted him. "Your interest in Mozart is obvious. Grob merely confirmed what I suspected. Your father-in-law wrote Grob about that. I gather that Mr. Pickering does not share your enthusiasm. I hope it is just Mozart's music that concerns you."

"Sir, I told you I am a composer. And Vienna is said to be the most musical city in the world. Where I can learn much about music."

"Nonetheless, to visit Salzburg you will have to get permission."

Jason asked, quite surprised, "Does everybody have to get it?"

"Everybody we deem necessary." Now Huber spoke with a curiously disembodied air. "All the duties, conditions, and regulations of the State must be obeyed without question." Then he continued like a schoolmaster questioning children that he knew were guilty already, asking the country, city, and date of their birth, their parents' names and places of birth, and their station in America, and finally, "Do you have any relatives or acquaintances in the Empire?"

Jason replied that they knew no one in the Empire, although he wasn't sure Huber believed him, but that he hoped to meet people who knew Beethoven, and possibly Haydn and Mozart, whose music he wanted to study.

Deborah added that Jason was a good pianist as well as a fine composer, although he felt she should have said bank clerk, except that Huber could use this against him.

Just as they assumed that the interrogation was over, Huber asked Jason, "Are you a student?"

Of Mozart, yes, he longed to shout passionately, but he replied, "No, except for Beethoven and his music. Why do you ask, Herr Huber?"

"You do not intend to enroll in a university here?"

"No, no! Why?"

"On your way from Paris did you stop off at Heidelberg?"

"Yes. It is on the route to Vienna."

"Did you have any associations with the students there?"

"Of course not!" Deborah blurted out. "Why are you asking?"

Huber said grimly, "The university students are our most trouble-some agitators. Especially in the German states, and in Heidelberg. We keep them under constant surveillance. I suggest you stay away from them here."

"We will!" she hurried to say. "Thanks for warning us, Herr Huber."

Then, as they assumed that their passports would be returned, Huber handed back their temporary visas, across which he had written,

"Approved until January 1, 1825." He said, "These will be good for three months. If you wish to stay longer, you will have to apply to me for renewal."

Deborah cried out, "But you said yesterday . . ."

"I said that your passports will be returned if you answer all the questions satisfactorily. You haven't."

"Doesn't the amount of money we have show that we are responsible?"

"It helps. But you also possessed a number of prohibited books."

Jason said, "I didn't know that they were prohibited."

"That is no excuse. Assuming that is true. You could be jailed for being in possession of the books that were taken from you."

Deborah asked, "For how long?"

"It depends on what is necessary for the safety of the State."

"Without a hearing? A trial?"

"Mrs. Otis, they are the corruptions of democracy. We will survive very well without them. You will have to register with the police as long as you are in Vienna. Twenty gulden, please."

"What for?" Jason felt a chill going up and down his back at the conditions Huber was setting.

"For each temporary visa. What do you intend to do about your driver?"

Jason hesitated, then asked, "What do we have to do if we keep him?"

"Pay for his visa. Guarantee his employment."

Deborah was shaking her head No, but if anything, that encouraged Jason to reject her advice. And Mozart had had a servant, he had read, even when impoverished. He said, "How much, Herr Huber?"

"Five gulden."

Jason paid it without another word even as he felt that Deborah could have shaken him in her anger. But where else, he reflected, could he find a servant who was so interested in Mozart!

Huber asked, "Have you met the ghost of Mozart yet at the inn?"

Jason answered, "I do not believe in ghosts."

"When you move, you will have to notify us of your new address."

"When will we get our passports back?"

"When we allow you to leave Vienna."

Wishing he could shatter Huber with a blow, Jason asked, "Is there anything else?"

"In Vienna I am public safety and tranquility. I am law and order."

Hans said he was privileged that Herr Otis had retained him in his employ, even as he wondered whether he had been wise to encourage this. He sensed that Frau Otis still disapproved of him. To show his gratitude, he offered his services as a messenger boy. So after they returned to the inn, Jason sent Hans to Anton Grob, suggesting an appointment. To their relief there was a prompt reply from the banker inviting them to his house on the Kohlmarkt the following evening.

However, Deborah was not finished with Hans. She reminded Jason that Hans had stated that he had relatives in Vienna. Didn't he intend to see them? And when Jason hesitated to ask Hans, she did. Hans replied, "Oh, I haven't forgotten them, Frau Otis. But I wanted to wait until I had helped you get settled before I visited them." And she had to be content with this, although she didn't trust his explanation, for Jason did.

Jason had not told Huber the truth. He felt that Mozart's ghost was all about him. And when Hans reminded him that the Collalto Palace, where Mozart had played first as a child of six, was just across the Platz Am Hof from the inn, he felt that this in itself justified Hans's presence, and he grew excited again. As Hans pointed out, it was very close; they could see the Collalto Palace from the inn. Jason had been too preoccupied before to absorb Hans's information, but now he had to examine it despite Deborah's reluctance to investigate what Huber had implied was forbidden. Yet she could not allow him to go alone.

Jason stood in front of the Collalto Palace, with Deborah beside him, and stared yearningly at the large five-story building and its many ceiling-high windows. He wished he could have been present when the boy Mozart had performed here. What an extraordinary occasion it must have been! Especially in view of what had followed. Had anyone foreseen that, he wondered, or appreciated Mozart then?

Suddenly he had an impulse to knock on the door and to inquire. Deborah said that was reckless, foolish, but Mozart was too much in Jason's heart for him to be careful. A liveried footman answered his knock.

Jason asked in German, "Could I see the chief steward? I have come from America and London and Paris to inquire about Mozart."

The footman understood him, which gave him satisfaction. Evidently his German was improving. And the footman didn't seem startled by his request, as Deborah expected, but nodded, as if this had happened before, and called the chief steward.

A very old man, tall and spare, with a long, gaunt face appeared a minute later, looking neither annoyed nor surprised. He introduced himself as Christoph Fuchs, chief steward to His Excellency, Count Collalto, and his German was easy to understand. His lean, dark features, which seemed bored, lit up when Jason asked, "Is it true that Mozart played here as a child?"

"Indeed." The chief steward regarded the eager young man with a humorous indulgence, but appeared glad to talk about it. "I heard him."

"But that took place over sixty years ago," Deborah said.

"It was an extraordinary day. One I never forgot. I was twenty then.

My father was chief steward at the time. It was like nothing I had ever experienced. He was such a brave, brave child."

Jason asked, "Did the nobles who attended appreciate him?"

"There was conversation during the entire performance."

"Did you ever see him again?"

"Many times. Years later, not long before he died, he resided just around the corner, on the Judenplatz. But then he had lost his connections with the nobility. One day about a year or two before he died, I saw him standing outside the Jesuit church next door, where one of his masses had been sung, and my master, Count Collalto walked by him. As if His Excellency had never known him. I don't think my master liked the way the Count was outwitted by a servant in *Figaro*."

"Did you?"

Christoph Fuchs smiled, but he didn't answer.

Deborah asked, "Did you speak to Mozart in front of the church?"

"After my master was gone."

"And did Mozart respond?"

"Dear lady, we used to eat in the same tavern."

"You really did know him well?"

"It was my duty to arrange all functions that employed musicians and tradespeople."

Jason asked, wondering if *he* sounded like Huber, "Did he ever complain to you about the way the nobility ignored him toward the end of his life?"

"He knew he was at odds with most of the nobility, but when the subject came up, he would look at you with his pale, gentle face and shrug, and go on composing music as if that were all that mattered."

"Do you think that he was aware that he was ailing?"

"Ailing? He composed two operas just a few months before he died."

"Then why do you think he died so young?"

"I have often wondered."

Jason wanted to ask him next about despotism and assassination, but he felt that was too risky to ask. He said instead, "Do you believe it was simply poor health? A kidney ailment, as his doctor implied?"

"I doubt it. Unless the doctor could have been responsible."

Jason felt his blood racing. But he asked, "How?"

"Through negligence, or some other reason."

Deborah said, quite upset, "Do you know what you are saying?"

"I knew the doctor."

There was a sudden silence while Jason and Deborah contemplated what the chief steward was intimating. Fuchs was peering at the Platz Am Hof as if to recapture the past; then he shook his head gloomily and pointed to the soldiers marching across the square. "Did you know that this used to be the Hapsburg jousting ground? And now the horses of the Imperial Cavalry make so much noise on the cobbles it is impossible to sleep. They still think they are fighting Bonaparte."

Jason asked, "Why are they so afraid of Napoleon? He is dead."

"His ideas aren't. Bonaparte was the epitome of the self-made man."

"Yet he became an emperor himself."

"By ability, not birth. But isn't your interest—Mozart?"

"Yes. We were talking about his death."

Christoph Fuchs said abruptly, "You want to know the truth?"

Ah, the great secret, Deborah thought derisively; but Jason felt compelled to go on, whatever the dangers, although he shivered as he asked, "Don't we always want to know the truth? Do you know something about his death?"

"It could have been the doctor."

Deborah said critically, "And you have a witness, of course?"

"Of course. Joseph Diener. He ran the tavern that Mozart frequented just before he died. Diener told me that he was the first one to notice Mozart's sudden turn of bad health and that he called the doctor and was with him to the very end."

"Is Diener alive?" Jason asked eagerly. Fuchs sounded convincing.

"I believe so. I am too feeble to go out much anymore."

"Where does this Joseph Diener live?"

"His tavern was on the . . ." Fuchs bit his lips in exasperation. "On the . . ." He gave a croaky sob, "Someone must remember. The doctor's name was . . ." He leaned against the door to collect his thoughts, and he said sorrowfully, "My memory recalls things that happened sixty years ago so clearly, and very little of what happened yesterday or the day before. But I remember Mozart, and Joseph Diener. His tavern in the 1790s was not on the Graben or the Kohlmarkt, but on another popular street, close to where Mozart was residing at the time. That was one of the reasons Mozart went there often. I sat there with him several times. He liked a glass of wine, when he was able to drink it. How could I forget that? He had a strange stomach. Some things he could digest without any difficulty, but others . . ." he shook his head in wonder. . . . "upset him very much. Those stupid doctors. Diener said . . . I wish I wasn't so tired."

"Did you know Salieri?" Jason asked, despite his promise to Deborah that he wouldn't ask about him.

"The Imperial Kapellmeister? Yes. Why can't I remember where Diener lived?"

"If I returned when you were less tired, say tomorrow."

"No. If I can't remember now, I won't tomorrow." Then his face lit up in a last flickering glow. "But if you could find the house that Mozart was residing in when he died. It was near Diener's tavern."

"How do you know?"

"Diener told me that he had to help Mozart home the last time Mozart ever went out of his house. And that it was a terribly painful journey, although it was a very short one. I never forgot Diener's story. He said that Mozart had collapsed in his tavern, and several weeks later our friend was gone." The chief steward's eyes filled with tears and he said, "Excuse me. I am not myself today. I have been told that I have to retire, and I have spent my whole life here. I wish I could remember some of Mozart's tunes. It is so strange." He shook his head in bewilderment. "You can be so close to something all your life, and then, all at once, you are all alone. All alone. And so tired."

The chief steward pulled on the bell cord by the door and before Jason could utter another word, the footman who had opened the door appeared and took Fuchs by the arm and led him back inside. And all that was left of the grand house was a musty smell and silence.

In the brilliant, sunny life of the Platz Am Hof, Jason recovered his equilibrium somewhat and said to himself, Somewhere in this city there must be someone who knows where I can find Joseph Diener and the doctor or doctors who attended Mozart at the end.

Deborah however, sensing what he was thinking, said caustically, "How can you trust Fuchs? A complete stranger. A senile old man."

"How can I trust anyone?"

She was shocked by the depth of his bitterness.

Later, when they went to bed, she came to him with a sudden emotion, standing above him nakedly, seeking to suggest the passion of a few days ago; and to her horror he turned his back on her. For a savage instant she wanted to kick him in the groin, a wild impulse that even as it made her feel abandoned also gave her a sickening sense of how little she truly knew herself. But she moved away from him instead, and said with a studied naturalness, "What's wrong? Don't you feel well?"

"Oh, leave me alone. Can't you see that I want to sleep?"

But he didn't sleep, and she knew it. Long after she had put on her nightgown and turned her face to the wall with an abrupt movement, to put a great distance between them, feeling hopelessly entangled in a lunatic asylum, she could hear him stirring restlessly. Had it been the danger? she wondered. The strain? The disappointments? Or was Vienna robbing him even of sensuality and nothing could compensate him for the loss? The thought that his growing involvement in Mozart could be making him impotent seemed for a moment a fit revenge for all that she had suffered, and she wanted to laugh, only it hurt too much.

Very late that night, when he was still tossing, she moved toward him, and at the sight of his profile, so vulnerable, so helpless, she put her hand to his face. To her surprise, she found that it was wet.

She exclaimed, "You're crying! You're quite unhappy, aren't you?"

"I don't know which way to turn. What have I gotten into?"

"You don't trust me?"

"Everything is so different from what I expected. But I can't turn back, Deborah, I can't."

"I don't expect you to," she answered. She thought no marriage could survive without a few lies, especially when your husband had to be a young lion and desired to understand everything, especially what was forbidden. She moved closer to him, so he could feel the warmth of her body and know that she was there.

14

Anton Grob

THE following evening Anton Grob greeted Jason and Deborah as if he had known them all of his life. He was a small, plump, round-shouldered man with snow-white hair and rosy cheeks and the smile of an elderly cherub. He took them by the hand as his liveried footman ushered them into his luxurious drawing room, and he almost embraced them with his warmth.

He said, "I've arranged a musical evening for you. I thought it would be appropriate for your introduction to Vienna. I am an amateur musician, and I felt that you might like to hear quartets by Mozart and Beethoven. After you've discussed your business, three of my friends, who are also amateur musicians, are joining us to play with me."

"Delighted," Jason replied. He didn't feel talkative, but he was relieved that the banker's German was easy to understand.

"Frau Otis, your father sounded worried about you. He asked me to inform him how you are."

"Fine, fine," she answered.

"You look very well. Despite the rigors of your journey. But he didn't tell me that he had such a beautiful daughter."

"You are very kind." Deborah was determined not to allow any flattery to influence her, but she was pleased by his admiration.

"Not at all. If you were my daughter, I would find it difficult to let you out of my sight. May I show you about my residence?"

Jason didn't respond, preoccupied with the problem of what could he *discuss* with the banker, but Deborah nodded.

Grob was the *bon vivant*, showing them about his drawing room. It was one of the largest and most lavish Deborah had seen, and she said so.

"And exactly square," he said proudly. "Forty by forty feet."

She said, "Your wine-red upholstered chairs are so palatial."

"You are perceptive. It is a royal red. A Hapsburg red."

As Grob led them around the drawing room as if it were a grand tour, she found it quite pleasing. She liked the walls with their white panels and gilt, the two magnificent mirrors on opposite sides of the drawing room, the handsome high windows looking out on a garden, the brilliant chandelier in the center of the ceiling. Grob must be rich, she thought. If she lived in Vienna this was the way she would like to do so.

Jason hadn't said a word; she wondered if he was still distraught.

Noticing her admiration, Grob said, "The chandelier is a replica of one in the Hofburg." But he was proudest that he was an art collector, possessor of many precious objects of art, which he showed them lovingly: a bust by Bernini, two seventeenth-century oak tables that had belonged to a Pope, a set of gold candlesticks attributed to Cellini, and a clock reputed to have been a childhood toy of Marie Antoinette.

He also admitted modestly that his mansion was cleverly located, on the Kohlmarkt just off the Michaelplatz, the heart of Vienna, and within walking distance of the Hofburg and St. Stephen's Cathedral. As he announced this, he glanced at Jason for approval.

Jason couldn't forget how miserable he had been last night. He felt he had tossed for centuries. It was as if he had been interrogating the darkness, as Huber had interrogated him, in an effort to find answers to the questions the chief steward had asked. The more he thought about Fuchs's comments, the more he felt he had to investigate the doctor or doctors who had attended Mozart in his last, fatal illness, and Diener's part in the affair. There was so much that he longed to ask Grob, but he told himself that he must wait for a favorable opportunity, if he asked the banker anything. Yet he had a feeling also that not a moment must be lost.

Grob seemed to sense his disquiet, for he said, "Perhaps this will please you, Herr Otis?" He took them into his music room and showed them his pianoforte, which was the latest model. And when Deborah expressed surprise that a banker should be so interested in music, he shrugged and replied, "That is not unusual. Every cultivated person in Vienna possesses a pianoforte. Would you like to try it, Herr Otis?"

"Not now." Jason's fingers were stiff; he wasn't in the mood.

"Perhaps this might change your mind." Grob hurried to a wall safe, and a minute later, holding it with an unusual affection and solicitude, he handed Jason an autograph of a Mozart sonata for the pianoforte. "It is the original," he assured Jason. "Look at it."

In his joy Jason felt that he could defy anybody. The notes began to sound in his head.

Grob suggested, "Play it."

Jason placed the score gently on the pianoforte and began tentatively. There was a sadness in the music he didn't expect. He was horribly out of practice, and his hands were dreadfully stiff, as he had suspected, but as he went on, he noticed that the music was in the form of a fantasia, and it was as if he were having a long, intimate conversation with Mozart.

Afterward Grob and Deborah applauded but Jason didn't tell them how the music had transformed him, for he had played clumsily, and they should not have lied to him. This sonata was an exquisite and splendid piece, with an astonishing vitality despite a curiously lingering melancholy, and he had performed it, for all his affection, like an amateur. But the music had loosened his tongue, and he asked Deborah, "How did you manage to choose a banker as musical as Herr Grob?"

"I asked my father to place our funds with someone who was interested in music. I said it was important. I told him that, Vienna being so musical, that should not be difficult. As it would be in Boston."

"And your father complied?" Jason was sceptical.

"Why not. He knew I would never forgive him if he didn't."

In this moment she looked very much like her father and Jason thought, Deborah has been shrewd to persuade Pickering to select Grob as our banker in Vienna. Pickering must care for his daughter after all, in spite of his icy demeanor. Perhaps she would be useful in more ways than he had expected when he had married her.

Grob said, "I'm happy that you are pleased with your wife's choice."

Jason said, "You seem to know a great deal about music."

"A great deal? I play. But so do many in Vienna. That is not unusual here. But to be musical—everybody that matters is."

"Were you alive in Mozart's time?"

"Indeed. I'm sixty. I was born in 1764. I'm virtually a contemporary of his. I was only eight years younger than he was."

"Did you know him?"

"Not personally. But I heard him play. And one of my friends, who will be here soon, studied with him. Herr Pickering mentioned your interest in Mozart. He said, begging your pardon, that you were infatuated with him."

"My father-in-law exaggerates. I admire Mozart. Don't you?"

"It would be regarded as an act of gross negligence in Vienna not to play Mozart."

"Do you know Beethoven?"

"I've had dealings with him, but I'm not a friend. However, I should be able to get you an introduction to him. Herr Pickering wrote, too, that you are to offer Herr Beethoven a commission to write an oratorio for Boston. I will be happy to do whatever I can on your behalf."

Pleased by Grob's considerateness, Jason asked, "Do you know Salieri?"

"We've met."

"Could you introduce me to him?"

"I fear not."

"Why not?"

"He is not well. He is not seeing anyone but intimate friends."

"I heard that actually he has gone insane."

"Insane?" Grob repeated that as if it were a great surprise. "He is not well, as I said, but out of his mind, that is not so. He has retired as Imperial Kapellmeister, but that is hardly a reason for such rumors. He has been Court composer for fifty years, longer than any other musician in history, and he has retired on full salary. I hardly think our Emperor would do this for a man bereft of his reason. But there is always gossip."

"Don't you believe any of it?"

"I believe that it is a mistake for a man with your gifts to waste his time on such idle and foolish speculations. I fervently hope that is not the reason you have come to Vienna."

Jason asked with apparent innocence, "What reason, Herr Grob?"

"To see Antonio Salieri."

"Why?"

"He is an object of reverence to the Royal family. They do not like such objects to be disturbed."

Deborah interrupted, "My husband has come to Vienna to see Beethoven."

"Is that the only reason?" Grob was polite, but skeptical.

"And to further his musical education."

"Then why does he wish to see Salieri?"

Jason hurried to comment, "I didn't say that."

"You asked to meet him. But never mind. I'm not a police official. I don't intend to embarrass you. It is a lovely day, isn't it?"

"I don't see why speaking to an ill musician should be dangerous."

"Did you say that to Herr Huber?"

"No."

"That was wise. He came to me the other day about you, the day you arrived. I knew that it was important when he came himself, and so quickly."

"Do you know him?"

"Only by reputation. He is close to the Commissioner of Police, Count Sedlnitzky, the most powerful man in Vienna next to Prince Metternich, yet Huber is authorized by the Prince to act independently if he desires. Huber is concerned with political matters. But I wouldn't worry. I assured him that you had come to Vienna with fine credentials. I pointed out that you had come to see Beethoven, that your interest in Mozart was just musical. And while he didn't admit it, I think he was impressed that you had a thousand gulden on deposit with me."

"It was my wife's decision to deposit that much money with you. I carry mine on my person."

Grob was shocked. "It could be stolen. You must deposit it in a bank."

"I will consider it."

"Sir, I will be devoted to your affairs. You can depend on it."

"Thank you." Jason's eyes sought Grob's. The banker's clear brown eyes met his directly, but he wasn't certain that he could equate this with trust. Suddenly he asked, "Could you get our passports returned?"

"I will try."

"I was amazed by the attitude of the police. Either our passports are good or they are bad. To be regarded as neither is absurd."

Grob murmured apologetically, "It must have been the books they found."

"Shakespeare?"

"We revere him, but at this moment some of the things in his plays are considered unfortunate. I'm sorry that you had such a distressing introduction to Vienna, but since Bonaparte, it is deemed necessary."

Deborah said, "I was so upset, I thought my legs would give way."

Grob replied, "Now I'm truly embarrassed. You must think that we are a most inhospitable people. You, of course, are accustomed to an equality of people in Boston. But our ways are somewhat different. War between Austria and France dragged on for many years. And everywhere there are disaffected Bonaparte veterans and inflammatory students. Our police have been given the task of combating the results of the French Revolution. Ever since Bonaparte appeared, our security forces have had to be enlarged. But this shouldn't affect you. Once the police know you are here just for musical reasons, there will be no further difficulties."

Yet while the banker's tone was soft, Jason felt that Grob was going to considerable effort to warn him. For as the other guests arrived, Grob added, "Don't try to see Salieri. And don't tell anyone that you even contemplated that. Everyone reveres Mozart now that he is dead, and I would leave it that way. Not everyone is as clever as you are."

Then there were no questions but just four men, all elderly, playing a quartet by Mozart and one by Beethoven that they had played for years. The music was performed better than Jason expected; the performers gave it a devotion that was heartwarming. The Mozart was moving, and the Beethoven surprised Jason with its intensity. The drawing room was an appropriate setting for the music; he could imagine Mozart coming through the door smiling with pleasure.

We live, reflected Jason, a life based upon selected dreams. Our view of the truth is dominated by what we need to believe. Mozart fits what I need. The purity and the perfection of his music are what I crave, even as I know that they will never be achieved in actual living. But I must indulge myself. For existence without his music, now that I have known it, would be intolerable.

Deborah thought that Mozart had gone deeper in the quartet than any of his music she had heard. Or was it, she speculated in a change of mood that was happening much more often now, that she was learning to penetrate her own skin? Deborah, who was proud of her ability to make up her own mind, was troubled by this. She was certain that they were engaged in a venture where they must exert every effort to be matter-of-fact, and circumstances continued to make that impossible. The strains of Mozart's music suggested many things to her, not all of them comfortable.

When Jason and Deborah applauded warmly and spontaneously at the end of the concert, lean, tall Fritz Offner, a music publisher whose age and parched skin caused him to resemble a living fossil, bowed slightly and smiled laconically and said nothing.

Ignaz Klaus, a wealthy grain merchant, set his purposeful jaw and declared, "When you play Mozart, very little else matters."

Diminutive Albert Lutz said, "Although I am a doctor, I have grown up with Mozart, and it is always an honor to play his music. I will always treasure that I studied with him."

Grob beamed with gratification and added, "After you hear Mozart's music, your mind and heart are so clean." He bowed his head in a gesture of reverence, and his friends followed his example.

They were all speaking very slowly and distinctly so that Jason could understand them, and he was bursting with questions. He asked Doctor Lutz, "Do you know the doctor who attended Mozart during his last illness?"

"No. I was just a medical student then."

"Did you have any idea that he was dying?"

"I did not examine him."

"Do you think he thought he was dying?"

"Very few of us do. We always think it will happen to someone else."

Jason asked, "Do any of you know where Mozart was living when he died?"

"What is the difference," said Grob. "At the time Mozart died, no one had to seek death out, it was never far away from an eighteenth-century household. I do not believe that he died from wickedness, as some say, but from naîveté, believing that his music might support him properly."

Doctor Lutz asked, "Herr Otis, are you writing a book about him?"

"It is possible."

Offner declared, "Such interest is no crime. When Mozart died, his autographs increased phenomenally in value. I could not be disinterested. They helped make my music publishing house's fortune."

Lutz said, "They helped make several fortunes. But not Mozart's. I never forgot my last visit to him. His situation was frightening."

"Do you think he died a natural death?" Jason asked impulsively.

"As I said, I didn't attend him. I was just a medical student then."

The four elderly men sat silently like effigies entombed in the past. The quiet was a conversation in itself, thought Deborah, a bond that united them. Yet Jason was not content, he would never be content, she told herself unhappily, until he proved that Mozart had been assassinated. Everything in him led in that direction. But what if he was wrong? It might be more than he could bear. And even if he found out what he wanted to know, would he be believed? As the questions piled up in her, she glanced over to Grob, who nodded slightly to indicate, Do not worry, I will direct the questions into suitable and sensible channels.

Jason asked, "Doctor, you said you never forgot your last visit. Why?"

"He was so ill. So poor."

"And you were worried about what was happening to him?"

Lutz hesitated, then to Jason's surprise, he noticed Grob motioning to the elderly doctor to continue. Why had Grob changed his mind? As Lutz resumed, Jason had the feeling that Grob was watching him as well as warning him. For an instant he even had the notion that the banker was using the doctor to set a trap for him. That Grob wanted to know how deeply he was involved in Mozart, and in what direction. Then he dismissed that notion. Ever since the encounter at the gates he had been suspicious of everyone, even Deborah. He must rid himself of these fears, or the cure would be worse than the disease. Doctor Lutz's reminiscence was pervasive, and Jason listened intently.

"It was a November evening in 1791. I remember the month because, as I stood in front of the house which Mozart lived in, I was very cold. Bitter winter weather had come with a startling and unpleasant suddenness, and I hoped that he had a good, warm fire in his rooms.

"I was upset as it was, for I had not studied the music he had given me a month ago to practise, I had missed my last few weekly lessons, and now I faced the disagreeable task of telling Mozart that I had to give up my music lessons entirely. I did not think that it would be a great loss to music, but I had a feeling that he needed my gulden very much.

"To my surprise however, Mozart didn't answer the door. Instead, someone else did, a man I had seen at a tavern that Mozart frequented. This man ran the tavern, and he asked me what I wanted.

"I said, 'I'm a student of Herr Mozart's, I'm . . .' but before I could finish, he interrupted me, saying, 'The Kapellmeister is not well, you had better return in a few days . . .' and I heard Mozart shouting from above, 'Let him in! I have little enough company as it is.'

"I asked, 'What is wrong?'

" 'He's been ill the last few days. His stomach. He cannot digest anything but soup and wine. And even then, he says, he has constant pain. I bring his meals to him, and try to keep him comfortable.'

" 'Where is his wife?'

" 'In Baden, for the baths,' the tavernkeeper replied. 'Mozart says that she must not be upset. That if she heard that he wasn't well, she would worry, and she mustn't, that her health is uncertain as it is.'

" 'But what about his own illness? Has a doctor seen him?'

" 'When he first fell ill. After eating dinner at somebody's house, he told me. He fainted the day after that dinner, but the doctor said it was from eyestrain and overwork. But the pain hasn't stopped, so now he doesn't trust the doctor. Aren't you the medical student who is studying with Herr Kapellmeister?'

"I nodded, afraid of what I might be getting into.

" 'Perhaps you can look at him. Diagnose what is wrong. I don't think his doctor knows.'

" 'But if his doctor doesn't know, how could I?' I said. 'I'm just starting my last year of school at the university and . . .'

"Mozart interrupted us, crying out from upstairs, 'What are you whispering about down there? What are you keeping from me?'

" 'Nothing, Herr Kapellmeister,' the tavernkeeper said.

" 'Then bring Herr Lutz up. And he can take his lesson.'

"But as we walked up the dark stairway to the first floor, the tavernkeeper whispered very softly to me, 'He is sitting up, trying to compose, to prove that he is not ill, but don't make him work. He is too weak. The effort could cause him to collapse again.'

"I nodded, and the tavernkeeper led me into Mozart's rooms. I was shocked by the change that had occurred since I had been there a month before. The silver service of which he was so proud was gone, and so were a pair of lovely candlesticks that I knew he treasured, and his music room was empty except for a pianoforte and viola.

"Yet he sat at a rolltop writing desk with a score in front of him, and while his clothes were shabbier than I had ever seen them and his shoe buckles were tarnished and even his fine, fair hair, of which he was proud and a little vain, was not carefully coiffured as it usually was, he was fully dressed, as if to show that he was well enough to work.

"But when he rose to greet me and to take my hand, he had to hold onto his desk to keep from falling. His face was so pale and emaciated it was shocking. And the music room was very cold, for there was only a little wood in the stove and it looked as if it were about to go out.

"Yet his handclasp was warm, although I noticed that his hands, which were inclined to be fleshy, even plump, seemed swollen despite his obvious loss of weight.

"He murmured, 'It is good to see you, Albert. I was beginning to think that I was never going to see you again. You've missed three lessons.'

"I answered, 'It is my last year of medical school, sir, and it is very important to me. I need more time to devote to my medical studies.'

" 'Of course! So some day you may be able to cure even me.'

"I bowed and said, 'It would be an honor.'

"He laughed, but he did not answer.

"I did want to help him, but how? I sensed that the two gulden I paid him for each lesson had become vital to him, yet it was clearly infinitesimal compared to what he really needed.

"Perhaps he sensed my disquiet, for he said, 'I have been working on a Requiem. Sometimes I think it is for myself, but they tell me that is foolishness, a hallucination. But I must not become bedridden.'

"He looked so gray with fatigue that I cried out, 'You must rest, sir!'

" 'Soon I will have plenty of time to rest, Albert.'

"The tavernkeeper interrupted, 'You are being too harsh on yourself.'

"But Mozart asked me pleadingly, 'You do want to study with me, don't you, Albert! I hate teaching, but to be without pupils!' He shuddered.

"So I, who had come to tell him that I could not continue with him, nodded yes.

"His face lit up with a smile and he said, 'At least I will have one pupil. I have no concerts, hardly any commissions . . .'

"The tavernkeeper reminded him, *The Magic Flute* is a great success.'

" 'And I can't see it!' There were tears in his eyes now. 'Do you know what it means not to be able to see your own opera? But I am not up to going to the theater. I am not strong enough, I am told. And you know, they are right.'

" 'You will be soon,' I said.

" 'You will come again,' he said. 'For your next lesson?'

" 'Yes,' I promised, 'Whenever you are ready for it, Herr Kapellmeister.'

"I could tell that Mozart was greatly moved. I wanted to steal away then, but he seized my arm, although his hand was trembling, and he said, 'My Requiem is nearly half finished. Do you have two gulden? I know that it is not customary to be paid in advance, but with the doctor . . . They inform me that there is not an empty seat at *Die Zauberflöte*, and I haven't received one gulden since it opened six weeks ago. Not an empty seat and I have to sit here and beg. . . .' I thought that he would break down and weep, and I hurriedly handed him two gulden, although I could not spare it.

"He said, 'Come next week,' and he dropped the two coins on his desk with an air of disdain and asked me entreatingly, 'You do have a genuine love of music, don't you, Albert?' Before I could reply, he added, 'You would be heartless if you didn't.'

"I thought then he was going to collapse from the exertion and emotion of the past few minutes, and the tavernkeeper motioned for me to go. But Mozart stood up with a tremendous effort of his will and joined me at the door, and said, 'One must always observe the amenities.'

" 'Thank you, sir,' I said.

" 'By the way, do you prefer being a doctor rather than a musician?'

" 'Medicine suits me better, sir,' I said modestly.

" 'If you could only cure me,' he said reflectively, 'I might agree.'

" 'When I graduate and I am in practice, perhaps I can, sir.'

" 'Perhaps?'

"Oddly then, it was I who needed reassurance. I said, 'I do hope, Herr Kapellmeister, that I have helped you feel a little better?'

"Mozart smiled wryly, then said, 'Albert, you are a doctor already. If your medicines do not work, you hope that your consolation will.'

"And then something occurred that I have never been able to forget."

Lutz's face was ashen and his hands trembled and he could not go on.

To Jason's surprise, it was Grob who asked, "What happened?"

"I've never told anyone," Lutz mumbled.

Jason turned to Grob, "You've heard this account before?"

"Several times. I thought that if Lutz told it to you, it might be helpful. Albert, what have you kept from us? Do you know something new about his death?"

"Oh, no, not that!"

But this fear, thought Jason, was ordinary, normal; it was what Lutz felt about his parting with Mozart that truly terrified him. The elderly doctor's eyes gazed into Jason's as if on the edge of some horror, a memory that even now sank into him with a knifelike sharpness.

Jason asked, "Did Mozart tell you what he felt was wrong with him?"

"Nothing like that!" Lutz cried. "Mozart clung to the door jamb to keep from falling and I thought, There is so much blood in him, yet inch by inch he is quite a small man, and then he said, 'It is amazing the number of doctors who commit murder.'"

Lutz continued, as if, once he had gone this far, he had to express all that he had hidden these many years. "Mozart had closed the door himself, but ever since, I have wondered whether I should have examined him. I was only a medical student, a last-year medical student, and there was so much I didn't know, but do you think I should have examined him?"

No one answered. All of them looked shocked and stunned.

Lutz rushed on. "Do you think that if I had examined him, I might have helped him? I could have gone back the next day, or the next. Instead, when I did . . ." He shook his head woefully. "It was too late."

Jason asked, "What had happened?"

"He was dead."

"How long after your last visit?"

"I don't remember exactly. Two, three weeks probably. I was quite distraught. Yet he had a well-known doctor. Experienced. Capable."

"Did you know him?"

"As I told you before, no! But I had heard of him. He was supposed to have excellent connections."

"What was his name?"

"I have forgotten. I was under a tremendous strain."

"Do you think that his body should have been examined?"

"Why?"

Grob frowned and Lutz looked so startled that Jason, who longed to ask the doctor if he thought Mozart's condition had shown any evidence of poisoning, decided not to venture such a grave, risky question. He said instead, "I just assumed that it was routine."

"Not unless there was a suspicion of murder," said Lutz.

"But you told us that Mozart said . . ."

Grob interrupted, "Mozart was probably feverish, and imagined things."

"Yes," said Lutz, "He probably was."

"Do you think he could have been saved?" Jason asked. "With different medical attention? Do you think the doctor could have been wrong?"

"How can I say!" cried Lutz. "I never knew what ailed him!"

Deborah said, "And that is why you feel so badly. You could have known what was wrong with Mozart, what, possibly, killed him, and you lost that chance. If you had known then how important he was to become . . ."

Lutz was horrified. "How can you suggest such an appalling idea?"

But Jason believed that Deborah might have a useful point. He asked Doctor Lutz, "What do you think caused his death?"

"There were several opinions. But what does it matter now?"

"Did you ever study music with anyone else?"

"After Mozart?" Lutz was shaken. "How could I?"

"Do you remember the name of the man who let you in?"

"He was a tavernkeeper, as I said. He lived nearby."

"Was his name Joseph Diener?"

"I don't remember. It was such a long time ago."

"Do you know where his tavern was?"

"Why should I? But he seemed to know Mozart rather well."

"Now you will tell me that you don't even remember where Mozart lived?"

"Of course I do, Herr Otis. On the Rauhensteingasse, near St. Stephen's Cathedral. I don't recall the exact address, but the street is clear in my mind. You could probably find the number of the house from the register of deaths in St. Stephen's, where the funeral services were held."

"Thanks."

Grob said, "Herr Otis, I hope you've found out what you want to know."

Jason shrugged noncommittally to hide the emotions seething within him.

Klaus blurted out, "It is no wonder that Mozart died impoverished. He was impractical and self-indulgent. Look how much our good friend Herr Offner has made from his scores. Why couldn't he have done the same?"

"It is an interesting phenomenon," said Offner. "The moment Mozart died, his scores doubled in value. In ten years they increased many fold. *Don Giovanni* and *The Magic Flute* are particularly popular."

"Yet he was so out of touch when he was alive," said Klaus. "He couldn't avoid unnecessary friction."

Jason suggested, "Herr Kapellmeister Mozart was an embarrassment?"

Klaus asked, "How do you mean?"

"With his views? His poverty? His way of life?"

"Essentially and candidly, yes. Did you know that he was a Freemason? Many tongues wagged about that."

"Enough, Herr Klaus," Grob cut in. "We mustn't gossip our lives away."

Grob asked Jason and Deborah to stay a few minutes after the others departed. But Doctor Lutz, too, desired to talk a bit more with the Americans. At the last moment, as the others were leaving, he had to go to the water closet, and he did not emerge until Klaus and Offner were gone. Then, ignoring Grob's efforts to silence him, he repeated, "Herr Otis, do you think I should have examined him?"

"If Mozart wanted you to," Jason replied.

"Who knows what he wanted. He was such a little man. How could he stand up to so many! I will never forgive myself for not having examined him. When I left him, I thought, he is a ruined man."

After Doctor Lutz's departure the next few minutes passed in a kind of dream for Jason, punctuated by Grob's comments to Deborah about the proper use of the money she had deposited with him. Jason felt immeasurably used up, as if the questions he had asked confronted him with more than he could face. But he returned to the moment as he heard Grob declare, "It is wise to view someone through another's eyes, although, I must confess, I have heard Lutz's story before."

Jason said, "You arranged this deliberately for my benefit?"

Grob replied innocently, "Isn't that what you wanted, Herr Otis?"

Yes, thought Jason, but not so calculatingly.

Grob said, "Your wife did deposit her funds in both your names. You are a fortunate man to have such a generous wife. Now, perhaps, you would like to place your own funds with me. There is no safer bank in all of Europe. Vienna is stable now, thanks to Prince Metternich."

"Can you get our passports returned?"

Grob sought to hide his irritation, but it crept into his voice as he answered, "I told you before that I would do my best."

"You get our passports returned to us, Herr Grob, and then possibly I can place my funds with you."

As Jason took Deborah by the arm to follow the others, Grob said, "You make interesting proposals, Herr Otis. And I will accept yours, if you accept mine. There is no evidence that Mozart died anything but a normal death. Accept it, you will be the better for it, and I should be able to get back your passports."

It was very late as they rode home in their carriage—Hans had called for them at a time arranged by Grob, and even Deborah was grateful that the carriage was waiting for them—and Jason tried to be calm, but it was impossible. He felt that Grob knew more about his interest in Mozart and Salieri than Grob should. Who could have told him? Suddenly he turned to Deborah and asked her if she had.

"How could I?" she exclaimed. "I never saw him before."

"You could have written him."

"My father did. But I didn't tell him to." Jason looked so offended, however, she wondered what she could do to regain his confidence. She had sat so quietly and politely all evening, even when she had been close to bursting. She had been rather proud of that, but now she felt humiliated and she cried out, "Grob did talk to Huber!"

"Grob must talk to many people."

"Huber must have told him about your interest in Mozart and Salieri."

"You think that I gave that away?"

"No, not really," she replied, feeling that whatever she said, she would be damned for it. "But Huber is very clever and so is Grob."

"You behaved as if you found Herr Grob quite charming."

"He is. But that doesn't mean I would trust him."

"You put a large sum of money in his hands. Was that to bribe him?"

That was ridiculous, she thought, but she was too tired and depressed to answer. Jason had declared that there was nothing more beautiful in the world than a piece of music by Mozart, but she disagreed. For her, in this moment, Boston would have been far more beautiful! How she wished she were home! And she could not forget Lutz's guilt and self-pity. Was Lutz using that? And Grob, too? If Jason would only calm down.

She made no effort in Jason's direction as he walked about their suite in the White Ox Inn, going from room to room as if somewhere he would find the answers he needed, while she lay in bed and could not fall asleep. If she could only become pregnant, she thought joylessly, or accomplish something that would involve him in her own feelings.

When he went to bed it was almost dawn, but he had come to a decision. Whatever the risks, he must go ahead with his plans to visit the people he had intended to: Beethoven, Schubert, Salieri if possible, and all those who had known Mozart intimately, but first of all, Ernst Muller, before it was too late. If it were not too late already, he reflected bitterly. At least Otto's brother shouldn't hide anything from him. He lay staring at his reflection in the mirror by his bed. He could hardly recognize himself in the pale light.

15

Ernst Muller

THE next day Jason told Deborah he was visiting Ernst Muller alone.

She had awakened depressed by the events of the previous night, but his news brought her to violent life. She felt he was saying this to punish her, and she replied, "I will not be left in this inn by myself."

"You stayed in London by yourself," he reminded her.

"I felt safe in London," she retorted. "I don't feel safe in Vienna. If you go without me, I will return to Boston."

"What about Huber? He has our passports."

"I will tell him whatever is necessary to get my passport."

"You would betray me, Deborah?" He looked shocked.

"You would betray me, Jason!" She sounded quite determined.

"It is irrational to be afraid to stay here alone for a few hours."

"That is not my reason and you know that very well. You want to punish me. You are angry that I deposited money with Grob. You are afraid I will use it to dominate you, and so now you are attempting to show that you don't need me, that you don't have to depend on me."

There was some truth to what she was saying, he realized, but he couldn't admit it, it would give her another advantage over him. He was tempted to let her go, but he must control his temper. He couldn't be sure whether she intended to carry out her threat and tell Huber why he was really in Vienna, but he couldn't take the chance. Moreover, if she did return to Boston, his resources would be strained to the breaking point. He was not even certain he had enough money of his own to stay in Vienna for the length of time that was essential. But Deborah must not know this, or she would use it. And suddenly he craved her sexually, although he couldn't admit that either. In her anger she was more beautiful than ever, with a subtle range of new expressions suggesting a developing, intriguing maturity. And she had not reminded him of the money she had given him for the coach. He said, "I didn't want you to go with me to Ernst Muller's because I didn't want you implicated in anything that could be held against you later. You are safer here."

He doubted she agreed with him, but she had the grace to look attentive.

"Ernst Muller may be under Huber's surveillance. Because of his interest in Salieri. I don't want to involve you any further."

She didn't believe him, but she didn't say so, sensing that could be fatal to their relationship. She remembered something her father had said to her at her wedding, "I hope you have the wits to maintain a decent superiority over Otis, as befits a Pickering." She was not sure she agreed with her father, but it was possible that she and Jason had different claims on each other. She said, "I appreciate your consideration. But you are my husband and my place is at your side."

"*Bravo!*" he cried sarcastically.

"I mean that, Jason, I do." She put her arms around him.

Her body was warm and passionate, and he felt a strong interior glow, like a fresh recognition of himself.

"After all, I shouldn't have been surprised by what we have encountered in Vienna. Da Ponte warned us and so did Michael Kelly."

"Then you do believe them?" Jason asked eagerly.

Deborah wasn't sure, but things were going too well finally to risk jeopardizing them, and she answered, "Perhaps much of what da Ponte said about the intrigues and resentments against *Figaro* were true. Your copy of Beaumarchais' *Figaro* was confiscated."

Jason had responded to her affection by returning her embrace, yet he still looked grim, saying, "It is the Mullers who trouble me. Otto warned me that I would encounter some difficulties, but not to the extent I have. He gave no indication that the State would be so opposed to any investigation of Salieri or of Mozart's death."

Deborah didn't like Otto, but she said, "Perhaps he didn't know."

"Perhaps." Jason released her suddenly.

"What's wrong?" Had she failed after all, she wondered bleakly.

"I must assemble all the facts I have learned that relate to the possibility that Mozart was assassinated." He sat down at a desk and began to itemize in writing the facts he felt were relevant to that.

She said, "This is dangerous. If these ideas are found on you, you will be accused of conspiring against the State."

"I will memorize them. Then burn them. As soon as they are memorized."

"You will take me with you, Jason," she pleaded. "I can't endure staying here by myself and waiting." She shivered fearfully.

Refreshed by her display of affection and need, he nodded.

She thought, All assumptions in marriage are fatuous. But she did feel a little more adequate. But only a little. Suddenly she was stricken with emotional weariness, and the day was just starting.

Jason decided to walk to Ernst Muller's address and told Hans to take the day off and added pointedly, "This will give you time to visit your relatives."

Then he said to her, "Now you will find out whether you have been right about Hans, and I don't want him to know where we are going."

But at the moment she felt drained. She would have preferred to rest, yet she had to accompany Jason on the Graben which led to the Weihburggasse, where Ernst Muller lived. Gradually, however, as he grew enthusiastic about Vienna again—the Graben was crowded with pedestrians and coaches, and, as he said, this was not a city of danger today, but the beautiful, romantic Vienna he had imagined—her spirits rose. She liked the sense of wealth that dominated. It was exciting to think of Mozart having walked here; someone looking much like him might be passing at this instant.

Yet notes of pessimism kept intruding. She thought, Between husband and wife extends a strong, tight rope that holds them together even when walking, and which they must accept if they are to survive together, for they are tied at the waist. She wondered if they would stay bound if there were no act of copulation. She didn't say this to Jason, for she felt that this might shock him. As they stood before Ernst Muller's door, she sought to be soft and appealing.

Ernst Muller was home as if he had been expecting them. He answered the door himself and escorted them to his rooms on the second floor. His quarters were simple by comparison with Grob's. The most attractive articles of furniture, Deborah observed, were chairs with backs in the form of a lyre. Everything else was plain, without pretension.

Jason had expected Ernst to resemble Otto; instead he bore an amazing physical resemblance to Grob. Ernst was short, plump, round-shouldered, with white hair and rosy cheeks. But there the resemblance ceased. Ernst was quick, abrupt, the opposite of charming. He had remarkably bright, penetrating eyes, and from the moment he greeted them, he gave Jason the feeling of having to get on with things, whatever the cost, impatient of disagreement and irritable with delays.

Yet Jason had so many questions to ask even as Ernst acted as if there were so little time, although Ernst did speak German slowly and distinctly to be sure that the Americans could understand him.

Jason asked, "Do you know an Anton Grob? A banker? In Vienna?"

"No. Why did you take so long to get here, Herr Otis?"

"It is a long journey. There were delays. Am I too late?"

"Oh, possibly not. You may have come just in time."

Deborah thought it wrong of Muller to give them the feeling there was no more time to lose, especially after what they had gone through, and she told him so. But the moment she was finished, he was saying, "Salieri is said to be failing. Did you get the news I wrote Otto?"

"Yes," said Jason. "Will I be able to see Salieri?"

F

"It will be difficult, but possible, I think. I have become friendly with one of his keepers, and at the proper moment and with the proper inducement something might be arranged. They call the asylum a hospital, but it is really a prison. There are bars on the windows and the gates are locked, but Salieri, I hear, as befits his services to the Hapsburgs, has a room to himself and two keepers in constant attendance."

Deborah asked angrily, "What about the risk?"

For a moment Ernst was speechless. Then he blurted out, "But that is why you are here! To talk to Salieri if I can manage it!"

"Of course," said Jason, seeking to mollify both of them. He was watching Ernst closely, trying to judge his sincerity.

"And Mozart's wife isn't well and his sister is bedridden."

Deborah asked, "Herr Muller, why do you need us to investigate the circumstances of Mozart's death? Why can't you do that yourself?"

He glared at her as if what she was suggesting was absurd, but he did take the trouble to explain. "Whatever I find out cannot be exposed, for the authorities would never allow me to leave Vienna. But you are Americans, you can depart whenever you please. Then, once you are out of the Hapsburg reach, you can tell the world what you have learned."

"That is not as simple as you suggest," said Deborah.

"What concerns my wife is what happened to us at the gates of Vienna."

"You mean the strictness of the examination by the customs officials?"

Jason told Ernst about the seizure of their books, of their passports being in the hands of Huber, and of the warnings they had received.

Ernst was silent for a long time. Then he said in English, "Yes, it could be dangerous."

Jason said, "You know English! Why didn't you use it before?"

"I wanted to find out how much German you know. It should be adequate."

"My wife's German is better."

"Good. You may need it."

"What about the difficulties? Why didn't your brother warn me?"

"He didn't know. He left Vienna many years ago."

"Why did he leave?" Deborah asked in German.

Ernst replied, "Your German is excellent, Frau Otis."

"Was your brother a political refugee?"

"No, no!"

But she wasn't sure that Ernst was telling the truth.

"The wars with Bonaparte had begun, and Otto wanted to find a more peaceful world, where he could earn a more stable living."

She said, "If your brother had told Jason about the dangers, Jason might not have come. And your brother knew that."

"It is possible."

"Then, in effect, he lied."

"In effect, Frau Otis, he was a human being."

She found Ernst Muller far too impatient to suit her. And he was not reflective and settled as she had expected, which dismayed her, as if this made him unmanageable.

He sensed her disquiet, for he said proudly, "I am four years younger than Otto. I am only seventy, and everyone tells me that I don't look that. I am still able to teach full time, and I can get about without any assistance. What else do you want to know? I did expect you weeks ago."

"Why are you and your brother so involved in this absorbing passion to unearth the mystery of Mozart's death? Assuming there is a mystery?"

"We want to see justice done, reason triumph."

She insisted, "It must be something else."

"Perhaps it is because Otto and I loved Mozart as a man and as a musician. And he helped Otto become a Konzertmeister."

Jason said, "Otto told me."

"And Mozart helped me, also. He was an unusually kind person. If not for his aid at a critical time in my life, I could have died."

Now no one interrupted Ernst as he reached out to embrace Mozart.

"It was 1787, at the time Mozart was composing *Don Giovanni*. But what concerned me directly was that I was to play first violin in a chamber orchestra he had hired to perform in his new quarters in the Landstrasse suburb. I knew it was a special occasion for him, for he had composed a new serenade to celebrate his fifth wedding anniversary, and the party was to be held in the garden. I had hesitated to accept the assignment, for I had been quite ill with a dreadful fever and chill, but he had asked for me—I had played for him at *Figaro* and for his subscription concerts—and he had a high regard for my work. I didn't want to disappoint him, and I needed the money desperately. I had fallen into debt, I couldn't afford a doctor, and my landlord was threatening to evict me if I didn't pay my back rent immediately. So the night of the concert I forced myself to dress, although I still felt feverish and everytime I coughed the ugly, hacking sound I made appalled me. If that happened during the concert, even Mozart might not forgive me.

"I was surprised to see Salieri at the garden party. I expected Haydn and da Ponte; Haydn was a dear friend of Mozart's and da Ponte worked with him, but Salieri's hostility to Mozart was well known. I felt that Mozart must have invited Salieri at da Ponte's suggestion.

"Salieri made me feel very uneasy. I had played in the orchestra for one of his operas, and it had been a frightening experience.

"From the first rehearsal, Salieri separated the German performers from the Italian and made it clear that he regarded us as inferior musicians and that he was using us only because he could not obtain anybody better. Inevitably a feeling of abrasiveness developed between Salieri and the German musicians.

"One rehearsal became especially stormy. News had just arrived in Vienna of the success of Mozart's *Figaro* in Prague, and there was talk that it would be revived in Vienna and Salieri was in a foul mood. Salieri, who guarded the palace gates like a grenadier lest any other musician might gain access, disagreed with our tempo from the first note. He had been sitting in the Royal box to try to judge how his music would sound to the Emperor and so that he could look down on us, but suddenly, in a vicious rage, he rushed into the orchestra pit and slapped the man sitting at the music desk with me, bringing a gory rivulet of blood to his mouth, and shouted, 'Pig! You squeal like a pig!'

"And when I protested—there had been nothing wrong with our playing, it was his music that was sour, without the melodic beauty of Mozart—he turned on me. He snatched my violin out of my hands and held it aloft over my head. I saw murder in his eyes and I thought he was going to brain me. Then I saw that his calculating mind had gained some judgment over his temper, and that he was realizing this was too public a situation for such an obvious display of violence.

"So he did the nastiest and cruelest act he could contemplate.

"With a deliberate gesture of disgust he smashed my violin against the music stand and broke it into many pieces. And while I longed to knock him to the floor and I was sick inside—I had saved a long time to buy this violin, one of the best in Vienna, and I doubted that I would ever be able to afford so splendid an instrument again—I fought to control myself. Salieri was Imperial Kapellmeister, I was working in the Imperial Opera House, and it was managed by his closest friend at court, Count Orsini-Rosenberg. If I dared touch Salieri, I could be thrown into prison, and I would surely be banned for life from all Royal musical activities, and there was no other way for a musician to support himself in Vienna then.

"I bent over to pick up some of the shattered pieces of my violin out of a feeling of affection for an instrument that had never betrayed me, and because I didn't know what else to do, and I had to do something to keep from hitting Salieri, and he kicked the scraps aside with contempt and snarled, 'That will fix you, you German swine!'

"I wondered if his rage was also because he knew I was a musician that Mozart favored, and a friend of Mozart's.

"I had only one thing left, my dignity. I sat without a word or gesture, although I had no instrument now, and I sensed that he could have murdered me for appearing so self-possessed, for he screamed at me, 'Go! Go! Before you drive me mad!' "

Ernst paused and Jason asked excitedly, "Did you leave?"

"I had no choice. And by the time I was able to buy a new violin, it was too late to rejoin the orchestra, not that Salieri would have allowed that. And since we were not paid for rehearsals, I fell deeply into debt, and then, because of that and worry, ill."

"Why were you worried? You had done nothing wrong."

"Salieri thought so. And he controlled much of the music in Vienna."

"What about Mozart?"

"Even when he became Third Royal Kapellmeister, after Gluck's death, he never had Salieri's influence. Salieri saw to that."

Deborah cut in, "Jason, you're distracting Ernst. Let him go on."

Jason resented her admonition, but he was eager to hear the rest of Ernst's story, so he motioned for Ernst to continue. He was shaken by what he had heard. Although it was a sunny day outside, the sky seemed to be darkening over Vienna and that emphasized his loneliness here, and his isolation from free ideas. He felt as if he were slipping into an incomprehensible world of contempt and hate, and that the only foothold he possessed was Mozart and his music.

Ernst resumed, "Remembering what had happened with Salieri, I wanted to hide when I saw him. But an air of informality reigned and while Salieri ignored my presence, Mozart took me by the hand to welcome me.

"His fingers were firm and beautifully shaped; his hands conveyed an exceptional sense of delicacy, and yet they were very strong. But I shouldn't have been surprised; he was the finest concert pianist I knew.

"He said, 'I hope you are feeling better, Ernst. I was sorry to hear that you have been ill.'

" 'I'm much better, Herr Kapellmeister,' I said, although I felt faint.

"But I was determined not to harm his music. I was relieved that dinner was served before the concert. I had not eaten properly for weeks, and the meal was just what I needed, a feast of oysters, roast pheasant, delicious glacé fruits, and champagne. And I was touched that we, the musicians who were to perform, ate with the guests. Most composers considered themselves above orchestra performers and kept apart in social situations. As I ate I felt better, but I still felt uncomfortable when I caught Salieri glaring at me. Apparently he had never forgiven me for what had happened at his opera rehearsal.

"So when the music began, I sought to play precisely. Mozart liked my clean style; he had complimented me for not scratching, for not making the same point more than once, and for avoiding what he called the false, flamboyant *bravissima* Neapolitan style of Salieri, which was replete with rises and falls, and which he liked to say kept the fiddler's hands in his audience's pockets, confusing the effect with the substance.

"We were playing a new piece that Mozart had composed for his wife, a serenade in G, which is known now as *"Eine kleine Nacht-*

musik," and he led it with such loving care that I knew it mattered deeply to him. I was grateful that I didn't disturb the music with coughing, although I almost choked in my efforts to prevent that wretched noise.

"When we finished, I thought it was one of the most melodic pieces I had ever heard, but Mozart's son, who had been sleeping upstairs, had been awakened by the music and had begun to cry, and I saw a sneer on Salieri's face. Salieri thought that no one was watching him, that everyone was focused on the child whom Mozart had brought downstairs, but I was.

"The next few minutes the child, Karl Thomas, held the stage, which pleased Mozart. Then suddenly I heard da Ponte say, I felt because he was bored with the child and wished to provoke an argument, which he enjoyed, despite his wish to get along with every important composer, 'Mozart, Maestro Salieri says that *Don Giovanni* is a foolish idea.'

"Salieri replied, 'That is not so, it is just that the story has been used a number of times already.'

"Haydn, who had been quiet—a plain, pleasant man in a brown waistcoat—but whose affection for Mozart was very evident, while Mozart regarded him with love, declared, 'I'm sure that Wolfgang's *Don Giovanni* will be amusing yet tragic, and as harmonious as all his other operas.'

"Da Ponte said, 'And might well outdo anything yet composed.'

"This must have annoyed Salieri, for he said, 'But the Don is immoral. He is a lecher, a murderer. No wonder the opera is not being done in Vienna. It would be offensive to the Emperor.'

"Mozart said, 'If it is a success in Prague, it will be done in Vienna.'

" 'If . . .?' Salieri paused, then offered his most gracious smile. 'You are a generous host, Maestro. I've enjoyed your table enormously.'

"But I wondered why Salieri had not eaten anything at the table until Mozart had tasted it first. And Salieri had shown a macabre interest in what Mozart could eat, and could not eat."

Ernst hesitated, then said, "This is something I have never forgotten."

Jason nodded; Deborah was motionless, thinking of how that fitted in with what they had heard in England. They waited for Ernst to continue.

"The orchestra was supposed to be paid the next day, but I stayed after all the guests left, and while I saw Constanze Mozart give me a look of disapproval, Mozart seemed pleased. I felt that he was so emotional about his new composition, he could have stayed up all night. When I asked him if he could spare a moment, he said, 'As many as you need, Ernst,' and drew me aside tactfully to give me the privacy I needed.

"Then I found myself unable to speak.

"He guessed what I was feeling, for he said, 'It is money, isn't it?'"

"I nodded, quite embarrassed.

" 'How much?'

"I shrugged. Drops of perspiration appeared on my forehead.

"He smiled, and handed me some money. I would have been grateful for a single kreutzer, and he had filled my hand with coins.

"He didn't want my thanks, however, for when I tried to express them, he changed the subject and asked what I thought of his new composition.

"I said, 'The serenade was extraordinarily beautiful and melodic.'

"His voice pulsed with emotion. 'I doubt the Court will like it, but it is good to please other musicians. It is the best way of knowing.' "

Ernst sighed deeply. "It was the greatest compliment I ever received."

Jason asked, "Did he give you two gulden?"

"Two? He gave me twenty, and something even more precious."

"What was that?" asked Deborah. What could have been more precious than money, she wondered.

"Mozart must have seen the tears in my eyes, for while his wife was calling him, saying it was time for bed, and I knew he prized his nights with her and I sensed that she was afraid he would give me money she felt he could not afford, he called back, 'I will be in soon, Stanzi.'

"He hurried into his music room and returned with writing paper. Then he sat down at a table where we had eaten earlier, and drawing music lines on the paper with his pen, he composed a minuet, working with amazing rapidity. He handed me the finished piece and said, 'This may repay you for what Salieri did to your violin.'

"I said, 'I can't take it, Herr Kapellmeister.'

" 'Of course you can,' he said. 'Give it to a music publisher. With my signature, it should be worth a few gulden.' He signed it, *Wolfgang Amadeus Mozart,*' and added, 'Not that they will doubt it. They will recognize my style, even if they don't understand the quality.'

" 'Why did you invite Salieri, sir? He is not your friend.'

" 'I know. But da Ponte requested it. He wants us to be friends. He thinks it would be useful. So I try, although it is probably a hopeless task. Are you strong enough to get home properly?'

" 'I'm fine now, sir. You've been most kind.'

" 'Settle your account with your doctor, and don't exhaust yourself with worry.'

" 'I hope you follow your own advice, Herr Kapellmeister.'

" 'Does anyone? If matters get difficult again, let me know. If *Don Giovanni* is accepted by Prague, it should be requested by Vienna.'

" 'It will be!' I cried.

" 'Perhaps,' he said, 'but I prefer not to have any final opinions until I finish a work. Make sure you get the best doctor in Vienna.'

"And only when I nodded did he say goodbye."

Jason asked, "How much did the piece he composed for you bring?"

"I don't know. I couldn't sell it."

"Do you have it now?"

"It is always close to me." Ernst took it out of a leather case with reverence and handed it lovingly to Jason.

The autograph was yellow with age but carefully preserved, and Jason was fascinated by the signature, so clear and distinct, as if written recently, while Deborah was discovering that she couldn't say a word.

Ernst said, "But I couldn't keep the music from the world, it sings with such assurance and beauty. I sold copies, but I've kept the original."

Yet when Jason wanted to play the minuet on the pianoforte, Ernst was abrupt, declaring, "You can do that later. Did you tell the internal security officer, Huber, that you were coming here?"

"No," said Jason.

"Good. There is no point in arousing a police officer's suspicions."

"Did you know the doctor who attended Mozart in his last illness?"

"I was out of Vienna then. When I returned, Mozart was dead."

"Did you know a Joseph Diener?"

"The tavernkeeper that Mozart liked? Yes. Is he still alive?"

"That is what I am trying to find out," said Jason. "I was told that Diener was with Mozart during the last few weeks of his life."

"I haven't seen Diener for years, but he could be alive. He was very young in 1791, when Mozart depended on him for some things."

"Do you know where his tavern is? Or was?"

"No. But I may be able to find out."

"I can't even find out where Mozart was residing when he died."

Ernst asked, "It was on the Rauhensteingasse, wasn't it?"

Jason said, "So I was told."

Ernst burst out laughing. "The Rauhensteingasse is just around the corner. Come, I will take you there. Now."

That excited Jason, but Deborah didn't join him and Ernst. Instead, standing motionless, she asked the elderly musician, "You said that Mozart saved your life. How?"

"After Salieri smashed my precious violin and I fell into debt and illness, I was quite desperate. If Mozart hadn't helped me, I wouldn't have been able to go on. I would have committed suicide."

She was silent for a long time. She felt she had nothing more to say.

But Jason wanted to rush out with Ernst, who was abrupt again, repeating insistently, "You must see where Mozart died."

Ernst was imperious, almost unbearable, thought Deborah, yet she followed him, for Jason was.

16

Mozart's Last Lodgings

RUHENSTEINGASSE, 970, where Mozart had died, was, as Ernst had said, just around the corner from his rooms.

They stood in front of the square, squat three-story house, and Ernst stated, "Mozart lived on the first floor."

Jason asked, "Did you ever visit him there?"

"Several times. The last time was after the opening of *The Magic Flute*. He was in high spirits. It had become a popular success, and he was hopeful that it would improve his situation. At that time he had no idea that Rauhensteingasse, 970, was going to be his last lodging."

"How long was it before he died that you visited him?"

"About a month."

"He wasn't sick then?"

"He was tired from poverty and overwork, but ill, no. He told me that this was a good apartment in which to compose." Ernst pointed to the five large windows on the first floor and added, "He liked them. He said it helped him look out on the world. He could see the Himmelpfortgasse from his study, from the window on the extreme left. He loved company, he composed often when people were around, and that autumn of 1791 he was alone often. So glancing out on the Himmelpfortgasse and the Rauhensteingasse while he composed helped him, he told me."

Remembering then what had happened at the Collalto Palace, Jason wanted to talk to the people who occupied Mozart's rooms now, but Ernst halted him, saying, "They didn't know Mozart. I tried it once and the door was slammed in my face. They regard the fact that Mozart happened to die in their rooms as an unnecessary nuisance."

"How could they?" Jason cried out.

"There are many people in Vienna who don't care about Mozart."

Jason was prepared for almost anything but that. What Ernst suggested was blasphemy. He thought of the multitude of people who must have passed Rauhensteingasse, 970, without having given it a glance, and anger rose within him. One of the jewels of Vienna had shone here, and there wasn't one sign of that, and all that could be seen was the face of ugliness. Jason longed to kneel here, to enshrine this house as a Holy of Holies, to embalm this house with Mozart; instead

F *

the wood was rotting and the plaster was yellow and cracked. What infuriated him the most was the indifference. There was not a spark of feeling here.

At first Deborah was touched by Jason's reverence and indignation, but gradually fatigue overwhelmed her and she said that she had to return to the inn and rest. Ernst was too energetic for her, and she didn't share Jason's sense of poignancy.

Yet when Jason said to Ernst, "A man I met, Christoph Fuchs, said that Diener's tavern was close to where Mozart died, and that if I could find the house I could find the tavern and possibly Diener—don't you think we should look for him now?" Ernst replied, "Later! We will look for Diener later! I have more important things to show you. While you are in the mood. That will convince you that Mozart was poisoned." Ernst clutched them by the arm and pulled them in a new direction.

Deborah thought wearily that Ernst, whatever his motives, was ready to use and misuse truth and untruth at the dictates of his immediate necessity. She said, "Herr Muller, you do not suspect the worst, you assume it."

Ernst merely smiled, but Jason exclaimed, "Deborah, you are unfair!"

Jason looked so ready for a passionate denunciation of her that she was quiet. The real accomplice was his need, she told herself; Jason had to trust Ernst because he had to trust someone. Without someone to trust, his task was hopeless. To keep his belief that Mozart had been poisoned within himself was too much of a burden to bear.

They had walked only a short time when Ernst sang out, "There it is, St. Stephen's, where the final services were held over his corpse."

Seen through Ernst's eyes and from the side of the magnificent south tower, it was as if they were viewing the cathedral for the first time.

Ernst said, "I wanted to show you that it is a very short distance from Rauhensteingasse, 970, to the cathedral. Perhaps three hundred yards."

Jason nodded, but Deborah looked as if she didn't understand.

"I also want you to know how the funeral went. It is significant."

"So hurriedly?" Deborah said. "Couldn't we have done it tomorrow?"

"Tomorrow things may be different. You surely wouldn't have begrudged following Mozart's corpse this far, would you?"

"No," said Jason. "I don't think so."

"Mozart's wife didn't come. Nor some of his best friends. Although the last rites were held close to his home and in the center of Vienna."

"Why didn't they come?"

"I was told that some people were afraid to attend Mozart's funeral because he had fallen into disfavor with the Hapsburgs."

"Assuming that was so, do you know why?"

"There were various reasons given. One view held that the nobility resented *Figaro,* others felt that it was because Mozart was a Free-mason, and it was also said that he had been too free with criticism of the Hapsburgs. And then there was the question of *The Magic Flute.*"

"What about *The Magic Flute?*"

"There were people who thought the Queen of the Night was based on the Empress Maria Theresa. It was not a flattering portrait."

"Who did come?" Jason asked as Deborah leaned wearily against the side of the cathedral. He wondered what Ernst was driving at.

"Van Swieten, Süssmayer, Albrechtsburger, and Salieri."

"Salieri?" Jason exclaimed. He was surprised. Even Deborah straightened up, almost as interested as Jason now.

"Yes. Albrechtsburger told me. He was so surprised to see Salieri there, he never forgot it. Salieri's hostility was well known to every-one."

"But Mozart's wife did not come to the funeral at St. Stephen's?"

"No. But it is Salieri's presence that matters as far as we are concerned. Evidently he intended to prove that he was a friend. And . . ."

Jason filled in, ". . . to prove that he was innocent."

"And very likely to make sure that the evidence was disposed of."

Deborah asked, "What are you insinuating, Herr Muller?"

"Once the corpse vanished, nothing could be proven. And if a man went so far as to commit murder, don't you think he would try to get rid of the body if he could? And Mozart's body did vanish. Completely."

Deborah said, "That doesn't prove that Mozart was murdered."

"Then why was no one at the cemetery? When the body vanished."

She said irritably, "I'm sure there is a reason."

Ernst said, "People always give reasons. But that is not an answer."

Jason asked, "What reason did the mourners give?"

"They said they left St. Stephen's intending to go with the body to the cemetery but at the city gate a terrible storm forced them to turn back. But I learned that the weather was mild that day."

"Then why did they turn back?"

"Herr Otis, that is the great question."

"You believe someone was responsible for no one being at the cemetery?"

"I think it was quite likely."

Jason said, "We should talk to those who were at St. Stephen's."

"Van Swieten, Süssmayer, and Albrechtsburger are dead."

Jason sighed. "I had wondered why Mozart's body vanished without a trace. Why no one was at the grave. It was what started this quest."

"If you could prove that Salieri was responsible for no one going to the cemetery, it would fit in with his confession."

"His alleged confession," Deborah cut in.

But Ernst felt so invincible with his probings, thought Deborah, nothing was halting him, for he insisted, "you must visit the cemetery now. See for yourselves how easy it was to reach. Do you have a coach?"

Jason said, "I gave my coachman the day off. I didn't want him to know that I was visiting you."

"That was sensible. We will hire a coach. But first you must see where the last rites were held."

He led them into the north side of St. Stephen's and into the aisle of the chapel of the Cross, where the funeral services had been held over the body of Mozart. There was no one else in this part of the cathedral, and the thought of Mozart lying here with only a few people in attendance made Jason very angry again, as if, once dead, Mozart had been given very short shrift. Yet he felt that mourning was a private and personal passion and as he stood before the famous crucifix that hung over this chapel it was Mozart who lay upon it and not Jesus.

It was too dark for Deborah inside the cathedral and it added to her feeling of apprehension. Jason appeared relieved by what Ernst had told them, as if that confirmed and justified his investigations, but she was even more afraid now of what they could discover. Yet she had to admit to herself that it was quite sad: Mozart had been so skilful in all kinds of music and there had been no witnesses at his grave. But what would *they* find at the grave? The possibilities made her shiver.

Once they were on the way to the cemetery in a coach that Ernst paid for, to Deborah's surprise, he freely admitted that their venture could be dangerous. It was as if he could only admit that after they had agreed to go to the cemetery with him, as if he needed that to convince him that they were going ahead with their investigations.

But even as he agreed now that they must be wary of the authorities and he stated, "There is no freedom under Metternich, he is too busy suppressing the results of the French Revolution, the only thing that keeps our tyranny from being intolerable is the police's lack of efficiency," he added, "Nobody will suspect anything if we go to St. Marx's cemetery. We could be visiting any one of a number of graves."

At the city gate he reminded them that it had been a short journey, yet everybody had turned back at this point.

Jason was affronted at this, and Deborah wondered if he was as tired as she was. She had felt oppressed by the narrow, curved, dark streets of the inner city that they had been riding through, but beyond the city gate they were in the country and she was glad, for the air was cleaner.

Ernst mentioned that they were passing by the Landstrasse suburb, where Mozart had resided when he had given him twenty gulden, but Jason didn't respond as Ernst expected and Deborah merely nodded.

As they approached St. Marx's a few minutes later, Ernst declared, "You see it isn't far, as I told you. Which makes it all the more puzzling and suspicious that no one followed the funeral here."

"Funeral?" Jason questioned. "I thought you said it was just one cart."

"One yellow cart, one yellow wooden box, one horse, one driver, and no one behind it. Not even a dog." Ernst's voice trembled with rage.

"It is incredible. It took us only a half hour to get here."

"And the road isn't bad. It has cobbles and is easy to ride on."

Deborah said, "Perhaps Mozart's death was such a shock to his friends that they couldn't endure another service. So they turned back at the city gate to keep their emotions from being stretched beyond the breaking point."

Ernst ridiculed that notion and regarded her as if she were betraying him. How could she have such doubts about his evidence?

Jason's silence seemed to agree with Ernst.

Yet she felt so exhausted by the extremes of emotion she had experienced the last few days, she believed that what she had suggested could be true. All the way to the cemetery she had been thinking what an emotional strain this journey had become.

Now they were standing outside the church of St. Marx's, a small, drab, humble edifice, and the caretaker answered Ernst's hurried interrogation, "Yes, this is the cemetery, too, but Mozart, no, I do not know anything about such a person. You say he was buried here?"

No one Ernst asked knew anything of Mozart.

It was as if a conspiracy of silence existed, Jason thought bitterly. The cemetery was not picturesque, as he had expected, but more rundown than the church. He felt he was in a heartless, mindless wasteland, a small, obscure graveyard where the foliage was wild and unkept. There were a few hedges, trees, and shrubs, but they were uncultivated. There were no flowers anywhere, not even on the occasional graves that had a tombstone. As they stepped on the gravel path, their feet made a harsh, ugly crunch. None of the graves looked cared for; a number of the tombstones had fallen or were tilted brokenly. When he tried to read the inscriptions he could hardly decipher the names, and then they were unfamiliar.

Jason had expected the cemetery to have the beauty of a park at least, but the grounds were unsightly and untidy, and they grew worse as he walked through them. Once in a while he saw a cross but when he sought to establish the geography where Mozart might have been buried, Ernst said, "Supposed to be buried. Remember, there is no exact spot."

Deborah asked, "You mean no one has any idea where the body was put?"

"There is not a trace."

"Not even in an ordinary grave?"

"Not anywhere."

"Have you been here before, Herr Muller?"

"Several times."

She felt they were walking about the cemetery in a daze, but now he led them up a gravel path to a large, flat, open area at the crest of a hill and said, "Here is where the common grave is said to be."

She said, "You mean this is where it is assumed he was buried?"

"It is believed that he was thrown into a common grave."

"But why? Surely he didn't have a pauper's funeral?"

"A third-class funeral. For eight gulden, fifty-six kreutzer. There was no money for a grave, so if he was buried, he was thrown in with a number of other corpses. With ten to a hundred other bodies."

Deborah could hardly bear to believe what Ernst was telling them, but Ernst was determined that they know all the facts, however painful they might be, and Jason was listening intently.

Ernst said, "They placed the bodies on boards a few feet deep."

Jason said, "And once the dirt was filled in, the bodies were consumed."

"By each other, and by the confusion. Do you understand now why the way his body disappeared is so vital to our investigation?"

"Isn't there any trace of the gravedigger?"

"They were temporary. They worked a short time, until they were paid, and then they vanished. This wasn't a busy cemetery. There wasn't much work. No one knows who the gravedigger was at the time. And it would have been easy to bribe him. Or to get rid of him afterward."

"Why was Mozart buried here?"

"This cemetery is part of the parish of St. Stephen's."

"The poorest part?"

Ernst nodded.

Deborah asked indignantly, "Why didn't his wife come?"

"Why?" Ernst smiled caustically, then said, "She stated that she was too ill. She didn't come to the cemetery until 1808, many years after Mozart's death." Ernst sounded as if he could never forgive her for this.

"But why didn't she come to the cemetery for so many years?"

Ernst sighed and murmured, "I wish I knew, Frau Otis."

"Do you think she was angry at Mozart? For a reason we don't know? She didn't even put a cross over his grave. Or where she might have thought it was. A simple wooden cross!"

"She said that she expected the parish to furnish the cross. Then later, when she was criticized for the lack of a cross, she said that she had ordered one to be erected. But there is none to Mozart in St. Marx's."

Jason asked, "Are you sure this is where the common grave was?" He wanted to pray for Mozart, but where?

"Only approximately. Within about a hundred yards, it is estimated. Because a large flat area such as this was the most suitable place for digging the long, wide trench that a common grave required. But the exact position has never been ascertained with certainty."

The sky had grown gray, and there was a threat of rain in the air now. Jason looked upward, as if somehow he could find an answer there, and he repeated, "No mark, no sign, no cross. It is unthinkable."

"But it happened. Once a body was in a common grave, it became unrecognizable. Any investigation of why the person died was impossible."

Jason was shaken violently. Deborah took his hand. He was grateful for her sympathy, but he couldn't stop his tears. He yearned to plant a flower here, or to dig, to act as if he were finding something of Mozart, to play a lovely pretending game that none of this had occurred and that it was just a nightmare. But the realization of the vast crater he would have to dig was appalling. And what would he find? Then he saw that Deborah was crying, and Ernst, too.

A sparrow flew over them, making a loud fuss. Something was creating a rattling noise on the gravel path, a field rat perhaps, for the bird was causing a shrill clamor in its effort to divert the intruder from its five babies in a nearby nest.

Ernst said, "Mozart couldn't even have a mass sung at his grave. Mozart who wrote wonderful masses for others."

"Was it because he was a Freemason?" Jason asked. "Was that the reason there was no cross?" He was trying not to weep, but it was difficult.

"A spoken mass cost a hundred gulden, a sung mass two hundred."

Deborah said, "But there should have been prayers at his grave."

"There weren't any. They cost twenty gulden."

Deborah said suddenly. "We had better go. I never thought Mozart's grave would be like this." She was terribly upset.

"In a moment," said Jason. He stood motionless as if somehow he could reach across the void that was so terrifying and yet so poignant and embrace Mozart, whose bones had been left here like a beggar man. But Deborah would say that was preposterous, he thought, roving in a graveyard for a body no one could ever find. If he had known it was going to be like this, he might not have come. He was overwhelmed with a feeling of bereavement and wretchedness. This cemetery was a house of pain. His heart was breaking all over again. Yet he had to stay a little longer. This place had become very dear to him. He knew he would never forget it.

Ernst was full of plans. He told Jason, "Your first step is to remove any suspicions. You must visit Beethoven and present him with the commission for the oratorio and attempt to become friends with him, even study with him, although both may be difficult, even impossible."

Jason said nothing. He didn't even lift his face. He stared at the ground in front of him, feeling that he had seen murder done.

Ernst continued, "And you should present the commission through this banker you mentioned, Grob, and move into more permanent quarters. If you approach Beethoven through the banker, it will avoid suspicion. Most important, don't talk about Mozart, talk about Beethoven."

Jason muttered, "It is unbelievable. No physical trace of the body. All obliterated. All mortal remains disintegrated, rotted away."

"When Mozart's body vanished, they thought they were eradicating all evidences of his life, instead they were making it more significant."

Even so, Jason felt that what had happened was monstrous, yet he stood as if the cemetery had cast a spell on him.

Ernst said, "No one talks about Salieri or mentions his illness in public, but in private there is much talk. One just must be careful who one discusses it with. Vienna is full of informers and spies."

The clouds had thickened, and Deborah said anxiously, "It is going to rain soon. We musn't lose our wits." Jason looked so strange.

"We're not very far from the coach," Ernst assured her. "I ordered the driver to wait near the entrance."

Deborah didn't look grateful or even thankful, but apprehensive.

Then Jason had to ask what had been on his mind ever since they had left England. "Herr Muller, do you know anyone who knew Catherina Cavalieri?"

"Ah, Salieri's mistress. I might. Why?"

Jason told him about Cavalieri's letter to Ann Storace concerning the dinner Mozart had eaten with her and Salieri, and her shock to learn that Mozart had died soon after. "What do you say to that, Herr Muller?"

"I'm not surprised. It adds confirmation to what we believe. It was said that Mozart's body swelled up during his final illness, which could have been caused by poison. I will look for someone who knew her."

It was starting to rain, and Deborah insisted they must go before they were drenched and caught a deathly cold, but still Jason paused, as if he could not allow Mozart to lie here alone. Then suddenly he bent down; and although the soil was turning to mud from the rain, which had become a pelting downpour, he scooped up a little earth, and felt that he was touching the body of Mozart.

Now he could follow Deborah and Ernst out of the cemetery of St. Marx's as she said sadly yet wonderingly, "Poor, poor Mozart."

17

A Question of Whom

DUSK was settling upon Vienna when they returned to their rooms.
But the questions remained. What had happened to the body?
Why had the mourners turned back at the city gate? Was Salieri
responsible? Why had the body utterly vanished? These questions
haunted Jason and although he felt as tired as Deborah, he hurried to
his writing desk to jot them down in the hope that the written word
would suggest some sensible answers. She lay upon their small sofa and
sought to rest, but she was sighing to herself, and he sensed that she
was troubled too.

After he lit the lamp, he could not write but sat silently and uneasily,
thinking that he had been deluded into believing that what he had been
doing had been his own free choice when, actually, he was the slave of
his actions rather than the master. He thought of the multitude of
bodies that had been disposed of without any further trace. He cared
little for the rituals of death and he felt that existence was indifferent to
burial, once flesh was without life it was without purpose, and so,
without value. Yet each time he reflected about what had happened to
Mozart, he was filled with revulsion.

Yet possibly, this was only interrogating the darkness. Suddenly he
rose and approached Deborah. She seemed to have become thinner.
She was still beautiful, but her features had become sharper, more
prominent, and she was tense. He took her by the hand, and they stared
at each other.

She asked, "Have I changed that much?"

"No, not really."

"Yes, I have. We both have. When we married, we inherited such
grand expectations, but now you are more concerned with disinterring
the past than living in the present."

There was nothing to be said in reply to such a remark. He released
her hand and returned to the desk. But when he went through his
notes, he had a feeling that they had been read. It was a strange,
unpleasant sensation. He asked Deborah if she had touched them.

"No. You get angry when I do. What's wrong?"

"I left my notes in a certain way. But they have been changed."

"You're sure?" She had a feeling of dismay.

"After all the warnings I was careful to arrange my notes in a special manner. To see whether these warnings should be taken seriously."

"You sound like a conspirator yourself."

"I may have to be." He walked around the room agitatedly.

A cry for help would have brought her to his side, but he seemed concerned only with his own judgments. She sat as if tied to the sofa.

He examined his books and then his clothes and said, "Someone has been reading my biography of Mozart. I left a marker at the page describing his death, and it has been moved. And I had some papers in the pockets of my greatcoat, and I can tell that they were touched, for they are in a different order now. Somebody has been here without our permission."

"Has anything been stolen?"

"Not that I can tell."

"Perhaps it was Hans."

"I will find out."

As Jason stepped into the corridor to fetch Hans, who was staying in the stable, Deborah cried out, "Don't be long!" but he wasn't thinking of that, for he could have sworn that a door closed suddenly in the hallway, as if someone had been watching their room. And after he left word with the innkeeper that their servant be called from the stable, he had a feeling that someone was skulking near their rooms, but while he didn't see anyone, he heard the creak of boards and the shutting of a door.

Deborah had another complaint. "They haven't given us any fuel for our stove. Do you think this was done deliberately? The fire has gone out. We could contract pneumonia in these conditions."

"So it was not a servant who was here while we were gone."

"It is getting so cold, I will have to wear my fur coat in bed."

"I will have Hans get some fuel and start the fire." Jason was annoyed; he felt that Deborah was distracting him. He had more important matters to consider. He had the sensation that things were closing in upon him, things that he could not see or touch or even anticipate, and for a moment the feeling of helplessness was overwhelming. But as he heard Hans at the door, that vanished. The instant he spoke to Hans, he should know whether their servant had been in their rooms.

Before he could ask, Hans said, "I'm sorry it took me so long to get here, but I was examining the new wheel, sir. It is not good. You will need another one if you intend to journey to Salzburg, Herr Otis."

"Were you in our rooms while we were gone?"

"Why would I do that, sir?"

"Someone was."

"Probably the hotel servants. They have keys, sir."

"Would they come in without our permission?"

"If they had to clean, sir, or make the bed."

Deborah said, "That was all done before we left this morning."

Hans shrugged.

She added, "And how did you know that we might go to Salzburg?"

Hans blushed momentarily, then said quickly, "You told me, Frau Otis."

But they hadn't, she was positive of that. *How had Hans known?*

She was irritated that Jason didn't share her incredulity, but said, "Hans, I would appreciate if you inquired downstairs whether any servants were in our rooms after we left this morning."

"Yes, sir. I will do my best."

She thought there was something pathetic in Jason's need to trust Hans, yet she had a feeling that if she overturned this, he might never forgive her. But she had to ask, "How are your relatives, Hans?"

"Fine, fine. They are fine," he answered hastily.

"Did you see all of them?"

"Most of them, Frau Otis. My uncle, several cousins."

"Where do they live?"

"Begging your pardon, Frau Otis, but you wouldn't know the neighborhood."

"I just might. Is it nearby?"

"The Landstrasse suburb, Frau Otis."

"And you walked there?"

"Frau Otis, I wouldn't take the coach. Not without your permission."

She didn't believe him. During the ride to St. Marx's she had observed that it was a long walk to the Landstrasse suburb, for she had been trying to determine whether the mourners who had turned back at the city gate could have done so for other reasons than Ernst Muller had considered.

Jason was impatient with her line of inquiry, interrupting her. "Hans, will you fetch fuel for our stove, ask downstairs whether any servants were in my rooms, and then I have a message for you to deliver."

"Thank you, sir. The storage for the coach and horses is cheap, and I can sleep in the stable. I will be happy to serve you in any way."

As Hans hurried out, she said, "Doesn't his relief that you are keeping him make you suspicious? I doubt he saw relatives at all." When Jason didn't reply, she blurted out, "Don't you have the courage to fire him?"

"You have enough half-facts to fill a book of attitudes. If I fire him now, assuming that he is not to be trusted, it will only make those who are watching us more suspicious. You must let me be the judge."

"What are you doing now?" she asked. Jason was writing busily.

"You will see." He continued until Hans returned with fuel. After Hans started a blazing fire, saying that the innkeeper had insisted that no one had been in their rooms, Jason handed him a letter and ordered him to deliver it to Herr Grob and to wait for a reply.

When they were alone again, he informed her proudly, "I'm asking Grob to arrange a meeting with Beethoven. It will indicate that I trust him."

"Do you?"

"Not necessarily. But if I offer also to deposit my funds with him, I should stop his mouth with it. And possibly get our passports back."

Deborah doubted that, but she said, "I still think that Ernst Muller is driven by self-interest. Like all the others."

"Naturally. But he doesn't deny it." Jason's voice took on a note of self-satisfaction. I assure you that your assumptions that I am naïve are wrong. I will use Grob to meet Beethoven, Ernst to meet Salieri."

"What about our rooms being searched? How can you avoid that?"

"We will move. Into private quarters where we will have no servants but our own. I must find Diener and the doctor who attended Mozart. Do you think any of the apothecary shops in Salieri's time sold poison?"

Jason didn't wait for Deborah to reply, but turned the key in the door to be sure that no one could enter. Then he picked her up bodily and carried her into the bedroom. Darkness was behind the windows, and with the uncertainties outside he had to feel something secure. After the pain and horror and grief at the cemetery and the sense of loss he had to express a gesture toward life. It had been such a sad day. But as long as he was active, he could go on. It was when he brooded that existence became impossible. Locked in her arms, he could even imagine that he was in an enchanted castle. When he kissed and embraced her and she responded fervently, he prayed that he be forgiven. Thirty-three years after death Mozart was still a living person, whatever could not be found, for his voice was everywhere; and still he wasn't sure that he loved her, but if she thought so now, it would suffice for the moment.

"Undress, please," he whispered. "Undress." That should end his doleful feeling. Perhaps she would support him even in his mistakes.

Their lovemaking lasted a long time. Deborah was astonished by Jason's passion, as if it poured out of him in a need to deny death.

But afterward, while an autumnal drizzle fell outside and Jason drifted into slumber, she heard him mumbling, "There is no body because it was poisoned. I have no choice." Yet Jason was so inert she put her fingers to his pulse to verify that he was breathing. How could she explain to anyone that his lovemaking was impossible to resist! He had such a fine, slim, loving body. It was the one shrine at which she could worship. The one time she felt fulfilled. But she could not sleep. What he had done had not lessened her worries but increased them.

The next morning she begged him to hide whatever he had written about Mozart. When he agreed to do so, she felt a little better.

18

The Ninth Symphony

G ROB was proud that he was on good terms with Beethoven. He felt that for a man of his taste that was as it should be. He saw Jason and Deborah at his office a few days later, as Jason had suggested, so that he would have time to communicate with the composer.

His bank was near his home and also on the Kohlmarkt, and he told them, "I've made inquiries directly to Beethoven. He is living in Baden, where he has been for his health; but he will be returning to Vienna soon, and he has agreed to see you in Vienna and discuss the oratorio."

So Beethoven was not living near the White Ox Inn, Jason thought, as Huber had stated. Had Huber lied? Or been misinformed? The last did not seem likely. But all he said was, "Thank you, sir."

"Since Beethoven is aware of my standing in the community, no doubt my support impressed him and added to his interest in your proposal."

"Is he concerned about money, Herr Grob?"

"From all the evidence, yes."

"What evidence?" Deborah asked.

"Just a few months ago he almost caused a scandal with his behavior."

"About money?" she asked.

"There were other problems, Frau Otis, as there are usually with Beethoven, but the amount of money he was to receive was a vital issue."

This sounded like Mozart's situation to Jason, and he was surprised; he had assumed that Beethoven had escaped such difficulties. He asked, "Did it concern his composing?"

"Two pieces he was trying to get played for the first time. But from the intrigues you might have thought it was an affair of state."

"What were the compositions?"

"One was a *Missa solemnis,* the other a choral symphony, the Ninth. In his efforts to get his two pieces performed, I thought he was going to turn Vienna into a battlefield. And a large part of his struggle was over the amount of money he was to receive." Grob motioned for them to be attentive while he resumed as if he were giving testimony in a courtroom.

"The affair began when Beethoven's friends heard that after years of silence he had finished a new mass and a choral symphony. Many people laughed at the idea that he could have composed anything new, for by now he was totally deaf. In reply his friends decided to arrange for a grand concert to show that he was still creative.

"The difficulties started at once. It was necessary to rent a theater for such large works, and the censor forbid that. The chief of police declared that it was blasphemous to sing a religious text in a theater. This should not have startled anyone, for a few years before Count Sedlnitzky had forbidden private dances during Lent, but it was also felt that the authorities were suspicious of Beethoven's motives, especially when it was learned that the finale of his new symphony was an ode to joy and was based on a text by Schiller. It was well known that his music, although allowed, was not necessarily approved by the authorities.

"So Count Lichnowsky, a friend of Beethoven's and an influential member of the Court, presented a petition to the chief of police, Count Sedlnitzky, for permission for the concert to be given in a theater.

"While this was being considered, there was intrigue over the theater. Count Lichnowsky convinced Beethoven that permission would be granted, for it was decided to use the Theater an der Wien for the concert. But Beethoven objected to the two music directors of this theater, and when he could not get the orchestra director he desired, he refused to consider the Theater an der Wien. He decided to rent the Karntnerthor Theater, although permission had not been obtained from the authorities.

"Now there were new quarrels. Beethoven said he was dissatisfied with the financial arrangements, particularly the price of admission, which he wanted increased. But permission for this had to be obtained from the Ministry of Police, and this was refused. Meanwhile, Beethoven had hired the theater and he had to pay for the orchestra, chorus, and all the other details of the concert.

"There was so much confusion, suspicion, and hostility among the various friends of Beethoven who were helping him arrange this concert, with his supervision, that no one seemed to consider the possibility that permission might not be obtained from the censor.

"But two days before the date of the concert, permission still had not been granted. Archduke Rudolf, the great friend of Beethoven, was in Olmutz; the Emperor was not in residence. In desperation Count Lichnowsky assembled the most influential people still in Vienna who were patrons of Beethoven, and they went to the chief of police, who informed them that Count Lichnowsky's petition had violated protocol, it had been sent by letter, and so it had been ignored.

"Count Lichnowsky begged Count Sedlnitzky's indulgence and explained that the mass was dedicated to Archduke Rudolf in honor of his installation as Archbishop of Olmutz and that it was a pious work.

"When Count Sedlnitzky didn't reply, Count Lichnowsky pointed out that a slight to music written in honor of the brother of the Emperor could be considered a slight to the Emperor.

"That, of course, made it a special matter.

"Count Sedlnitzky thanked Count Lichnowsky for calling this aspect of the music to his attention and said he would give his answer tomorrow.

"Dress rehearsal came the next day, just twenty-four hours before the scheduled performance, and no one knew what was going to happen.

"Beethoven, who often acted as a law unto himself, was in despair. He was pacing around the entrance to the Karntnerthor Theater, muttering, 'No concert! No concert! I shall never compose music any more! It is not worth this anguish!' when there was a message from the chief of police. Count Sedlnitzky had written Count Lichnowsky, as befitted the latter's position, saying that in view of the fact that only three hymns of the mass were to be sung, and the title was not to be used, no profanation was intended, and so permission for the concert was being granted."

Jason interrupted, "Was Beethoven pleased?"

"He was furious. He said he was being treated as a servant. He swore he would not allow his work to be done under such intolerable conditions. But when he was reminded that he had declared the new symphony was his greatest work, and that after this performance he expected to sell it for a thousand gulden, he agreed to allow the concert to go on."

Deborah was more interested in the outcome of the grand concert. She asked, "Was the music a success? This mass and choral symphony?"

"It depends on the point of view. Everyone wondered whether anybody would attend after the commotion and the threat of censorship, and thus, official disapproval. Instead, because of the attention that had been aroused there was not one available seat except for a single conspicuous absence. The Royal box was empty and no member of the Imperial family was in attendance, which was an obvious indication of Royal disapproval, although the official excuse was that the Emperor was not in residence.

"Conveniently, I reflected, but I was glad I was in my box. It was a stirring sight to see the theater crowded to the doors. The fact that the concert almost had been prohibited had stimulated the public's curiosity and they had come expecting something sensational.

"In my box with me were the three friends you met at my residence.

"Fritz Offner, in particular, was watching with great curiosity. He had published Beethoven's work with profit, and he was interested in whether the new symphony would be worth publishing. Despite Beethoven's reputation, Offner was a cautious man who recalled to the kreutzer what every piece earned.

"As I saw the composer take his place by the side of the conductor—Beethoven stood on the right, where, according to the program, he was to set the tempo at the start of each movement, although we all knew that this was impossible, he was so deaf—Offner nudged me and whispered, 'Beethoven may be a poor risk. With his poor health he is not likely to live much longer, and once he dies and his novelty wears off, his music might very well decrease in value.' "

Grob halted and said to Jason, "I'm telling you this because it relates to your present situation. You must be prepared to bargain. Despite Beethoven's fame, his needs could overcome his pride, which can be frightening, and give you an advantage that you might not have otherwise."

Jason asked, "Do you agree with Offner's opinion?"

Grob smiled sardonically and said, "Who can tell about the vagaries of public taste? Beethoven will ask more than he will expect to receive. Do you know how much you are willing to pay for the oratorio?"

"I'm not sure," said Jason. "It depends on circumstances."

Deborah asked, "Why do you think the chief of police changed his mind and allowed the concert?"

"Probably after he was sure that the music was not treasonous."

"How could he tell that without hearing the music?"

Grob regarded her indulgently. "It was no secret in Vienna that someone in the orchestra would be in the service of the police."

Jason cried indignantly, "A spy? An informer?"

"That is one way of putting it. However, I suspect that Count Sedlnitzky, as chief of police, was determined not to be taken by surprise. Once he was reassured about the music, after the dress rehearsal, he also didn't wish to offend Beethoven's powerful patrons, at least no more than necessary. And he is proud that he is an informed man. When I glanced about the theater to see who was in attendance, I saw him—surrounded by his staff as if he were an archduke—sitting in the rear of a box that commanded an excellent view of the theater, yet hid him from the view of the general public."

"What about Beethoven?" asked Jason. Count Sedlnitzky's shadow grew larger and darker each time he was mentioned, and Jason longed to be free of it. "Did you like his new compositions?"

There was a moment of silence as Grob reflected. He was proud of his judgments. He spoke quite slowly now.

"I have never cared much for religious music, so it was not until the new symphony began that I really listened. I realized at once that Beethoven had not accommodated himself to public taste, but had composed music that was solemn yet volcanic and quite relentless in its intensity as if he were shouting, *'Despite my deafness I've won. I've won and damn it all!'* And I found myself staring at his head.

"Beethoven, who was still standing by the conductor, was peering at the score as if to make certain it was being played as he had written it, yet I was sure that he couldn't hear a note. Then his head turned sideways as if somehow the ear that still possessed a slight remnant of hearing would capture a few of the sounds that eluded him otherwise.

"I thought that each time his music was played a part of him hoped that he would hear at least one note. But that was only a dream.

"When the symphony ended and the applause rose in a great storm of sound, one of the loudest bursts of noise I had ever heard, Beethoven stood unmoving, his back to the cheering audience, not hearing a thing.

"Just as it was becoming more than any of us could bear, Caroline Unger, who had sung in the symphony, stepped forward from before the curtain, where she had been acknowledging the tumultuous applause, and took Beethoven by the arm and turned him around so that he could see the waving handkerchiefs and the clapping hands. Suddenly his body, which had been stranded in a frozen waste of silence, groped forward, understanding now what was happening, and released itself from the ice with an abrupt bow.

"Mysterious instant, when he stood staring back at the waving, shouting audience and saw gleaming through the darkness a light as bright and as warm as the sun. I shall never forget it.

"The response to his bow was a prolonged crash of applause like the sound of thunder. Caroline Unger, whom he liked, nudged him again to acknowledge it. And as he did, the shouting and waving increased so passionately that suddenly I heard the chief of police cry out, 'Silence!'

"I was surprised, but I thought that for once Beethoven was fortunate in his deafness, he who stood like Orpheus in the Underworld.

"The crowd chose to ignore Count Sedlnitzky's command, as if, for once at least, they could disregard the censorship and release their emotions in a torrent of applause. It was the custom for the Imperial family to be applauded three times, but Beethoven was applauded five times.

"Doctor Lutz whispered, 'Sedlnitzky will wish he had prohibited the music after all. They will never be able to halt its future performances now.'

"The program was repeated several weeks later without any interference."

Deborah asked, "Did Beethoven make as much money as he expected?"

"No. He was grievously disappointed. After the excitement subsided, he was told that while the receipts were over two thousand gulden, after all the expenses were paid off, only four hundred remained for him. It made him very angry. But it could also make him more receptive to the oratorio. Herr Otis, have you come to a decision about your own funds?"

"Yes. I expect to deposit them with you. When I get settled."

"Splendid. You will not regret it."

Grob beamed so beneficently it gave him the courage to ask, "You would do me a great favor if you could speak to Huber about our passports."

"You realize now that Mozart died a natural death?"

Jason nodded, afraid that if he spoke he would betray himself, but he felt the color rising in his cheeks.

If Grob noticed, he didn't indicate it. He said, "I will do what I can."

"Thank you. I'm thinking of moving from the inn, and it is a nuisance to have to report to the police every step I take."

"The rooms are not comfortable?"

He couldn't tell Grob that they had been searched. He nodded again.

But Grob said, perhaps out of vanity, perhaps to show that he must not be underestimated, "Indeed, you will be more comfortable in your own rooms. Then you will be the only one who has the keys."

Jason was aghast. He felt himself turning pale.

Deborah said quickly, with a presence of mind that was a relief to Jason, "Herr Grob, you mentioned earlier that Beethoven's behavior almost caused a scandal. But from what you told us, I don't see how."

"He shouldn't have questioned the censorship. Public decency must be observed, and he could have caused public disorder. His music could have been used to create a public demonstration. His republican sentiments are well known. The outburst of applause was suspicious."

"Because he had two pieces of music performed?" Jason couldn't keep the scepticism out of his voice.

"It wasn't the music. It was Beethoven's resisting authority. That was what the audience was applauding as much as anything else. And the music would have been played eventually. Probably."

Jason wondered if Vienna's musical world was habitable. Until now he had thought so, but Grob had such a look of annoyance despite his effort to be diplomatic that the threat was plain. Or were they sparring still, talking in different languages, although he was pleased at how well he was understanding German, and without any help from Deborah.

But suddenly Grob was contemplative again, saying, "You must hear Beethoven's music yourself. It is being played next week, with a symphony by Mozart and a piece by Schubert, a new, youthful composer. When you meet Beethoven, if you can talk about his music it will please him. I will take you to the concert myself."

Sensing that Grob was offering him his hand, and that, whatever the difficulties, he was being useful, Jason said, "You are very kind."

Grob said proudly, "We are the most musical people in the world."

Jason said softly, "That is why we came here."

"Of course. You are a determined young man." After a long pause, Grob added, "As a demonstration the concert could neither fail nor succeed. But while the audience did show an excess of zeal, I must admit that the symphony gave them some reason. Sometimes I thought it was just a mass of notes and sometimes I thought it would never end, and I still don't know whether it is music one should or could enjoy, but curiously, its effect lingers on. When I heard it, I felt it was a crying out, Beethoven informing the world of his suffering in spite of the Ode to Joy, but now I realize that it was not a cry for help, for he knows that no one will help him or halt his suffering, that it was not even a cry of despair, no matter how melancholy he was, but a need to shake off his fears, a cry from the heart, a cry that must be heard with hope as well as sadness."

Jason almost asked Grob whether he would have felt this way if they had not been listening, but somehow he didn't, feeling that the answer was better left unsaid. Yet Grob had tears in his eyes.

19

A River of Life

ONE WEEK later the symphonic concert took place. It was given by the Austrian Philharmonic Society in the Karntnerthor Theater, and the program was the overture to *Rosamunde* by Schubert, the Symphony in A Major by Beethoven, and the Symphony in G Minor by Mozart.

"An all-Viennese program," Grob said reverently as he escorted Jason, Deborah, and Doctor Lutz to his box. "Vienna loves the symphony. We play this kind of music better than anybody else. We are the home of Haydn, the father of the symphony, and Beethoven, the master of it."

From the moment Jason entered the theater he was filled with wonder. This was the first symphonic concert he had ever attended. He had never seen so many musicians in an ensemble before. There was no such orchestra in Boston, or anywhere in America. He was fascinated by the precision with which the ensemble followed their leader. Then he was startled; Ernst Muller was playing one of the violins. Deborah saw Ernst, too, and she nudged Jason to keep that to himself, and he did.

Yet he couldn't take his eyes off Ernst. Why hadn't the elderly musician told him about this concert? There was so much to learn here, also. The more he listened, the more he wanted to listen and to absorb.

After the overture to *Rosamunde*, Doctor Lutz declared, "Schubert is a born melodist, he knows how to write a tune."

Jason nodded. He was pleased by the tenderness of Schubert's music. Beethoven, however, he realized quickly, was a different matter.

Before the Symphony in A Major began, Grob informed Jason knowingly, "This is Beethoven's seventh symphony. It was a triumph when it was first performed. An excellent piece. Rather patriotic, actually."

But Beethoven's symphony was far more than that, Jason thought, imperious rather than beautiful, dynamic rather than melodic, music without moderation, yet with a power that was compelling. This was a man to be reckoned with, the symphony stated that with every note, pursuing its uncompromising goal with an originality that bent the music to Beethoven's own personal use with a passionate expression.

Jason was quiet during the intermission while the others chattered busily. His heart, which had gone to Mozart's music swiftly, held back from embracing Beethoven, although he had been stirred. He had a feeling that Beethoven would not welcome such an attitude, as Mozart would. Yet the Symphony in A Major rang in his head, although he could not sing it to himself with pleasure as he could much of Mozart's music.

Deborah was surprised by how much she liked Beethoven's symphony. He spoke with such strength. She admired that. No wonder, she thought, he desired such a large price for his works.

The very first notes of Mozart's Symphony in G Minor filled Jason with amazement. Never had he heard any music that moved him so deeply from the first note. This symphony surpassed anything he had ever heard. It was as if Mozart had given his soul to this symphony. Here was a voice singing in the darkness, then emerging into brilliant sunshine. If God sang, Jason thought, He would sing like this. The emotion in this music shook him to the core. He felt perched in space, between heaven and hell, with a glimpse of both. *What a remarkable piece of work was Mozart!*

When the Symphony in G Minor was applauded enthusiastically, Doctor Lutz shook his head sadly and said, "And to think that this composition was never played in Mozart's lifetime."

Jason found this hard to believe. He said, "That is incredible. He was not an obscure musician when he composed it. Was he?"

"No. From the age of six when he became known as a child prodigy, he was one of the most famous musicians in Europe. And most of his music was played when he wrote it. Often that was the reason he composed it, for a concert that was being given or where he was to play the pianoforte. He was the finest pianist of his time, and he wrote most of his pianoforte concertos for his own performances."

"Are you certain he never heard this Symphony in G Minor?"

"Positive," Doctor Lutz said mournfully. "The last three symphonies he composed were not discovered until after his death. He never heard them except in his mind."

"Why? The G Minor is the most wonderful music I have ever heard."

"The reason is unknown."

"What a terrible thing to have never heard this symphony played!"

"And yet he went on composing."

Jason took a deep breath, then asked, although he saw that Grob was listening intently, "Do you think that the fact his last three symphonies were not played had anything to do with the circumstances of the time?"

"What do you mean?" Doctor Lutz asked. The applause had stopped and the audience was leaving, and Deborah stood up to go, quite restless.

"Herr Grob told me how Beethoven's Ninth Symphony almost wasn't played. Because of political circumstances."

Grob said, "That was different. I think we had better go."

"In a moment. Doctor Lutz, do you think the reasons were political?"

"Not in the sense that Beethoven's difficulties were."

"In any sense?"

Grob interrupted, but smiled indulgently to show that he was amused rather than annoyed, "I thought, Herr Otis, you were not going to involve yourself in such matters?"

"I'm not. But not to have had such beautiful music played when it was composed is inconceivable."

"Many things are inconceivable. But they happen. Come, there is a good coffee house nearby where we can discuss your visit to Beethoven."

Yet as they left the theater, Doctor Lutz fell behind Grob and Deborah and said softly to Jason so he wouldn't be overheard, "Anton thinks the following theory is foolish, but I've held it a long time. I have always felt that the reason Mozart was neglected the last few years of his life had nothing to do with him actually. It was the time. By 1789 the French Revolution had begun with the fall of the Bastille, and by 1791, the year of his death and grossest neglect, Marie Antoinette was imprisoned and threatened with execution, which happened later. She was an Austrian princess and sister of the Emperor. Naturally the concern of the Imperial family was for her, and their own safety. The revolution in France had become such a danger that the nobility, particularly the Imperial family, had neither the time nor the interest to be concerned with a mere musician. His fate was not of the slightest consequence to them, especially compared to Marie Antoinette's peril. This was why Mozart was so neglected, and why he died so young. Once he was ignored, he became impoverished and he was unable to support himself; and his fatal illness was a result of these unfortunate circumstances."

"You're saying that Mozart was a victim of the French Revolution?"

"Essentially, yes."

"Yet you implied that he could have had many enemies."

"Who may have injured him. But if anything killed him, it was the revolution in France. Mozart was a victim of his time."

Jason realized that Lutz was convinced of that. And possibly, he reflected, the circumstances of the time had conspired against Mozart and had hurt him. But that still left many unanswered questions.

The coffee house was near the Karntnerthor Theater, and there was attractive grillwork over a wide, wooden, handsome door. The interior was spacious and well lit, with lamps located over many of the tables.

There was an abundant choice of things to drink, Grob pointed out,

Bavarian beer, noble Sexard wine, black coffee, white coffee, sugared water, hot punch, and brandy.

Grob was well known in the coffee house, for a waiter led him to a familiar round table which commanded a view of the entire main room.

He liked to see who entered, and he said, "Schubert comes here occasionally. Did you like his music, Herr Otis?"

Grob had seated himself between Jason and Deborah, with Doctor Lutz on Deborah's side, and obviously he wanted Jason to declare himself.

Jason said, "Yes, I found Schubert's music charming. Thank you very much for taking us to the concert. Much of it was a revelation."

"Schubert is a promising young composer. Did you enjoy the Beethoven symphony?"

"Is Beethoven as imperious and demanding as his music?"

"He likes to think himself impregnable, and when he finds that he isn't, he gets upset. He is returning to Vienna next week, and I'm arranging for you to visit him. Frau Otis, did you like the concert?"

"Yes. Particularly the Beethoven." She had been so moved by the Mozart Symphony in G Minor she felt that was a private matter and she didn't want to discuss it.

Jason asked, "Herr Grob, have you spoken to Huber about our passports?"

"I promised I would."

"What happened?"

"Herr Huber said he is considering your request."

"But he did not return them?"

"Not yet. But that should only be a matter of time, Herr Otis."

Deborah asked, "Did he tell you when?"

"It is a mistake to try to change the way the police work, Frau Otis. They have their ways; and if you accept them, there should be no further difficulties. If everything goes smoothly, you could have your passports back soon. Herr Huber was impressed by my appeal."

She said, although she wasn't sure it was true, "We know you have done your best. It gives us pleasure to have you as our friend."

"Thank you. And I hope you will accept my humble advice. If you move, I would inform Huber. He will know in any case, and if you should fail to tell him, it could give an unfortunate and awkward impression."

Jason said, "I will keep Huber informed. Does Beethoven know that I want to see him to commission an oratorio?"

"I didn't communicate that directly. I thought you could do that better yourself. But the fact that I made the inquiry impressed Beethoven. He admits that he is in need of money, and the knowledge that I am representing you in this matter must have been decisive. Beethoven is very much aware of the reputation of my banking house, and so he said he would be happy to make your acquaintance.

However, he is a man of many moods. Don't be surprised if he changes his appointment several times, or his attitude during your meeting."

As Grob went on with what Jason felt was self-adulation, his attention returned to the Symphony in G Minor. On reflection it was even more beautiful and sublime. Overwhelmed with emotion upon hearing it, now he yearned to go back to this music again and again to experience the wonder of it. Why hadn't Deborah said anything? Didn't she like it? He could never forgive her if she didn't.

Deborah asked Grob, "Then you think Beethoven will be receptive?"

"He let it be known, thanks to my recommendation, probably yes."

Doctor Lutz, who had been reflective like Jason, said suddenly, "Herr Otis, I believe Mozart offered his Symphony in G Minor to several music publishers—Fritz Offner, for one—but they refused to consider it."

Jason said, "That is amazing. The one time I would regret dying is when I would realize that I would never hear the G Minor symphony again. Don't you agree, Deborah?"

She didn't know how to answer. While she liked the G Minor symphony better than anything else of Mozart's that she had heard, she resented the way it was usurping Jason's emotion. It was a direct threat to her. Jason was even more infatuated with Mozart than before, and worse, more in love with Mozart than with her. Yet now that she had heard this music, it was increasingly difficult to dispute that; the G Minor had reached her like none of Mozart's other music had. But she must continue as if nothing had changed when, in fact, much had changed. She could not add to his regard for the symphony, or tell him how much she liked it herself. So she equivocated. Jason was looking very impatient, and she said as calmly as she could, although she felt anything but calm, "It is interesting music. Almost like a river of life. But I would like to hear it again before I say anything further."

20

The New View

LATER that week Jason found rooms on the Petersplatz which he felt were suitable for his needs. He didn't tell Deborah of this decision, but took her to see them after he decided to rent them. The Petersplatz was a short distance from the Platz Am Hof and as they walked toward the rooms, he kept the purpose of this journey from her. It gave him great satisfaction that he had chosen these quarters without her help.

They moved silently along the Graben, then into the Petersplatz, which was a small square just off the Graben, and around an old church, St. Peter's, and suddenly Jason halted.

Deborah felt that she had collided abruptly with an inexorable fact. She had hoped that this walk would dissolve the barrier between them, that they would be able to talk freely to each other again, for he had been distant ever since he had heard the Symphony in G Minor, as if, once more, she had betrayed him because she could not share his enthusiasm. She had tried to walk as closely to him as she could without appearing to be a woman of the streets, but he had hardly spoken.

Now, however, he was talkative. He stood before a gray, square three-story house, much like the one Mozart had lived in last, and he stated in a rush of emotion, "I have rented five rooms here. The landlady lives on the ground floor; we will have the entire first floor; the second is empty, which will make our quarters quiet; and Hans can stay in the attic. There is a small stable a few doors away for our carriage and horses, and a garden in the rear of the house just for our use."

His decision had been duly delivered, she thought, without a word from her. She felt humiliated that he had committed himself without her, and she could not allow herself to look impressed. She replied, "It doesn't look very attractive. The church, which will be directly in our view, is one of the ugliest buildings I've ever seen, a lunatic mixture of gray and yellow, more Turkish than anything else, with its fat, round cupola, yet somehow, also, a poor imitation of St. Peter's in Rome."

"It is a fine location. We will have the privacy we desire, the Petersplatz is secluded, without the noisy bustle of the Graben, yet we are centrally located. We are just off the Graben, the heart of Vienna."

"What about the light and air?"

"The house faces south and west so that it has sun and warmth. And unlike the damp, dark, narrow streets you dislike so, the Petersplatz is as open and spacious and light as any location in Vienna."

She shrugged, still determined not to be impressed. She did like the location; it was what this move portended that oppressed her. Once they moved into this house it could become their permanent residence.

"We are also within walking distance of Ernst Muller and Grob, and just a few doors away from where Mozart lived and courted his wife."

"Did Muller show you this house?"

"What's wrong with that?"

"You saw him without me?"

She made that sound like an accusation, and that angered him. But he didn't reply. He resented her proprietory need to know his every act, to be with him always; he was pleased that he had avoided this and had found these rooms by himself, after Ernst Muller had suggested them.

She said, "I thought you didn't trust Muller?"

"I don't, in some things. Come, I'll introduce you to our landlady."

Now Deborah felt betrayed as well as humiliated that Jason had made this vital decision without consulting her, but she feared that if she refused to accept this decision he would abandon her, and so she followed him.

The door was of heavy wood, and he had to bang on it to be heard. She wondered if Jason was improvising a prison for her, but the *Hausfrau* who answered his knocking introduced herself at once as Martha Herzog and greeted them warmly. The landlady was short, frail, her skin wrinkled like parchment, but she was voluble, telling Deborah immediately that her husband and two sons had been killed in the Bonaparte wars, thanks to the Hapsburgs, and that the only thing she had left was her house, and yes, Herr Mozart had resided just a few doors away.

Then Jason led Deborah upstairs to the rooms he had rented. The ancient stone stairway was unlit and as she climbed up with a clumsy awkwardness, she felt assailed by the gloom and the darkness.

Outside the entrance to the rooms Jason paused and kissed her deliberately, as if to use this as a final persuasion, but she neither responded nor recoiled; there was no excitement in her, only a growing and consuming weariness. Unsmiling, she followed him in. If he had just compromised a bit, asked her, "Could we have a two-week trial here?" But to be confronted with a *fait accompli* was too much to accept willingly.

The first room—"our reception room," Jason said—was small and plain, and she was not impressed. But the next one—"the living room," he announced proudly—was a different matter.

It was pleasing even to her critical eye. Large and square in shape, it gave her a sense of space which she liked. The chairs were of white brocade, there were two fine oak tables, and a small chandelier in the center of the ceiling, but then she saw the marks of boots on the red velvet chaise-longue and she was dismayed. "Where a French officer slept." Jason informed her, "during the occupation of Vienna by Napoleon."

He was proud of the French windows that faced the Petersplatz, and he announced, "We will have sun all afternoon."

She was surprised by the music room. It contained an imposing black pianoforte and many books, including some on music.

"A musician lived here," Jason declared, "and put in the furnishings himself. This was to be his permanent home."

"What happened to him?"

Jason frowned, then hesitated and didn't reply.

"He is in prison? Sick?"

"No." Jason sighed, then said, "You will find out eventually. He died a few weeks ago. That was why these rooms were available. He was a friend of Ernst Muller's, who directed me here."

Deborah's pleasure at the wisdom of his choice evaporated. The thought of living where someone had died, of putting her flesh where his flesh had been, was a reminder of her own mortality and she wanted to flee.

Jason maneuvered her into the bedroom and he said happily, "In addition to being able to play and to compose here"—which, in her mind, fitted her fears that he was visualizing these rooms as a permanent residence—"we have a lovely garden in which to read and to relax."

The bedroom, which was in the rear of the house, looked out on a charming, fertile garden and a small, attractive courtyard. She stared at the trees, the fountain with the stone nymphs around it and the figure on top that appeared to be Venus and from whose mouth the water flowed. She saw birds and flowers, and Jason regarded the garden lovingly.

"But what about the bed?" she asked. "Is it comfortable?"

"It is excellent. It has a solid mattress and heavy blankets. The musician who lived here liked his comfort."

"What did he die of?"

"I don't know. Besides, does it matter? We're fortunate that such fine rooms are available."

He sounded heartless, she thought; he would have resented it if anyone had said that about Mozart. But she tried to be practical. "What about the heat? Winter will be here soon, and I don't intend to freeze."

"You haven't been very observant. There is a stove in each room."

Oddly, she had not recalled seeing any. Had she been so distraught?

"We even have our own water closet. Opposite the bedroom."

She sat down on the bed, thinking this was preposterous; Jason was planning to live here a long time and he didn't have enough money for more than a few months' expenses, whatever the rent.

He said, "Aren't the rooms lovely? What more could we want?"

But she could not allow him to become inordinately fond of these rooms. They were threat enough as it was. She asked, "How much is the rent?"

"I can afford it. Don't you like them?"

His tone was so plaintive, suddenly she couldn't say no. While she kept her head down so that he couldn't see the doubt in her eyes, she whispered, "They are better than the inn."

"And with Mozart having lived just a short distance away, it gives one an extraordinary sense of his presence. As his G Minor symphony did."

She nodded.

Jason beamed. He must feel as Mozart felt. And here he should.

She felt that the barrier could be dissolving between them; and when he said, "I made sure that the bedroom looked out on the garden so that it would be quiet, that the rooms would be finely furnished," she tried to look impressed. In those circumstances she also found the courage to say, "It would make me happy if you allowed me to pay at least half the rent."

His face darkened, but she went on swiftly while she had the chance.

"Jason, dear, you must realize that I have never reproached you for what you have done. I have never mentioned money unless it was essential. But in your own way you have made this trip very expensive. That is no disgrace, but a fact. If you intend to use only your own money, you will come to your journey's end with these rooms."

"That is a risk I must take."

"I don't see why. It is no crime to have ample means. Oh, I know that often you seem displeased with that, but once you married me and set forth, you should have accepted that situation."

Possibly there was truth in what she was suggesting, for he had contemplated staying in Vienna; lately he had not even thought of Boston, not even during the horrid moments, yet he yearned to refuse her in icy tones. But at the rate he was spending money he had enough for just a few months now, and it was becoming more likely that he would have to remain longer. If only she didn't make her money sound so important!

"Once I contributed to your quest, I would feel a part of it."

"You paid for the coach."

"And that didn't lessen your freedom, but added to it."

He reflected a moment, then said, "That's true."

"You could consider my share of the rent a loan if you don't want to feel obligated. And return it later, after we are back in Boston."

But he made no effort to accept the money she was offering him.

In her exasperation she cried out, "How will you get back to Boston? You admitted you didn't have enough money to return, and now that things cost twice as much as you expected, the gratuities, the bribes, the ... "

He cut her short curtly. "I'll manage." He didn't take her money.

After they moved to the Petersplatz, Jason arranged to see Huber.

Police Headquarters were just around the corner, which Jason said was a convenience, but Deborah found that frightening. Yet this time they were ushered into Huber's presence without discomfort or delay.

Jason whispered, "Grob must have put in a good word for us."

Huber rose to greet them and asked them to be seated and said, "I'm glad you obeyed my advice to report your new address promptly. Herr Grob informed me that you have arranged to see Beethoven."

"Yes, sir," Jason answered. "As soon as he returns to Vienna."

"An oratorio should occupy him usefully. Do you have a text for him?"

"Text?" Jason had been waiting until he spoke to Beethoven, but Huber was waiting demandingly. "I've several in mind."

"I trust you will have a sacred subject for him."

"I will do my best, sir. Is Beethoven told what he should compose?"

"Sometimes. How long do you intend to stay at your new address? Since you are our guests, we wouldn't want you to abuse our hospitality."

"Three months. Or possibly, a little longer. With your permission."

"Longer?"

"Negotiations may take time. I hear that Beethoven can be difficult."

"Indeed." Huber wrote down their address on the Petersplatz.

Jason asked, "Herr Huber, did you know that Beethoven was in Baden?"

"Yes."

"But you said, sir, that ... "

"That the inn was near him. I remember. Does that trouble you?"

"Oh, no sir," Jason said hurriedly. "But you are so efficient, I ..."

"You were living close to Beethoven. Emotionally."

"Yes, sir. If our passports could be returned, it would be appreciated."

"I'm sure it would be." Huber made no effort to get them.

"You said that once everything was in order they would be returned."

Huber stood up, signifying that the interview was over.

Jason was furious, but he hid that, while Deborah was so cast down she blurted out, "What do we have to do to get our passports back?"

Huber replied, "Did you enjoy your visit to the cemetery?"

Jason exclaimed, "Then it was your people who searched my rooms!"

"Your rooms?" Huber was irate. "What is your proof?"

"My notes were in a different order than when I left them."

"Are you certain?"

"Positive. I made sure I left them a special way."

Huber said icily, "Some people are more inefficient than others."

Jason felt that Huber's anger was because his spy had been found out.'

Huber asked, "Was anything stolen?"

"No."

"We do not steal in Vienna. We are not inhuman. If you could tell me who took you to the cemetery, your passports could be returned."

Deborah wanted to tell Huber, but Jason said quickly, "He was a servant, sir, who merely showed us the way. I didn't think there was anything unusual in visiting a cemetery. It is an historic place."

"Only for one reason, Otis."

"I thought I might put up a cross. As an expression of my respect."

"You don't remember the name of the man who took you there?"

Jason hesitated. Then as if he had been trying to remember but had failed, he said regretfully, "I'm sorry, sir, but I don't."

Huber asked, "Did you find out what you wanted to at the cemetery?"

"It is very sad, sir. No grave, no cross, no record of the burial."

"But that has been accepted by the world. As you should."

When Jason and Deborah reached their rooms and they were sure that no one could hear them, she said that Huber had been warning them and that they should be grateful and heed him. But Jason felt that the police officer had revealed so much because of other reasons, possibly as a threat, or for reasons not yet clear. Jason could not sit still. He said that he had to see Ernst Muller at once and tell him of Huber's knowledge of the visit to the cemetery. Instead of being tense and worried as Deborah was, he seemed to welcome Huber's remarks as a challenge. She had a new fear that he was starting to enjoy the role of a conspirator and that the outwitting of Huber had become a game as well as a necessity.

He informed her proudly, "Another reason I rented these rooms is because there is a rear exit through the garden that nobody knows about except our landlady, and she has promised to keep it a secret. Should anybody be watching us, as I suspect someone is, they won't even know that we are gone. I musn't involve Ernst any more than is essential."

And although Deborah felt desperate, hearing this, she refused to be separated from him. She insisted on visiting Ernst with him this time.

Apparently they were not followed, for as they entered Ernst Muller's residence on the Weihburggasse, they saw no one on the street.

Ernst expected Jason. They had made an appointment for this hour, and Ernst assumed that they would be delighted with their rooms.

Deborah asked him who had lived there before them, and he didn't want to discuss that, saying, "The previous resident's death was sudden, sad, and unexpected, and will only depress you."

"Did you know about the secret exit? Is that why you suggested it?"

"Private exit, dear lady. Don't you prefer to move about unwatched?"

He was regarding her with quizzical amusement, which added to her irritation, and she snapped, "I presume that you also have an explanation for not telling us that there was an important concert taking place and that you were participating in it."

"I didn't know that you were that interested. Frau Otis, is it necessary for me to tell you everything I do before you will trust me?"

She flushed, although she was still not satisfied with his explanation; but before she could retort, Jason said impatiently, "Deborah, you're wasting time. Ernst, Huber knows that we went to the cemetery."

"And that I went with you?" Ernst looked alarmed.

"No. I said a servant took us there. He doesn't know it was you."

"Fine, fine." Ernst sighed with relief. "You are learning."

Learning to protect him at their own expense, Deborah thought bitterly. Muller was even more conspiratorial than Jason, and it made her unhappy. He was prowling up and down his room like a predatory animal, looking much younger than his years, while Jason waited attentively.

Then Ernst said, "I've learned that the three Weber women are all in Salzburg. I'm almost sure I can arrange for you to talk to them, and perhaps even to Mozart's sister, Nannerl, who has been failing. But you must have a reason for approaching them."

"I'm writing a book about Mozart. As a memorial to him and his music."

"No. Constanze's present husband, Georg von Nissen, is doing that. We need a better reason."

"Do you think I will be able to get permission to visit Salzburg?"

"If Beethoven accepts the commission for the oratorio, that should lessen Huber's suspicions. And that should take some time, so it would be natural for you to visit one of the most beautiful towns in the world."

"And Mozart's birthplace," Deborah reminded them. "Of which Huber is very much aware."

Ernst said, "Many people visit Salzburg for that reason. But you need a better one to see the Weber women, especially Constanze."

Jason suggested, "If I brought her something. Say, from America."

"A present," Ernst said reflectively. "Possibly a gift of money. You could tell her that it was from admirers of Mozart's music and an expression of respect for her as his widow."

Jason exclaimed, "An excellent idea!"

"It would not have to be very much."

"You decide on the amount. You will know what would please her."

Deborah was appalled. Jason looked as pleased as Ernst now that he had agreed to this scheme; he would never have enough money to return to America. She asked suddenly, "Ernst, could we hear music by Salieri?"

He looked affronted, shocked.

She was not to be put off, saying, "Since we have been judging Mozart by his music, don't you think we should do the same with Salieri?"

"But you won't like his music."

"Don't you think we ought to judge that for ourselves?"

"He is hardly ever played."

"Even though he is still alive?"

"His music hasn't lasted."

"I still think we must judge for ourselves. Don't you, Jason?"

Jason nodded in agreement, and although Ernst looked unhappy at the idea, he said, "I possess a sonata for pianoforte and violin by Salieri. If your husband is willing, we can play it now."

Jason had the feeling, playing Salieri's score, that he was violating Mozart, then he told himself that this was absurd. Salieri's music was dull, uninspired, with slabs of sentiment that left him uninvolved.

Deborah listened in the hope of hearing the grace, the assurance of a master, driven by a desperate need to prove Ernst wrong, and the more she heard the more she was bored. This sonata by Salieri was a tidy piece of craftsmanship and a musical vacuum. Only once did the music become melodic and pleasing, in the second movement, and suddenly she knew why. It was an imitation of Mozart.

When the piece ended, Jason and Deborah exchanged a glance of understanding and Ernst said in a voice unusually patient for him, "I didn't want to play Salieri because I dislike him. But perhaps you needed this view. Now you know why he envied Mozart so."

21

Beethoven

WHILE Jason waited for Beethoven to see him, he occupied himself with music and sightseeing. Mornings he practised pianoforte sonatas by Mozart and Beethoven and worked on one of his own; afternoons Hans drove him and Deborah about Vienna to see the interesting sights of the city.

He told her that this would show Huber, if Huber was having them watched, that they were engaged in innocent diversions, but she felt that he was trying to prove to her that Vienna and their new rooms could be hospitable, and she was not convinced, still uneasy about their situation, although she enjoyed some of the sightseeing.

One of his secret dreams was the hope that the closer he came to Mozart, the more like Mozart he would become. Ever since he had become aware of his life and work, he had felt a communion with his spirit. Yet he couldn't tell her that from the moment he had touched Mozart and his music, he had a dearly cherished dream of becoming a great composer; she would laugh at him. But Jason felt that he was still young enough, still formative enough to achieve this ambition, and there was so much fine music to hear in Vienna. So he practised and composed in equal measure. But when he finished his sonata for pianoforte and played it for her and asked her how she liked it, there was a strain in her.

She felt a conflict between duty and affection and she was silent. His new piece was too much like Mozart for comfort.

He sighed, "Truth naked and unashamed. Is that too much to expect?"

"It isn't a question of truth. How do you feel about your work?"

"I admit I've been influenced by Mozart. But I didn't imitate him."

"I didn't say that you did."

"What you didn't say conveyed more than what you did say."

There was another silence. Jason felt that he was learning a bitter lesson: there never would be the communion between them that there was with Mozart; Deborah would never regard him as a musician as well as a lover and a husband, and it was useless to seek to convince her.

As he stood up and closed the pianoforte with sudden formality, she

G *

said, "I'm sorry," seeing how deeply he was annoyed and feeling the shadow of disaster approaching, "but if you need reassurance . . ."

He halted her. "I don't wish to exact anything from you." He was wounded by her lack of understanding, but he couldn't admit that. Then, deciding to play his sonata for Ernst, he felt better. Ernst, he was certain, would take his composition seriously and be a comfort to him.

The sightseeing was less of a strain. For the first time Vienna was almost delightful, almost enticing. They viewed the Schönbrunn and Hofburg Palaces and they agreed that these were magnificent in their baroque splendor. They visited the Burgtheater, where Mozart operas had opened, and the Theater an der Wien, which first had housed *The Magic Flute*, and Jason sought to recreate those moments as if they had been magical, and Deborah accepted that as appropriate. He was impressed by the fact that Vienna was much smaller and compressed than London, which sprawled, while Vienna seemed to grow inward only. He found that useful and exciting; while she hid her distaste for the dark, narrow, crooked streets that were so much a part of the city and the oppressive feeling of being confined within a walled fortress, and she pretended that this was part of his hunt for the truth and a stimulating adventure.

Several experiences made a vivid impression on Jason. On the advice of Ernst, he saw the small house on the Schulerstrasse where Mozart had composed *The Marriage of Figaro*, and where, according to Ernst, Mozart had been happiest in Vienna, and the Palace of the Teutonic Knights at 7 Singerstrasse where Mozart had defied with great courage and considerable peril the Archbishop of Salzburg, Prince Colloredo.

The two locations were near each other and Jason insisted on walking down the Blutgasse to 7 Singerstrasse, which, he felt, Mozart must have done many times, in an effort to relive Mozart's feelings.

Jason imagined Mozart leaning against the yellow plaster wall of an old house on the Blutgasse, which was barely more than an alley, to jot down a theme that had occurred to him suddenly, and as he did passersby paused to stare at him, not because he was Mozart, but because he was doing something that they would never think of doing. Then, reflected Jason, Mozart must have brushed off the plaster marks from his coat and entered the square within the palace at 7 Singerstrasse with satisfaction. Here where he had been humiliated, he was returning in triumph.

Jason told Deborah of these speculations, and he was pleased that she nodded and listened as if they were of consequence.

She didn't think they were important, but she was determined to avoid any more quarrels. Her feet hurt from so much walking, yet she hid that, too, although she was glad that he decided to return to their rooms on the Petersplatz, which was a short distance away.

As they sat in their garden later—it was almost November and the days were growing cold, but there were still some leaves on the trees and Jason felt in a mellow mood—he said, "This is an ideal location. We can walk to so much of the city. And it is vital to get a sense of the Vienna that Mozart knew. I've learned many things lately."

She still differed with him about that, but she said, "Yes."

"And nothing has been touched while we were away. We are safe here."

"I hope so." Hans was approaching, and the less said before him, she felt, the better.

Hans took his hat off, which he did always in their presence and when Mozart's name was mentioned, and said humbly, "Herr Otis, I have a message for you from Herr Grob. His coachman gave it to me."

Jason read aloud the note Hans handed him:

> *Beethoven can see you now. I will call for you tomorrow afternoon to take you there. Pleasing to relate, he seems happy, even eager to see you.*

Yet Jason was nervous as they drove to Beethoven's rooms on the Johannestrasse the following day. Like so many addresses in Vienna, it was within walking distance, but Grob insisted that they go by coach.

Grob was bursting with advice, declaring, "Don't be startled if you find Beethoven's rooms untidy, even dirty and disorderly. His troubles with housekeepers are notorious. And he is always moving. Every year he has a different address, sometimes several. And you must be careful about the questions you ask him. The most innocent query can provoke an explosive reply. But you must not be timid or reverential. Respectful, yes, even admiring, but not obsequious, he hates that. And remember when it comes to money, bargain. Beethoven will expect that."

But how could he bargain with Beethoven! Jason was appalled by that idea, and his heart was beating very fast. He thought himself prepared, but now he was not certain. He held a package under his arm which he intended to present to Beethoven as an expression of his homage, a large bottle of the best wine he had been able to buy, for Ernst had told him that Beethoven loved wine. When Deborah and Grob had asked him what it was, he had refused to tell them. It must be his own surprise.

He had written a note with this gift, with Ernst's help, as a toast to Beethoven and so the composer could avoid asking him to write it down.

Ernst had warned him that this was important; anything that would lessen Beethoven's self-consciousness about his deafness was wise.

Now, the closer Jason came to Beethoven, the more he felt he had to defer everything else to convincing the composer to accept the commission. That was vital to throwing Huber off the trail. Deborah sat silently by his side in Grob's coach, while Grob had placed himself across from them.

Jason couldn't tell what Deborah was thinking or how she intended to act, which added to his nervousness, but surely she must comprehend the importance of this meeting, and perhaps she might not be too much of a hindrance, with her recent efforts to please him.

Just before Grob knocked on the door of the house in which Beethoven was living, he announced, "I have just received four hundred gulden from Herr Pickering, in the name of the Handel and Haydn Society of Boston, to be paid to Herr Beethoven for the composing of an oratorio. Herr Pickering says that the money is to be paid at my discretion."

Both Jason and Deborah were surprised, as Grob expected and desired. Before they could ask any questions—Jason was outraged that Pickering had placed such a condition on the payment of the money, and Deborah was shocked by her father's lack of faith—Grob knocked on the front door and it was opened by a young man dressed fashionably in a blue-and-yellow-trimmed frock coat, whom Jason judged to be about thirty.

Grob, who knew him, introduced him as "Herr Schindler."

Schindler was expecting them, for he handed Jason a gold-engraved visiting card, which said, *"L'ami de Beethoven."* Then he led them up winding stone stairs to the second floor, warning them, "Beethoven won't hear a word you say, even if you shout, so as soon as you enter, be prepared to write down anything you want to tell him." Outside the door to Beethoven's rooms, Schindler handed each of them a notebook and a large carpenter's pencil.

Deborah looked puzzled. Grob scribbled something which he hid from the others; while Jason wrote: "Dear Herr Beethoven, I appreciate your gracious permission to visit you. Your Symphony in A Major has made a profound impression on me, and I would consider it a great privilege and honor to introduce it to Boston and to America."

Beethoven didn't hear them enter, although he was expecting them. He was sitting by his Broadwood pianoforte and staring out the window at the trees in the courtyard outside, deeply preoccupied.

Like a belligerent statue, thought Jason: Beethoven's fist was clenched; his jaw protruded so that the lower lip extended perceptibly beyond the upper lip. The firmness of purpose was unmistakable, as were the size and strength of his head.

Yet as the visitors stood for a moment in silence while Schindler approached Beethoven to announce them, Jason was grateful for this opportunity to observe Beethoven without the latter's knowledge. He noticed that the hand which rested on the pianoforte caressed it affectionately. And he was fascinated by the contradictions in Beethoven's appearance. At first glance the composer was ugly, almost repulsive. His skin was dark, pockmarked from smallpox as were so many of his generation, and yet his cheeks were very red, almost florid. His features were so heavy and blunt they looked coarse. His nose was short and square; his jaw was wide and ridged with deep furrows; his eyes were small and deeply set. But when Schindler nudged Beethoven so that he would realize that his guests had arrived, his expression altered. Animation illuminated his brown eyes when he saw that one of them was a beautiful young woman and that Jason Otis was youthful and attractive also, as if youth and good looks appealed to him, and his features were pleasing in this instant.

Jason handed Beethoven the bottle of wine with the enclosed note on which he had written *"In homage to Herr Beethoven,"* and added what he had inscribed outside the door, and the composer's animation increased.

Beethoven stood up with sudden feeling. His fist unclenched and he took the wine with the same affection with which his other hand had caressed the pianoforte. He said, "Obviously you are not a red Indian or a savage of any kind. We must drink to your health. Schindler, get some glasses!"

Schindler hurried to obey Beethoven's order, and Jason saw that the composer was shorter than he had expected, about five feet four, and stout with a bulky squareness. And when Beethoven walked toward Deborah and kissed her hand gallantly, he bulged perceptibly in the rear, his buttocks sticking out like two uneven mountain crags, and he moved with a hobble. But now Jason was aware of his high, broad forehead, which was unusually large and which suggested a nobility of thought. As Beethoven smiled, an unexpected softness appeared on his face; and his interest in his visitors gave his features a quality of uniqueness that possessed its own truth and beauty, as if his personality had overridden nature, even nature's unflattering aspects, and his appearance manifested a significance that had to be regarded respectfully.

Beethoven said to Grob, "Why didn't you inform me that such an attractive young lady was going to visit me? I would have taken more care with my person. I don't believe that men should look like peacocks, but beauty should never be ignored."

Grob shrugged, but Beethoven wasn't really interested in his answer.

Beethoven turned to Deborah and asked her, "Are you musical, too?"

She wrote without hesitation, "Yes."

"Did you like my A Major symphony, too? Like your husband?"

She wrote, "Indeed. I wouldn't have missed it for the world."

Beethoven beamed, but then suddenly he was sad, muttering, "They so rarely play my music in Vienna now. It is Italian this, Italian that, and Rossini is the public's God. Is it the same way in America?"

Jason wrote, "Handel and Haydn are our favorites. And Beethoven." He was relieved that his constant use of German was making him more fluent in the language and that Beethoven spoke so distinctly he had no difficulty understanding him.

Beethoven was pleased by Jason's comment, and he replied, "Handel is my favorite, too," but before he could speak further, Schindler returned with glasses, and Beethoven motioned for Jason and Deborah to sit with him at a large, square oak table, ignoring Grob and Schindler.

Deborah was embarrassed by Beethoven's treatment of Schindler and Grob, and she took each of them by the arm so that they would have to sit beside her. And she was startled by Beethoven's indifference to appearances. She wondered where Schindler could place the glasses and the wine, for the table was crowded with pencils and notebooks, music paper and pen and ink, a rusted old yellow ear trumpet that looked unused, and many books.

But Beethoven, oblivious to everything but the moment, swept everything into the center of the table, although that increased the chaotic appearance of the room, and with an imperious wave of his hand he ordered Schindler to deposit the glasses and wine on the table.

When she pushed her glass toward Schindler, Beethoven gruffly told him to fetch two more glasses. She noticed that Beethoven's black suit was so rumpled it looked as if he had slept in it, or possibly, that it was his entire wardrobe. She saw a violin behind the pianoforte; otherwise the living room was like a huge second-hand shop, with objects strewn about in the most careless and disorderly profusion. There were dirty underclothes in a corner, unhung pictures in another; she was taken aback to see a *pot de nuit* under his secretary; straw spilled out of his sofa; its cushions were torn and wine stained; and his chairs were scratched and chipped. A way of living as distraught and as disheveled as his hair, she reflected, which rose above his high, domed forehead like a great, tangled, wild gray bush. His hair looked as if it had never been combed nor cut, nor washed either; yet suddenly Schindler excused himself, whispering to Deborah, "Water is leaking from his wash basin, which he doesn't hear. He took a long time at the water basin today, although you would never think so from his appearance. He wanted to be especially clean, and he can throw water on his face and head for hours. He thinks it is healthy, but some people believe that is why he became deaf, the constant cold water on his head and ears. . . ."

Beethoven shouted suspiciously, "What are you saying behind my back?"

Schindler wrote, "I was telling Frau Otis that the water is leaking."

"Fix it then, but don't whisper. First however, fill the glasses!"

After Schindler did so and went to fix the water, Beethoven didn't wait for him to return but proposed a toast: "To our visitors from America!"

"And to Herr Beethoven," Deborah wrote and handed that to him.

For an instant she thought she saw tears in his eyes, then she thought, No, he is too much of a curmudgeon for that. Yet he emptied his glass with one gulp and brushed his eyes with his arm.

Then he declared, "Now to business."

Grob gave Beethoven what he had written a few minutes before, and Beethoven, despite Grob's indication that this should be kept between themselves, read it aloud, "Herr Otis' offer for an oratorio must be taken seriously, for I have just received a cash draft from Boston."

Beethoven turned to Grob, asked, "How much?"

Grob wrote, "Four hundred gulden."

"It is not enough," said Beethoven, "but it is a start."

Jason wrote, "How much do you want, sir?"

Beethoven wished that the young American's German was better, as was his wife's, but at least he could understand it, and he answered, "Competition for my work is most intense. Five publishers desired my *Missa solemnis,* and there would have been more if I had been willing to bargain. I would have been bombarded with offers."

Jason wrote, "Sir, what sum would you deem appropriate?"

"A thousand gulden."

Jason recoiled. Elisha Whitney had told him that five hundred was the most the Society would pay, and Grob was shaking his head to say No. As Jason wrote, "The Society is honored by your interest, but . . ." the banker whispered, "You must bargain, remember."

Beethoven snatched the notebook from Jason's hands, not even bothering to read what he had written, and stated, "You are conspiring against me. Many people do. Vienna is a land of intrigue. I will compose the oratorio for England, where people are honest."

Deborah looked so distressed that Beethoven was concerned. He asked her, "What is wrong, Frau Otis?"

She wrote, "We have come thousands of miles to see you. To have it end in failure is heartbreaking." She was on the verge of tears.

Jason longed to embrace her, she was so moving and effective. Beethoven replied, "Dear lady, you must not be grim. It spoils your beauty. But I am busy and my health is uncertain. I have been ailing for many months, so that whatever I undertake, I must, on my honor, be sure that the compensation is adequate. It is not profit I wish, but merely sustenance to go on. You understand, Frau Otis?"

She nodded in agreement, smiled, and patted his hand approvingly.

"If you put in a good word with your husband, perhaps something can be arranged. If he will compromise."

Deborah turned to Jason, who motioned for her to continue, and she wrote, "You are most gracious and kind, sir."

Grob wrote, "Herr Beethoven, how much do you want for an oratorio?"

"I am not an investment!" Beethoven cried out angrily. He stood up abruptly. Jason and Deborah rose also, believing that the composer wanted them to depart, and he said, "Wait a moment. I prefer to discuss this matter without any merchants present. Herr Otis, you are a musician, aren't you?"

Deborah nodded again, this time fervently.

"Tell your husband to put his price in writing, and then I will consider it. Music publishers and bankers are my natural enemies. We must discuss this matter just among the three of us. Frau Otis, would you be free for dinner tomorrow evening?"

She waited until Jason said "Yes," and then she wrote, "We would be honored, sir."

Beethoven said to Grob, "I will discuss the oratorio with the Americans my own way, if you don't mind."

Grob shrugged, but he didn't disagree.

Beethoven asked, "Frau Otis, do you have your own carriage?"

She wrote, "Of course. Can we be of any service to you?"

"Indeed. Could you fetch some veal tomorrow evening? And fresh fish? I adore both, but my cook is abominable and I am not sure she will be here."

She wrote, "Who will cook the meal, sir?"

"Schindler, if necessary." Beethoven roared with laughter at that idea.

Schindler however, who had just returned to the living room, looked dismayed, and said, for the moment forgetting Beethoven's deafness in his own distress, "It would be calamitous. We have lost two kitchen maids and housekeepers in the last week, yet he insists on playing the host."

There was an instant of terrible silence, as if Schindler had committed the most grievous sin. Then Beethoven said in tones of the deepest melancholy, "And people wonder why I am so suspicious. Even my friends are always conspiring against me."

Schindler wrote, hurriedly, "I meant no harm, Master. I was merely telling your guests trivialities that would bore you."

"And taking advantage of my disability, as men do. What did Schindler say, Frau Otis?"

She paused, and Schindler wrote, "I said, Master, that we do not have the facilities to serve dinner. Your housekeeper gave notice yesterday. This morning the new cook ran away when you scolded her."

"Then find someone else. There should be somebody in Vienna who is willing to serve Beethoven."

Deborah wrote, "We will, sir."

He replied, giving his knee a great thump, "You do have character, Frau Otis. We will cook the meal ourselves tomorrow if we have to, even if we have to teach ourselves. You will not forget the veal or the fish, will you, Herr Otis?"

Jason wrote, as he wondered how he could supply Beethoven's request, "I will get the best in Vienna, sir."

"And bring your text for the proposed oratorio."

Before Jason could finish writing, "I don't have any," Deborah wrote, "Of course, sir. My husband has written much music for the Society. He is passionately eager that the text be worthy of your music."

Beethoven pressed her hand warmly, but was silent.

Jason was at the door when without conscious thought but unable to resist the impulse, he wrote, "Dear Herr Beethoven, forgive this question, but ever since I started this journey from Boston I have wondered, whom do you consider the greatest composer who ever lived?"

"Handel."

Jason wrote, almost in anguish, "What about Mozart?"

Beethoven paused, then said, "He is not an easy composer to discuss. Remind me, tomorrow, to tell you how I met him."

His eyes seemed to grow misty, and Deborah patted his hand again to show that she cared.

Schindler and Grob were in the passageway when Beethoven motioned for Jason and Deborah to linger. When he thought the others were out of hearing, he whispered, "If you could bring some more of that wine, it would be appreciated. Schindler says that it is not good for me, but sometimes it is such a comfort. And make sure the banker does not find an excuse to come along. He is much too mercenary to suit me."

Jason had to persist now, writing, "Sir, have you ever considered why Mozart was thrown into a common, unknown grave? How terrible it was?"

Beethoven growled, "He was a victim of the Viennese disease. Indifference." His voice became melancholy as he added, "But dreadful as that was, his fate was not as terrible as mine. My hearing—there is nothing left."

22

An Oratorio for Boston

THE following day was a frantic one. Jason felt that the fate of the oratorio depended on how cleverly he satisfied Beethoven's request, and he and Deborah spent most of the day scouring Vienna for a succulent joint of veal and for the finest fresh fish, and used Hans, but without any success. None of the food they found seemed good enough for Beethoven. They returned to their rooms so despondent their landlady asked them why.

When they told her, Frau Herzog laughed. She said that their problem, which had begun to assume immense proportions, could be solved quickly and easily, that she knew just where to shop. She took them to a market just around the corner from the Petersplatz, but in a secluded side street hidden from the main thoroughfares of the city.

Frau Herzog was partial to schwartsreuter, a trout found in the Salkammergut lakes near Salzburg and shipped to Vienna for those who could afford it, and she persuaded Jason to buy this delicacy.

After she obtained a large, fresh joint of veal free of fat, she insisted on cooking it herself. She overrode Jason's objections that there wasn't enough time, that Beethoven had stated he would cook it. Frau Herzog declared that the poor hungry man had not wanted to put such a burden on them, but that it was no burden to her; she would roast it well done as he must desire. This created another crisis. Jason said this would displease Beethoven—Jason preferred his own meat rare—but Deborah felt intuitively that Beethoven liked his meat cooked Frau Herzog's way, as a fellow German, and supported their landlady. The fish was a different matter, it was left uncooked, but it was kept fresh.

The preparations took longer than the landlady had promised, for she felt this was a grand occasion. Jason was distressed, for they were late already and he was sure that Beethoven would never forgive them for keeping him waiting, but finally everything was ready and she was packing the veal in her best dish, to be certain that the meat was properly covered and would stay warm, and she was saying, "Herr Composer will be pleased, I'm one of the best cooks in Vienna," when there was a knock on the door. Schindler stood there, and before Jason could ask him in, he said, "Herr Beethoven cannot see you tonight. But possibly later in the week. Saturday, perhaps."

Deborah's impulse was to decline, but Jason replied hurriedly, "Of course. Saturday evening. Unless we hear to the contrary."

"Yes. And don't forget the veal and the fish. Fresh fish."

Schindler was gone before they could ask him what to do with the food they had prepared already. Jason was disappointed by the postponement, while Deborah reminded him that Grob had warned them on the drive home yesterday, "Just because Beethoven has invited you to dinner, don't assume that it will go smoothly. I hear it rarely does. He could change his mind in an instant, his feelings can veer like the wind."

However, Jason had felt Grob was saying this because he was irritated by Beethoven's preference for them, but that the banker could not show such feelings. When Jason had tried to discuss Pickering's conditions, the banker had refused to discuss them, except to say that if Beethoven agreed to compose an oratorio for a reasonable sum—Grob didn't say what, although he implied that five hundred gulden might do—he would not raise any objections. And much as Jason resented Pickering's conditions, he had to be content with this.

Now Deborah was saying, "I don't think we ought to go Saturday. The same thing could happen at the last moment."

"But he liked you. Preferred you."

She shrugged and said, "He likes young people around."

"And attractive women. I think he is not so much indisposed as eager to impress us with his ability to be hospitable. Schindler probably convinced him that to serve dinner without a housekeeper or maid, and on such short notice, was obviously impossible. But by Saturday he will have had enough time to obtain the right help, to prepare properly."

"You may be right," Deborah admitted grudgingly.

Jason had a sudden impulse then. "Yet we will be there tonight in a way. I will have Hans deliver the veal and fish in my name."

"Our name," she interjected.

"If you wish. It will demonstrate that we care and are not offended." Jason added a bottle of wine to the package and sent it to Beethoven with their compliments.

Saturday night Jason and Deborah arrived at Beethoven's rooms with mixed feelings. There had been no response about their gift.

Hans had told them that a young man of about his own age had answered the door—he believed it was Beethoven's nephew—and had taken the food and wine without a word, as if such incidents had occurred before and were not worth commenting about. "But," Hans had added, "I noticed that he smelled the veal, for his nose wrinkled up"—Hans was proud of his powers of observation—"and he seemed to approve of what he smelled."

"Let us hope that Beethoven did," Jason said to Deborah as he ordered Hans to wait in their carriage on the Johannestrasse in the event that Beethoven would not see them. He carried a package similar to the one he had sent a few days ago, but he was determined not to present it unless the composer was receptive, and he held it under his greatcoat so that it would not be seen. Outside the door he paused to adjust his cravat.

This amused Deborah. She said, "I don't know why you should worry about your appearance. Beethoven doesn't worry about his."

"He is not interested in such things."

"Nevertheless, I would be more flattered if he were not so untidy. I feel it is an expression of his indifference to people. Perhaps to us."

"Indifference, yes. But not to us. Why should a man like Beethoven waste his time on keeping order in his household or such trivialities as his clothes, especially when he has someone else to do it."

"It doesn't justify his allowing himself to look like a shabby old man."

"You don't understand. Beethoven has such an overriding need to be creative that housekeeping bores him. Some people live for cleanliness, which takes a lifetime of practice, but a man like Beethoven, driven by creative energies unrelenting and constant, must be compelled to express them continuously. Keeping this tremendous volume of energy in order is his necessity, not cleanliness or housekeeping. For him, those chores are dull, boring, uncreative, and worst of all, repetitive, without any hope of surcease, and a waste of time, for there is never an end to dirt. So he has no time or energy for these things. He has to conserve himself for his composing, which goes on in him constantly, even without his knowing. He is attached emotionally to his music, not to his living quarters or the way he dresses. That is why he moves so much, but he never departs from his creativity or his composing."

"Mozart never behaved this way."

"Mozart wasn't deaf. Didn't you notice, Deborah, that even though Beethoven told us himself that he can't hear anything, he was straining to hear us? He kept inclining his left ear, his best ear, in our direction, as if, somehow, he would hear something. Think of what a strain that must be, what a torture, especially for a man whose whole life is lived in a world of sound. No wonder he is in such a state of tension and agitation; no wonder he is irascible. It may be why he cancelled our previous engagement. He couldn't endure feeling humiliated before people whose good opinion he desires."

Deborah didn't want to be carried away by Jason's emotion, but she couldn't ignore what he was saying. She resolved to be more observant, and more understanding. Yet she couldn't be too encouraging or Jason would disregard her feelings, and so she said, "What you say is interesting, but not necessarily true."

Jason knocked on the door, and Schindler answered quickly, handed them the usual notebook and carpenter's pencil, and led them upstairs.

Beethoven was standing so that he faced the door so he would know when they entered. The instant he saw them he hurried toward them and exclaimed, "I thought you would never arrive!" He took them by the arm and escorted them to his table, seated them on each side of him, and said, "How did you know I preferred my veal well done! Only a woman could have been aware of that. Frau Otis, you are a genius. I have been unable to afford veal lately, yet I have a special appetite for it. And I haven't had schwartsreuter for ages and it is my favorite fish."

When Jason brought forth a similar gift, Beethoven sat silently and shut his eyes to hide the extent of his emotion, while Schindler said, "You couldn't have brought him anything he craves more. He couldn't see you before because we had no help, but your food was a godsend. We obtained a new housekeeper yesterday. Her cooking doesn't satisfy him, but yours does, Frau Otis. He thinks that you are marvellous."

Neither Deborah nor Jason corrected that as Beethoven said, "The veal was so skillfully cooked, I knew you must be people of great taste."

Jason unwrapped the package and revealed he had included champagne.

Beethoven regarded Jason as if he were a Midas and declared, "Herr Otis, you are a man of sensibility. And the kindest of people."

Deborah noticed that Beethoven was wearing a neat brown coat which matched the color of his eyes, that the *pot de nuit* was gone and so were the dirty underclothes. But there was still much dirt in the corners of the room, and papers and books were strewn about carelessly. Yet after what Jason had said, cleanliness no longer seemed important. What did concern her was that when Beethoven went to get the wine glasses himself, to express his affection for them, he almost lost his balance and fell.

Impulsively she cried out, "You are not well, Herr Beethoven?"

And when she saw his bewildered, anguished expression as he sought to hear her and failed, she knew that Jason had been right. His deafness created a constant strain and torture, and worse, a feeling of frustration and rejection. As quickly as she could she wrote down what she had said and handed it to him while Jason took the wine glasses from him.

Beethoven replied, "It is living in the city. It upsets me."

But as he sat down, he had to clutch the table to keep his balance.

Frau Otis had almost guessed one of his worst afflictions, thought Beethoven; he must be more careful from now on. Some things he had to admit because there was no hiding them; but others he had concealed even from his closest friends, and certainly from Schindler, who despite his willingness to serve him, was officious and prying. But a man must be allowed some privacy, or he would never have any peace. Much that had happened to him since he had begun to lose his hearing had caused him sorrow. The deafer he had become, the more imperfect his balance had become. Many times since he had lost his hearing, a fast movement, a quick turn of the head, a gust of wind, or someone bumping into him had caused him to be dizzy, and several times it had caused him to fall.

He remembered vividly and with shame the time he had been bumped by a stranger on the Kohlmarkt and had lost his balance and had sprawled on the street in a ludicrous fashion. People had laughed, he could tell from their expressions, and while he had not been able to hear what any of the passersby had said, he was sure they had whispered to each other, "Poor old Beethoven, drunk again," when he was never drunk but dizzy.

But no doctor seemed to understand this. He wondered if Mozart had had such troubles with doctors. Had they misunderstood Mozart's ailments, too? Or not understood them at all?

After the fall on the Kohlmarkt he had felt ashamed and humiliated, and his embarrassment had lasted for days. Worst of all was the fear and the knowledge that he would fall again. As he had several times since, when he had moved suddenly and impulsively.

For an instant he almost blurted this out to the young Americans, they looked so sympathetic, especially lovely Frau Otis, but then he was afraid that even they wouldn't understand and behind his back mock him or feel sorry for him, which would be the hardest of all to endure.

Schindler opened the champagne. Beethoven ordered him to sip it first, and when he saw the surprise on Jason's face, he added, "Papageno knows what suits my stomach. There are some things it cannot absorb."

Jason recalled Schindler's card, *"L'ami de Beethoven,"* and thought, To establish this Schindler would take almost anything, even abuse, but he must never allow himself to fall into such a position.

Only after Schindler had sampled the champagne did Beethoven taste it. Then he proposed a toast: "To the oratorio for Boston!"

Jason and Deborah joined him, and Jason wrote, "You will do it."

"I have thought about it much these last few days, and if certain conditions can be agreed upon, I might be able to compose it."

Jason wrote, "What conditions, sir?"

"How much will the Society pay for it?"

Jason wrote, "I am honored by your interest, sir, but they will not pay a thousand gulden, although I am sure that this is a fair amount."

"That was for Grob's benefit. The banker insists on bargaining, so I gave him something to bargain. But we are friends. What will you pay?"

Jason wrote, "The Society authorized me to pay five hundred gulden."

Beethoven looked annoyed, and Deborah wrote hurriedly, "My husband wants to please you, sir, but his hands are tied by the Society. As it is, it was his idea to approach you."

Beethoven patted her hand and said, "Dear lady, I know that your husband is endowed with the most excellent qualities." He took a second sip of the champagne, after they did, then turned to Schindler and snapped, "I hope you told the housekeeper to heat the veal, not cook it."

Schindler nodded.

"You had better make sure," Beethoven ordered.

Schindler took the hint and went into the kitchen.

Beethoven whispered, "He doesn't have to know everything I do. If I do the oratorio for five hundred gulden, can I have the money in advance?"

Although Jason wasn't sure that Grob would agree, he wrote, "Yes."

"What about the text?"

This flustered Jason, and Deborah wrote, hurriedly again, "Dear Herr Beethoven, my husband considered several, but he decided finally to wait until you were consulted. He felt you should make that decision, that you would know best what text would be suitable." Jason, reading what she wrote, added, "Perhaps a biblical subject, like those of Handel."

Beethoven declared, "Handel is the greatest of us all."

Jason couldn't resist writing, "What about Mozart, sir?"

Beethoven answered, "Haydn and Salieri were my teachers."

Jason wrote, "But you said, sir, that we should remind you to tell us of the time you met Mozart."

"I did?" Beethoven glanced at Deborah for confirmation.

She nodded her head yes and pressed his hand warmly, although she wished it weren't so rough and hairy.

He hesitated, then said abruptly, "After we eat." He shouted, "Schindler, I can't wait forever for dinner. Our guests are hungry, too. What kind of a host will they think I am if I don't serve them soon. The veal was cooked already unless the housekeeper is determined to spoil it."

But when Schindler emerged from the kitchen a moment later, he was pale and stricken, as if he were about to announce a catastrophe.

Beethoven yelled, "Don't tell me, Papageno, she's spoiled the veal?"

Schindler wrote, "She has had an accident."

"She burnt it, the idiot!"

"Worse," Schindler wrote. "She let the fire go out. We will have to wait until she can start it again, and that might take an hour."

While Beethoven glowered angrily, Jason wrote, "Sir, we don't mind waiting. You could tell us about Mozart now."

Beethoven shouted, "What is there to tell! I came to Vienna to study with him, I met him once, then I had to return suddenly to Bonn, and when I was able to come to Vienna for good he was gone. A candle snuffed out."

Jason wrote, "Were you surprised by the suddenness of his death?"

"Everybody was. He was only thirty-five. Only fourteen years older than myself. And once I was mature, it wouldn't have been much of a difference. We might have become friends."

Jason wrote, "Sir, you must have wondered why he died so suddenly."

"What was there to wonder about! He was improvident."

Jason wrote, "Was that the only reason for his early death?"

"Possibly not. Certainly he depended too much on noble patronage. It is why I resolved never to become a victim of the nobility."

Jason wrote, "What about Salieri?"

"What about Salieri?" Beethoven's face grew red, almost apoplectic.

Jason wrote, "Some people think he might have caused Mozart's death."

"How idiotic!"

Jason wrote, "Yet it is said that Salieri confessed to that, sir."

"I know. The rumors are everywhere. But they are only rumors."

Schindler interrupted to write, "Yet you have speculated about that."

"Speculated, yes, why such rumors developed. But I have never believed them. Do you believe them, Frau Otis? Is that why you are here?"

She wrote, "We are here to meet you. And to discuss the oratorio."

For the first time, however, Beethoven regarded her suspiciously.

Sensing that, Deborah wrote, "But naturally, we are interested in your view of Mozart. As one master about another."

Still Beethoven hesitated, and then, driven by a force that transcended everything else, he cried out, "How could I forget my meeting with Mozart!"

23

Beethoven and Mozart

WHEN he saw they were listening intently, he continued with a great rush of emotion. "All my growing up was directed toward what Mozart was. My father was determined that I become another Mozart, as if there could ever be another—the stupid, drunken, irresponsible fool! But in his mind I was to be another child prodigy, wasting myself on people who would regard me as a freak, famous—like the child Mozart, for how I could amaze rather than for how I could satisfy musically. I hated that and I fought my father's influence every chance I got, although he punished me constantly.

"Yet, loving music, and influenced by my grandfather and by my first teacher of consequence, Christian Neefe, I studied hard, and when, at the age of fourteen, I was appointed second organist in Bonn with a yearly salary of one hundred and fifty gulden, I felt quite grown up.

"Several years later, when Neefe arranged for me to visit Vienna with the hope of studying with Mozart, I was tremendously excited.

"I knew much of Mozart's music by heart. He was regarded in 1787 as the greatest living musician; and while I felt that some of his court music was too rococo for my taste, I was devoted to his compositions for the pianoforte—they were so lucid, precise, and controlled.

"But when I said goodbye to my mother there were tears in my eyes, for she looked so frail and aged, and we loved each other dearly—I loved her more than anybody else, for I could always trust her, she never betrayed a confidence, a hope, a dream—and so I left Bonn with mixed feelings.

"However, once I was on the road my excitement returned. Vienna was the capital of music and I had a letter of introduction to Baron van Swieten, who was a close friend of Mozart's. Only Neefe had made one mistake. Neefe had sent me off in the middle of winter. The roads were mud, ice, and sleet. I had to ride in the public stagecoach, for I couldn't afford anything better, and while I was wrapped in furs, I was always chilled and my hands hurt often from the cold.

"But finally, in April, I was in Vienna and van Swieten said he would introduce me to Mozart. He was a solemn middle-aged man, going bald, which he hid with a large wig, but he was very influential, a famous patron of music, who held important positions with the Emperor.

"The day I was to meet Mozart I was very nervous. What could I say to such a man? I had learned, too, that he was composing an opera for Prague—I discovered later that it was *Don Giovanni*—and that he was troubled by his father's illness. His father was dying, and he was deeply attached to his father, unlike me, and I was afraid that he would have no time for me. But I sensed that van Swieten wanted to get the meeting over with, that he was doing it mostly to impress Neefe with his influence, and so, despite my fears, I knew I must seize this opportunity now.

"At the last moment, as we were preparing to visit Mozart, the Baron asked me, 'Couldn't somebody else hear you, boy?'

"I was only sixteen, although I looked older with my dark skin; but I resented his patronizing tone. So, while I wanted to sound polite and grateful, I blurted out, 'I want only Mozart!'

"Van Swieten was annoyed, and I heard him mutter to himself—my hearing was satisfactory then—'I am not sure Mozart feels the same way'; but he called his carriage after he was certain that I was dressed correctly.

"This surprised me. I didn't expect a man like Mozart to care how people dressed. But van Swieten was resolved that I look like a proper little gentleman, although I felt like a court flunkey in a green coat and breeches, and a dark wig to go with my complexion.

"Mozart was residing on the Schulerstrasse and as we entered the small courtyard before his rooms and we climbed the winding staircase to the first floor, I thought, No matter what well-conceived plans I create, it will happen differently from what I expect.

"Mozart's wife, Constanze, a slight, short dark-haired woman with bright, dark eyes, nice slim ankles, and a good figure, admitted us.

"But Mozart was surprised and irritated to see me. He was in the middle of composing, and he had forgotten that he was to hear me. He exclaimed to van Swieten—the Baron had led me into Mozart's music room, to show his familiarity with the composer—'Who is this, van Swieten?'

"'Ludwig van Beethoven,' van Swieten answered. Mozart looked puzzled until the Baron added, 'Neefe's prodigy from Bonn.'

"'Oh!' Then as I stood in front of Mozart feeling unprepossessing and stupid, I sensed that Mozart felt this, for he half-apologized, saying, 'My father is very ill, and it is not a good time for me.'

"Van Swieten expressed his regrets, which eased Mozart's irritation. Then the Baron said he would pay for my lessons, although I felt that Mozart didn't believe him and neither did I, for van Swieten had exhibited penuriousness on several occasions since I had met him.

"Mozart stood up as van Swieten introduced us formally, and I was startled by his smallness. He was considerably shorter than I was, and I was only sixteen and not tall for my age. He was also quite pale, as if he rarely spent time in the outdoors I loved so much. As Mozart fondled his fine fair hair—he was not wearing a wig since he had been composing—I sensed that he was rather vain about his hair.

"Not knowing what to do, I thrust out my hand and shook his. Violently, I am afraid, for he seemed to shrink from my grasp. For an instant I thought he was going to dismiss me after all, but after more discussion with van Swieten he agreed to hear me perform on the pianoforte, reluctantly, I felt.

"I insisted on playing one of his sonatas and I could tell when I finished that I had not played quietly enough to suit his taste, for he compared me to his favorite pupil, Hummel, who was only nine.

"Afraid that all was lost, I cried out, 'May I improvise, Herr Kapellmeister.' I sounded so insistent—actually I was terrified—he nodded, but, I felt, even more reluctantly than before.

"Once I was improvising I felt at home; and where I had been cautious with his sonata, I played my improvisation with all my power. I doubted that he would enjoy this, or even like it, it was so different from his own style, but I had to express myself my own way.

"When I finished he gave me another theme to improvise.

"Composing was my great love, and encouraged a little, I played with all my heart. This time when I finished, he sat silently for a long time. Just as I was sure that I had failed to convince him of my worth and I felt miserable, he said something that I have never forgotten."

Beethoven paused to savor this memory, but when he saw the entreaty in Deborah's eyes, he resumed, "Van Swieten asked Mozart what he thought of my improvisations, and he said, '*Listen to him carefully. His music will make a fine sound in the world.*'

"I was very excited by his praise, but I couldn't show that—I was proud. Yet when van Swieten asked Mozart to teach me, I asked also. After some deliberation Mozart agreed to accept me as a pupil and told me to return in a week and then he would arrange a schedule of lessons.

"I replied that I was more interested in composition than in playing and that he was my favorite composer, and he said, 'I hope you still feel that way when we finish,' sarcastically, I felt, yet hopefully, too. I was happy, although I hid that, believing that would indicate weakness.

"Van Swieten drew Mozart aside to discuss a commission, and I heard Mozart declare, 'I will not bargain. I want two hundred gulden for the opera or nothing.' Yet in the next breath I heard him whisper to the Baron, 'This boy from Bonn will make a splendid pupil in composition if he is interested. I will teach him for nothing if it is necessary.'

"I glanced about his music room, which I thought was going to be my salvation. It was long and narrow, with naked cupids on the ceiling and they embarrassed me. Yet I realized I would always remember his music room—they call it the *Figaro* room now, for he composed that opera there—and the cupids, despite their suggestiveness. But at

220 THE ASSASSINATION OF MOZART

sixteen it was easier to stare at the table upon which he had been composing and at its green cloth, almost the same pattern as my breeches, the yellow quill pen, the white candle, and the dusty violin.

"A moment later Mozart was saying goodbye to me. My last view of him was of a slight, small, pale man in untidy breeches, half dressed, an inconspicuous-looking person until he smiled. Then, as he regarded van Swieten affectionately and begged him, in a beautifully melodious voice, to forgive his brevity, but next week he hoped he would have more time to spare, I thought he had a lovely, endearing smile."

24

Beethoven and Salieri

BEETHOVEN halted, very emotional.

Deborah wrote, "Dear sir, what happened then?"

"I never saw him again."

"Why?" she wrote.

"I had to return home, My mother had become quite ill. A little later she died. By the time I was able to come back to Vienna, he was dead."

Jason wrote, "Do you think that Mozart died a natural death?"

"Probably. You could see that he was a bad manager, why he fell into debt. He could turn down a commission for two hundred gulden that he needed urgently, yet in the next breath offer to teach me for nothing. Which would have been a mistake. No wonder he died impoverished."

Jason wrote, "Sir, do you feel the same way about his music?"

"Young man, Mozart had a wonderful instrument—himself. His music was his personality. He was able to convert his inner pain and joy into genuine feeling and express great happiness or break your heart with the beauty and sensibility of his art. He never abused his ability, although he may have abused his body. His music teaches us many things." Beethoven bowed his head reverently in memory of Mozart and his music.

Jason honored this for a minute, but then his impatience was too much for him and he wrote, "What do you really think of Salieri's confession?"

Beethoven said angrily, "Salieri was my teacher."

Jason wrote, "But what about his confession. He is in an asylum."

"He is mad."

Jason wrote, "Perhaps he was always mad."

Beethoven jumped up abruptly and said curtly, "I must see how that idiot of a housekeeper is managing. If she doesn't serve the dinner soon, I will die of starvation." He hurried into the kitchen.

When Schindler was sure that Beethoven was out of sight, he showed them one of Beethoven's conversation books and what he had written in it.

Salieri has cut his own throat, but he is still alive. He maintains that he poisoned Mozart. He is quite deranged. In his ravings he keeps claiming that he is guilty of Mozart's death. He insists on confessing to this crime, and it is said in Vienna there is a priest who heard his confession. The odds are a hundred to one that Salieri's conscience has spoken the truth. The manner of Mozart's death confirms this statement.

Jason cried out excitedly, "Then you agree with me, Herr Schindler?"

"Yes."

Deborah asked, "But what about the police? Aren't you afraid of them?"

"They wouldn't dare touch Beethoven. It would cause a scandal."

"But he doesn't believe that Salieri had anything to do with Mozart's death. He is quite positive about that."

"On the surface. But he doesn't really trust Salieri."

"Are you sure?"

"Ask him about the time he visited Salieri in the hope that Salieri would recommend him for an appointment as a Royal Kapellmeister."

"How?" asked Jason. "Every time I mention Salieri he gets angry."

"Your wife will find a way. He is fond of her. He has been in a state of nerves all day, anticipating your visit. And your proposal excites him, even as it worries him. He wants to compose the oratorio for Boston, as much to show Vienna that he can still do it and that his work is still in demand, yet composing is very difficult for him now."

Deborah asked, "Herr Schindler, why do you dislike Salieri?"

"When Beethoven lost his hearing totally, Salieri stopped seeing him."

"Do you think Beethoven has any doubts about the way Mozart died?"

"Yes, I'll show you proof of that." But when Schindler went to fetch this, he heard Beethoven returning and he said, "Later. Before you leave. It would make him angry if he knew what I was doing."

Beethoven stood in the doorway, shouting, "What are you intriguing against me now, Papageno? The moment my back is turned you talk about me."

Deborah wrote, "Dear sir, we were discussing Salieri."

"He is as good as dead. You should allow him to rest in peace."

Deborah wrote, "Yet you feel he taught you more than anybody else?"

"Definitely. Frau Otis, you write an excellent German. Much better than your husband's."

She wrote, "Then you believe that Salieri has been misunderstood?"

"Yes. It is not unusual for musicians to quarrel. When I studied with Haydn we quarreled, but that doesn't mean we poisoned each other."

Deborah wrote, "Thus, if you could give us your impression of Salieri, it would be very kind, and it should end our interest in him."

"And then we can eat. The meal is almost ready. That idiot of a housekeeper has managed finally to get the fire started."

Jason was upset by what Deborah had suggested, and he wrote, "Sir, could you tell us about the time you asked Salieri to recommend you for a post as Royal Kapellmeister?"

Beethoven was displeased by this question, but when Deborah looked interested he grumbled, "Papageno has been gossiping again. It wasn't as he says it was, but it might be of some value to you. It will convince you that Salieri might be capable of intrigue, but certainly not murder."

Beethoven sat down, and when he resumed speaking he was very thoughtful.

"By the time I returned to Vienna it was the end of 1792 and it was too late to study with Mozart, for he was dead. So I became a pupil of the composer closest to him, Haydn, who had come back from England. But we did not get along, and some time later I started to study with Salieri.

"He had a fine reputation as a teacher, he had been in the Imperial Service for many years, and he treated me sympathetically and taught me more than anybody else, and he charged me only a nominal fee. I assumed that he was my good and genuine friend, and wherever I went, I signed myself in gratitude: *'Ludwig van Beethoven, pupil of Salieri.'*

"By 1814, when the rulers of Europe assembled in Vienna for their Congress, my reputation surpassed Salieri's but I continued to sign myself that way. Eight of my symphonies had been performed, and another I had composed to celebrate the defeat of Bonaparte, *Wellington's Victory at the Battle of Vittorio*. Most of Vienna's best musicians participated in its premiere. I conducted; Salieri led the artillery; Hummel played the snaredrums; Meyerbeer manipulated the thunder machine. And soon after, my final revision of my opera, *Fidelio*, was performed and acclaimed, for it was assumed that it commemorated the triumph of the Hapsburgs over Bonaparte, a misapprehension I was warned not to correct.

"Yet I was uneasy. While everyone was telling me how fortunate I was that my patrons had assured me that I would have an allowance of four thousand gulden a year for the rest of my life, a munificent sum for a person of my humble wants; inflation, medical expenses, and missed payments put me into financial want. When I was not paid for several months and I heard that a situation as Royal Kapellmeister was going to be vacant, I decided to apply for it, although I had doubts about the worth of Imperial patronage, especially after Mozart's experiences.

"I made an appointment with Salieri, who seemed most qualified to aid me. He was the First Royal Kapellmeister; he had served the Hapsburgs for nearly fifty years; even Metternich and the Emperor listened to him, although neither had much interest in music. And while the waltz dominated public taste, Handel's *Samson* was being sung in Vienna also, and so I felt there was some hope for me.

"Salieri's rooms were on the Kohlmarkt, where he had lived for many years. As I gave my card to his footman, I saw the latter's eyebrows rise. Perhaps the *'Ludwig van Beethoven, pupil of Salieri,'* had provoked him. But he motioned for me to wait, although rather rudely.

"I knew these rooms, yet I never ceased to marvel how a musician could manage to live in such luxury. Salieri had decorated his white walls with panels of deep red and gilt trimmings, like the Hofburg Palace, and the crystal chandeliers and parquet floors obviously had cost a fortune.

"By the time Salieri appeared, over an hour later, I was in a bad temper. He insisted on addressing me in his poor German—even worse than yours, Herr Otis, although he had resided in Vienna for almost fifty years—instead of writing out what he wished to say.

"I could still hear somewhat in those years, but I was so afraid that I would misunderstand what he said or miss it altogether that I strained too hard to hear and the tension made me irritable and edgy. I could feel my jaws snapping uncontrollably as I inclined my left ear, my best one, toward him, and I thought, Mozart would have been more considerate.

"But after Salieri apologized for being late, crying out, 'I am so busy I could use another Salieri to fill all my engagements,' which I heard, for he was shouting in his enthusiasm, he threw his arms around me and hugged me so tightly I could feel the many medals that covered his coat scratching my chest, already sore from the gout. He was dressed in the height of fashion, with a high collar, ruffles of the purest silk. His hair was combed so that a forelock fell over his forehead, for wigs were no longer the mode and his face was carefully rouged and powdered, with the largest amount of powder devoted to his large nose. But instead of hiding its bulbous look, it called attention to that.

"He muttered something I didn't hear, and I had to say, 'I didn't hear you, Maestro,' which was embarrassing and added to my discomfort.

"He repeated, shouting this time, 'It is good to see you, Beethoven!'

" 'Thank you, Maestro.' I decided to get to the issue at once and keep the conversation to a minimum before I felt too uncomfortable from not hearing. 'I have been thinking of accepting a Royal appointment.'

" 'Good!' he yelled. 'From whom? Who is the lucky prince?'

" 'I'm not sure. I thought you could advise me.'

"Salieri frowned and didn't answer.

" 'Or help me,' I added.

"He mumbled something and when he noticed that I hadn't heard him, he smiled cynically and shouted, 'What can I do, Beethoven?'

" 'Recommend me to the Emperor. You are close to him.'

"He shrugged, but he also beamed as if that were a great compliment.

" 'As your pupil,' although I hated myself for having to stress that.

" 'Of course!' he cried. '*Fidelio* is composed in the Italian style, as all good operas should be. You have learned my precepts properly.'

" 'I have been told there is a vacancy in the Imperial Court.'

" 'Would you be interested in an assistant's post?'

"Salieri looked surprised as he asked, but I didn't want to appear difficult, so I said, 'If it were to someone as worthy as yourself.'

"Just as I thought I had convinced him to help me, he said, 'What about the four thousand gulden you were guaranteed by your patrons?'

"I explained, grateful that, at least, I could hear him without too much strain, 'With inflation and the cost of the war, they haven't been able to pay me regularly. And the last few months, with their preparations for the Congress of Vienna, not at all.'

" 'But the war is over now.'

" 'The costs remain. And the inflation. And the nobility are spending so much money for clothes, grand balls, they have none for me.'

"Then, even as Salieri seemed sympathetic, he said loudly, to be sure I heard this, 'I am delighted to help you, but your republican sentiments are well known. They are not regarded favorably by the Court and they could create difficulties. You have not kept them secret.'

"I felt this was a reprimand, but I managed to conceal my anger as I pointed out, 'My battle symphony, *Wellington's Victory at the Battle of Vittorio,* was performed before thousands of people in the Redoutensaal and the Empress of Russia and Austria and many notable personages, including yourself. I was honored that you directed the cannonade.'

" 'It was impressive,' he declared with self-satisfaction.

"I could tell what he had said by reading his lips, at which I had developed some proficiency; and I nodded and remarked, 'So there should be no objection to me as an official musician.'

" 'Beethoven—official musician! The wild, uncombed bear—tamed!' Salieri roared with laughter, thinking that I hadn't heard him.

"But I had inclined my left ear close to him; and by one of those occasional vagaries that permitted me to hear unexpectedly, possibly because his voice had become very low, but not soft—I could still hear low bass tones most of the time—I knew what he had said. However, I ignored the sarcasm and asked, 'Maestro, you will recommend me?'

" 'I will do what I can. I will approach the proper authorities.'

" 'Should I get in touch with you?'

" 'No.' He escorted me to the door, kissed me on both cheeks, and shouted, 'It will not be necessary to call on me. I will call on you.'

Beethoven halted to wipe his brow, which was dripping with perspiration. Even now, Jason thought, these memories troubled him.

Then he remembered where he was and he said, "I wonder if you know, Frau Otis, what an effort it is to hear when there is no life left in your ears. It is horrible. Like being an infant again, having to learn all over again, but with no hope that things will really improve. If you are lucky, you . . ." He stopped, unable to say what he was thinking.

When he resumed soon after, he said, "I waited and waited to hear from Salieri, but when weeks passed without word from him, I felt I had to do something. Finally, more in desperation than in hope, I decided to approach him, although I had not heard from him. I had been told by my dearest patron, Archduke Rudolf, that the post in the Imperial Court was about to be filled, and if I were to arrange a rapprochement with the Court it would have to be done quickly."

"I knew from my experience as a pupil that Salieri always came home for lunch at one in the afternoon, which he said was the most important meal of the day, and that he did this rigidly and punctually. So I appeared at his rooms at that time.

"The footman tried to stop me at the door, shouting, 'The Maestro isn't in, Herr Beethoven,' but I pretended not to hear him, for once grateful for my deafness, and I hurried into his dining room. Salieri was sitting at the table with an attractive young woman, whom I didn't know—but I assumed it was his current mistress, for I knew it was not his wife or one of his four daughters—and he was startled when he saw me. I carried a notebook and a giant carpenter's pencil with me so whoever had to speak to me could write it down, and as I approached Salieri I thrust them at him. But he ignored the notebook and pencil as if they were offensive and shouted, 'What do you want, Beethoven?'

" 'You said you would inform me when you had news.'

" 'When I had news,' he replied loudly. But he did have the grace to rise from his chair while I stood like a log—only a log couldn't run away as I wanted to do now, my courage and resolution gone—and he leaned close to my ear and said harshly, 'You know I can't write German. It is an abominable language for expressing emotion. Do you like mushrooms, Beethoven?' Before I could answer, he added, 'Not all mushrooms are eatable. Some are deadly poisonous. But I know about such things,' he said proudly. Then he seemed to remember that I was still a person of some importance, and he invited me to join him and the young lady at lunch, although he didn't introduce me and she didn't say a word.

"I started to apologize for coming so suddenly, but he dismissed that, declaring—I could hear him by straining, 'Artists like us, with our solitary, sedentary occupation, are overcome with restlessness.'

"But when I didn't touch any of the food, too disturbed to eat, he yelled with sudden irritation, 'You can be poisoned by wrong food, bad food, but my food is the best! Why aren't you eating?'

" 'I'm not hungry, Maestro,' I said. 'I just ate.'

"That was not true, but Salieri seemed to accept that. But I noticed that he touched nothing until his companion tasted it first, and I wondered if this was the real reason she was his guest.

"I asked, 'Maestro, did you discuss my situation at Court?'

" 'Indeed!' he cried. 'Exhaustively!'

" 'And how was my petition received?' I asked.

"Salieri frowned.

" 'Unfavorably, Maestro?' I ventured.

" 'Everyone acknowledges your ability, and I have been praised for bringing that forth.'

"I sensed that he didn't wish to answer me directly; yet I was grateful that he had been considerate enough at least to seat me so I was close to him and he faced my good ear, where it was less of a strain to hear him, and I said, 'So, Maestro, the answer is No?'

"He replied, 'You wouldn't want to lose your independence.'

" 'What was the real reason I wasn't acceptable to the Court?'

" 'The hostile things you've said about the Court are resented.'

"I thought of Mozart then, who, I had heard, had suffered from the Court because he had spoken the truth. I was overcome with anger, and so I snapped, 'Who said I was unreliable? The chief of police?'

"Salieri didn't answer, but he looked guilty.

"I said, 'The Austrian Empire contains many enemies of music.'

" 'It is remarks like that which make it difficult to help you.'

"I said, 'Is that why Mozart had so many difficulties?'

"Salieri said emphatically, so I could hear him accurately, although his sallow features flushed and he was agitated, 'I bow to no one in my admiration for his art. All this talk about rivalry is nonsense. I attended his funeral. I was very upset when he died. I still take off my hat at the mention of his name. I would happily have changed my fate for his. I have never forgotten how he was buried. It was terrifying. The day he was buried there was such an awful storm, it was no wonder that we couldn't go to the cemetery.'

"I recalled that when Haydn had died I had followed his coffin over terrible, desolate roads to the cemetery, and in a storm, although I was ill, in pain, and poorly dressed, while the French army, occupying Vienna, watched and thought I was an idiot. But it was the least I could do.

"Salieri said, 'I appealed to the Emperor on your behalf, but he had never forgotten that you refused to take off your hat in his presence.'

"I said, 'That was years ago.'

" 'And he is very busy entertaining the great princes assembled in Vienna,' Salieri added. 'Affairs of great importance are being decided.'

" 'No doubt,' I said. 'Like making the Empire into a vast barracks, now that Bonaparte has been defeated.'

" 'That's what they mean. You should be more careful of what you say.'

" 'Maestro, are you a police informer too? Or your guest?'

"She hadn't said a word, but now she started to speak. Salieri checked her and said, 'Beethoven, you are too forthright.'

" 'Like saying the Emperor's public audiences are public deceptions.'

"Salieri shuddered as if I had uttered a sacrilege.

"Then his guest reminded him that he had an appointment with his hair dresser, who was appallingly busy with all the crowned heads in Vienna, and that the *friseur* could not and would not wait. I was not supposed to hear that, but I did, and offended, I rose so suddenly I got dizzy and fell headlong on the floor. I wished I could move as slowly as a snail, but I am too impetuous by nature for that. As I picked myself up I could see a look in Salieri's eyes, saying, Good God, Beethoven, why don't you behave yourself, why do you have to drink so much—when I had not had a drop of wine all day. But Salieri did have the sense to say, and loudly enough so I could hear him, 'Are you ill, Beethoven? I will send you home in my carriage if you like. I would be honored to do so.'

" 'Thank you,' I said, 'but I am fine. Just a momentary faintness, from the warmth of the room.' It was overheated and possibly that was the reason. 'Then I can assume there is no hope for me at Court?'

"Salieri shook his head sorrowfully and stated clearly, 'None, I'm afraid. Your music is deeply appreciated, and it is felt that an official appointment would only tie your hands and lessen your art.'

"When I smiled as if I accepted that, he was amiable again. He took me by the arm and escorted me to the door of his dining room.

"He said, speaking into my better ear, 'I hope you will forgive my not escorting you to the street, but I am very busy. I have an appointment this evening with the Emperor, and I must not keep him waiting.'

"I smiled, not knowing what else to do; and he assumed I was feeling friendly again, for he became confidential. 'You should see, Beethoven, how many of the rulers worry about being poisoned. I think the most vital men at Court are the official tasters. It certainly seems to be the most dangerous, and courageous, post. With my knowledge of poisons,' he boasted, 'I could be of considerable use to them.'

"Salieri couldn't seem to stop talking now, as if he felt that this could be the last time I could ever hear him, for he rushed on in a torrent of loud volubility, 'If you were a composer of waltzes, Beethoven, there would be no difficulty, but your music is too stormy for their ears.'

" 'Are there other reasons,' I asked.

" 'Count Sedlnitzky is disturbed by your criticisms of the government.'

" 'He prefers that I practise the official Hapsburg rhetoric?'

" 'You could be more tactful. My dear Beethoven, why do you have to state openly that you are a republican?' But when he said goodbye, he embraced me and kissed me on both cheeks.

"At the door to the street I realized I had left my notebook and pencil in the dining room and that I might need them to get home. I hurried back there, keeping my balance with difficulty, and found that Salieri was in the music room with the young woman. They didn't hear me, their backs were to me, but I could see them through the red drapes. I approached them and as I put my good ear to the crack between the drapes, I could hear Salieri saying to her as if he were uttering a Royal proclamation, 'It is incredible to think of that wild, hairy beast at Court as an Imperial musician. The Emperor cannot stand ill people around him. Can you imagine him having to lean close to that coarse German face and screaming a Royal command in its ear. The Emperor would be so nauseated, so uncomfortable we would all suffer.' "

Beethoven was in the present now, muttering, "At that moment I wished I was totally deaf, but now that I am, I have regretted that wish, and I have prayed that it could be undone."

Jason thought there was nothing to say to that, and he was silent.

Deborah reached out to touch Beethoven, to show her sympathy for what he had suffered, and he recoiled as if he could not endure pity.

Self-conscious about how much he had revealed, he rushed into the kitchen and returned triumphantly with the veal, shouting, "It is done, finally." And when he saw Jason hesitating to eat, he declared, "I hope you enjoy eating, young man. Without it, we are lost."

However, he ordered Schindler to taste the wine and food first, and when Schindler did and nodded approvingly, he commanded him to serve them. Beethoven ate and drank with great gulps and a hearty relish, the veal accompanied only by potatoes and red Austrian wine, all of which Schindler had to sample first. It was as if Beethoven had emptied himself of all ideas and only the eating and the drinking mattered.

His table manners were terrible, thought Deborah, virtually non-existent. He didn't say a word during the meal, and when she wrote, "Don't you think that Salieri behaved very badly," he didn't answer.

But after dinner and while Schindler was in the kitchen, Beethoven blurted out, "That wasn't the worst thing Salieri did. When I discussed the affair with the Archduke Rudolf, he informed me that Salieri had never approached the Emperor at all on my behalf, or anyone at Court."

Jason wrote, "Yet you still believe that he didn't hurt Mozart?"

"Many people harm us. Sometimes those who are closest to us."

Deborah wrote, "What do you think of Salieri's music?"

Beethoven said, "He was a fine teacher, he understood form and structure very well, and he was quite clever. But among ourselves we called him Signor *Bonbonieri,* for his compositions were bonbon music, Viennese confectionary in the Italian style, and of little consequence."

Jason wrote, "Salieri is supposed to have felt that way about Mozart."

"Mozart!" Beethoven was furious. "Did you ever try correcting Mozart?"

Jason shook his head no.

"It is impossible. The man made no mistakes."

"None?" Deborah wrote sceptically.

"None that mattered. How long do you intend to remain in Vienna?"

Jason wrote, "Until you finish the oratorio for Boston. How long do you think that it will take, sir?"

"That depends. First, I must be certain that it is worth doing. If Herr Grob will place five hundred gulden in my name in his bank, I should have the oratorio for you by the end of the year."

As Jason nodded yes, Deborah looked critical, for Grob had guaranteed only four hundred gulden. He whispered to her, "I will make up the difference, if that is necessary."

Beethoven shouted, "You must not talk behind my back. Is it any wonder I am suspicious! Aren't there any honest people in the world?"

Deborah wrote, "We were discussing the terms."

"I want the deposit as an expression of good faith."

Jason wrote, "Of course, and we will expect it by the end of the year."

"I will try. But I cannot work properly at night anymore. My eyes are too weak, and I cannot read properly without sunlight to see what I am doing."

Jason wrote, "Perhaps we can help you."

"No! It is not that I am arrogant, but I must do it myself. An oratorio will take time and effort to write. Lately it has been difficult for me to compose. I think and ponder, but it is very hard to begin. I am terrified of starting such a large work. I am always judging myself, sometimes harshly. But once I've started, once I've dipped myself into the body of the work itself, it goes fine enough."

Jason wrote, "We will wait."

"You will have to. I must have a text that stimulates me, something moral and elevating. I could never write the operas Mozart did. *Don Giovanni* and *Così fan tutte* are licentious, and so is *Figaro.*"

Deborah wrote, "Sir, you indicated that the Bible would suffice for a text. As it did for Handel."

Beethoven nodded approvingly and said, "I will write about a Hebrew prophet whose power consisted of moral authority. Jeremiah, perhaps. He has fascinated me often with his lamentations of doom. I feel that man must be warned to give up his wicked ways or we will all face an Armageddon. Or should I write in condemnation of Original Sin? I hear that Original Sin is fashionable in New England."

Schindler returned from the kitchen agitated. He informed Beethoven in writing that the housekeeper needed bread money and that she said she could not keep it down to ten kreutzer a day as Beethoven insisted.

Beethoven retorted angrily, "But twelve kreutzer a day is too much. Two rolls a day for her is more than I can afford. Such an increase would amount to over eighteen gulden a year."

Schindler wrote, "She will quit if we do not satisfy her."

"So she will quit! Is that so unusual? Frau Otis, Papageno thinks that no one who speaks English as a native tongue can count to three. I must watch every kreutzer or I will end up as impoverished as Mozart."

Deborah wrote, "Do you think that is the only reason he died when he did?"

"We know that he died young; everything else is conjecture."

Schindler wrote, "And what do I tell the housekeeper, Master?"

"Nothing. I owe her no explanations. Herr Otis, what are your plans?"

Jason wrote, "We plan to visit Salzburg. It should take a few weeks."

"Good. You will see where Mozart was born."

Deborah wrote, "But first we must get permission from the police. They confiscated our books, our passports," and as Beethoven looked sympathetic, reading that, she wrote, "Could you recommend us to the authorities?"

He smiled grimly and said, "I would like to, but I am already in poor repute with the police and that doesn't improve with time. They watch me closely. Oh, I know," he insisted, waving aside Schindler's gesture that this wasn't so. "I see it in many ways. My views are too strong for their stomachs. There are police informers everywhere. They encircle us with their webs like spiders, and to break out is not easy."

Jason wrote, "Is that why you have your food sampled, sir?"

Beethoven replied, "It is a common practice."

Schindler wasn't his friend, Jason thought, he was his official taster.

"I don't even trust my housekeepers," said Beethoven. "The Italian disease, poisoning, is still prevalent in Vienna, and one must be wary."

He rose to indicate that the evening was over. As they followed him to the door, Jason wrote, "Did you know da Ponte?"

"Only by reputation, which wasn't good. A most licentious man."

Deborah wrote, "Won't you want a written agreement for the oratorio?"

"Dear lady, don't you trust me? I trust you."

Jason nodded.

"I have given you my verbal assurance. And I must not waste paper.

Paper is costly. I have to scribble for my bread, to support me during the writing of a great work. I have not received a single kreutzer of my annuity for a long time."

Beethoven stood like a chunk of rock and Deborah knew that she would always remember this evening and the short, stocky, corpulent composer, overflowing with nervous energy despite his age and ailments, impatient of fools and quick to misunderstand, yet sensitive and intuitive to friendship, looking pleased when praised yet also uncomfortable, not certain whether to trust it or accept it, yet knowing that praise was his due, knocking on the door of life with an inner ear that heard and selected and that was always forming music in his mind.

He said, "These are not happy times. We live in the past, believing that it is always better than the present. Our age is one of bleakness, and I must have some money before they put me under the dead leaves."

Jason wrote, "Aren't there any contemporary composers you respect?"

Beethoven exclaimed, "Papageno, give them young Franz Schubert's address. He was Salieri's best pupil, next to me, and the scores of his I have read indicate that he has a true lyrical gift."

While Schindler went to get Schubert's address and to write it down, Beethoven stared at them a moment. Then he cried out with a sudden release of emotion and energy, "How good to meet young persons who care!"

He took each of them by the hand with a burst of passion and said, "Papageno will show you to the door. I avoid the stairs as much as possible these days. And keep in touch with me, and in a few weeks I will be able to estimate when the oratorio will be completed."

At the street Schindler showed them an old print. Their carriage was still there, and Hans had fallen asleep. Fortunately however, he had tied the horses to a street post.

As they stared at the print, Schindler whispered, "Beethoven may not agree that Salieri poisoned Mozart, but this scene is of immense importance to him."

The print was yellow with age and wrinkled from constant handling. It was of a funeral cart carrying a corpse in a small black box and entering the deserted cemetery of St. Marx's, followed only by a stray dog.

"It is a drawing of Mozart's funeral," said Schindler, "and this tuneless maddening situation has haunted Beethoven for years. He carries this with him always."

25

Interlude

O N THE drive home Jason told himself that he must reward Deborah for the clever way she had encouraged Beethoven to be hospitable to him. Yet even as he was excited by the success he had had with the composer and with Schindler's disclosure of Beethoven's involvement in the tragic circumstances of Mozart's funeral, he was oppressed by the grimness of the print and he longed to shake himself free from that memory.

As soon as they reached their rooms he courted her, kissing and fondling her as thanks for having helped him to obtain Beethoven's promise to compose the oratorio. When she responded to his fervent expressions of affection, he undressed her and when she was naked he came to her with such passion she could hardly bear it. But while she lay beneath him this time, at his insistence, as if this were his right, his assertion of masculinity, she wondered how much of his outpouring of emotion was his true self, was actually love.

He sensed her doubts as she hesitated momentarily in her response, and abruptly he felt unwanted, rejected, and so, impotent, interrupted rudely at the height of his devotion. Unable to continue, he hated her in this moment for spoiling his desire.

She realized this as he was about to withdraw. Quickly then, knowing intuitively that this could create a dreadful breach between them, she embraced him passionately and pulled him down upon her.

Her voluptuous avowal of him erased his feeling of rejection and his impotence. Once again he sank into her, but forgetfulness didn't come.

The most conspicuous image in his mind was the old funeral print and the empty procession entering the cemetery, and her body became a grisly casket. He was tormented with guilt that he could be making love after the shock of the print, as if that were a profanation of Mozart, and the sexual act seemed meaningless. Even as she clung to him with the requisite emotion and pleaded for more, he thought, I am not really thanking her or expressing love; I am hovering between life and the grave and seeking to exorcise death. As if to take that to bed with them was unbearable.

Then he felt her warm mouth on his, her sensuous hands on his

H *

shoulders pulling him closer. Her passion quickened enormously, and in his need to respond and to keep pace with her, there was a new emotion in him. She made him feel alive and triumphant, and he forgot everything else. But afterward, as they lay in each other's arms, he decided that she had done this deliberately, to show him that she could drive everything else out of his mind.

She said, noticing his distraction, "You still don't trust me."

"It isn't that. But you've been so sceptical about my search."

"I'm still with you, Jason dear."

"Even if that means sacrificing your cherished beliefs?"

"I'm not certain what I cherish anymore. Except our marriage. Life has become so many fragments. And so hopelessly entangled."

He was surprised that she was trembling. He asked, "What's wrong?"

She whispered apprehensively, "The roof gets lower and lower, and sometimes I feel that we are trapped and that there is no escape."

"You are afraid despite the proof that we are here because of Beethoven?"

"Yes. He may not keep his word."

"You are tired. You were very good with Beethoven. And helpful."

"Because you showed me how to understand him." And in her understanding of the composer she felt closer to Jason, and when he continued to praise her, quite flattering now, she stopped trembling.

He caressed her and added, "There is light ahead. And we are nearly there. After we return from Salzburg, I should be able to put all the pieces together. We will just have to make the final effort."

He had been generous, she decided. He had come to her with an openness and affection he had not shown before, grateful for the way she had aided him with Beethoven, and for such favors she must be appreciative.

So she embraced him and he continued to respond. But suddenly he felt exhausted, only he couldn't admit that. The need to assert life in the midst of death had been almost too much for him, and there were moments when he felt, too, that his quest was impossible.

Yet when the sun shone brightly the next day and his fatigue was gone, Jason felt better. Deborah was also in a more cheerful mood, refreshed by a good night's rest. As they entered Grob's office, she assured Jason that she would support him in whatever course he followed.

Grob was not as enthusiastic about Beethoven's agreement to compose the oratorio as Jason was. The moment Jason finished telling him that the composer had said Yes, he asked, "Did Beethoven put that in writing?"

"No. He said that his word was good enough."

"No one's word is good enough. And certainly not Beethoven's. He

promised five different music publishers his *Missa solemnis,* and then
gave it to none of them. You should have gotten his promise in
writing.''

Jason cried out desperately, "But he has already started work on it.
And I've come thousands of miles for it.''

Grob looked sceptical, but he said, "What terms did you agree to?''

"Five hundred gulden.''

Grob was surprised. "You must have bargained very hard.''

"Not particularly. I told him what I could pay and he agreed to it.
But he did insist that the money should be paid in advance.''

"That is impossible. Beethoven's unreliability is notorious.''

"You will not be taking any risk. He said that the money should be
placed in his name in your bank as an expression of good faith. You will
not have to release it until the oratorio is completed.''

"What about the text?''

"He will use the Old Testament, probably something about
Jeremiah.''

"Jeremiah should be safe. He should satisfy the authorities.''

"Beethoven stated that the oratorio would be very devout.''

"But can he finish it before you leave Vienna?''

"He said he would. He assured me that the moment the money is put
in his name he will start work. He said he has several musical ideas.''

"How long did he say the oratorio would take to compose?''

"Two, three months at the most.''

"That's unlikely. With his poor health, his age, and his deafness he
never finishes on time anymore. Are you prepared to stay longer?''

"I am prepared to stay as long as is necessary.''

"That may be longer than you anticipate. Beethoven never considers
anything finished as long as it is in his hands. To obtain possession, you
may have to forcibly take the oratorio away from him.''

Deborah said, "Then you will deposit the money in Beethoven's
name?''

"I can't deposit more than four hundred gulden," Grob answered.

Jason said, "Elisha Whitney told me the Society would pay five
hundred.''

"Who is Elisha Whitney?''

"The Society's Director of Music.''

"He has no authority. Herr Pickering authorized me to pay only
four hundred gulden. At my discretion. I cannot make up the difference.''

As Jason hesitated, Deborah said hurriedly, "I can.''

"No," protested Jason. "It is my responsibility. Herr Grob, will you
put five hundred gulden in Beethoven's name if I make up the
difference?''

"I have the right to refuse you," Grob reminded him.

"I know. But you wouldn't, would you, sir?''

"When are you going to deposit your funds with me?"

"Next week," Jason said hurriedly. "Before we leave for Salzburg. I have only a hundred gulden with me now. I brought that in case . . ."

"You needed it," Deborah blurted out, feeling he still didn't trust her. "You assumed you would make up the hundred gulden from the beginning."

"I didn't. But one must expect some problems." To prevent any further objections being raised, Jason handed Grob a hundred gulden.

Grob accepted the money, although he said, "I will put five hundred gulden in a Beethoven account, but it must be understood that the money is to be paid only when the oratorio is completed and delivered."

"Can I inform Beethoven about that?"

"If you wish. I will, in any event. Did he talk about anything else?"

Deborah said quickly, "No, not really."

"Nothing else?" Grob was sceptical. "Not even politics?"

"No," said Jason.

"And, of course, Mozart wasn't mentioned at all?"

"Oh, yes," said Jason, "Beethoven talked about his music and how much it influenced him." He added innocently, "Don't you think it did?"

Grob replied, "It isn't what I think that matters, and you know that."

When they returned to their rooms, Jason hurried to where he had hidden the rest of his money and he was relieved to find it was as he had left it. Yet as he counted it anxiously, Deborah sensed that he was in an agony of apprehension, for when he finished he looked unhappy. She didn't want to anger him, but she had to ask, "Is it less than you need?"

"Less than what I thought I had." He felt he had been wasteful, and yet how else could he have proceeded, he wondered.

He was grateful that she didn't offer him any money, but asked, as if it were his sole responsibility, "Do you have enough to go to Salzburg?"

"Yes. We will just have to live less expensively."

"As long as we stay alive," she joked, "we mustn't worry."

He couldn't consider that a joke. Somebody had hit him hard as they had walked along the Graben, and he doubted that it had been an accident. The man had vanished into the crowd before he could see who it was, and since his back had been turned, he had been unable to tell whether it had been an arm or a shoulder that had pushed him violently. But if he had been Beethoven with the latter's faulty balance, he realized, he would have fallen to the ground, perhaps in the road itself, and would have been in danger of being trampled to death by the carriage that had sped by them.

Aware of this, he was afflicted with melancholy at the realization of his own limited abilities and the possibility that there were many powerful enemies about them, and worse, unseen and unknown and thus impossible to defend against. But this, too, he must hide from her.

Deborah was saying, "Somebody has been here while we were gone. There is an odor of tobacco in the rooms."

Jason called the landlady, but Frau Herzog had seen no one, not even Hans, who, she said, was attending the horses in the stable nearby.

Deborah said, "Perhaps it was Muller. Does he know about the garden?"

"Indeed," said Frau Herzog. "He has used that entrance often."

Ernst was practising a sonata when Jason knocked on his door. But instead of looking absorbed and animated, he appeared tired and distracted, as if he were trying to use the music as an escape and wasn't succeeding.

He wasn't surprised to see them, and he stopped at once, answering Deborah's query. "Yes, I was in your rooms. I was wondering why I hadn't heard from you. Have you given up the search? Was Beethoven discouraging?"

She was upset that their rooms could be entered without anyone knowing it, but she said, "You are the one who looks discouraged."

"My brother is ill."

Jason asked, as he felt saddened by the news, although somehow Otto seemed far away now, even emotionally, "Do you know what is wrong?"

"His letter didn't say, but I suspect it is old age."

"Did he ask for me?"

"Briefly. That is why I know he is ill. He talked mostly about his ailments and how cold and lonely it is in Boston."

Deborah asked, "Why didn't you leave a note?"

"And incriminate myself if you're being watched? I'm not that foolish."

"Yet you suggested these rooms because you said they would be safe."

"Nothing is totally safe in Vienna," Ernst said. "Herr Otis, did you have any luck with Beethoven? Did you discuss studying with him?"

"I never had the chance," Jason replied. He was annoyed; that was not the reason he had visited Beethoven, and Ernst should have remembered. Was Ernst becoming senile, untrustworthy? Ernst was depressed, listless. "We were busy discussing the oratorio and Mozart and Salieri."

"You had two meetings with him."

"Who told you?"

"Frau Herzog. But not what happened. Except that she cooked for him."

Deborah announced proudly, "Beethoven will do the oratorio for my husband." She told him the details, including Grob's assent.

Ernst wanted to know what Beethoven had said about Salieri.

"Beethoven informed us that Salieri boasted about attending Mozart's funeral as an expression of his respect, but that Salieri claimed he didn't go to the cemetery because there was a terrible storm that day."

"That's a lie, Frau Otis; the weather was mild that day. It proves I am right about Salieri. Did Beethoven give you any other evidence?"

"He thinks we ought to talk to Schubert, who studied with Salieri."

"That can be arranged. Are you ready to go to Salzburg? With the oratorio settled, you can pursue your investigations without suspicion."

Deborah wasn't certain, but she waited for Jason to answer.

As Jason wavered, Ernst said impatiently, "There is nothing to be afraid of now. They will assume you are going on a musical pilgrimage."

"What about Salieri?" asked Jason. "When I was not in Vienna, you wrote urgently that I should come swiftly before Salieri died. And what about Cavalieri and Diener and the doctor who attended Mozart during his last days?" There swept over him a torrent of emotion as he realized that he had become so involved in Beethoven that he had almost forgotten his earlier intentions and certainly had neglected them.

"I haven't been able to locate Diener or the doctor," said Ernst, as if failure was so humiliating it was impossible to admit. "But you may in Salzburg. Sophie was with him when he died, and his wife. And Cavalieri should be known by Aloysia. Aloysia was her understudy."

"They are all there?" Deborah asked critically.

"Yes. I've managed it through friends in Salzburg who know the three sisters. The Weber women have assembled there because they have heard about the visitors from America who wish to inquire about Mozart. I understand that Sophie and Aloysia are staying with Constanze at the moment. This is the time to see them. Each of them feels that what she has to say is vital. And they will tell you much about Mozart."

"Is that the only reason they are willing to talk to us?"

"They assume also, Frau Otis, especially his wife, that you are coming to pay homage. Herr Otis, you must prepare a gift for Constanze and Mozart's ailing sister, Nannerl. It doesn't have to be much. Fifty gulden from admirers of his music in America should be enough."

"Fifty gulden!" exclaimed Jason.

"That should be generous enough," Ernst assured him.

Generous, indeed! Jason cried out, "Must I? Is it essential?"

"I'm not sure they will see you otherwise. Say it is an expression of respect for those closest to him. They will appreciate the compliment."

Jason asked, "What about my chances of seeing Salieri? You gave me the impression that he didn't have long to live."

"His health, I hear, has improved. Moreover, there is nothing I can do." Desperation crept into Ernst's voice. "The keeper I know is ill and I have to move cautiously. If it is found out that I am trying to arrange a meeting with Salieri, the consequences could be grave. I daren't risk approaching the others. You will have to wait to see Salieri."

"Then you think we ought to go to Salzburg now?"

"At once. It is only about three hundred miles, more or less; you have your own coach; and if you go before the snow falls, which usually starts in December, the trip shouldn't be too difficult."

Ernst turned away as if everything was settled, and Jason asked him to listen to the sonata he had composed. The elderly musician was annoyed, as if it were an unwelcome intrusion and he didn't want to risk passing judgment, and he said, "I'm very busy." But when he saw the insistence in Jason's eyes he agreed to listen.

Only it was impossible to escape from Mozart now, Jason thought. As he played, he realized that he had imitated him, like Salieri. That turned the pianoforte into a wretched rack upon which he was torturing himself, and he performed unhappily, without the excellence he craved. As he finished he felt that whatever ability he had developed in the past had vanished with his stiffening fingers.

Ernst listened in silence, although toward the end he began to stir restlessly. When the sonata was over he said hurriedly, "You must leave for Salzburg. By the time you return, Salieri's keeper ought to be better and a meeting should be possible to arrange."

But there was no evading it. Jason had to ask, "What do you think about my composition?"

"You are here to find out who killed Mozart, not be another Mozart."

In this moment Jason hated Ernst, not sure he could survive him.

Deborah hadn't said a word, and now the three of them sat as if they were listening for some other sound. Perhaps that would avoid any further provocations, thought Jason, yet he asked, "You don't like my sonata?"

"It is natural that your music should resemble Mozart's. Do you intend to see anyone else before you depart for Salzburg?"

"Schubert, possibly. Beethoven suggested that."

"Good. Schubert studied with Salieri, but his music shows a strong preference for Mozart. I will write Salzburg that you will be there soon."

Jason could hardly wait to go. It was as if Ernst had betrayed him, and even Mozart had, too, luring him into a world he could never inhabit. Yet it was such a promised land, one that he could not resist.

26

Schubert

As SCHINDLER led Jason and Deborah to Bogner's Café, which was Schubert's favorite coffee house and where Schindler hoped to introduce them to the composer, Jason was puzzled. He had a feeling that he had been here before, but when? Then he remembered. Bogner's Café was on the corner of the Singerstrasse and the Blutgasse, and between the Palace of the Teutonic Knights, where Mozart had defied Prince Colloredo, the Archbishop of Salzburg, and the rooms on the Schulerstrasse where Mozart had composed *Figaro*. This was Mozartland, he reflected.

He felt easier then, more at home. However, before Jason could ask Schindler whether the latter was aware of this, Schindler paused in front of the café to tell them what he thought of Schubert.

But for the moment all Jason could think of was how he had arrived here. It had begun the day after he had seen Ernst. Unhappy about that meeting, he had had to do something affirmative. He had sent Beethoven six bottles of Tokay wine as an expression of his admiration—and, as Deborah had said, to seal Beethoven's agreement to compose the oratorio.

Jason had written with this present, *"In the hope, dear Herr Beethoven, that this will fortify you against the disorders of time."* The composer had responded quickly with a thank-you note, calling the wine, *"a rare and noble gift,"* and had stated emphatically that on further thought he had decided that Herr Otis and his charming wife must talk to young Schubert, for the latter had spent much time with Salieri and should be able to provide them with useful information; and that he was sending his factotum along to introduce them to young Schubert. And even Deborah had felt that this was an order they could not ignore, and so Jason had postponed the departure to Salzburg.

Apparently Beethoven had spoken highly about them, thought Jason; for Schindler had greeted them effusively, and now, discussing Schubert, he was excited about this meeting. He was saying, "You praised Beethoven very carefully and just at the right moment, but Schubert is different. If anything, he resents praise, even when it is well meant."

Deborah asked, "Why?"

"It has to do with his distaste for intrigue. He feels that praise is always given for self-advantage, and he disdains intrigue, yet to succeed musically in Vienna intrigue is essential, particularly when so much rubbish is performed and praised. But Schubert is little known."

"Do you like his music?" Jason asked.

"Oh, yes, I respect him as a composer."

"But not as a man?"

"He is stubborn, impractical. He should give pianoforte lessons to support himself instead of depending on his composing. But he hates teaching, he says that it interferes with his composing. He insists that he has to create in the mornings, when he could be teaching, that the afternoons should be given over to meditation and the evenings to pleasure. He loves to spend his evenings in cafés, and always with friends. He doesn't like being alone. It is no wonder that he never has any money. It is ridiculous, spending so many nights here."

Yet the contents of the café seemed harmless enough to Jason. All he could see as they entered the front door was a large room capable of seating about fifty people in conditions of some crowding and discomfort. There was much smoke, the strong smell of beer, and the loud clatter of glasses and dishes. Schindler pointed to a man sitting by himself at a round table, who was staring reflectively through thick spectacles into an empty wine glass. "Schubert," he whispered, and when Schubert saw Schindler, he rose to greet them.

Schubert was small and insignificant looking, thought Jason, with a chubby, full face, a high forehead, and long, curly dark hair, almost as tangled as Beethoven's. As Schindler introduced them, Jason noticed that while Schubert wore a knee-length brown frock coat and a darker brown cravat around his white collar to match the color of his hair and eyes, his crumpled clothes looked as if he had struggled unwillingly into them. He was almost as untidy as Beethoven, with food and wine spots in abundance on his coat and shirt. Schubert was quite short also, about five feet tall, and obese, and dripping with perspiration, as if it was not easy for him to meet strangers. But what surprised Jason the most was that the composer was not much older than himself, about twenty-seven or twenty-eight at the most.

Deborah was taken aback that, as he leaned close to her to see her better, obviously very nearsighted, his breath smelled strongly of beer and tobacco and his teeth appeared neglected.

But his voice was soft, musical, and he seemed relieved that they didn't start off by flattering him, but wanted to talk about Mozart.

"He set such a standard!" Schubert exclaimed. "It is almost unattainable. Only Beethoven has reached it. Do you know Mozart's G Minor symphony?" And when Jason and Deborah nodded yes, he cried out, "It is as if the angels are singing! But Mozart is very difficult to play well. His music is ageless."

Jason asked, "Do you play Mozart, Herr Schubert?"

"When I can, Herr Otis. But not as skilfully as I would like to. Since I do not possess a pianoforte, I am out of practise."

"How do you compose?"

"If I need a pianoforte, I borrow the use of it from a friend."

Schindler said, "Herr Otis is a great admirer of Mozart."

"Marvellous," Schubert said. "I love him so much."

"And he is a friend and protégé of the Master's. Beethoven has become very fond of this young couple. They have brought him much happiness."

"Beethoven deserves all of our devotion!" Schubert cried, and he embraced Jason and firmly deposited a kiss on each cheek, adding in his enthusiasm, "I used to dine at a café like this just so I could view Beethoven, usually from a distance. That is how I met Herr Schindler."

Jason was embarrassed by Schubert's demonstration of affection, and he wished that Schindler hadn't exaggerated his relationship with Beethoven, but he was pleased, too, for Schubert had become a man with a miraculously mobile face that had been transformed from sadness to joy.

Schubert was eager now that they join him at his table. Feeling he could trust them, he was in fine spirits suddenly, explaining, "I am so glad to be back in Vienna. I have just returned from Hungary and the Esterhazy estate, where I taught the Count's family during their summer retreat. A few kreutzer earned to buy bread and apples, but Hungary is a dull place. I never could work there for a quarter of a century like Haydn did. I am waiting for my friends, but this a good time to talk, before the beer drinkers and the sausage eaters have arrived. Frau Otis, what wine would you like? Tokay? Moselle? Nesmuller? Or Sexard?"

"Whatever you prefer," she said, and she was surprised that he ordered a bottle of Tokay, for Schindler had warned them that Schubert was usually impoverished; yet the composer waved aside Jason's offer to pay, although he had just enough money to pay for the wine. And she was upset by his obesity and his absorption in his drinking. But Schindler had told them also that Schubert was most communicative over a glass of wine; otherwise he was apt to be silent.

He drained his glass quickly, and he was impatient when they didn't keep pace with him. When he saw her expression, he declared, "The water is so bad, we must take no chances. It could poison you." Then he lapsed into silence, puffing on his pipe and staring through his spectacles out the window of the café as if a dark cloud had fallen upon them.

Jason said he adored Tokay and insisted that they must have more.

But again, when Jason offered to pay for the wine, Schubert wouldn't allow it. The composer took manuscript paper from his pocket, and he converted it swiftly into a song and handed it to the waiter as payment.

The waiter accepted the song without question and brought more Tokay.

Schubert's spirits improved once more; and when Jason said, "Tokay is costly," he replied, "I write music to live, not to make a living."

Yet he had said that, Jason thought, without any sense of pride.

Schubert was concerned that Frau Otis was still upset. He asked her solicitously, "Aren't you comfortable? This is a hospitable café, especially in the evening hours after one's work is done."

She was disturbed by a man staring at them from a nearby table, who had eyes for no one around him but them, and she asked, "Do you know him?"

Schubert peered through his spectacles, sighed sadly, and said quietly, but without surprise, "Very well. He is a police inspector. And a spy."

Deborah cried out, "Doesn't he have any pride? He is so obvious!"

"He wants to be obvious. He wants you to know that he is there."

"But why? We've done nothing wrong."

"The police are always watching. Especially some of us."

Jason asked, "Herr Schubert, why should you be under suspicion?"

"Some years ago friends of mine belonged to student organizations."

"What has that to do with you, sir?"

"Student organizations are regarded with suspicion. One friend of mine who was active in a student union in Heidelberg was expelled from the university, and after he was interrogated he was deported."

Deborah asked anxiously, "How does that concern you, Herr Schubert?"

"I was his friend. At the time he was arrested my rooms were searched."

Schindler interrupted, "Franz, I wouldn't pursue this matter further. It is not such an unusual situation and you've been free."

"They confiscated all my papers so they could examine them to see whether I had any political associations with my friend or with the student organizations to which he belonged, and when they returned my things, several of my songs were missing. I have not seen them since."

Schindler said, "So you composed other songs, new songs."

"But not these songs. And the title of the opera I composed, *The Conspirators,* had to be changed to *Domestic Warfare.* A terrible title. A mockery. Do you think they will forbid dancing next?"

"Franz, don't be foolish."

"They forbid dancing during Lent. I think they did it to me deliberately because they knew I liked dancing so much."

Deborah asked, "Herr Schubert, isn't there anything you can do?"

"I meet my friends here so that the police will not think that we are a secret society—secret societies, especially ones like the Freemasons, are forbidden—and drink Tokay. Herr Otis, do you like swimming?"

"No, I'm afraid of the water." Mortally afraid, thought Jason.

"I love swimming, but it is regarded with suspicion by the authorities. They say, *'It gives rise to associations that are difficult to supervise.'*"

There was one consolation in this, thought Jason as he saw Deborah growing restless; it should lead them to Mozart and Salieri. He asked, "Sir, have you ever wondered about the circumstances of Mozart's death?"

"It was a great pity."

"Nothing else, Herr Schubert?"

"What else was there?"

"Do you think his death could have been precipitated by someone?"

Deborah wanted to hush Jason, afraid that the police inspector could hear him, but Schubert assured her that was impossible; they were too far away and the café was too noisy. He was puzzled by the question.

Schindler said, "Franz, Herr Otis wonders if Salieri ever talked about Mozart's death when you studied with him. You did for a number of years."

"Maestro Salieri was my teacher, not my friend."

"But Salieri must have referred to Mozart's death?" Jason exclaimed.

"Why?" Schubert said sceptically. "Because he is ill now?"

Jason said, "It is reported that he confessed to poisoning Mozart."

"Many things are reported in Vienna that are not true. Do you know that this reputed confession exists? Or is it just a rumor?"

"Salieri was Mozart's enemy. I do have proof of that."

"Maestro Salieri disliked anyone who threatened his own position. But that doesn't make him an assassin. Where is your proof?"

"I'm developing it. Step by step. That's why I wanted to talk to you."

"Salieri was an old man when I studied with him, and that was years ago. And long after Mozart died. I never knew Mozart."

"But Salieri did. And he must have spoken about Mozart."

Schubert didn't answer.

"Not even though, once Mozart was dead, he was the most important composer in Vienna, and obligatory for a young composer to study?"

Herr Otis was shrewd, thought Schubert; that was true. Suddenly he was reflective. He had been fascinated by Mozart's music from the first moment he had heard it. He could hear it now, even with all the noise in the café. The police inspector seemed to be leaning toward him, as if to listen to what he was saying, but the florid middle-aged man was too far away. Yet part of Schubert wanted to disengage himself from this conversation, afraid that it was leading him into dangerous realms. He had heard the rumors, too, that Salieri had fallen ill and then insane and had been confined in an asylum after confessing to a priest of poisoning Mozart. But no one he knew had seen Salieri since, although there had been a Court announcement that the Imperial family had retired Salieri on full salary as an expression of gratitude for his services. Hardly a gesture, Schubert assured himself, appropriate for an assassin. Or had the Hapsburgs been part of the plot, too? Had they been accomplices by connivance? But that was too risky to consider, and he shuddered, knowing that he didn't dare voice such conjectures. But Salieri, he knew from his own experience, was capable of quick hostility.

Jason asked, "Salieri never resented your regard for Mozart?"

Schubert hesitated.

"You must have been influenced by Mozart, as Beethoven was."

"I couldn't avoid it."

"And Salieri resented that, didn't he, Herr Schubert?"

"It led to the worst moment I had with him." This was blurted out in a spurt of emotion, and then Schubert was relieved; he had yearned to talk about this ever since it had happened. When he saw that they were listening intently, he went on, although his voice dropped so that no one could hear him except those at his table. He felt as if he were releasing himself from a rope that had threatened to choke him for a long time.

"In 1816 a Sunday was set aside to commemorate the fiftieth anniversary of Maestro Salieri's arrival in Vienna. He was to be awarded many honors, including a gold medal that was to be presented in the name of the Emperor, but the festivity that concerned me was a concert to be given in his home by his pupils. And I had been asked, as one of his foremost pupils in composition, to write a cantata to celebrate the anniversary of his fiftieth year in Vienna. This was regarded as a great privilege. Salieri had taught most of the leading musicians in Vienna, and twenty-six of his students had been invited to his concert, and yet my composition was to be one of the featured pieces.

"Thus, when I was summoned to appear at his home one afternoon a week before the concert, I was excited. It was unusual for a student to see him in his home—I had never been there myself—and I arrived with a mixture of anticipation and apprehension. I was almost nineteen, and I felt that the cantata was the best piece I had composed. I was eager to find out what he thought about it, for there was no other reason he would order me to see him at his home. Yet I was nervous, too, for if he didn't like my work, it could be disastrous. He was the most influential musician in the Empire, with the power to recommend or destroy.

"A sumptuously dressed footman led me into Maestro Salieri's music room, and I was dazzled by the appointments, the most magnificent I had seen outside the Royal palace, but before I could become accustomed to these surroundings, Salieri appeared through the French doors.

"Suddenly I was frightened. I had been choirboy in the Court choir until my voice had broken when I was fifteen, and then I had become a student in the Imperial and Royal Seminary and had two classes a week with Maestro Salieri to study counterpoint. But never had I seen my teacher so angry. His features, which were usually sallow, were flushed and his black eyes glowered, and he seemed to tower over me, although he wasn't much taller than I was. He held my cantata in his hand, and before I could speak, he cried out in his bad German, which I always found hard to understand—but while he had lived in Vienna since 1766, he spoke hardly anything but Italian, except to those of us who didn't understand it—'You've been listening to the wrong music!'

" 'How, Maestro?' I cried. Was this why he had summoned me here?

" 'You've written most of this cantata in the barbarous German style.'

"Salieri pushed my cantata under my nose, knowing that I was very nearsighted. As I strained to see through my spectacles, his sentiments were quite plain; for now I saw that he had crossed out whole passages that I had composed. It was a terrible feeling, as if a large part of me had been mutilated, but I was quiet.

"He said, 'I wanted to speak to you privately, before your self-indulgence goes too far and carries you out of reach. If you continue to commit such eccentricities, I will not be able to recommend you. I couldn't risk it.' Suddenly he was being indifferent to me.

"I asked humbly, 'Maestro, may I look at my mistakes?'

" 'Indeed,' he said, almost contemptuously, and handed me the cantata.

"I was stunned. Every passage he had destroyed had been in the style of Mozart, where I had sought to capture his grace and eloquence.

"I was still studying his corrections when I heard him laugh harshly and declare, 'I suppose, however, that once one is born a German, he will always be a German. Your cantata also contains the howlings that some people prefer these days, but whose vogue will die soon.'

"I realized that now he was referring to Beethoven. I had sold my school books to hear *Fidelio*, but how could I tell him? In this dreadful moment I wanted to flee, but I knew that if I did, all chances of advancement in Vienna would vanish, and so I bowed my head, more meekly than I felt, and asked, 'Maestro, what have I done wrong?'

" 'You've failed to set this score in the Italian style.'

"But that was old-fashioned, I longed to retort; and if Mozart and Beethoven were my models, I was like most of the other students. But I said, 'I didn't mean to, Maestro. Only I like Viennese sounds.'

" 'Hideous sounds,' he declared. 'I cannot allow this piece to appear at a concert in my honor. It would disgrace my teaching.'

"By now I was hopelessly in love with Mozart, but I realized more than ever I could not admit this. It was common knowledge among the students that any trace of Mozart's influence had to be exorcised from our texts, although publicly Salieri professed the greatest admiration for Mozart's music. I had accepted this as the natural envy of one composer for another, but now I wondered if his envy went deeper than this.

"Salieri said, 'If you cannot find adequate music without these nauseous influences, I cannot allow your music at my concert.'

"I felt I was sitting on blazing coals. In my despair I asked myself, Should I give up composing? Wasn't it too hard to please? But Mozart spoke to me with such a divine voice that within me, even as I listened to Salieri, I was humming one of Mozart's melodies; and as I contemplated the prospect of never composing as I wished, the pain was unbearable. So I did something which I have always regretted. I asked supplicatingly, 'Maestro, what can I do to show my contrition?'

" 'It is too late to alter your cantata and manipulate it in the Italian style. You will have to write something simpler. A trio for pianoforte.'

"I nodded, unable to speak. I preferred composing for the voice.

"Using the weight of his authority, he added, 'A few words in a poem as an expression of gratitude for what I have done for my students would be useful and would help me overlook your ill-intentioned cantata. I can only recommend students who have cooperated with me.'

"I agreed, and Salieri walked me to the door of his music room, indicating that the discussion was over."

Schubert halted, still stricken by the memory, and Jason asked, "What happened at the concert for Salieri?"

"My trio for pianoforte was played. It was in the Italian style, and he praised it. But I felt like a cheat. Verses I wrote eulogizing him and stating how much we owed him were read and applauded. It sounded sincere, but I was embarrassed. I couldn't remove the pain I had felt when he had exorcised Mozart and even Beethoven from my music. If I couldn't heed them, there was no point to music. It was very discouraging. I kept wondering whether it was wise to want to be a composer."

Jason waited a moment to allow the others to absorb what Schubert had told them, then inquired, "When did you leave Salieri?"

"The same year."

"Did he recommend you for any posts?"

"Oh, yes, for several."

"Did you get any of them?"

"No. Each time he recommended others, too."

"Who did get the posts?"

"The students he recommended the most."

"Didn't you resent that?"

"I didn't like that he favored someone else behind my back, saying that those students were the best qualified, but what could I do. He did allow me to introduce myself as his pupil, which was a great honor, and I consoled myself that there would be other opportunities."

"Were there? Did you ask Salieri for any other favors?"

"Some years later when I heard that there was a position vacant in the Imperial Court I applied for it, but I was informed that my music didn't appeal to the Emperor, that it was not in the Imperial style."

Deborah asked, "What did Salieri have to do with that?"

"He was the Imperial Musical Director, and he had great influence with the Emperor. Everyone knew that the Emperor never appointed anyone without consulting Maestro Salieri first."

"So, in effect," said Jason, "it was Salieri who turned you down."

"Officially, no. Unofficially, yes."

"And you didn't mind?"

"Of course I did. But what could I do about it? Cry out to the world? That would have been useless. There is no one who understands the pain of others. We are always imagining that we are living together, when actually we are far apart. Moreover, if I had those posts now I couldn't retain them. I have such pains in my left arm these days I cannot play the pianoforte at all. Composing is all that is left to me."

"Is it rheumatism?" Deborah asked solicitously. Schubert was so mournful suddenly, it was appalling.

He grimaced, drank to their health, and said impetuously, "I have a serious complaint, but I suffer it. From the greatest exaltation to the utterly absurd is but a brief step, and we must accept that." As he saw several of his friends standing at the entrance to the café, he asked, "Would you like to meet them?"

Deborah waited for Jason to answer, and he hesitated. For a moment it sounded interesting; but Schindler looked noncommittal, and too many people already knew why he was here, he thought, so he shook his head no.

But as Schubert rose to say goodbye, he seemed to want to talk about Mozart as much as Jason did, declaring with passion, "You never know what inner misery tortures someone else. Perhaps this afflicted Mozart and hastened his end. And if he confided that in anyone, it would have been his wife. Because a man composes beautiful music doesn't mean that he is happy. Think of a man whose health will never be good again, and who in his despair makes it worse. Imagine an artist whose glowing hopes have died, for he has come to realize the ultimate impermanence of things, particularly himself. Imagine the unbearable poignance that brings to every smile and embrace. Or when he falls asleep each night, he is not certain he will awake the next day. Imagine thinking of yourself dead when you are still young. Imagine that there is neither a heaven nor earth, but that soon you are to be enclosed in an eternal night, alone and apart."

Schubert had become sombre, and Jason sensed that he was talking about himself as much as he was about Mozart.

Schubert continued sadly, "Most of us are afraid to think of our own death, but when you sense that it is near, as Mozart did, as some of us do, even though you are still young and active, how fearful that is. How likely it is that in his terror he may have hurried his own end, and been an accomplice in that. As some of us are."

Jason asked, "Then you do not believe that Salieri had anything to do with Mozart's death? Even if he has gone mad? And feels guilty?"

"It is easy to feel guilty. And Salieri has reason to. As for going mad, for some it is not such a long distance to travel."

"Then you accept his madness, Herr Schubert?"

"I accept that everyone has a breaking point and that his could be reached a little quicker than most."

Schubert's friends were standing by the table. Jason, troubled by what he had just heard, was in no mood for trivialities, and he felt surrounded by amateurs, gifted perhaps, but dilettantes in essence, clustering around the artist like the drones about the queen bee.

After the proper goodbyes were said, they pushed their way through the crowd. It was annoying to Jason, for it was as if a wall had risen to make their departure painful. He had a nasty moment when he felt a sharp, painful elbow in his ribs. It was impossible to tell where it came from, he was surrounded by so many people; yet Deborah was on one side of him and Schindler was on the other, struggling as he was to reach the door.

But finally, they were almost at the door, slightly nauseated, when someone stumbled and bumped into Jason. He thought the man was drunk, but the man apologized profusely; and then he heard another man sneer, "Schubert! A tavern politician!" He turned around to see who it was, but that man disappeared into the crowd. For an instant Jason thought someone was touching him; he could have sworn that there was a hand on his chest—but no, it must have been his imagination, he told himself, for when he glanced around no one was there. Both men were gone in the crowd now. Yet, for a moment . . .?

Jason and Deborah were climbing the stairway to their rooms on the Petersplatz when he realized suddenly that he had been robbed. The money he had been carrying in his inner coat pocket was gone.

Schindler had left them down below, and it was too late to run after him. Then he realized how it must have happened, crying out, "I thought the man who stumbled against me was drunk, but he must have been the pickpocket while the other man distracted me. Something terrible has happened, Deborah. All of my money is gone!" He felt as though a knife had been thrust through his heart.

She was about to put the key in the door, but Jason was standing as if transfixed. Shocked, she retorted irritably, "You weren't carrying all of your money on you? How could you be so reckless?"

"I was carrying most of it. After the way Ernst Muller was able to enter our rooms, I was afraid to leave much of it here."

"You are sure that you didn't lose it?"

"I don't see how. I've been extremely careful." He looked again, and said, "It is all gone. Every penny." He was appalled.

But she insisted on searching their rooms in the hope that he was mistaken, although he assured her that he wasn't. When he went to where he had hidden his money, there was just the little bit he had left.

She started to undress, to hide her agitation. Suddenly he said he was going back to the café, and without another word he was gone.

She was terrified then, sure that he wouldn't return, that someone must be watching them still and now was their opportunity, although what they would do she had no idea. But she would have done almost anything to avoid being alone, and she thought of calling Hans, whom she disliked, or Frau Herzog, who would talk too much. Instead, full of misgivings, she put all her clothes on, even her coat, and sat on the bed, knees tucked under her chin, shivering and struggling to keep from sobbing, and feeling very weak, on the verge of fainting.

Jason hurried back to Bogner's Café. It wasn't far, but he was surprised by the darkness of the streets. It was after midnight and he had a feeling he was being followed, but he didn't care; he must get to the café before it closed and the people left. He was too late, however for when he reached the café it was dark and no one was about.

It wasn't fair, he cried to himself. He was panting heavily, and he felt the sweat forming on his forehead, although it was November and chilly. But he saw no one behind him, which was a small relief. Then he realized that he had left America with almost two thousand dollars, his earnings from the Handel and Haydn hymn books, a small fortune, and now virtually all of it was gone. He felt trapped, as if his quest had eaten away a large and vital part of his life.

Yet when he returned to their rooms, he tried to hide his inner torment and appear composed. Deborah had all the lights lit, grateful that they had so many candles and lamps, but even the bedroom was dingy now, and as she heard him enter, she looked up slowly and hesitantly as if she could not believe that it was Jason. Then instead of reproaching him for poking his nose into this business, she collapsed in his arms, sobbing as if her heart would break, while he wondered what he could say to her. He felt that they were surrounded by sinister forces, while she was behaving as if she had been violated.

27

Neither Praise nor Blame

THERE was no choice now. Jason had to accept the use of Deborah's money. But he also had to report the robbery to Huber, in addition to requesting his permission to visit Salzburg.

They were admitted to Huber's office quickly, after the usual bribe, and the internal security officer greeted them almost cordially—Jason assumed that was because Huber knew of the arrangement with Beethoven—and he offered them a glass of wine. It was not as tasty as the Tokay that Schubert had given them, but Jason thanked Huber for his hospitality.

Deborah had warned Jason to get permission to visit Salzburg first, before the internal security officer could become irritated, and not to mention the police when he spoke of the robbery, for surely that would offend Huber, but the robbery had upset Jason too much for him to be cautious. He blurted out what had happened in the café and stated, "What makes it worse, a police inspector was present."

Huber, who had been lounging in his throne-like seat, stiffened until he was as straight as the high back of his chair. His gray eyes became like two small stones and his smile vanished, and he said sharply, "Otis, are you implying that the police were responsible for this theft?"

"I didn't say that, sir. But a police inspector was there."

"How do you know that this person was one of my men?"

"Herr Schubert, the composer, told me."

Huber made a gesture of contempt.

"And this man was watching us. Like a spy."

Huber laughed as if that was absurd. "Do you think we are so obvious? If one of my men had been watching you, you wouldn't have known it."

Jason insisted, "He was watching somebody."

"Schubert, possibly. Schubert is politically unreliable."

Deborah sensed that Huber was growing irritated, but she was so grateful that Jason had accepted her money she sat silently, determined not to aggravate him, however she differed with him, and pretended to sip Huber's wine as if they were really his guests.

Yet that was difficult to believe now; for Huber didn't offer them a second glass but sat angrily, as if the implication that his men could have been involved in a robbery was offensive.

"And I was robbed," Jason repeated. "Probably in the café."

"Probably in the café? You're not even sure where it happened."

"I'm almost sure. I was jostled there. It must have happened there."

"It could have been one of Schubert's friends. Schubert keeps bad company, unreliable company. Have you spoken to him about it?"

"I haven't seen him since."

"Maybe he did it himself. He is quite poor. He is always in need."

Jason was outraged by Huber's sneer, but he sought to control himself, answering, "Schubert insisted on paying for everything himself."

"To cause you to be gullible, perhaps."

"No. If anyone was involved in the robbery, it was the inspector. There is no reason to assume that he is any different from everybody else."

Huber brought his hand down on his marble-topped table so hard Deborah thought he would crack it, and he nearly overturned his nude Venus in his anger as he snapped, "How dare you make such an assumption, Otis?"

"What assumption, sir?" Jason answered innocently.

"That my men would indulge in such a vulgar business. We represent the Crown. We are responsible only to Prince Metternich and the Emperor."

"Oh, I have no doubt that he did it without your knowledge."

"Indeed!"

"That is why I brought this affair to your attention. I thought you would be as offended as I was. And that you would correct it, sir."

Huber was irate once more, but most of all with himself. He had done something he considered unpardonable: he had shown emotion. He must not allow this to happen again, ever. But as his face became expressionless, he was filled with hatred for this young American who had prodded him into self-exposure, although it had been only for a moment. And Otis had not even had the decency to offer him a present, when his favors had earned him one of the finest collection of jeweled snuffboxes in Vienna and many other valuable trinkets. They would pay for their neglect, he resolved; he would see to that. Master and servant, he thought contemptuously; that was the way of the world, and he must never allow that to alter. He sat behind his desk, not indicating what he was thinking, but many ideas formulated in his mind. He was positive now that the only reason they had visited Schubert was to discuss Salieri. Why else would anyone wish to visit a misfit like Schubert! Surely it was not to study with him, and Schubert was too poor to bargain with. But if it had been one of his men who had robbed them, he would have his head. He despised such inefficiency; it was stupid and unnecessary. If these Americans were as disruptive as he suspected, the trap could be set in a better, more innocent way. He didn't need such fools in his employ. He had sources of information close enough to supply him with a dossier on all their movements, he reflected gloatingly, sources that would be afraid to betray him. There was much that he was starting to comprehend. He was proud that he had the patience. And the skill. Even for these rich Americans. How gratifying it would be to catch them in an act against the State. Now nothing else mattered more. He felt much better then.

Jason asked, "Sir, do you think you could help me recover my money?"

"It is not a police matter," Huber replied curtly.

"Not a police matter?" Deborah cried, shocked by his attitude.

"You have no proof. Is there anything else?"

She hurried to remind him despite her dismay. "The reason we came here is to get your permission to visit Salzburg, as you suggested."

"As I ordered. How long do you expect to be gone?"

Jason said, "A few weeks. Until Beethoven finishes the oratorio."

Huber sat silently, his eyes fixed chillingly beyond them, and Deborah had a feeling that he didn't believe a word they were saying.

Jason added, "We have kept our word; we have arranged for Beethoven to compose an oratorio for the Handel and Haydn Society of Boston. Think of the prestige that will bring Vienna."

"Prestige?" sneered Huber. "Do you think that will protect us against seditious influences? Are you still reading revolutionary works?"

"You told us that we shouldn't."

"Do you think I assumed that a wayward American like you would listen? Have you finished Beaumarchais' *Figaro*?"

"You confiscated my copy. At the city gates. Remember?"

"Copies can be obtained in Vienna, secretly. Are you still infatuated with Mozart's *Figaro*?"

"It's a great opera, sir."

"I doubt that. Nobody goes to hear it anymore."

"Then why do you dislike it so, sir?"

"It is full of provocations. The aria *Non più andrai,* for instance, ridicules the very foundation of the Empire, our army. But at least you had the good sense to ask my permission to visit Salzburg. Otherwise you could have been arrested."

Deborah said softly, "We have done our best to be obedient, sir."

"No doubt. Is that why you are going to Salzburg?"

Jason said hurriedly, "We have decided to make it a second honeymoon. We've been told it is one of the most beautiful cities in the world."

"I know all about the scenery. Are there any other reasons?"

Jason replied slowly, "It is Mozart's birthplace."

"Obviously. And you expect to pursue your musical studies there?"

Deborah wanted to halt Jason before he incriminated himself further; but Jason thought this line of questioning was innocent, and he answered, "Yes. Mozart and Beethoven are my musical models."

"Not Salieri?"

"No!" Jason was surprised. "No one studies Salieri."

"Yet you continue to make inquiries about him. Why?"

Jason was silent, and Deborah, sensing that was most incriminating of all, volunteered, "Salieri taught Beethoven. His influence is important. May we have our passports now, Herr Huber, so we can go to Salzburg?"

Huber sat motionless, and his thin lips barely moved as he said, "Do you have enough money with Grob to maintain you until you return to Boston?"

"I believe so, Herr Huber. Don't we, Jason?"

"I don't know," he said abruptly, proudly. "It is my wife's money."

"If you don't, you will have to return to America. At once." Suddenly Huber felt elated; perhaps the robbery had been sensible after all.

Jason said quickly, "I'm sure my wife has enough."

"I hope so," Huber said grimly. Whatever they professed, he would verify it with the banker. "If not, the consequences could be unfortunate."

Deborah repeated, "May we have our passports now, Herr Huber?"

"Not yet. Where are your temporary visas?"

Jason handed them to Huber, and he was stunned when Huber wrote across them *"Politically unreliable"* and returned them, saying, "These will suffice to get you to Salzburg and back."

As Huber saw Jason's shock, he said in an icy tone that made Deborah's blood run cold, "You shouldn't mind, Otis. Your friend Beethoven is also politically unreliable, and so is Schubert. As your idol, Mozart, was."

Jason longed to oppose this accusation with all of his sensibility, but he was quiet, afraid that he would say the wrong thing. Deborah said, thinking someone had to be practical, for Jason wasn't, "Can we go by the public post, if we want?" She was determined not to use Hans.

"The express coach to Salzburg leaves only once a week, and then it stops at Linz and takes a very long time. And it is poorly sprung; often axles are broken, coaches are overturned, and many of its passengers are bruised and battered. Your own coach would be safer."

"Is that an order, sir?" she asked.

"Advice. As a friend. I want you to avoid discomfort and danger."

"What happens if the weather should be bad and delay us in Salzburg and we get back to Vienna after the first of the year, after our visas have expired? Or if Beethoven should be dilatory in his composing?"

"You will have to apply for a renewal of your identity papers."

"What happens then?"

"We will cross that bridge when we come to it."

"Is there any alternative?" she cried out.

"Leave Vienna for good and we will return your passports."

Yes, sir, she yearned to reply. But she knew that if she said this it could end her marriage, and so she glanced at Jason appealingly.

Huber declared, "Beethoven could mail you the oratorio."

When Jason didn't answer, Deborah asked him, "Have you decided, Jason?"

He said, "I must see Beethoven's finished oratorio before I can accept it. Herr Huber, what happens if these visas are stolen? Or lost?"

"Without identity papers you will be thrown into jail."

Jason put them into his inner pocket, where he had kept his money, and said, "Then I must be more careful. May we go now, sir?"

Herr Huber extended his hands in a gesture that was expansive for him and said, "Of course. As long as you don't infringe on our hospitality. Or threaten our security." He escorted Deborah to the door and said to her, "Frau Otis, you are such an attractive woman it causes me to wonder how you could have involved yourself on such a hopeless quest. Especially when, with your money, you could have such a pleasant life. The wisest thing you could do would be to leave Vienna. Before it is too late."

Jason pulled her out of Huber's office before she could respond.

But on the street he noticed that she was staring at him with an expression that was close to despair. He sighed deeply and said, "You should not have to ask me *why* any more. If that isn't clear to you now, it never will be." Yet when she still looked apprehensive, he added, "It is natural for a policeman to speak of danger, and Huber is, above all, a policeman. Besides, he is trying to get our secrets out of us. If you want me to use your money, you must trust me, you must allow me a free hand."

She smiled, attempting to hide her returning fears and doubts, and said, "You must see Grob as soon as possible, to expedite our trip to Salzburg."

Yet Jason was not appeased, for in spite of all they had gone through together lately and the fact that she had behaved better than he had expected, there were still moments when he wasn't sure he could trust her.

At Grob's office the next day Deborah assumed the role of the agreeable wife and assented to everything Jason said. She was startled that the banker was not surprised by the news of the robbery, but after Grob reproached Jason for not heeding his advice and leaving the stolen money with him, she was pleased that he congratulated Jason on her foresight.

He explained to a puzzled Jason, "Frau Otis' good sense in depositing her funds in both your names makes the business formalities simple."

"I hope so," said Jason.

But then Grob shook his head woefully. "To think of all that money in the hands of a thief! What a waste! How tragic!" He dismissed the possibility that the police might have been involved as ridiculous, crying out, "Herr Otis, we are not barbarians! Vienna is the most civilized city in the world. It must have been one of Schubert's tavern companions."

"That's what Huber said."

"Obviously."

"And when I criticized the police he censured me."

"Naturally. He is a proud man and he doesn't like being opposed. Agree with him and you won't have any more trouble. Herr Otis, how much money do you want to take with you to Salzburg?"

"That depends on how long it will take Beethoven to complete the oratorio. Have you heard from him lately?"

"No. But I put five hundred gulden in his name. To be given to him when he delivers the oratorio. As you've heard, he can be unreliable."

"That's what Huber said."

Grob shrugged. "Everybody knows that."

"He stated that Mozart was politically unreliable, too. Do you know why?"

"There could be many reasons. I wouldn't worry about that now. Schindler told me that Beethoven is working on the oratorio. You may be lucky; he may finish this work for a change. How much money do you want?"

Jason glanced over to Deborah, who motioned, As much as you want, and he said, "Five hundred gulden. That should take us to Salzburg and back."

"Easily," said Grob, "especially since you are taking your own coach."

"Our own coach?" exclaimed Deborah. That had not been decided yet. Grob must have spoken to Huber, whatever the banker professed.

"Yes. To go by public post when you can afford your own is foolish. And you have such a fine coach and experienced driver at your service."

At their rooms Deborah was still against using Hans, and Jason replied that her fears were groundless. He called Hans into their rooms to show her that he was having his own way, and he told him to buy a new wheel and a spare one for the journey to Salzburg. She interrupted, asking Hans, "How are your relatives?"

"Fine," said Hans.

"Why haven't you introduced us to them?" she asked.

"They are peasants. You would have nothing in common with them."

That added to her suspicions, for Hans was eager to go now, saying, "I must order the wheel if you are to leave for Salzburg in a few days."

Jason agreed, cutting Deborah short.

When they were able to leave for Salzburg within a week, Jason was positive that this justified his confidence in Hans. He had obtained a letter of introduction to Constanze from Ernst Muller, but he had not told him about the robbery, preferring to avoid more criticism and eager to reach the next stop on his quest. He was certain that Constanze could give him information that no one else could.

Yet at the gates of Vienna, despite the precautions Jason had taken, they were halted by the guards. And when the guards read the words *"Politically unreliable"* on their visas, they searched their luggage thoroughly and asked insolent questions, although this time nothing was found that could be confiscated. Jason had left all of his books in their rooms on the Petersplatz and had packed only clothes, addresses, and the letter, which was read, noted, and returned without comment.

Only after they were through the gates did Deborah's uneasiness lessen. Jason was more relaxed then, too, invigorated by the clear, bright blue sky over their heads, and he said, "We must make the most out of this visit. Whatever happens."

"Have I blamed you for anything?" Deborah cried out.

"No," he admitted grudgingly. "But you might."

"We must not praise or blame each other. As you said, whatever happens."

Jason didn't answer, preoccupied with the landscape. For even as Deborah was speaking more reassuringly, the countryside was becoming wintry, and while their coach was riding comfortably, it was growing cloudy ahead of them, and he had to warn her before she became panicky and made the trip even harder. He said suddenly, ominously, "There is a threat of snow in the air now. We could be riding into a heavy storm."

J

28

Salzburg

THE STORM did not materialize that day. Jason was relieved, for it had been his decision to take this route to Salzburg and to go at this time of the year despite the warnings of Frau Herzog, who had said that the weather could be wretched. Deborah sat beside him reflectively, and he felt she was humoring him for the sake of peace, which added to his determination to show her that he was right. The road outside of Vienna was good and Jason, who had memorized the biography of Mozart, pointed out to her the Schönbrunn Palace as they passed it, saying, "Mozart played there triumphantly as a child," and when they rode through the town of Parkesdorf with its many villas, he declared, "This is where Mozart said goodbye to his beloved father for the last time."

She merely nodded, not really interested. She was thinking that Jason was so committed to his quest he had to act in a headlong, confident manner. But would he have accepted her reason for writing her father the day before their departure, she reflected, urging him to send her another thousand gulden as soon as possible. Afraid that Jason would have objected, called her disloyal, and halted her, she had kept this letter a secret. But the possibility of being penniless in Vienna appalled her. She felt that would give Huber a power over them that they could not oppose, but that as long as they possessed money Huber would have to move carefully.

By the time they stopped at St. Polten for the night, Jason was very much aware of Deborah's mood of reflection. Although she lay next to him in bed, she was unusually quiet. He wondered if she realized that he was afraid to be reflective, that if he thought about all the dangers and the difficulties, he might not find the courage to continue.

The next day the sky fell upon them with a vicious downpour that threatened to flatten them against the earth. But Hans drove on, as if it were essential for him to go on, thought Deborah. Hans was so eager to serve them it added to her suspicions. In the middle of the afternoon one of their horses developed a limp because of a bad shoe, and the coach teetered and slithered dangerously and almost overturned. Jason ordered Hans to halt at the next post stop, where they changed horses; but a few miles later one of the fresh horses threw his shoe.

Quite upset himself, Jason sought to soothe Deborah, who sat trembling, for the coach had almost overturned again, and now he told Hans to slow the horses to a walk until they reached a blacksmith.

The gaunt, elderly blacksmith, who also ran a small store, would not guarantee that his work would last until they reached Salzburg. He said, "Once these roads become slippery, anything can happen. It was conditions like this that caused Maria Theresa's coach to overturn. She was flung out on her face, and it was scraped so badly on the loose gravel she was scarred permanently, ruining what little was left of her beauty. You are such a nice-looking young lady, it would be a shame if anything like that happened to you."

She asked apprehensively, "Do you really think that is possible?"

"Of course. It was rumored that the Empress' coach had been tampered with. By political enemies. Have you checked your wheels?"

Jason asked the blacksmith to do so, and when he found that the new wheel was out of line, he fixed it. Jason hid this from Deborah, knowing that it would add to her distrust of Hans. But now he ordered Hans to drive carefully all of the time, and he watched him closely, too.

As the weather became worse, Hans drove more cautiously. Approaching Linz, which Jason considered halfway to Salzburg although Deborah reminded him that in actual miles it wasn't, the weather was so bad that Hans slowed the horses to a walk again. Rain and snow blotted out everything around them. One of their coach wheels threw up a rock which ricocheted through the window where Deborah was sitting, shattering the glass, and jagged pieces of glass just missed her eyes. She thought she was going to faint. But icy air blew into her face, and the appalling cold caused her to shiver uncontrollably. Jason hastily hung his coat across the broken window, which lessened the wind but not the cold.

He sat shivering, too. Deborah put her head through the shattered window, ignoring the jagged glass, and shouted to Hans, "Hurry! Before I freeze to death!" Anything was better than that, she thought.

Hans whipped the horses despite the slippery road, and while the coach almost went off the road and she sat with her eyes closed and she was sure they were going to die and she prayed that it would be quick and not like this ghastly cold, they reached Linz without any further mishaps.

Jason agreed to wait there until the weather improved. When it stopped snowing the next day and he was able to hear Mozart's overture to *Don Giovanni*, his *Sinfonia concertante* for Violin and Viola and Orchestra in E Flat, and his last symphony, the "Jupiter," his spirits improved and he told Deborah that it had been a marvelous interruption. Every seat at the concert in the opera house was taken, and each piece was applauded emotionally. Jason realized with gratification that this audience, too, remembered that Linz had fond musical memories of Mozart.

Deborah was deeply moved by the sombre beauty of the *Sinfonia concertante,* as Jason had been, but she shrugged. Jason was saying that Mozart had written this music with nobility, but she doubted that there was nobility anywhere in the world, and she did not want to encourage his love of Mozart further—it was overwhelming enough as it was.

The overture to *Don Giovanni* aroused Jason's desire to hear the entire opera, but the *Sinfonia concertante* caused him to wonder what had made Mozart so sad and reflective, and he was puzzled that no one knew where the title of the "Jupiter" symphony had come from.

By now he was sick of travelling, but she would not believe him, he thought. But inwardly rebellious, he prepared for the rest of the trip with the utmost care. He had a blacksmith examine every nut and bolt in the coach; each horse was shod with new shoes; the window was fixed with the heaviest glass available; and he went over all of this himself, trusting no one's judgment anymore, even looking at the axles, hearing that this was a source of accidents, too. And to protect Deborah from the cold he bought her a fur coat, a hooded fur hat, fur gloves, and boots lined with fur, although that reduced his money by a hundred gulden.

Hans, who feared that he had lost all circulation, his legs had become so numb, wanted to quit, but he was afraid that the consequences could be even worse. The only thing he could do, he decided, was to act naturally, to dress more warmly, avoid the bad weather whenever he could, and obtain more heat. So he suggested that they furnish him with turf.

"Turf?" repeated Jason. "What is that?"

"It is a little stove in a wooden box which contains a small earthen pan with turf that is heated. You keep your feet in it, the heat lasts a few hours, and when it goes out you can heat it again. Strangers to it don't like it at first, because if you are not used to it, it can give you a headache, but it is better than being frozen. May I have some turf?"

Jason nodded, and purchased turf for the three of them.

They resumed the trip to Salzburg when the sun shone. It was straight ahead of them, for they were moving almost directly west now—in the direction of Boston, too, Deborah thought with a sigh—and it was low on the horizon, in their eyes, but none of them minded. And on an empty part of the road Hans halted the coach so he could relieve himself.

Deborah started out of the coach to stretch her legs and suddenly there was a thunderous roar and in her shock and fear she fell off the step, scraping her shin. A moment later an irate man appeared out of a field, brandishing a gun, followed by a retinue of servants.

Baron von Staub was furious. How dare a servant use his private hunting preserve to relieve himself! No wonder he had thought the driver was a deer; it was certainly not his fault. If the sun hadn't been hazy, he shouted at Jason, he would never have missed such a fine target.

Deborah hurried over to translate, for the Baron spoke German with a provincial accent, and Jason was having difficulty understanding the burly, florid old man with his swollen neck and imperial whiskers.

At the sight of Deborah the Baron regarded her admiringly, examined the coach with respect, studying the coat of arms on it, and said to her, "You are a countess, no doubt. The coat of arms indicates that your husband is in the Hapsburg service."

She nodded, hoping that he would believe her.

"I'm Baron von Staub. We have the best meat in the Empire. In such wild country it is fleshy, Countess. I would be honored to have you and your husband as my guests to dinner."

"Thank you, but my husband has an urgent engagement in Salzburg."

When Deborah told Jason how the Baron had been fooled, he praised her quick thinking; but her shin ached painfully, and she prayed that they would finish this journey without any serious injury.

They entered Salzburg on the Linzerstrasse. The afternoon was clear, and in the bright, sunny air the town was superbly attractive. It was amazing, Deborah reflected; just a short time ago she had felt near death and now she felt magnificently alive.

Salzburg was the most beautiful town that Jason had seen, and he was full of admiration. Mountains encircled Salzburg, framed Salzburg, and dominated Salzburg. There was snow on the peaks, but none on the ground, for which he was thankful. A town to paint, to write about, but he had been told that Mozart had despised it, yet he wondered if that was correct. This had been Mozart's home. How could Mozart have disliked his home? The farther he was from Boston, the more he craved Boston. When he had started out, he had never thought he would feel that way. How could Mozart have hated Salzburg, Salzburg was so beautiful.

He told Hans to pause on the bridge that crossed the Salzach River and separated the old town from the new, and Deborah said, "Do you think that Mozart ever felt he owned Salzburg as the town now feels it owns him?"

"I doubt it," said Jason. "He ran away from it whenever he could. But Salzburg, visually, is one of the scenic wonders of the world."

She thought, I will have to hold down his enthusiasm or it will lead us into more dangerous waters. Yet she had to admit to herself that the town was an impressive sight. The old part of Salzburg nestled against the curve of a mountain, the Monchsberg, and on top of it was the castle of Hohensalzburg, situated like a royal crown, commanding and dramatic.

Ernst Muller had recommended a small inn on the river, and Jason liked its location. He rented the entire top floor. Their reception room faced the Salzach and the new town, while the bedroom looked out upon the old town, and as Jason lay on the bed to try it out, he could see the Hohensalzburg and the portion of Salzburg where Mozart had been born.

He yearned to clutch at everything that was reminiscent of Mozart, but Deborah wanted to rest. And as he stood up to rush off to Constanze's address with the letter of introduction that Ernst had given him, Deborah said, "If you arrive uninvited, you could antagonize her and she won't tell you anything. Or even see you." A quiet Alpine dusk was deepening over Salzburg, and she added, "You must give her time to get ready for visitors. Pretty herself up a little, compose herself, so she will not feel surprised. Otherwise she could be resentful, uncooperative."

This sounded sensible to Jason, and he followed her suggestion. After Hans put the coach and horses in a nearby stable, he sent him to the address for Constanze that Ernst had given him. He added a brief note to the letter of introduction, writing:

> As one who has been deeply moved by the beauty of Mozart's music, and your devotion to him, I have come to Salzburg to pay my respects to the one who was nearest and dearest to him.

Constanze's address was within walking distance, and Jason waited eagerly yet anxiously for her reply, while Deborah tried to nap. But she, too, was a mixture of anticipation and apprehension, and she could not sleep.

Hans returned quickly, looking upset.

"What's wrong?" asked Jason. "Was it the wrong address?"

"No," said Hans. "I knocked on the door and a maid answered and said Frau Constanze von Nissen lived there."

"Did you give her the two letters?"

"Yes. But after the maid took them, she slammed the door in my face."

"Didn't you request an answer?" Jason cried desperately.

"Just as you instructed me, Herr Otis. But I had barely gotten that out of my mouth when the maid yelled, 'Frau von Nissen will answer when and if she deems that suitable,' and I was left empty-handed."

Jason's impulse was to accost Constanze at once, but Deborah warned him again that such an act would be rash, perhaps even fatal, although like Jason, she wondered if Hans had actually delivered the letter.

So Jason sought to control his impatience, but when there was no reply in a few days, he decided to go to Constanze's address himself. He was surprised that Hans had not told him how difficult it was to reach this house. As he climbed the narrow lane on the Nonnberg, it was so steep in spots he had to assist Deborah to keep her from falling.

The maid who answered his knock regarded him with indifference. When he asked, "Did you receive two letters for Frau von Nissen recently?" she nodded; and when he said, "Can I expect a reply soon? I'm Herr Otis from America?" the maid looked aloof and shrugged.

Deborah, who had been silent, asked suddenly, "Is she home?"

"No."

"Is she out of Salzburg?"

"No."

"Where is she?" Jason asked.

The maid stood like stone and did not answer.

Impulsively, he placed twenty-five gulden in an envelope, sealed it carefully, and wrote:

Dear Frau von Nissen, this is just a modest token of appreciation for your services to Mozart and his music from your admirers in America. We have come a long way to meet you, and if we could have the privilege of seeing you while we are in Salzburg we would be honored.

He added his address as a postscript.

The next morning there was a reply from Constanze, apologizing for not having been able to see them as yet, but if they would be patient she would be happy to meet them soon, and she would notify them when.

But as a week passed without word from Constanze, Jason felt desolate. Without the Weber women, the quest was doomed. Had they been warned not to see them by Huber, he wondered? Or were there other reasons?

He tried to muffle his fears by visiting everything associated with Mozart, and Deborah was grateful that the November weather remained clear.

She said, as they tramped around Salzburg and Hans drove them through the nearby countryside, "The air is so dry, sweet, and healthy, I feel reborn, and the silvery light that is so typical of late autumn gives everything such a soft yet heavenly clarity." She admired the ancient castles, the magnificent estates, the dignified churches, far more numerous than she had expected, the handsome marble façade of the cathedral, its spires which dominated the old town, the elaborate baroque squares, the monumental fountains, the many statues, and the beautiful views which were everywhere, and always, the mountains around them wherever she gazed.

Jason preferred the house on the Getreidegasse where Mozart had been born. One morning, by giving the servant who answered his knock two gulden, a small fortune to the servant, he was allowed to enter when no one was home. He noticed that the upper floor where Mozart had lived was just old wooden planks, but that the other floors were parquet. But then he had to leave, for the residents were approaching, and the servant said that they disliked strangers. He also visited the house on the Hannibalplatz where Mozart had spent the last part of his life in Salzburg, but this was even more disappointing, an echo of many houses that Jason had seen in Vienna, without distinction or beauty. He was fascinated by the solidity of the Residenz, the Archbishop's palace, which had been so much a part of Mozart's growing up, and intrigued by the dark, narrow, crooked streets of the old town that had known Mozart's footsteps, but the endless looking made him very tired, and his mind was strewn with too many unsolved clues for sightseeing to appease it.

Two weeks after they had arrived in Salzburg he lay on his bed and he did not want to get up, unable to look at another castle or church or any reminder of Mozart. December was tomorrow, and he was afraid they would never be able to return to Vienna before their visas expired. He felt he ought to take matters into his own hands and approach Constanze, even without an invitation, but Deborah continued to advise patience. He stared at the Hohensalzburg, which had dominated a Mozart as full of life as he was; and he wondered if the castle had depressed him, too. Yet as he lay there, near where Mozart had lain, it was as if they formed one body, one awareness. But to speak of this to anyone else was madness.

Deborah said irritably, "Aren't you getting up?"

He answered, "Do you think that the maid pocketed the money?"

"It is possible. Now I know how much the endless travelling must have drained Mozart of his essential energy and shortened his life."

"It is not what killed him," he said suddenly.

"Is that why you are lying in bed? Why you can't get up?"

"I feel surrounded by a world of sham."

"Because no one has acknowledged your presence in Salzburg?"

"I can't wait forever." He sat up abruptly. "But I do not regret this journey, no matter how it turns out. Do you?"

"No," she said, knowing it would be fatal to say anything else.

He regarded her affectionately, and in this instant he could not imagine life without her. A knock on the door brought him out of his reverie. It was Hans, with an invitation from Frau von Nissen to visit her tomorrow afternoon, that is, if they were still in Salzburg.

29

Constanze

Dearest, Most Beloved Wife of My Heart:
I simply cannot express with what eagerness I am looking forward to seeing you. My one wish is that you will be returning from Baden soon. When I recall how happy we were together, the days without you are lonely and melancholy indeed. My precious Stanzi, love me for ever as I love you. I kiss you a million times and I await your return passionately.
Your ever loving
Mozart.

These lines ran through Jason's head like a musical refrain from a Mozart opera while he and Deborah prepared for their visit to Constanze as if they were going to visit Mozart himself. He had memorized these words from letters Mozart had written to his wife in the last few months of his life, and they added to Jason's expectancy.

Deborah wore her most stylish clothes, and Jason dressed in a blue waistcoat and gray trousers because they were Mozart's favorite colors.

Finally the much anticipated time was at hand; and as they climbed the steep, winding lane leading to Constanze's house, he wished they had wings. Although the day was clear, the climb was tiring and he was breathless.

"Look!" cried Deborah, pausing to regain her own breath. Her heart was beating faster with excitement, and she wondered how an elderly woman like Mozart's widow could navigate this arduous walk. "We are next to the Monchsberg and directly under the Hohensalzburg. What a splendid location! Do you think it was given her because she was Mozart's wife?"

"I don't know."

"Do you think that she will finish with us quickly?"

"Deborah, we haven't even met her and you are talking about it ending."

"You have read everything that you could find out about her. Especially whatever letters of Mozart that are available."

"His letters are full of love and a remarkable richness of emotion. But that doesn't mean that Constanze shared his feelings. I can't find anything that she wrote."

"Perhaps she didn't always agree with him. Jason, suppose she asks us to come back and to see her several times?"

"Then we will see her several times. As long as that is necessary."

"That could bring us back to Vienna after our visas expire."

"I've been aware of that." Sarcasm crept into Jason's voice.

"What a gracious remark!" Deborah's voice sharpened, too.

"It wasn't a gracious comment!" he retorted.

"Returning to Vienna after our visas expire could be a terrible risk."

"We've taken such risks since we started out. We'll manage, somehow."

She didn't want to sound reproachful, so she was quiet. A delay could have one advantage, she thought, whatever the other difficulties it caused; it would give her father time to answer her request for money. And she was curious about Mozart's widow. By now she felt like part of his family, and his widow must have been closest to him. Yet as they resumed their climb and she saw the fortifications of the Hohensalzburg directly above them, she recalled that it was also a prison, and she followed Jason with a sinking heart. He had such a look of reverence in his eyes she was sure he would regard Constanze too romantically for their own safety.

He continued without another word until they reached the house. He was torn between anticipation and trepidation. Constanze had sung one of Mozart's masses, but suppose she was without any of Mozart's musicality? He blurted out, "I have no choice, Deborah! I have to stay here as long as there is any information to be unearthed."

"You may not find out anything vital. You may be disillusioned."

"I know. I've been aware of that from the beginning. But I must try! Don't you understand, I must try!" His cry came with an emotion he had not shown before. "Either I prove that he was poisoned, or I leave convinced that I was wrong. And I'm not certain of either yet."

Deborah tried to have strength for both of them, knocking on the door for him. The maid who admitted them was stiff, with a snobbish air, but she did expect them and she escorted them into the reception room.

And as the maid went to inform Frau von Nissen of their presence, he whispered, "You had better pray for me, for I may have some uncomfortable questions to ask."

Ever since Deborah had learned about the last few weeks of Mozart's life and what had followed, she had wondered about many things. And all of a sudden she was reciting them to Jason as if she had written them down in a mental notebook and now she needed answers, too. "If Mozart was still well known at the time he fell ill, as you say he was, why didn't he get the best medical attention? And why was Constanze away in Baden at that time? Then the medical diagnosis of the fatal illness varied so. And why didn't his wife attend the funeral? Or have his body examined since there was doubt about what had really killed him? And why didn't she go to the cemetery with the body?

I would have made sure that he had been properly buried, storm or no storm. But you tell me that Constanze didn't go to the cemetery for many years after he died—1808, I believe, seventeen years later. And why didn't she put up a cross where he was supposed to be buried? Even nearby? It is almost as if she boarded up his memory and abandoned him. Whatever she says now."

Deborah's emotion had mounted as she had spoken, and he felt an affinity in her that had never existed before.

Before he could respond, her conflicting emotions caused her to lose heart again and she said, "Perhaps we ought to leave these questions unanswered. If you ask them, you could alienate her, get nothing at all from her, and drive her straight into the arms of Huber."

"Treat her only with reverence? Ask nothing that is embarrassing?"

"Yes. Otherwise, she will think that you are meddling."

Jason looked thoughtful, apparently interested in her suggestion.

"It is just your welfare that I am concerned about."

Suddenly he felt that she was lying.

She continued, "You are hunting something that is unattainable."

He said, "You are as bad as Huber."

She said sadly, "You don't trust me."

"I don't trust anyone."

"Not even the questions I suggested, Jason?"

"I've thought about them, too. What about the doctors who attended him in his last illness? Who did hire them? Who made that decision? And were they qualified? And did she know Cavalieri? Or Salieri?"

"She must have known Salieri."

But Jason couldn't acknowledge that she knew more about Mozart or the circumstances of his death, and he was silent suddenly, abruptly.

Deborah glanced around the reception room in an effort to be casual, while Jason walked around restlessly, staring about him in the hope that these surroundings would give him a clue to Constanze's nature. He thought her rather assertive about Mozart. There were pictures of Mozart throughout the reception room: a portrait of a mature Mozart appearing reflective and sad, a picture of a youthful Mozart and his sister playing a duet with their father watching them proudly, another portrait of the boy Mozart dressed in the court costume of a Hapsburg archduke and wearing a tiny, gold sword, but none of her with Mozart.

Deborah was attracted by the elegant gray velvet chaise longue and its border of gold braid, the shiny parquet floor, the fine marble windowsills, the porcelain placed upon the mantel with an orderly precision, and what she felt was the heart of the room, two rows of lighted candles around a cabinet shaped like a coffin, containing a keepsake of Mozart.

All this was forgotten as Constanze approached. Actually, it was a grand entrance, Deborah thought, for she walked in very slowly, not because she was feeble, but to be sure she had their complete attention.

Constanze was not as old as Deborah had expected, nor as attractive as Jason had assumed. Deborah saw a small, slight, pale woman past middle age, with pointed features that had become more pointed with time. She wore a beautiful white dress, however, youthful for her age, with a silk-lace trim; and the short, flowing sleeves and low-cut neck revealed the slim, compact, and still surprisingly sensuous figure of which Mozart had been quite proud and which she still treasured.

Jason could not get over his surprise at how old Constanze was, until he realized that Mozart had been dead thirty-three years, although sometimes it seemed like only yesterday. He realized that Constanze must be in her sixties by now, although her skin had remained smooth and soft.

As Constanze saw that her visitors were young, attractive, and far better dressed than she had expected, her dark eyes shone, and Jason remembered how much Mozart had liked them.

He bowed low as Mozart had bowed for Maria Theresa, and he introduced Deborah and said, "It is a great honor to meet the wife of Mozart."

She smiled as if she had heard this before and said in a clear German, "Wolfgang would have been pleased by your homage. Have you come to buy some of his music? I still have a number of his original scores."

Jason was surprised. "What gives you that impression?"

"You left twenty-five gulden with my maid."

"That is an expression of our admiration, Frau Mozart."

"Frau Nissen. Von Nissen. I remarried years ago. In 1809."

"I'm sorry. I was so excited by meeting Mozart's widow, I . . ."

She cut him short. "If you don't want a score, what do you want?"

Deborah explained, "We want to meet the person closest to Mozart."

"You are not writing another book about Wolfgang, are you?"

Constanze looked so suspicious that Deborah felt that was what had delayed her invitation, and she hurried to say, "My husband is a composer who has come to study your husband's music at its source."

"He came all the way from America just for that? I've heard that Americans are much addicted to the noisy part of the orchestra."

"He also had an assignment to obtain a commission from Beethoven."

"Did he obtain the commission?"

"Yes," Deborah said proudly. "Beethoven is writing an oratorio for the Handel and Haydn Society of Boston, which my husband represents."

Constanze seemed impressed, and she said, almost confidingly, "Nissen is finishing a biography of Wolfgang, the authorized account. It is nearly done, and it is going to be the best one ever written, from my own lips."

Jason asked, "Is that why you couldn't see us before, Frau von Nissen?"

"My husband was leaving for Munich and Mannheim to negotiate for the publication of the book there, and we have been very busy."

Deborah noticed that Constanze held a little gold-beaded handbag with ornate red hearts on it, and she fingered it nervously as she might her rosary beads, and it looked quite expensive.

And when Deborah admired the handbag, Constanze said proudly, "Wolfgang gave it to me. As a present. For our wedding anniversary."

Yet she showed no sign of emotion as she spoke of him, thought Jason.

Deborah said, "We heard that Mozart was a generous man."

"Very. I only married again to fight off loneliness. Although Nissen is a good man. Why have you really come from far-off America?"

Jason was dismayed by her bluntness, and he equivocated, "We want to touch anything and everything that was close to Mozart."

Her eyebrows rose sceptically, but she didn't comment.

Jason added, "I understand that he had a loving nature."

"Oh, he liked being pampered a bit. Especially by women."

"But the people I talked to who knew him said . . . "

She cut in, "No one knew him like I did. What did they say?"

"They talked about his sweetness, his good nature, his amiability."

"He was the best musician of his time. Everybody loved him."

"Everybody?" asked Deborah.

Constanze regarded her as if she were impudent.

Jason said, "Frau von Nissen, no one is loved by everyone."

"He was," she said disapprovingly.

"Even by the Court?"

"He was a great favorite at Court as long as the Emperor Joseph lived."

"And afterward?"

"They were involved with the difficulties in France. Even I had to flee from Vienna in 1809, when Napoleon came. That was when I wed Nissen."

Jason asked, "Then you don't think that the Court had anything to do with his death?"

"How?" Constanze was suspicious again.

"Through their indifference. The new Emperor and the nobility did ignore Mozart, didn't they? Toward the end of his life?"

"Many were indifferent. But not everyone. The last few years of Wolfgang's life were the worst I ever spent." Her face was suffused with melancholy so that they would realize how much she had suffered. "When he fell ill the last time, I knew that something dreadful was going to happen. I never faced anything more difficult."

"Was Salieri indifferent?" asked Jason.

"He is ill. I know what illness is. I was ill for a long time. All during my marriage to Wolfgang. And when he fell ill, it was the final cruel blow."

"In what way?"

"I've just managed to survive. And to endure," she whispered sombrely.

For thirty-three years, thought Jason, yet now she appeared in good health. He asked, "Have you been ill much since then, Frau von Nissen?"

"No, fortunately. Nissen has taken excellent care of me."

"But you didn't marry him until 1809."

"Once you are a public figure the most scandalous things are said."

"People can't help wondering about Mozart's death. He died so young."

"At thirty-five?" she said questioningly.

"It was young. And so suddenly, unexpectedly."

"He had the best medical attention," Constanze declared strongly.

"You knew the doctor? You hired him? He was qualified?"

"Qualified! Closset was the most fashionable doctor in Vienna!" Constanze exclaimed indignantly. And now Deborah was worried that Jason was going to drive Constanze into silence with his questions, but instead, her breath came faster, her eyes gleamed, and she stared at them as if they had dragged dirt into her immaculate house. She had a need to justify her behavior that transcended restraint and caution. She cut short Jason's next query and snapped, "I have never forgotten the moment I discovered that Wolfgang was critically ill. Anyone who thinks that I was neglectful should face the same crisis. The same unexpected, sudden emergency. Yet abandoned by those I needed the most." Constanze had their total attention now, and that encouraged her to rush on, yet Jason had the strange sensation that she was not speaking to them but at them.

"It was November, 1791, and I had stayed on at Baden past the season at Wolfgang's insistence. I was taking the baths for my health, and the waters were good for all sorts of things—gout, rheumatism, palsy, cramps, afflictions of the nerves, chronic distempers, headaches, maladies of the eye and ear, and difficulties of the bowels. Wolfgang and I were great believers in the value of the baths, so I knew I was pleasing him.

"Thus, when I received a hurried communication from my younger sister, Sophie, that Wolfgang had collapsed and might be very ill, I knew it must be serious, and I rushed back to Vienna. It didn't take long, for Baden was only fourteen miles away; and when I arrived at our rooms on the Rauhensteingasse, he was in bed and unconscious.

"Sophie was by his side, and she told me that he had been sick for several weeks, and I was angry at him for not informing me. But my sister had been smart; she had called our family doctor, Closset, as soon as she had learned about Wolfgang's illness."

Jason interrupted, "Was Closset a good doctor?"

"The best," she said impatiently. "I told you that Closset was the most fashionable doctor in Vienna. He was just a little older than Wolfgang, and by the time he was recommended to me, a short time before, he was one of the most important doctors in the Empire. He had many famous patients. He was Prince Kaunitz's personal physician with a yearly fee of one thousand gulden; he attended Field Marshal Loudon, our greatest soldier and hero; and he was consulted by the Royal family. I knew what I was doing. He spoke French and Italian fluently."

Jason asked, "Who did recommend him to you?"

"Baron van Swieten. The court librarian and censor."

"Was the Baron close to the new Emperor, Leopold."

"Not in the way he had been to Joseph. Why do you ask?"

"I was just wondering. What did Closset say was wrong with Mozart?"

"That was the strange thing." She sighed. "I don't think he was sure."

"What do you think it was, Frau von Nissen?"

She shook her head in perplexity. "This is what I found most trying."

Deborah nudged Jason to be quiet, and he waited for Constanze to go on.

Constanze said reflectively, "Sophie told me that Wolfgang had fallen ill after a meal he had eaten. I wondered what it was, for he had to be very careful what he ate, but I couldn't ask him, for when he recovered consciousness and saw me by his side, he was so glad that I couldn't upset him. But later Sophie told me that he had become nauseous, and virtually everything he ate now caused him to vomit. I thought that something he might have eaten could have poisoned him, and Wolfgang must have thought so too, for one night he fainted again, and when he recovered consciousness and saw Closset at his side, he cried out emotionally, 'Was I poisoned, Doctor? By bad food? By Salieri?'

"Closset looked uncomfortable, as if such questions embarrassed him, and he said, 'Absurd. Impossible. You're upset, Mozart.'

"Wolfgang replied, 'But my stomach hurts so.'

"Closset said, 'All illnesses settle in the stomach.'

"And when Wolfgang continued to complain about his cramps, Closset said that it was his fever he had to cure, and he gave him drugs for that. For a few days I felt that Closset was right, and I think that Wolfgang felt the same way, for he was feverish.

"Only his fever didn't abate and his hands began to swell and he couldn't even hold a score—he had been working on his Requiem, which he was saying now was for himself—and his stomach cramps grew worse and he fell into a violent physical depression and he started to talk about poisoning again, and so I summoned Doctor Closset again.

"This time Closset came with a Doctor von Sallaba, whom he brought for consultation. This was reassuring, for Sallaba, although he was young, too, was even more famous and fashionable, the chief of the Vienna General Hospital. Sallaba nudged Wolfgang in the ribs, ordered him to exhale and inhale, although Wolfgang could hardly breathe at all—Sallaba was an expert on the heart while Closset was an authority on fevers—and then they moved into a corner of the room for discussion.

"Wolfgang lay there white-faced, expecting the worst. As the doctors prepared to depart, they called me over, and Closset said in a solemn voice, 'I am sorry, Frau Mozart, but there is no hope.'

"Sallaba had to catch me to keep me from fainting.

"After they revived me, Closset said mournfully, 'The fevers have progressed too far. There is nothing we can do anymore.'

" 'And his heart has been affected, also,' Sallaba added. 'It is only a matter of time now. There is also a deposit in his head.'

"What could I tell Wolfgang? I could hardly stand myself. And when I told Sophie what the doctors had said, she was puzzled as well as shocked.

"Sophie said, 'But all the symptoms indicate that it is his kidneys that are damaged. His dizziness, vomiting, the constant fainting, and now his body is beginning to swell in addition to his hands.'

"But I had to lie down before I collapsed, and a week after the doctors had spoken to me, just one week, Wolfgang was dead."

Constanze halted, apparently overcome by her memories. But she had not talked about Mozart, thought Jason, she had talked about herself. He had expected to learn more from her than from anyone else, and so far she had told him the least. Yet however difficult she was, he must not lose his presence of mind. He asked, "Where is Doctor Closset now?"

"Dead. He died in 1813. From a fever, I believe."

"And Doctor von Sallaba?"

"Dead. He died a few years after Wolfgang. But they were the best doctors in Vienna. I am sure I did whatever I could for Wolfgang."

"We're sure you did," Deborah said consolingly. "It must have been a frightful ordeal, Frau von Nissen."

Constanze gave her a look of gratitude and said, "My sister, Sophie, who was with me during those terrible days, can verify that these doctors were the most respected in Vienna."

"I'm sure they were," said Jason, taking his cue from Deborah. "But you said that his symptoms indicated his kidneys were affected. If he were poisoned, wouldn't it be his kidneys which would be most affected?"

"I was a poor widow," Constanze answered. "And in poor health. And one doesn't question the doctor of the Chancellor."

"And now both doctors are dead?" repeated Jason, as if he could not believe it. Suddenly much of his evidence seemed forever out of reach.

"Long ago. But enough! Even now, it hurts too much to talk about his death. My consolation is my two sons. What a blessing they have been!"

Deborah asked, "Will we have the pleasure and honor of meeting them?"

"My older is in Italy, and my younger is in Poland. I gave Wolfgang the best medical attention in the Empire. No one can blame me."

"Of course not," Deborah said reassuringly. "You were wonderful."

"I did my best."

"But what about Mozart's last few hours?" asked Jason. 'The night he died? Was there anything unusual about his passing?"

Constanze started to weep, sobbing, "I can't talk about it."

"I'm sorry," said Jason. "I didn't mean to upset you."

"But you did." Constanze wiped the tears from her eyes and asked, "You are sure that you don't want to buy one of Wolfgang's original scores?"

"It would be a great privilege," said Jason, "but we came for other reasons."

"So I see." Constanze's voice grew cold and she stood up. "I take a bath every afternoon; we have brought special waters from Bad Gastein, which is nearby. They are not as beneficial as Baden's, but they are good for the skin. I don't want to be rude, but I've told you all I know."

Jason doubted that, but Constanze's mouth had tightened, and he sensed that she would not talk any more about the fatal illness and death, even though he had more things to speculate about, not less. Yet he needed something else, or he would feel like an utter failure. He said, searching for something sensible to say, "Ernst Muller told us that your other sisters knew Mozart well, too."

"Ernst Muller?" Constanze repeated his name with obvious distaste.

Deborah asked quickly, "You don't like him?"

"He borrowed money from Wolfgang. And he never paid it back."

"I know," said Jason. "He told us."

"That doesn't excuse it. Particularly from a poor widow with two young children to raise."

"How much was it, Frau von Nissen?"

"I'm not sure. Fifteen, twenty . . ."

"Twenty-five gulden?" Jason interrupted.

"Yes. That's it," she said hurriedly.

Jason handed her the other twenty-five gulden he had intended to give her on Ernst's advice. "Ernst is sorry you've had to wait so long."

"Thirty-five years! It is not coming from your own pocket, Herr Otis?"

"Ernst Muller gave me strict orders to present this money to you."

Constanze took the money without another word.

Deborah asked, "You don't like the Mullers, do you, Frau von Nissen?"

"What is there to like? They took advantage of Wolfgang when he was alive, flattering him so he would use them, and now stirring up trouble."

"I don't understand?" said Jason.

"Smearing his death. Oh, I know they have put you on this hunt."

"What hunt?"

"To prove that Salieri was responsible. They've always hated Salieri."

Jason cried, "Didn't Mozart?"

"That was different. He had reasons." Then she corrected herself. "All the opera composers disliked each other. That was natural."

"Even for such a gentle person as Mozart?"

"He was human. And Salieri assumed that every composer of his generation was in competition with him, except Gluck, his sponsor."

"Then Mozart was right in thinking of Salieri as his enemy?"

"Wolfgang had many enemies." Constanze's mouth tightened again.

"But he did distrust Salieri?"

"Do you trust everyone, Herr Otis?"

Jason was silent, and Deborah suggested, "Perhaps his early death was the fault of the doctors. Perhaps they did make the wrong diagnosis."

"No!" said Constanze. "They were the best in the Empire. If they were wrong, anybody would have been. We must let Wolfgang rest in peace."

But where? a voice shrieked inside Jason, and suddenly he didn't feel so impotent. He had a feeling now that Closset and von Sallaba had contributed to Mozart's death, not directly perhaps, by assassination, but in their own way, by negligence and stupidity and indifference. They were innocently irresponsible, he thought, or possibly not so innocent and very responsible. As Constanze led them to the door, he asked, "Frau von Nissen, may I trouble you with one more question?"

She was annoyed, but she paused, curiosity stronger than irritation.

"Did you know Catherina Cavalieri?"

She looked blank.

"Cavalieri sang Constanze, the lead in *The Abduction from the Seraglio*."

"Oh, her! Yes, I knew Cavalieri."

"I was told that she was Salieri's mistress."

Constanze shrugged as if that was a matter of no consequence.

"Did you know her well, Frau von Nissen?"

Before Constanze could reply, she was interrupted by the entrance of another elderly woman, who swept into the reception room imperiously, waiting obviously for the right moment to make *her* entrance.

Constanze was furious, but she was forced to introduce the intruder. "My sister, my older sister, Madame Aloysia Lange."

So this was the Weber whom Mozart had fallen in love with first, Jason thought, and the great beauty of the family. But the beauty was gone, he realized. Aloysia regarded them with a calculating look and a cynical smile and her face reminded Jason of a hatchet, with a sharp jaw, chin, and nose, and heavy makeup which made her wrinkles more conspicuous.

Aloysia said, "I knew Cavalieri intimately. I understudied her in the original production of *Seraglio* and sang with her on many occasions."

Constanze added testily, "My sister used to be an opera singer."

Jason had the feeling that Aloysia had been listening in the next room, waiting for the appropriate moment to enter, and he asked her, "How do you think Cavalieri regarded Mozart? Favorably? Unfavorably?"

Aloysia said, "It depends on what he gave her to sing. I remember . . ."

Constanze cut in. "Herr Otis, this afternoon has exhausted me."

"I'm sorry, Frau von Nissen. We could return tomorrow."

"Not tomorrow. Tomorrow I am going to the baths."

Aloysia said hurriedly, "I could tell you what you want to know about Cavalieri. I knew her better than my sister did."

But Constanze was adamant in her determination to end this conversation. She stated, "I will let you know when I can see you again. In a few days, perhaps." She ushered Jason and Deborah out before they could utter another word.

30

A Matter of Some Consequence

THE VISIT to Constanze left Jason agitated and discontented. He spent the rest of the day sorting and arranging what he had learned about Mozart's death from his widow, but the more he sought to put her facts in order, the more he felt on shaky ground.

He was unable to sleep that night. Constanze, instead of clarifying his views, had made them more confused. She had added to the multitude of impressions struggling for ascendancy in his troubled mind and had contradicted many of them, and he didn't know what to believe. And she had been so impatient with him. How could he like her?

He lay in bed and stared out the window at the Hohensalzburg, which towered threateningly above him in the bright moonlight, and he was in a panic. His head felt like a floating bubble with nothing in it. He was reaching for strands of knowledge, but when he touched them they broke, or withered and dissolved like cobwebs in his hand. The moon gave the ancient fortress a foreboding grayish whiteness, and it shone like a medieval monster. Then the moonlight was in his bedroom and formed a silver triangle on the foot of his bed, the light so strong he saw the faces of Wolfgang, Constanze, and Aloysia at each end of the triangle, with Wolfgang's at the apex and the two sisters pushing up toward him on a ghostly beam in their struggle for supremacy. But while the light was like a lamp in the room, it did not lighten the dark in Jason's mind, but silhouetted a crowd of remembered and confusing words.

"Dearest, Most Beloved Wife of My Heart!"

But had Constanze felt the same way?

"The days without you are lonely and melancholy indeed."

Had she responded as Mozart had?

"My precious Stanzi, love me for ever as I love you."

And had Constanze done so?

"I kiss you a million times and I await your return passionately."

She had been in Baden when Mozart had needed her the most.

The next morning Jason was grateful that Deborah didn't ask him why he had been unable to sleep. He tried to reconcile his fears and his need to continue his search by walking along the river that day in the hope that the fresh air would bring clarity to his mind. Deborah was determined to stay attached, and she sought to adjust her mood to his.

They moved out of Salzburg this frosty day to where the Salzach curved. The country air had a tingling freshness, and there was the pungent fragrance of wet leaves still clinging to tree and soil, and this was comforting. And it was as if Jason had come out of an embryo into the largeness of life. The sun was above the mountains now, warming them, and he said, "I thought I would like her, I thought because . . ."

"Because Mozart did?" Deborah interrupted. "But you didn't?"

"Not much."

"Not enough?"

"I don't know what to believe. Just when Constanze says something that convinces me that my suspicions are correct, she contradicts it. One moment she says Mozart was loved by everybody, the next she declares he had many enemies. She denies that Salieri could have harmed Mozart, then tells me that Mozart thought he was poisoned. It is confusing."

"Isn't most evidence?"

"No. I did learn what his symptoms were when he fell fatally ill."

"And you did find out the identity of the doctors."

"And that they were dead," he reminded her. "That wasn't very helpful."

"She told you their diagnosis. What they thought caused his death."

"But they contradicted each other, too. And Ernst insisted that Constanze would welcome me with open arms, that they were good friends, and you saw how she dislikes him. His letter of introduction was worthless. Now I don't know how much to believe of what he has told me."

Jason was so disappointed that Deborah, instead of expressing gratitude that he had come to share her distrust of the Mullers, was sorry for him and sought to console him, saying, "You must be forgiving."

"Of whom?" he asked suspiciously.

"Of yourself. And of Constanze. You musn't blame her too much. If I were in her position, I would feel defensive also."

He didn't agree with her. He felt that a part of him belonged to Mozart, but did Constanze?

Just as the frosty December air had cleared his head, Jason was sure that Mozart's music would do the same. When they returned to the inn, he stopped at the desk in the entrance and asked the proprietor, "Where can we hear some Mozart, Herr Raab? An opera, preferably."

Herr Raab bowed deferentially, for Herr Otis must be a rich man to rent an entire floor, and for an indefinite time, and said, "I'm sorry, sir, but there is no opera in Salzburg."

"No opera?" Jason was shocked. "Where Mozart was born?"

"Begging your pardon, sir, that was why he left Salzburg for Vienna."

"But there must be much Mozart played in Salzburg?"

Herr Raab shook his head mournfully. His face was mottled with age, and his long, wrinkled features drooped sadly. He said regretfully, "Not much, sir. Salzburgians have always resented that Mozart left Salzburg, and then they are not very musical. As Mozart said himself."

"Did you know him?"

"Almost everyone my age did. I was born in 1754, two years before he was. And Salzburg was small, and he brought fame to the town with his tours. My father was always telling me that I could be another Mozart if I would only practice the violin, but I knew I would never be another Mozart. I still play, but only as an amateur. Tonight we are playing Mozart in the home of my doctor—he is the leader of our chamber group—and if you would like to hear us, we would be happy to have you."

"There isn't any other Mozart being played in Salzburg?"

"Not at the moment, sir. We don't get many visitors in December, and the local inhabitants, except for a few of us, aren't interested. Most of our residents are gratified that Mozart made Salzburg well known, but are indifferent to his music. He is too special for many of them."

"Do you think that his widow will come to your concert?"

"She never has. She doesn't mix much."

"Then why does she live here since Mozart didn't like Salzburg?"

"Nissen says it is easier to work here. In Vienna she is bothered by people who want to talk about Mozart. But in Salzburg nobody cares that much. They take Mozart for granted. And it is cheaper here."

"Do you know her sisters?"

"I have seen them about."

"Are they living with her?"

"I think so. But her house in the Nonnberg is secluded. Why don't you visit Mozart's sister, Maria Anna von Berchtold zu Sonnenberg?"

"I will, but I wanted to see Mozart's widow first. Are they friendly?"

"Not really. I doubt Mozart's sister ever forgave him for marrying a Weber. Everybody knows. It was the talk of the town when it happened."

"And what did the town say when Mozart died?"

The innkeeper shrugged. "Not much. Death was common. As it still is. Over half of the Viennese die before they are twenty. The city is full of typhus, smallpox, dysentery, and consumption. It is why I live here."

"But I have reason to believe that Mozart died of a kidney ailment."

"One malady or another, what is the difference! I even heard that he died of a nervous fever. Doctors say many things when they don't know. Herr Otis, we would be honored if you attended our concert tonight."

"Can we walk?"

"Probably, but the streets are dark. You will be happier in your coach."

"And safer?"

"Perhaps. But we do not have much crime here. Not like in Vienna."

As Raab wrote down the address of the concert, Jason noticed a man sitting in the entrance of the inn and staring at him. When he stared back, the man looked away. Disturbed, Jason asked Raab, "Who is he?"

"A guest."

"I have a feeling that he is spying on me."

"Are you in trouble with the government?" Raab was alarmed.

"Of course not," Deborah volunteered hurriedly. "But my husband was robbed in Vienna, so naturally he is especially careful now."

The innkeeper was relieved, although he sighed mournfully and said, "That is typical of Vienna. They are much more lawless there. But I run a respectable inn. We are very careful to whom we rent our rooms."

The stranger had not moved. His eyes had come back to them, when, thought Jason, the man assumed that they were not watching him. He said to Raab, "What is his name?"

"Bosch, he said. He arrived about the same time as you did, Herr Otis, maybe an hour before or after, I don't remember."

"What is his business?"

"He didn't say, or tell me how long he is staying. A week or two, maybe. He has a room underneath you. Herr Otis, are you under official surveillance? I wouldn't want to antagonize the authorities."

"I'm here because of my love for music. What is dangerous about that?"

"You never know. The police are very strict these days."

"You are wise to be cautious," Deborah assured the innkeeper. "Do you have many guests at this time of the year?"

"Not usually. But there is always somebody stopping here on the way to Linz and Vienna, or going to Innsbruck, Augsburg, and even Mannheim and Munich. I suspect Herr Bosch has not seen an American before, and he is curious. Some people in Salzburg have never seen an American."

Hans interrupted, "Do you need me, sir?"

Jason was startled. Had Hans been listening? He had not heard Hans approach, Hans had been preternaturally still. He said coldly, "Why?"

"I have friends in Salzburg, sir, and I would like to see them."

"You told me that you had never been here before."

"That's true, Herr Otis. But they lived in Mannheim at one time."

Deborah asked, "Do you know that man sitting there?"

"I never saw him in my life!" Hans sounded utterly sincere.

Yet she could have sworn that they had exchanged glances.

Jason said, "You are free now, but we will need you tonight, to drive us to the concert."

"It will be a pleasure, sir."

The stranger's eyes followed Hans out the door, but he didn't move.

Doctor Friedjung resided at the foot of the Nonnberg, not far from Constanze, in a house that pleased Jason and Deborah with its elegance. Raab greeted them at the door, and when Hans saw him, he asked Jason, "Could I hear the concert, too, sir? I love Mozart, as you know, and it is very cold outside."

Jason hesitated, and Raab said, "We do have a place for the servants, Herr Otis. In the rear. And these December nights get very cold."

Jason nodded, and turned to meet Doctor Friedjung, who was waiting for them in his music room. It was designed like a small concert hall, and the ten chairs for the orchestra faced places for fifty people to sit.

Doctor Friedjung regarded them with an expression of triumphant eagerness and said how honored he was that they could attend his humble musicale in his poor home. But Jason thought it was one of the most luxurious houses they had been in and that the doctor stood before them with an air of bravery, as if it took great courage to play Mozart where the composer had been born and had been so well known. Jason noticed also that Friedjung's hands were muscular and limber, more like those of a musician than of a doctor. He was of Raab and Mozart's generation, but his skin was younger looking than the innkeeper's, with a remarkable tone for a man of seventy. He was short, like most of the men Jason had met in Vienna, with regular features, gray-blue eyes, and snow-white hair.

As a lover of Mozart Doctor Friedjung had programed three pieces by Mozart: a country dance in B Flat Major, a divertimento in B Flat Major, and the Symphony in B Flat Major.

"All works that Mozart composed in Salzburg," Raab whispered as he sat down beside them, adding, "With your permission, Frau Otis."

She nodded, and Jason asked, "Why are the pieces all in the same key?"

Raab said, "It's simpler. The doctor doesn't like to take chances."

Jason said, "Aren't you going to play also?"

"I have colic and the doctor is afraid it will spoil the music."

"Shouldn't you be in bed?"

"No. Colic is common in Salzburg, and many other stomach complaints. And the doctor thinks that good music is the best cure."

Jason turned around, curious to see if Hans was in the rear, and observed the stranger who had aroused his suspicions at the inn slip into the music room and seat himself several places away from Hans.

But when he mentioned that to Raab, the innkeeper said, "I invited him. There's nothing else to do, and he says he likes Mozart. As you do."

For once however, Mozart's music didn't involve Jason. Friedjung conducted without restraint, and most of the music was scraped rather than played. There was none of the magical Mozartian atmosphere Jason had come to expect: Raab had been charitable when he had referred to the musicians as amateurs—they were more like novices. It was such a poor performance he felt desolate. Yet as Friedjung accepted the applause from the audience, Jason thought, The premise is simple: praise, praise, praise! So he applauded, too, and nudged Deborah, sitting beside him absentmindedly, as if her attention were far away, to join him. Jason would have liked to have ordered all the violinists in the chamber orchestra to practice scales, but when the doctor asked him if he had enjoyed the concert, he replied, "Interesting. Most interesting."

"A great success," ventured Raab. "Don't you think so, Doctor?"

Doctor Friedjung bowed modestly.

"But I would have ruined it with my colic."

"It is a seasonable illness in Salzburg," Doctor Friedjung said.

Jason felt that the performance had been so inept that it would have sent Mozart, usually the gentlest of men, screaming from the concert.

Raab suggested that Doctor Friedjung, Herr Otis, and Frau Otis join him in a late dinner at his inn. He said, "As my guests. To celebrate the concert. The Golden Goose is famous for its fowl. Our livers of geese are a great delicacy." As Jason hesitated, he added, "Mozart loved them. My father, who owned the Golden Goose before me, told me that Mozart ordered them every chance he got."

And when Friedjung was agreeable—it would give him a chance to discuss his conducting—Jason and Deborah accepted the innkeeper's invitation.

But Jason's first question was, "Doctor, did you know Mozart well?"

"As well as most. Do you have trout, too, Herr Raab?"

"Of course, Doctor. Trout was one of Mozart's favorite foods also."

Jason ate the livers of geese while Deborah had the trout with Raab and Friedjung. Hans had his dinner in the kitchen, as was the custom. Hans had appeared to enjoy the concert, for he had been listening attentively whenever Jason had looked at him, and that pleased Jason. There was no sign of the stranger, and Raab said that he had probably gone to bed, for there was nothing else to do in Salzburg at this hour.

It was easy to get the doctor and innkeeper to reminisce, however, when Jason said flatteringly, "How much you both must know about Mozart."

The doctor said, "I have often wondered whether the Archbishop's hostility hurt him. It was one of the things that drove him away."

"Yes," said the innkeeper. "I remember when Colloredo was so critical of Mozart's music, Mozart got sick here, right where you are sitting."

"I remember that incident, too," said the doctor. "The concert was given at Colloredo's palace. After the concert ended, Mozart, who was twenty-four and mature for his age, had to approach the Archbishop and ask him supplicatingly whether his music had pleased, although it was common knowledge that they disliked each other. But Mozart, as Colloredo's servant, could not reply as Colloredo scolded him for writing heavy, tiresome music when he had desired a light and gay divertimento."

Jason asked, "Do you remember what the composition was?"

"A *sinfonia concertante*, I believe."

"For violin and viola?"

"Yes. A sad piece. But afterward, as Raab said, Mozart was so upset by Colloredo's words, he got ill here. I know because I had to attend him. It wasn't serious: nerves, tension, disappointment, and . . ."

Jason stopped listening. The *sinfonia concertante* was incomparable music. He liked it as much as any piece of Mozart's he had heard.

Silent music filled the air and Jason was sitting in a ghostly palace lit with crystal chandeliers, and Mozart was standing under them, saying to Jason, "This chamber is for dancing. I always put a dance in my music. Hear the steps. Even in my *sinfonia concertante*. Any donkey could follow. Even Archbishop Colloredo." Then Mozart's fine clothes fell off of him and he was dressed like a Court flunkey, in the livery of a servant, and holding a violin. But instead of playing it, he waved the bow as a conductor and it was not an orchestra that followed him, but the audience, the nobles with their jeweled swords, the Archbishop with his symbols of his office, the well-to-do in their powdered wigs. And even as Mozart seemed to have possession of the situation, his audience turned on him, advancing toward him with drawn sword until the points touched his throat, one drop of blood, two . . .

Jason closed his eyes, unable to witness any more, and when he opened them, slowly and reluctantly, Friedjung and Raab were sitting in front of him and there was not a trace of Mozart. The livers of geese were succulent, and Deborah seemed to be enjoying her trout. Raab urged him to have a second helping and he did, his mind on Mozart. There was Moselle on the table and he drank some wine, but where was Mozart?

He felt better as he dropped his head and the others faded from view. He wondered if Deborah would think he was foolish, imagining Mozart sitting here. But why not! Mozart had sat here. One must find happiness in the stomach, or in love, or wherever he could, even in his imagination, and make himself immune to the cruelties of men.

In his imagination he found himself asking, *"Did you love Constanze as you said you did, Wolfgang?"* and Wolfgang nodded vigorously.

"And did she love you the same way?" And the answer was the same,

but there was a trace of indecision now.

"*Did she make any great sacrifices for you?*"

"*She bore me six children.*"

"*But she was always sick.*"

"*She was always pregnant.*"

"*Is that why she can't talk about your dying hours?*"

An expression of terrible sadness appeared on Mozart's face. Then Jason's imagination heard him say, "*She gave me love when I was alive.*"

But that was as if Deborah were speaking.

Jason looked up and saw her staring at him strangely.

"What's wrong?" he cried.

"You look so far away," she answered. "In another century."

He wanted to explain, but his hands went to his stomach. Pain was thrusting through his flesh as if pushed by the sharpest of knives, and he doubled up with cramps so violent he thought he was going to die. He had to vomit and the doctor and the innkeeper with one motion, as if they were familiar with this situation, motioned out the door, and he ran to the back. But while he vomited with a wrenching, convulsive harshness, the pain didn't go away. He was dizzy, hardly able to stand, and Doctor Friedjung said he must lie down, and the two men helped him upstairs, Deborah having hurried ahead to arrange the bed. But when he lay down, he still felt awful. Nausea swept over him in waves, and he wanted to vomit again. He had pains in his legs, arms, and fingers. Then he was assailed with alternate diarrhea and vertigo, and he thought he was going to faint. Doctor Friedjung dabbed his head with cold water, but Jason felt that a horror had come to fullness within him, dedicated to pain, demanding that he suffer, suffer, suffer. As if there was a creature within his stomach clawing at his flesh and seeking to tear him apart. He didn't faint, although he wanted to—in the hope it would end his torture. What fury had let loose this ravenous energy within him, he wondered in his anguish, and he writhed to be free of this body that had betrayed him. The doctor gave him something to drink, and his vomiting and diarrhea increased. Deborah cried frantically, "Do something, Doctor, please!" and Friedjung said, "I have," and gradually, Jason's body rejecting in haste, expelling the only relief, the only comfort, the worst of the pain subsided. Now he lay on the bed in a sick stupor, his head aching, his throat burning, very thirsty, never had he felt so thirsty, water was the greatest luxury, and when Deborah gave him some it was as if she had saved his life.

And he could speak again; and when Doctor Friedjung asked him, "Do you have an unusual taste in your mouth?" he nodded and said, "Metallic."

Doctor Friedjung brooded a moment, then asked, "And your throat?"

"It burns," he whispered.

"And you are very thirsty?"

"Very?"

Deborah asked fearfully, "What are you getting at, Doctor?"

"We must keep an eye on him." He examined Jason's body and looked relieved, adding, "At least, his body hasn't begun to swell."

Deborah couldn't put into words what she was thinking, but Jason murmured, "You think I could have been poisoned?"

Doctor Friedjung didn't answer.

"Is that why you wanted to see if my body had swelled?"

"You did have severe cramps."

"Dreadful cramps."

"And felt faint, nauseous, thirsty. Interesting symptoms."

Deborah said, "Could the food have been poisoned?"

"A little bit of poison never killed anyone."

"Was it the goose livers?"

Raab said strongly, "We have the best cuisine in Salzburg. Goose livers just don't agree with Herr Otis, as they didn't with Mozart."

Deborah turned to Doctor Friedjung, asked, "Can food poison you?"

"Indeed. But your husband had other symptoms."

Jason lay a few yards away while the doctor drew Deborah aside to discuss his condition. He watched their lips, but he couldn't tell what they were saying, although the doctor was stressing something.

Friedjung was telling her, "Some of the symptoms suggest arsenic." She tried to hide her shock for Jason's sake, but she grew so pale the doctor had to reassure her. "Everyone absorbs some arsenic in his body. But that doesn't mean that it is going to be fatal."

"Are you suggesting that arsenic was put in his food deliberately?"

"I'm not suggesting anything. But his symptoms are those I have found where arsenic has been absorbed. Your husband is lucky; he will recover."

"You're sure?" She looked at Jason, who was staring at them.

"Yes. If it was going to be fatal, I would have known by now. I will give him a drug which will help him sleep, and tomorrow, except for soreness and a bad taste in his mouth, he should be better."

Doctor Friedjung turned to Jason, who was waiting eagerly yet apprehensively, and said, "You ate some food that didn't agree with you."

"Poisoned food?"

"Possibly. After all, we ate the same meal, but a different food, trout. The livers of the geese might have been tainted."

"Deliberately?"

Raab was offended, but the doctor said, "It's difficult to know. Poisons can develop in some foods without outside help."

Jason lay back, too exhausted to ask any more questions.

The doctor said, "Everybody absorbs some poison with what he eats, but in most instances the body is able to throw it off."

Deborah said, "Then you believe that it was an accident?"

"Yes. But you were lucky that I was with you at the time."

Raab said emphatically, "It couldn't have been my food!"

Jason said earnestly, "Herr Raab, I'm sure it wasn't your fault. But perhaps somebody in your kitchen . . ."

"No! My wife and oldest daughter do all the cooking!"

"Maybe someone else was in your kitchen at the time."

"Only your servant, Hans Denke, and you trust him, don't you?"

"What about the man who was watching us, Bosch?"

"You are a bit delirious, Herr Otis. Bosch went upstairs while we were eating. Begging your pardon, sir, but you were very excited hearing Mozart; that is what upset you. I saw the same thing happen to Mozart, as we told you. He got so sick he couldn't hold anything on his stomach."

Friedjung said, "It was the incident we mentioned earlier. When he was criticized by the Archbishop. I had just become a doctor, and I was called in because I was eating here. Herr Otis, I wouldn't have eaten at the Golden Goose all these years if I didn't trust the food."

Jason asked, "Just when did Mozart get sick here?"

"It was when he had come back from Paris like a prodigal son, after the death of his mother, in an effort to placate the Archbishop and his father."

"When he felt like this, what did you suggest as a remedy?"

"I put him on a strict diet. As you should do now."

Deborah asked, "Was there any other remedy for Mozart?"

"Yes. To leave Salzburg before it killed him."

"You're saying that somebody or something here was murdering him?"

"Not in that sense. But he was so unhappy and he felt so little sympathy here that inevitably, if he had remained in Salzburg, I am convinced that it would have shortened his life. And perhaps did, anyway."

Deborah wondered if the doctor was warning them also. Before she could ask, he gave Jason a drug to help him sleep, wrote out a diet, and said, "I don't know how it is in your country, but we still live in an age of poisons. We call it the Italian disease. An inheritance from the Borgias. Although it is not as bad as it used to be."

Deborah asked, "Were you able to help Mozart?"

"Sometimes all a doctor can do is to make his patient comfortable."

A moment later they were alone, and Deborah sat down beside Jason, determined to reassure him, stating "I really don't think you were poisoned, not deliberately. Otherwise, why didn't they do it to me?"

"That would have been too obvious."

"But I know almost as much as you do."

"You wouldn't pursue it like I have."

Hans stood in the doorway and mumbled, "I just heard that Herr Otis was sick and I wondered if there was anything I could do."

"Thanks," said Deborah, and went to dismiss him, but Jason halted her, and asked, "Was there anybody in the kitchen besides yourself?"

"Only Frau Raab and her daughter."

"And yourself?"

"You told me to eat there, sir."

"Yes. And what did you eat?"

Hans hesitated.

Jason said, "I can always find out from Frau Raab."

"Livers of geese. There were some left over, after they served you."

"And you had no ill effects?"

"I'm used to them, sir. I've eaten them many times."

"Good. Then we can depend on you. From now on, you will eat with us."

"But I'm a servant, sir!"

"Exactly. And you will serve us by sampling all of our food first. At least, as long as we remain in Salzburg." Jason lay back, exhausted again, but grateful that the vomiting and diarrhea had stopped and much of the pain was gone. Yet he was still suspicious, for the pain had started too quickly and spontaneously to be ignored, and now, after a terrible expenditure of energy, he wondered how much more he could endure.

31

Aloysia Lange

ALOYSIA LANGE was proud of herself. Despite Constanze's refusal to
tell her where the young Americans were staying, she had found
them. But it had been difficult. She had gone from inn to inn, and
just when she had felt hopeless, she had thought of the Golden Goose.

But Herr Otis was so pale! Had her sudden appearance startled him
so?

A week had passed since Jason's illness, yet he still felt weakened and
shaken by the experience. He had been unable to find out anything
more about the dinner that night, except that Raab's wife had cooked
and served it. Bosch was still at the inn, although he had seen him only
twice, and then briefly. Deborah continued to say that he should accept
the poisoning as accidental—if it was poisoning—as the doctor had
done, although in her heart she was not sure that the doctor was right.

Jason had seen Friedjung a few days ago, and the doctor had said
that his patient was recovering nicely. When Jason had asked, "Could
the geese have been poisoned?" Friedjung had replied, "We musn't give
Salzburg a bad name. Naturally, animal life could be diseased, but
poison, it is rumored constantly. Quite near this inn stands the home of
Paracelsus, the greatest physician of his age. When he died suddenly,
mysteriously, it was said that even he had been poisoned. But there is
no proof, for when he died in 1541, he was the only one qualified to
judge."

Raab had broken into this remembrance, knocking on the door of
the reception room, where Jason and Deborah had been going over
Jason's notes on what they had learned in Salzburg, to inform them,
"Herr Otis, there is a lady downstairs who would like to see you."

Jason had asked hopefully, "Mozart's widow? Frau von Nissen?"

"No. It is her sister, Madame Lange, the singer."

Before Jason had been able to say, "Show her up," Aloysia had
appeared behind Raab, she was so anxious to talk to them. And after
Constanze's reluctance to speak to them, Aloysia's eagerness was
astonishing.

Jason did have the presence of mind, however, to thank Raab, and to
close the door behind the innkeeper, in the event that Constanze's sister
had something confidential to tell them.

Deborah was fascinated by Aloysia's appearance. She stood like a statue, obviously to impress them by putting herself on a pedestal, yet her severe features had an icy cast, more like cold marble than warm flesh. Her appearance was more suitable for a young woman than for an elderly lady in her sixties. And while it was early in the afternoon, she had come in an opera cloak and as she handed it to Jason imperiously, she stood revealed in a gown appropriate for evening wear or an opera performance, bouffant in style, high-waisted, with her shoulders bare to her low-cut bodice and heavily powdered. Yet she asked, "Are you students?"

Jason said, "University students?"

"Yes."

"Why?"

"You are young. Passionate. Impulsive. Critical of things."

"No, I'm not a university student, but a student of Mozart. A musician."

"I hoped so. I need a musician's understanding. Like Mozart gave it. The authorities are keeping the students under constant surveillance." Her voice took on a triumphant note. "My little sister wouldn't tell me where you were staying. She said that she didn't know, when I was sure that she did. But I found out, without her help."

Deborah asked, "Why wouldn't she tell you, Madame Lange?"

"She was afraid I would tell you the truth about her and Mozart."

"Is that why she dismissed us as soon as you entered?"

"Yes. She is more interested in preserving her illusions."

Jason cut in, "Then what she told us was wrong?"

"In most respects. Mozart didn't really love her the way he loved me. I was his first, best love. She was his second best. He fell in love with me first, and proposed to me first. No wonder she doesn't give me my due; it is terrible to be second to a sister."

Aloysia spoke with such an outpouring of emotion it was impossible to halt her, and as if she had waited for this opportunity for a long time.

Aloysia was remembering when Mozart had courted her, when one smile from her had brought him to his knees. She couldn't tell them that these memories filled her with melancholy and self-flagellation. That she would never get over the fact that she had had immortality offered her and she had said No. Worse, somebody she considered inferior had gotten it, her little sister. For while she hadn't wanted Mozart at the time, she hadn't wanted her sister to have him. *"He was mine!"* she yearned to shout, but they would laugh at her. She said, "When Mozart proposed to me, I was beautiful." She dug into her handbag and handed them a picture. "My husband, Joseph Lange, painted it when we married. I was twenty."

The carefully preserved miniature was a relic from another age, but it told eloquently why Mozart had fallen in love with her. Aloysia had been beautiful, thought Jason, with sharp, perfectly formed features.

But Deborah felt that even then the tall, slender, gray-eyed, dark-haired loveliness possessed the same hardness that had come to dominate Aloysia in old age, and that Aloysia was in competition with her, with anyone who might, like Constanze, have something Aloysia desired.

"My husband, Joseph Lange, was supposed to be an actor, but he was a better painter. His portrait of Mozart is the best I've ever seen."

Jason asked, "You didn't like your husband's acting?"

"He moved like an ox on stage, while I was as light as a feather."

"And you are sure that Mozart loved you best?"

"Yes. He proposed to my little sister only after I turned him down."

"Do you regret that?"

"I had bad advice. My mother and Mozart's father were against my marrying him. It was the only time they ever agreed."

"If Mozart loved you so much, why didn't you say Yes anyway?"

"I was very young. Sixteen. Who knows her own mind at that age."

"Then why are you here now?"

"To set the record straight. You are writing a book about Mozart."

"I am not. I pointed that out to your sister."

"Then why is she afraid to see you? Nissen's book, while it flatters Constanze, will be read because her authority is behind it."

Deborah said, "She insisted that she was devoted to Mozart."

Aloysia smiled cynically.

Deborah said, "When she spoke of his death she broke down and wept."

"She should have. She wasn't there."

Jason said, "But she gave us the impression . . ."

"That she was with him during his last hours. But she wasn't."

"We heard that before, but we were so shocked that finally we didn't believe it. Where was she, Madame Lange?"

"In another room, prostrate, feeling very sorry for herself."

"We heard that too, but it was hard to believe. Perhaps she was sick."

"She was sick all during her marriage to Mozart, to keep him attentive, and since then she hasn't had one sick day. She's clever in some things."

Deborah asked, "Were you at his bedside, Madame Lange?"

"It would have been wrong. I was married to someone else, and in view of our earlier attachment, it would have caused a scandal."

"Perhaps Constanze was always ill because she was always pregnant."

"She had to satisfy him in some way. And she certainly didn't satisfy him musically. Like I did. And could have in many other ways."

"Why are you so critical of your sister?"

"Frau Otis, she didn't even go to the cemetery when he was buried!"

K

"We know. Did you?"

"If I had been married to him I would have. But my little sister didn't even bother to put up a stone."

"How could she since the body vanished and the grave was unknown?"

"She could have found a place. Approximately. She didn't get to the cemetery until 1808 or 1809, and then only because Nissen forced her to go, saying it wasn't right for her to stay away any longer. He was about to marry her after living with her and he didn't want any more gossip."

Suddenly Deborah longed to reject what Aloysia was saying, even if it was true. She had doubts about Constanze, too, and she knew that Jason was critical of her, but she was sickened by this kind of talk.

Aloysia raced on, "It was Nissen who made Constanze go to the cemetery and put up a cross. As I said, for the sake of appearances."

"Perhaps she can't bear cemeteries," Deborah suggested.

"She can become involved in cemeteries when it suits her purpose. She appropriated Leopold Mozart's grave in the St. Sebastian cemetery in Salzburg. Constanze put our Aunt, Genoveva Weber, in it with Mozart's father. I presume she feels this is suitable bècause both were parents of composers. Our Aunt was the mother of Carl Maria von Weber. And I hear that Constanze is going to use the grave for herself and Nissen. You see, her monument will be far larger than that of Leopold Mozart. I doubt she will leave him any space at all. Yet he hated Constanze."

Jason said, "But I thought you didn't like Mozart's father. He was against your marriage to Mozart, and he didn't help you as a singer."

"I didn't need his help and Mozart would have wed me, whatever his father did, if I had said Yes. Constanze's behavior is a disgrace."

"Madame Lange, did you know Doctor Closset?"

"The best-dressed doctor in Vienna! Of course! I would never have used him. He was more interested in his fee than in anything else. Once he knew that Mozart was impoverished, I'm sure he lost interest."

"Do you think that Closset was responsible for Mozart's death?"

"Many people were responsible."

"Who, in your opinion?"

Aloysia was silent suddenly, overwhelmed with a torrent of emotion that surprised her. So many things had happened that were unforseeable. Much of the tragedy of Mozart's death had not been *what people had done*, she reflected, but *what they had not done*. There was a deep ache in her now. Perhaps she had really cared for Mozart as much as she had said she did. He had been such a little man, such an insignificant-looking man, but his music had been the support of her life. And perhaps she would be remembered as his first love, even if Constanze remained better known.

Deborah said, "If that is too difficult to discuss . . .?"

"Many people walked away from Mozart at the end. Doctors,

Constanze, van Swieten, the Royal family, the nobility, da Ponte, almost everybody abandoned him.' '

"Even Madame Lange?" Deborah suggested softly.

"Even Madame Lange," Aloysia whispered, "in her lack of consideration. But I didn't think it could happen. It was so sudden, unexpected."

Jason said, "You didn't mention your sister Sophie."

"She was with him when he died."

"Do you know what his symptoms were?"

"Sophie said violent cramps, vomiting, diarrhea, and a swollen body."

"Did she think he was poisoned?"

"I don't know. Constanze wondered about it, but Sophie has a kind of innocence that, even today, views matters differently from how I do."

"Do you think he was?"

She regarded Jason suspiciously and said slowly, "That's not something to be discussed publicly. Are you involved with the police in some way?"

"No!" Jason hurried to say. "If anything . . ." He halted abruptly.

"Are you in trouble with them? Under surveillance?"

"Of course not! Our visas are quite in order. I'm simply trying to find the truth."

"That is an exercise in futility." Aloysia walked to the window and stared at the Salzach river, which was silvery in the late afternoon sun. "Soon, this week, next week, it will be snowing. It will hide many of our deceptions. Herr Otis, his grave is a quagmire that could suck you in."

"Perhaps. Madame Lange, did you know Catherina Cavalieri?"

"Very well. I sang with her in *Seraglio, Figaro,* and *Don Giovanni.*"

"I thought she sang the original Constanze in *Seraglio.*"

"I understudied her. Mozart wanted me, but he was forced to take her."

"By Salieri?"

Aloysia retorted contemptuously, "Mozart hated Salieri."

"Should he have?"

"Salieri did everything he could to harm him."

"Do you remember how?"

"He was the one who ordered Mozart to be given only eight hundred gulden when Mozart became a Court Kapellmeister, instead of the two thousand Gluck had received. It was a clever way of making sure that Mozart would remain poor. And he must have been the person who told the new Emperor that Mozart had made slighting remarks about the Emperor's lack of taste."

Deborah asked, "What is your proof?"

"The Emperor gave Salieri the choice commissions, not Mozart."

"Then why did Mozart use Cavalieri if she was Salieri's mistress?"

"She was a leading member of the Royal Opera Company, which was supported by the Throne. Mozart had to use her."

Deborah persisted, "Was she beautiful? Like yourself?"

Aloysia answered scornfully, "Some people thought so, like Salieri. He was notorious for his interest in divas, since castrati were useless for his purposes and going out of style, and Cavalieri was buxom, in the opulent Teutonic manner, and very obedient to his wishes."

Jason said suddenly, struck with a new possibility, "Could Cavalieri have been a spy for Salieri? Since she sang frequently for Mozart."

Aloysia paused, seeking to recall proof of that.

Jason hurried on, excited by what he was suggesting, "We were told that Salieri and Cavalieri had dinner with Mozart not long before he died."

Aloysia said, "That's not unusual. I had dinner with them, too."

"But Mozart fell ill the day after he ate with them, and two weeks later he was dead. At the height of the success of *The Magic Flute*."

"I know."

"You were at that dinner, too?"

"No. But I had dinner with Salieri and Cavalieri a few days before. They told me that Mozart had invited them to hear *The Magic Flute*."

"Yet if Cavalieri was a spy, why did she write Ann Storace about this dinner, and express her shock at Mozart's sudden death afterwards?"

A sad expression appeared on Aloysia's face and she said somberly, "Cavalieri might have been a spy. As I was. An innocent one."

Aloysia paused, then said, "But I didn't suspect anything when Salieri invited me to his rooms for dinner. He said that he wanted to discuss his new opera with me, and that Cavalieri would be there, too, to show he had no other purpose in mind."

Jason and Deborah sat side by side in silence, and as Aloysia rushed on, Deborah's hand stole out and gently eased into Jason's, and she was grateful that he didn't pull away.

"It was an evening in November, 1791, and I arrived at six. I recall the time because Salieri insisted that I be there promptly. The usual footman admitted me, and Salieri greeted me at the door to his music chamber, his favorite room. I was surprised that Cavalieri was not there yet, and I must have shown that, for Salieri apologized, saying, 'You know how Cavalieri is, always late.' But I had a feeling it had been on his orders. I wondered what intrigue he was planning now. Perhaps he was going to give me a role he had promised her. My heart beat a little faster then. I didn't like his music much, but any opera composed by the first Royal Kapellmeister would have the Court's attention, unlike *The Magic Flute*, which had been ignored by the Court, and thus also by the nobility. Salieri led me to his pianoforte and asked me to look at a score.

"Yet while his voice was soft, he was bursting with something, for even though he was fashionably dressed and his features were heavily rouged and powdered in the French style, there were vivid worry lines under his dark eyes and his wide mouth twitched, and he jumped up and suggested that I sit at the pianoforte. It was not to play music, but so he could look down on me, for standing, I was taller than he was, and he hated that.

"He said in Italian, 'I am honored that you could come, Madame Lange.'

"I knew he hated to speak German, so I replied in Italian, 'I am the one who is honored, Maestro.'

"He asked, 'Do you like the score of my opera, Madame Lange?'

" 'Indeed!' I said, although he had not given me time to examine it. But with Salieri you never knew what game he was playing. 'It should add to your renown. I've admired your work a long time.'

" 'And I have admired your work, madame.'

" 'But the role seems suitable for Madame Cavalieri, too.'

" 'It suits your voice better. But that will be our little secret. That is, unless you are occupied with your brother-in-law's work.'

" 'How could I be? *The Magic Flute* is running very successfully.'

" 'So I've heard.' He frowned, then smiled beneficently. 'But there is always the possibility of following someone in it, if it runs long, or having something else offered you by your brother-in-law.'

" 'It is my sister Josepha who is singing the Queen of the Night.'

" 'What does she think of the opera?'

" 'Maestro, she has two very successful arias. She likes it very much.'

" 'And Herr Mozart? I hear he has been having some trouble with his food.'

" 'That's not unusual,' I replied. 'He's had trouble for years.'

" 'With certain wines, I believe, and livers of geese, which he adores?'

"Surprised by his question, I asked, 'Are you having Mozart to dinner soon?'

" 'No. You know he and I have had our differences. I've tried to warn him that he is going in the wrong direction, but he ignores me. I told him that if he wrote an opera about Freemasonry the Emperor would never forgive him. Leopold is far more conservative than Joseph and detests Freemasonry. But Mozart didn't heed me, and everyone knows that the role your sister is singing, the Queen of the Night, is a criticism of Maria Theresa. *The Magic Flute* has ended his prospects at Court forever.'

" 'Maestro, why are you telling me this?'

" 'You're a sensible artist. You would never offend the Court.'

"That was true, I thought; but then I was bewildered again, for he began to ask questions with an interrogative persistence.

" 'Have you seen Mozart lately? Much?'

" 'Is his health as uncertain as it is rumored?'

" 'Is he really so dedicated to Freemasonry?'

" 'Is his opera still playing to full audiences?'

" 'Does Josepha have any idea how long it is going to run?'

" 'Is he planning another one?'

" 'Do you think that will help his stomach?'

" 'It can't be too bad, if his wife is still in Baden?'

" 'Who does cook his meals these days?'

" 'Or is he eating in inns now?'

" 'Does he actually trust other people's cooking?'

"I answered Salieri as best I could, and he rushed on breathlessly, apparently pleased by what I had told him.

"He informed me, 'I met Closset at Court the other day. Closset had been called in for consultation about the Emperor. Leopold hasn't been feeling well, and there is a fear that he is being poisoned.'

" 'Who is suspected?' I asked.

" 'The Court is afraid of the revolutionaries in France who are holding the Emperor's sister Marie Antoinette a prisoner. They believe that subjects of the Emperor who are in sympathy with the French have put poison into the Emperor. Closset tells me that Mozart's stomach is most untrustworthy. Would you agree, Madame Lange?' I nodded, not knowing what else to say. I hadn't seen Mozart for some time, but I didn't want to sound ignorant. 'Cavalieri tells me that you still see him often, since he writes songs for you. She is always after me to write some for her, but I have to conserve my strength for more vital matters. The Emperor consults me on all musical matters, as you may have heard.'

"The clock struck seven. A moment later I heard a knock downstairs, and soon after Cavalieri swept in, but when Salieri reproached her for being late, she blurted out, 'You told me to come at seven, Salieri!'

"They always called each other by their last names to show that they were professional with each other and to give themselves distinction.

"Salieri shouted, 'You always misunderstand me!' But he calmed down after she said, 'I accepted Mozart's invitation to hear *The Magic Flute*.'

" 'And he will have dinner with us afterwards?' Salieri asked eagerly.

" 'Probably. As you suggested, I didn't mention it, so that when we invite him after we see *The Magic Flute*, our enthusiasm for his opera will make it more difficult for him to say No.'

"But Salieri had denied he was having dinner with Mozart. Yet it was so natural to expect intrigue from him, I didn't give that much thought.

"Cavalieri was proud of herself, announcing, 'I've found out what he can eat and cannot eat, so you can be a good host. And Madame Lange can confirm that. She knows Mozart's diet, and what he can't resist.'

"When I denied that, she snapped, 'But isn't that why she is here?'

"I thought Salieri would kill her then, he gave her such a harsh look. But a minute later, as he led us to the dinner table, he held each of us by the arm and said, 'I want my invitation to surprise Mozart. That is why I denied it earlier, Madame Lange. I am sure that your brother-in-law is just as eager for a reconciliation as I am.'

"His dinner was sumptuous, everything tasted delectable, and Salieri was generous with the wine. By the end of the evening the three of us had blended into a cozy familiarity, drinking over and over to each other's health; and I thought that Mozart would be lucky to be the guest at such a fine meal, for good food always made him feel better, and perhaps this would end their enmity. But a few weeks later Mozart was dead. And I wonder now whether I told Salieri things that I shouldn't have."

Deborah's hand had sunk deeper into Jason's as Aloysia had gone on, and she could feel his fingers tighten emotionally. But he was determined to remain controlled, she reflected, and she was proud of him as he asked quietly, "Did you talk to Cavalieri after Mozart died?"

"Yes. But never about our dinner. Or the dinner she had with Mozart."

"Then why did she write Storace about it, and not talk to you?"

"Storace was not a rival. And maybe she was afraid Salieri would find out if she spoke to me. But she had so much guilt she had to unburden herself to someone. I'll never know. She has been dead a long time."

"And your sister Josepha, who sang in *The Magic Flute*?"

"Dead."

"Did you get the role from Salieri?"

"No. Neither did Cavalieri. Soon after, they began to drift apart."

"Yet you have never thought about that dinner before?"

"Many times. But I didn't connect it with Mozart's death. Constanze was in Baden when he was Salieri's guest, Sophie looked in on him only occasionally, at that time I wasn't seeing either of them often."

And nobody had wanted to investigate, thought Jason, afraid that it would jeopardize their own safety.

Aloysia was very tired. Her rejection of Mozart was with her always these days. She was never free of it anymore. The more famous he became, the more it was with her. And now there was no end to his fame. His fame would last as long as life, and that filled her with self-hate and a sudden desire to punish herself. She said bitterly, "How could I be concerned? I'm just an old retired opera singer with no record of what I've done except a few yellow newspapers and faded memories. My husband left me long ago, no one has given me love for many years, and now I try to support myself teaching children who have no talent or genuine interest in music, but take lessons so their parents can boast that their children have cultivated tastes. I'm known now as the woman who could have married Wolfgang Amadeus Mozart and didn't, and today I have to depend on the charity of a sister whom I don't like and who doesn't like me, but who will not throw me out because people would talk about that and she is more afraid of that than anything else. But what I told you about Salieri and Cavalieri is true."

"I believe you," said Jason.

But when Deborah didn't speak, Aloysia said, "You don't like me."

Deborah replied, "I don't think that is what we've been talking about," when she knew that, to a large extent, it was all that Aloysia had talked about.

"Salieri never got over his jealousy and guilt. And never will."

Jason asked, "Will we see you again, Madame Lange?"

"What is there to see! If Constanze finds out what I told you, she will never forgive me. But if I told Salieri things I shouldn't have, I didn't mean to." Aloysia left then, as suddenly as she had come.

32

At This Time

B UT Jason kept trying to visualize Aloysia as Mozart had. He thought that she must have possessed a lovely voice for Mozart to have composed for it. Many men must have pursued her when she had been young and beautiful. And she had told him much that fitted what he suspected, yet vital links in the chain were still missing. Deborah couldn't get him to eat until he went over everything that Aloysia had said, weighing what he believed and what he couldn't trust. Then he ate with a preoccupied air, after Hans tasted the meal first. This had become their ritual and little was said, and then it was to discuss the weather. Hans mentioned that Herr Raab felt it was going to snow soon and had warned him that a storm could make the road back to Vienna impassable, and he asked, "Do you know, sir, when you intend to return to Vienna?" Jason replied, "Soon, in a week or so," and lapsed into silence.

The Salzburg weather had been cold, often windy, but clear, with one bright sparkling sunny day after another; but Hans seemed eager to depart and he couldn't desist, saying, "Herr Raab informed me that once it snows, it will be difficult to get back to Vienna by the end of the year."

Jason looked up abruptly, "Why are you so concerned about that?"

"Don't our visas expire at the end of the year, sir?"

"That is not your problem, Hans."

"They could investigate me, too, sir. Or even arrest me."

"Don't worry about that. I will take care of it."

"But Herr Otis, it is dangerous to drive on such roads in winter. There were times I was afraid we wouldn't reach Salzburg safely."

Jason said bluntly, "Then quit, and we will hire another driver."

"Oh, no!" That prospect appeared to frighten Hans even more than the perils of winter travel. "I wouldn't think of deserting you, sir. I just thought you would want to know about the difficulties of the weather."

Deborah found Jason up early the next morning, even more eager to pursue his inquiries, and he said, "I wish I could talk to Constanze once more."

"You can, if you want to," she assured him. "Now that Aloysia has seen us Constanze should be willing to talk to us again, if you are willing."

"But Aloysia said that Constanze must not know that she visited us."

"And relinquish one of her great triumphs?" Deborah laughed. "Aloysia will make sure that her sister knows she saw us, one way or another. Then Constanze will be unable to allow Aloysia to have the last word. You'll see."

Jason wasn't as certain as Deborah, but he thought it was possible. As he wrote down a list of people he still wanted to talk to, he was grateful that since he had been robbed she hadn't mentioned money. He went over his list: Constanze, Sophie, Friedjung, Mozart's sister, and, if they were still alive, Diener and Salieri. The last name made him tremble, and he didn't mention that to Deborah. After he wrote down Salieri's name, he crossed it out. But when she continued to stare at him, he got up and walked over to the window.

Deborah was regarding him affectionately. She was pleased with his growing distrust of Hans and with the skilful way he had questioned Aloysia. When she had decided to marry Jason, she had feared that he would embarrass her with his youthful indiscretions, particularly his fervor for causes like Mozart. Her father, upon learning that Jason intended to go to Europe, had accused him of nervous instability. He had warned her that Otis only desired her because she was wealthy and marriage to her would be extremely advantageous for a poor bank clerk, and while she had denied that indignantly, her father's accusations had troubled her, and in moments of doubt had remained with her. But now, she felt, Jason was maturing. He would be twenty-five in a few weeks and soon she would be twenty-four, and she felt that their many experiences were developing new qualities in him. For while Jason still looked younger than he was, with his fair hair and complexion, and his sensitive, mobile features and impulsive enthusiasms gave people the impression that he could be outwitted easily, she thought, That is no longer true. And his sensuality had not disappointed her, except when he had been distracted. Most of the time, especially in the brisk, pungent climate of Salzburg, he had been quite satisfactory sexually. And while she couldn't always agree with his passion for Mozart, now she shared some of his devotion.

He exclaimed, "Hans is talking to Bosch! I told you Bosch is a spy!"

"Because he is talking to Hans? That is no proof." But she followed his gaze out the window. Bosch and Hans stood on the riverbank, and Bosch asked Hans a question, and suddenly he nodded and walked away hurriedly.

Jason declared, "Bosch is probably asking about us."

At dinner Jason asked Hans, "What did Bosch want to know?"

Hans was eating slowly. Meals were a painful chore—he was afraid he would say something he shouldn't, and he said with apparent surprise, "Who?"

"The man you were talking to at the river. This afternoon."

"Oh, that man! Why, sir?"

"He could have been the person who poisoned me."

"Oh no, sir. I'm sure that you weren't poisoned. I ate the same food, and I had no ill effects. It must have been your stomach."

"What did Bosch ask about me?"

"Not a thing, sir. He merely wanted to know where he could hire a coach, and I sent him to the stable where I keep our coach and horses."

"Did he tell you his business?"

"No. Except that he is a traveller."

"A traveller?"

"Aren't you, sir?"

"Yes," said Deborah. "How long is he staying in Salzburg?"

"He didn't say."

"Or where he wants to go with the coach he intends to hire?"

"Frau Otis, should he have told me?" Hans asked innocently.

Before Deborah could reply, Jason rose hurriedly from the table.

"Is it your stomach?" she cried.

He nodded, and ran outside. He was pleased that Deborah and Hans accepted his pretended cramps as genuine; perhaps then he could fool the doctor, too. He was determined to have another talk with Friedjung about poisons, particularly arsenic, and it would be less suspicious if he went as a patient. When he returned to the table, he said to an alarmed wife and a worried servant, "It is not nearly as severe an attack as last time, but I had better not eat anything else, not tonight, at least."

Since no one else had been upset by the roast chicken, although Hans and Deborah had eaten it, too, Deborah insisted that Jason visit the doctor again, and he assented, although apparently unwillingly.

Friedjung thought Jason's cramps had been caused by nerves. "You are in an obvious stage of agitation, although you try to hide it."

"But you intimated earlier that I could have been poisoned."

"You intimated. I was merely curious about your symptoms."

"You did tell my wife they indicated I could have been poisoned."

Friedjung looked annoyed, saying, "What are you afraid of, Herr Otis?"

Jason longed to tell him, but Deborah gave him a warning glance—Do not tempt providence—and he replied, "I have heard so much talk about poisons that naturally it comes to my mind."

Friedjung stared at his office to collect his thoughts. It was as decorative as his music room, lined with bookcases on one wall, busts of Handel, Haydn, and Mozart on his mantel, and large French windows that faced a lovely garden and fountain. He said, "I didn't have to be a doctor. My father, while not of the nobility, was able to acquire wealth as a merchant, selling food to the Archbishop. But I didn't want to be in trade. I would have preferred to have been a musician, but I realized that I would never be a Mozart, and moreover, I didn't like being regarded as an inferior. So, I took my degree as a doctor of medicine at Heidelberg. And while I was offered a practice in Vienna, then as now the center of music and medicine in Europe, I decided to remain in Salzburg. It was more peaceful, quieter, and healthier, and I could indulge myself in music and my other hobbies. But medicine has been less active here. Not having to support myself with my practice, I have done much reading, and one of the subjects I have found fascinating is poison. It has often dominated history and changed it."

Deborah said, "You did mention to me the possibility of arsenic."

"It is a favorite poison. But I referred to it in a general way."

"You did say that some of his symptoms suggested arsenic."

"Did I, Frau Otis? I don't remember."

The doctor sounded so innocent, Jason almost believed him until Deborah said, "Yes, you did, Doctor. Several times." And as Friedjung looked annoyed, she added, "But perhaps it is a subject you don't know much about. We wouldn't have come here if my husband hadn't gotten ill again. And I heard that arsenic is usually more effective when it is given in repeated doses, over a length of time."

Jason turned to Deborah in surprise, asking, "How do you know?"

"I've done some reading, too. But if the doctor doesn't know . . .?"

As she had hoped, Friedjung's vanity got the better of his prudence, and he replied, "It is a subject I've given much attention to. Arsenic is the most common form of poisoning that exists. It is easy to give, for it is rarely detected. You can buy it from an apothecary; it can be slow or quick, depending on the nature of the dose. One can drop it in wine or sprinkle it on food. And you never see it or taste it."

Jason asked, "Can you tell when it has been given? Afterwards?"

"No one can be sure. But I know more about it than most doctors."

"Is it possible some doctors would not know the symptoms?"

"Yes. To sense its presence takes experience and instinct."

"Is there ever an occasion that you are sure that someone has been given arsenic?"

"Not without examination of the body after death. But even then it is difficult. And once the body is gone, the quest is hopeless."

"Then if someone poisoned a victim with arsenic, it would be important to them to hide the body?"

"You are obvious, Herr Otis."

"Why, Doctor?" Jason sought to appear surprised and innocent.

"Ever since Mozart died and his body vanished, there have been rumors that he was poisoned, possibly with acqua toffana, a form of arsenic."

"What do you think?"

"What is there to think! Once the body is gone, there is no evidence."

"Doctor, what are some of the symptoms of arsenic poisoning?"

"Usually cramps, thirst, vomiting, diarrhea, vertigo, body swelling."

Shivering, Jason asked, "Like some of the symptoms I had?"

"Some. But this time, fortunately, they were far less severe."

Deborah asked, "Then you don't think it was the same thing this time?"

"A stomach ache, as much imagined as anything else."

So the doctor was suspicious after all, thought Jason, and he hurried to say, "But some of my pain was the same."

"Yet not nearly as severe. And there was no indication of arsenic."

"How does one look when they die of arsenic? How can it be identified?"

"Herr Otis, you could be walking on dangerous ground."

"I won't tell anyone what you've said."

"It doesn't matter. I can always say that I was giving you medical advice, to prevent it happening to you. But if this knowledge is found on you, in view of certain circumstances, it could be incriminating."

"I'll memorize what you tell me. They won't know it is in my mind."

Friedjung dusted off an old book and turning to a familiar page, he read: *"Arsenic poisoning is seldom detected and yet it is common. It is found in the Bible, in ancient and medieval history, and very much in our own time. In 1659 a Neapolitian woman named Toffana, having developed a solution in Naples which possessed an arsenic base and which, when given in moderate doses by wives as a means of getting rid of unwanted husbands, was so highly successful, reducing the male population of Naples alarmingly, she was stopped by the police. But her invention, known as acqua toffana, became so popular because it was so difficult to detect, that it was reputed to have been the most widely used poison in the eighteenth century."*

Jason asked, "How does one look after aqua toffana? Or arsenic?"

"Essentially the same. At death the belly is protuberant, the eyes are fixed, the nostrils half-inverted, the legs heavy, then cold, stiff, and numb, and boils often break out and the body is swollen."

"If this was the way Mozart looked, why wasn't it investigated?"

"These symptoms are much like those in kidney failure."

"Is there any difference, Doctor?"

"Not really in the symptoms. But in kidney failure there is one vital difference between it and arsenic poisoning and acqua toffana."

Deborah listened intently while Jason asked eagerly, "What is it?"

"If Mozart had kidney failure, he would not have been able to compose for weeks before he collapsed and he would have been unconscious for a long time before his death. But if it was poison, the attack, particularly the final one, would have been much more sudden."

"I think . . ." Jason started to say, but Friedjung halted him.

"You must not think. You must know. Whatever I've told you concerns only you. If you quote me to the authorities, I will deny every word."

"Doctor, I will not violate any of your confidences."

"It won't matter if you do. It will be your word against mine."

"But if you are absolutely sure . . ."

"I'm not even sure you were ill. You look fine now. Your food could have been spoiled the other night, that's all. One piece can be and not another, and poison is a relative thing, affecting some more than others."

Deborah asked, "Then why did you answer our questions, Doctor?"

"I too have wondered whether Mozart was poisoned. And it is possible. But you cannot prove that. There are no final answers to the questions you ask."

33

The Sisters

W HEN the second invitation came from Constanze, although it arrived later than Jason expected, it was presented in a summary tone, more like a summons than a request. And while it was beginning to snow as Jason and Deborah started out for her home on foot, and Hans repeated Raab's warning about the weather, Jason replied, "It is too late for that now," and strode on. The snow was becoming heavy, but he was afraid that if they didn't go now the invitation might be withdrawn; as it was, he had waited longer than he had wanted to. A week had passed since they had visited the doctor, and he had begun to think that Deborah's prediction would not come true. He had spent the intervening days writing down his observations so that he would know what to ask Constanze, and he had put off approaching Mozart's sister, feeling it would be more appropriate to see Constanze again before this final visit in Salzburg.

Deborah believed, however, that Constanze had learned that Aloysia had visited them, but that Constanze had waited a few days so that she would not appear too eager. What worried Deborah was their visas. Now it was evident that they would not be able to return to Vienna before their visas expired. But she no longer discussed this with Jason, as if, at least by her show of confidence, she would remove his tension if not his fear. And there wasn't anything she could do about it. Perhaps this inquiry into the causes of Mozart's death was a quicksand, she reflected; but she was in it, too, for after the doctor's remarks and her encounters with the Weber women it had become impossible for her to do otherwise.

By the time they reached Constanze's house on the slope of the Nonnberg, they realized they were in the midst of a storm. A white blanket had fallen upon everything around them, and walking had become slippery and exhausting. The wind was blowing hard, driving the swirling flakes into their faces; yet Jason thought he saw Bosch standing in the arched entrance of a house that was within sight of Constanze's. But when he peered up the steep, winding lane, the man threw a scarf around his face, concealing all of his features but his eyes, and stepped back into the rear of the entrance before Jason could be sure. He didn't tell Deborah; he felt she was nervous enough as it was about their present situation.

This afternoon they were admitted to Constanze's reception room as if it were a ceremonial chamber. She appeared at once and began, thought Jason, like she was making an official statement in court. She was as anxious to speak to them as Aloysia had been, although he felt that she was scolding them. Constanze wore black, so they would know that she was in mourning. She looked sad so there would be no misunderstandings today about her feelings toward Mozart, and she said immediately, "I couldn't allow you to leave Salzburg without clearing up some misconceptions."

Jason bowed and said, "We are grateful for this privilege."

"I am the one person who knows the truth about Wolfgang. I was the one who shared his bed, his table, his work, his happiness, and . . . "

"His misery," interrupted Jason.

Constanze glared at him and said severely, "What do you mean?"

Schubert had said Mozart might have had an inner misery which had led to his early death; but when he expressed that, Constanze cut him short.

She said indignantly, "Wolfgang was very happy with me. He said ours was the most suitable marriage he could have made. But my sister never learns. The arrival of anyone interested in Wolfgang acts upon her like a physic, and she develops diarrhea of the mouth. I am sure she boasted that she was telling you the truth about Wolfgang. But she was wrong. As she was when she rejected him. Only she will never forgive me for that. I was the one he loved the most. Did she tell you that?"

Jason shrugged, not wanting to violate any confidences.

"Aloysia hasn't liked me for a long time. Ever since I wed Wolfgang. She didn't want him, but she didn't want anyone else to have him."

"Yet she is living here?" said Jason.

"She has no other place to go."

Deborah said, "Under the circumstances, you are kind to take her in."

"Thank you. Did she talk about how I neglected his grave? About my not going to the cemetery?"

Neither of them answered.

"Of course she did. She tells that to anyone who will listen. Is that why you came to Salzburg? If it isn't to write a book or to buy a score? It can't be just to kill time. No one comes to Salzburg for that reason."

Jason said, "We want to find the truth."

Constanze regarded him critically, then burst out laughing.

"What's wrong with that? Is it such an impossible quest?"

"Herr Otis, you are very young. Too young to be a Don Quixote."

"I will be twenty-five soon. And I have learned much lately."

"No doubt," she said sarcastically. "Such as hoping to impress me by wearing the same colors that Wolfgang did. That is not enough."

"You said you were the one person who knows the truth about him."

"It is why I saw you before. But then you spoke to my sister."

"She spoke to us. She visited us. We had no choice in the matter."

"Once Wolfgang proposed to me, I was first in his heart."

Deborah said sympathetically, "Frau von Nissen, I'm sure you were."

"Do you really think so? You don't believe Aloysia?"

"Of course not. Everyone said how much you loved Mozart." Deborah hoped that Jason would forgive this exaggeration, but she did want to help him, and Constanze had become less severe. "And we were told that he loved you even more, better than life itself."

Warmed by Deborah's compassion and feeling now that they could speak as one woman to another, whatever the inadequacies of male comprehension, Constanze began to cry and said, "I was so shocked when Wolfgang died I threw myself on his bed and begged to be buried with him. And I would have done it, if not for my sister Sophie, who persuaded me that the best way to preserve him was to preserve his memory."

"Was that why you were unable to visit the cemetery?" Deborah ventured cautiously. "You were so ill, so distraught, Frau von Nissen?"

"Exactly. I was prostrate. I was in bed for weeks."

"I would have felt the same way."

"I knew Aloysia talked about my not going to the cemetery. She never forgave that, although she didn't go herself."

"Perhaps she was ill, too."

"Ill? She was in the prime of life. But my sister has so much vanity she deluded herself into believing that Wolfgang still loved her."

Deborah thought, The sisters are obsessed with each other. Jason was quiet, realizing that Constanze needed no encouragement now to talk.

"Yet I was fortunate, I had him during the best years of his life, although my sister and his father could never accept that."

Deborah said, "But when he died, you must have been very bitter."

"I was. We had gone through so much in such a short time. When he died, I couldn't even pay for his funeral. Van Swieten had to assume the expense. Without his aid, Wolfgang would have ended in a pauper's grave."

"But he did, didn't he, in a way?" said Jason. "His body was thrown into a common grave. If it was put into any grave."

"It wasn't a pauper's grave. It was a third-class funeral, which was better. There was a cart, a coffin, and men who cost three gulden, and services at St. Stephen's which were eight gulden, fifty-six kreutzer. I remember that very well. I have a good memory for such details, and van Swieten reminded me of it many times. Yet without van Swieten,

Wolfgang might not even have been buried. I was penniless. But a third-class funeral is not a pauper's funeral. A pauper's is the poorest you can have. It would have been a disgrace. It would have broken my heart."

Deborah was confused. She felt more sympathetic to Constanze than Jason did, but some of her own shock and dismay remained. When she had learned that Constanze had not accompanied the body, she had found it almost impossible to believe. Some facts drained her imagination, and this was one of them. And finally she could not believe it. Now she was hearing it again from Constanze, but that didn't make it easier to believe. She wondered, Could Constanze have gone into shock because the doctor she had called had allowed Wolfgang to die? Could she have blamed herself for his death for that reason? That could have made her powerless, unable to perform the simplest act, and going to the cemetery could be complicated.

Constanze said, feeling that Frau Otis, at least, would understand, however Herr Otis disapproved, "So, as I told you, I was unable to go to the funeral. When Wolfgang died, I went out of my mind; and during the funeral I put myself into his bed, hoping I might die from the same illness."

Deborah asked softly, "Why didn't more of his friends go to the funeral?"

"They were afraid they would have to pay for it."

"What happened afterward?"

"How could I go afterward? Once I went it acknowledged he was dead?"

"But shouldn't somebody have put up a cross?"

"Where?"

"Somewhere in the cemetery," Deborah suggested.

"I thought the parish or the priest would."

"When they didn't, would it have been better than never having done it?"

Constanze paced around her reception room, looking worn and frail, as if she were still suffering, and said, "So I would have gone to the cemetery the following year? Or the year after? Where was Wolfgang's grave? Here? Or here?" She said this in a voice choked with emotion, and she took several steps to illustrate. "Or was it here? Or over there?" She pointed to the cabinet shaped like a coffin which contained a keepsake of Mozart. "I have a lock of his hair in there. It is all that is left of my husband's person. How could I stand where I wasn't sure? How could I kneel and pray when I didn't know where to pray? How could I say, My precious Wolfgang? What has happened to you? I would want him to hear me, to know I was there. But how could I be sure? And now nobody knows where the body is!" She lost her composure and began to weep.

"I'm sorry," whispered Deborah. "This must be a terrible ordeal."

Jason was far away. From the start of Constanze's explanation, he had been thinking of Mozart, and gradually Mozart appeared in his mind with a ghostly familiarity. When he began to criticize Constanze, Mozart sighed and cut him short, saying:

"I don't know what she did and I don't care. I loved her and that was enough. That is all that matters, that is all I know."

"But the neglect . . ."

"I loved her. That is all I know, that is all I want to know."

"Yet the shortness of your life . . .?"

"It went so fast, I tried to realize, to notice. Did I? I suppose."

"Your growing fame? Is that any consolation?"

"If it brought me back. What is it worth otherwise?"

"Constanze says . . ."

"I don't know and I don't care. I loved her and that was enough."

That sang like an intimate musical refrain in Jason's imagination, and Deborah cried out. "You look so strange! What is wrong?"

Tears came into his eyes, and Constanze, thinking that he was crying because of what she had said, added, "Don't cry, it doesn't do any good."

Jason murmured, "What worries me is why nobody went."

"They were too busy. Too concerned with themselves." Constanze was touched by Jason's emotion, and she added passionately, "I never dreamt that I would not live out my whole life with Wolfgang. I thought we would grow old together. When I went to Baden that autumn he was in good health."

"You are sure he was in good health then?" Jason was excited again.

"I wouldn't have gone otherwise. We had many plans. If he had lived, he would have re-established himself. *The Magic Flute* was his first great popular success. He would have been the envy of all the opera composers."

"And he was not sick until his final collapse?"

"No, Herr Otis."

"Didn't he have any premonitions of disaster the last few months of his life? Wasn't he afraid that someone was poisoning him? Da Ponte told me that there was much intrigue against him and Mozart."

"Da Ponte intrigued so much, he assumed everyone else did."

"But Michael Kelly and Thomas Attwood talked about how certain foods and wines upset your husband."

"Neither one has kept in touch with me, although Attwood used to write me as long as he needed the connection."

"Do you think that certain foods upset Mozart?"

"Unquestionably. But that didn't kill him."

"What did, Frau von Nissen?"

"Wolfgang always cherished me. He cracked like a heavily used bowl."

"Is that why he talked about poison?" When Constanze denied that,

Jason reminded her that she had mentioned it herself. She looked troubled and confused, and he thought, Constanze wants to make sure that her place in the Mozart pantheon is secure; nothing else matters much.

Deborah, however, put her hand on Constanze's consolingly, and said softly, "Mozart's memory must possess you so poignantly that it must be very painful to speak of his death, but in justice to yourself . . ."

"Myself?"

"Yes. Before we received your gracious explanations, we heard many ugly rumors about why Mozart died. Some said he was a libertine."

"That was nonsense. He had many enemies who spread that rumor."

"We heard other rumors that he died of neglect," Deborah continued.

"Neglect by the nobility, perhaps, but months before he died he was possessed with the notion that he had been poisoned. He wondered if someone was trying to kill him. He would get a sudden stomach attack, and then, just as he felt fine, another attack would occur."

"Did he refer to any particular poison?"

"He believed someone was giving him acqua toffana."

"Why that poison?" Deborah found it difficult to keep the excitement out of her voice, while Jason sat intently, eager for Constanze's answer.

"It was known to be in common use. It couldn't be detected, yet his kidneys seemed affected. But he had had no trouble with them until then."

"Yet you still don't believe that Salieri did it?"

"No, Frau Otis, although many others did."

"Yet if they were enemies, why did Mozart accept his invitation?"

"Wolfgang's greatest ailment was loneliness. He hated being alone. When I was in Baden or he was traveling, he wrote me often how much he missed me. That in itself would have caused him to accept Salieri's invitation. Then he was probably excited by the success of *The Magic Flute,* particularly with Salieri at his side, too excited to go to bed, and Salieri's table was noted for being sumptuous, and Wolfgang, who had been unable to afford food he liked, might have been tempted by this. There could have been many reasons. But you must speak to my sister Sophie. She was with him when he died. I will call her."

As Constanze went to fetch Sophie, Jason thought, It is remarkable how Deborah has persuaded Mozart's widow to talk, and better yet, has asked the right questions, questions I couldn't have improved on. But he hesitated to praise her, afraid that she would take advantage of it. So, although he felt like embracing her as an expression of his gratitude, he walked over to the window and looked out, one of his favorite ways of hiding his feelings. It was snowing so heavily there wasn't a trace of any living thing outside. He couldn't even see the houses on the other side of the lane. Yet even as he realized that it would be wise to leave now, before it became difficult to return to the inn, he could not relinquish the opportunity of meeting Sophie.

Constanze came back quickly with Sophie, introduced her as Frau Haibel, and said, "I'm going to leave you alone. It's too painful to hear about Wolfgang's last hours, and Sophie will verify what I told you."

"If I can," said Sophie. She looked anxiously after her departing sister, yet she didn't try to halt her, as if that would have been futile.

Sophie wore a simple dark gray dress which was old and frayed but very clean. She was between Aloysia and Constanze in height; her features were round, plain, and wrinkled, but softer and smaller than her sisters'.

Jason asked, "Whom did he prefer? Each of your sisters says it was her."

"Constanze. He was always fond of Aloysia's voice, but once she turned him down, he never could care for her in the same way."

"Are you sure? You must have been very young when he first met Aloysia?"

"Ten or twelve, I don't remember exactly. I am the youngest. But later, when he became attached to Constanze, I was older. I envied her. I thought she was fortunate to have such a good man to look after her."

"You liked his disposition, Frau Haibel?"

A glow came into her gray eyes, and she was enthusiastic for the first time. "He was gentle, kind, full of fun, and devoted to Constanze."

Jason felt that of all the sisters he could trust her the most, and yet he had to be sure. "How can you be positive he preferred Constanze?"

"It was in every word he wrote. In every thing he did. When she was away, he was desolate. There was no one in the world like his Stanzi."

"Do you think that she felt the same way?"

Sophie hesitated, then said hurriedly, "Of course."

"Then why wasn't she at his side when he died?"

"Aloysia must have told you. She has always been jealous."

"But you were at his side."

Sophie exclaimed, "I had to. I loved . . ." She floundered, and blushed. "We were fond of each other. But that isn't why you want to talk to me."

She was so overcome with emotion Jason felt sorry for her, and he said more gently, "I didn't mean to upset you, but I did wonder how you felt about Mozart. Often sisters-in-law don't approve of brothers-in-law."

"Wolfgang!" Sophie was shocked. Her lips quivered. "The cruelest thing that ever happened to me was when he died. I'll never forget it. There was so much I wanted to do, and so little I could do."

"But you did your best. Even Aloysia admits that."

"Perhaps. I've never been sure. So many things went wrong."

"When did you realize that Mozart was critically ill?"

Sophie's face darkened and she said sadly, "It was some weeks after the opening of *The Magic Flute*. I had not seen him for a few days, since he had taken my mother and me to hear the opera, but that didn't worry me. He had been in such high spirits because of the success of *The Magic Flute*. It was his first popular triumph in Vienna, and he felt that his poverty and neglect were ending. He had plans to write another opera for Schikaneder. Wolfgang was delighted with the way the audiences had come to love *The Magic Flute*, particularly Papageno. Even his health was better. In the last six months he had had sudden stomach attacks, usually of cramps, followed by vomiting and diarrhea. But they cleared up when he ate carefully, and he blamed these attacks on tension and overwork. He had been unhappy composing *La Clemenza di Tito*. He felt that the Emperor, for whom the opera was being written, was indifferent to his work; and Wolfgang disliked the libretto, he felt it was old-fashioned. But the success of *The Magic Flute* had revived his spirits. Only one thing troubled him. He had to compose a Requiem and because he didn't know who it was for, he did say that he was writing it for himself, but I felt it was because the idea depressed him and he was resisting it in that way."

"What about Constanze?" interrupted Jason. "Where was she?"

"In Baden, with their oldest son, Karl. Their baby, Franz, was with my mother. But though he missed Stanzi terribly, he kept saying that she must stay in Baden so she could rest until she got better."

Deborah put her hand on Jason's to halt any further interruptions, but he was listening now as attentively as she was. The reception room had taken on a deathly stillness, and Sophie's memories became as real as themselves.

"My mother and I were living not far from Wolfgang's house on the Rauhensteingasse, and we were about to sit down for dinner when I heard a knock on the door. It was a waiter from Diener's tavern, and there was a frantic note in his voice as he said, 'I am glad I found you in, Fräulein. Your brother-in-law, the Kapellmeister, seems quite ill, and Diener is very worried. He says you must come at once.'

"I was annoyed. Much as I cared for Wolfgang, I was young, I felt it wasn't my responsibility, but the waiter regarded me so imploringly, I went. By the time I reached Wolfgang's rooms, Diener had put him to bed, lit the stove, and sent for the doctor. But I was alarmed, for while the bedroom was still cold, Wolfgang's head was burning and he was in a coma.

"I asked Diener if this was his first severe attack, and he said, 'No. But much the worst. He told me he got sick after he ate with Maestro

Salieri, and fainted the next day, but when he asked the doctor if he had been poisoned, the doctor laughed at him and said he was suffering from eyestrain. But since then he has hardly been able to eat anything. He has been living on soup and wine, which I have been bringing to him, for he hasn't been going out lately. Then today he staggered into my inn and ordered wine. When he couldn't touch it, I knew he must be very sick, and so I brought him home and sent for you and the doctor.'

"The waiter Diener had sent to the doctor stood before us, mumbling, 'Closset doesn't want to come. He says Mozart already owes him money.'

" 'I'll pay him,' I assured the waiter, but when I put my hand in my pocket I realized that in my agitation I had run out without a kreutzer.

"Diener gave the waiter two gulden for Closset and said, 'Tell him to hurry. That it is an emergency.'

"I promised Diener that I would pay him back, but he merely smiled and said, 'The Kapellmeister tells me that, too, but I can't let him go hungry. We had better call his wife, whatever the doctor says.'

"Diener was right; for Wolfgang was unconscious for two days, and when he came out of his coma and saw Constanze by his side he was glad.

"Now I had a daily routine. I visited Wolfgang and Constanze each day, pretending that I had come to clean, searching for dust even when it wasn't there, trying to be casual even when I was most worried; and each time Wolfgang was alone with me, he said, 'I'm failing, Sophie, I'm failing. My body keeps swelling and my stomach aches so. But don't tell Constanze; she won't be able to bear it.' And I wondered how much more he could endure. He was having repeated attacks of cramps, boils were breaking out on his hands and feet, and however he lay he was in constant pain.

"One afternoon I entered his bedroom without his hearing me, which was unusual, for he had the most acute hearing, and I thought, Wolfgang must be very ill indeed if he has trouble hearing, and he was staring at his hands woefully as if they had become corrupt and betrayed him.

"When he saw me he cried out with terror in his voice, 'Look, Sophie dear, now I am really bankrupt! I will never be able to play again!'

"Horrified, I thought, He could be right. His fingers and hands had swollen out of shape the last few days.

" 'Soon I won't be able to move my fingers, my precious fingers. I can barely move them now. Sophie, am I going mad?'

" 'No, no, no!' I denied vehemently. 'You are the most rational of men!'

"He smiled sadly and said, 'Without work, I will die.'

" 'It is just that your illness manifests itself in strange ways.'

" 'Sophie, do you think I have been poisoned?'

" 'Of course not!' I cried, although I wasn't sure.

" 'That's what Constanze says. She doesn't want me to know the truth. She wants to protect me. But it is too late.'

"I asked, 'What does the doctor say?'

" 'Closset? He keeps saying, 'There is nothing to worry about.'' He does that because he doesn't know what is wrong. But I think I've been poisoned. My cramps, vomiting, diarrhea, swollen body. I have all the classic symptoms. It is the perfect way to eliminate me. Salieri may be a genius after all.'

"His words sounded in my ears like the notes of one of his sonatas, as if I was listening to the beat of his heart. But unlike what some people said, this music was not light and gay but grim, with an uncanny agitation, an agitation that was fatalistic. I was not supposed to know much about music like my sisters Josepha and Aloysia, who were opera singers, or Constanze, who would have had a fine voice if she had studied, but anything he composed now, I thought, would be dominated by an inevitable resignation.

"He asked me wistfully, 'Where are you, Sophie? You seem far away.'

" 'I was thinking of the sonata you wrote in Vienna in the summer of 1781, before you married Constanze. You said that it was a declaration of love to both of us, but I always felt that you were mocking me.'

"He said, 'I have never mocked you.'

"I said, 'You never finished it.'

" 'It wouldn't have been fair to Constanze, would it, Sophie?'

" 'I didn't answer. I wasn't sure that I could be that fair.

"He said, 'You were shocked by what I said about being poisoned.'

"I replied, 'You mustn't think such dreadful thoughts.'

"He said, 'And you musn't think I don't care for you. I do.'

"Then I was sure he didn't love Aloysia. I realized that he couldn't love anyone who didn't love him. In his quiet way he had a fierce pride.

"Thus, you can imagine how horrible I felt when a terrifying look of suffering appeared on his face. Wolfgang was trying to turn around, his position had become so painful, but his swollen body and his boils caused him to groan and mutter, 'Isn't there any relief?'

"I spent the next twenty-four hours sewing a nightgown for him that he could put on from the front, so that he wouldn't have to turn around. He was pleased with it, for it lessened his pain and discomfort.

"The next few days he seemed more cheerful, for Constanze had arranged for three musicians to stop in on Sunday and perform his Requiem with him.

"I decided not to visit him on Sunday; I would be a distraction, although he wouldn't say that. But I knew he would prefer it that way, and so, on Sunday, I tried to relieve my own anxieties with some coffee.

"I lit a candle, but I couldn't stop thinking about Wolfgang. I found myself staring into the flame, wondering how he was, and suddenly the flame went out although it had been burning brightly a moment before.

"Frightened, I hurried to dress, putting on my prettiest dress—Wolfgang always liked me to look my best, he loved pretty clothes—and I had just finished when Süssmayer, Wolfgang's protégé, rushed in, crying out, 'Mozart is worse! Your sister begs you to come at once!'

"Yet when I arrived at his house, he didn't appear critical. He was surrounded by three musicians who were performing his Requiem with him. He was singing the alto part, and that seemed to lift his spirits.

"Before I could feel better, however, Constanze took me into the next room and whispered tearfully, 'Thank God you've come. He was so sick last night I didn't think he would be alive today. Please, you must stay with him now. He likes you.'

"When I found my voice, I asked, 'What does the doctor say?'

" 'He called in another doctor, and they told me that his condition is hopeless. But you mustn't tell him. As it is, he believes he is under a sentence of death, and it depresses him terribly. You must cheer him up.'

"So as I walked into his room I had a smile on my face, but it didn't fool him. His voice had failed him totally, he didn't have the strength to sing a single note, and he looked as depressed as I had ever seen him. The three musicians had left, after saying they would return next Sunday to resume where they had stopped. When he saw me, he pushed the Requiem aside and wept, sobbing, 'I'm nothing, nothing. Without music I'm nothing.' He motioned for me to sit beside him and he said, 'Dear Sophie, it is kind of you to come. You must stay tonight. You must see me die.'

" 'You're depressed,' I managed to say. 'You had a bad night.'

" 'I already have the taste of death on my tongue. Who will look after Stanzi when I am gone?'

" 'You will be better,' I forced myself to add. 'After you rest.'

" 'Rest?' He looked as if he had been disemboweled as he clutched his stomach. 'I can't rest. Sometimes I have such pain it is indescribable.'

"What could I say to him? He trembled in a terrible paroxysm of pain, and I felt overwhelmed, longing to help him and unable to do anything.

" 'I've had these cramps ever since I ate with Salieri. And I had been feeling much better.' His pain eased for a moment, and he rushed on while he could. 'I thought I was over my attacks of cramps of the last few months. Until I had that supper with him.'

"I asked, 'Do you recall what you ate at Salieri's?'

"But his thoughts were elsewhere, as if he had to explain his visit to Salieri before he died, and he said, 'I wondered whether I should accept Salieri's invitation to supper, but he had accepted mine. And he and Cavalieri seemed to like *The Magic Flute*. There wasn't a single aria that didn't bring forth a *Bravo* from him and applause from her. And it had been some time since I had had a decent meal, and I was too excited to go straight home after the performance and to an empty house. I needed company desperately, and they were both musicians. Cavalieri had sung my music very well.' Then this effort to speak was too much for him, and he was silent.

"That night he was much worse, and we called a doctor and a priest.

"It was difficult to persuade a priest to come, although St. Stephen's was nearby. I don't know whether it was because they were afraid they wouldn't get paid, because they disapproved of Wolfgang being a Freemason, or they felt that he was a pagan because of operas like *Don Giovanni* and *Così fan tutte,* but finally I shamed a young priest who confessed that he liked music to come.

"Süssmayer had gone to fetch Closset, who was at the theater hearing *The Magic Flute*—Wolfgang had given him tickets for calling the other doctor—and Süssmayer returned distraught and told me, 'Closset says he can't come until the opera is over.' He added, whispering so Wolfgang would not hear him, 'Closset says it will make no difference anyway.'

"Constanze had lain down in her room before she collapsed. Wolfgang wanted to know where she was, and I told him.

" 'Isn't she well?' he asked weakly.

" 'She needs rest,' I replied. 'She didn't sleep much last night.'

" 'Yes,' he said mournfully. 'I kept her up.'

" 'No, you didn't. But you haven't been well lately.'

" 'Dying, Sophie, dying. There are scores of my last three symphonies in my safe. Don't let them be destroyed. They might be played some day.'

"Then he fell into a coma, and by the time Closset arrived, I was afraid that he would never talk again. But while the doctor was washing his hands, saying, 'I don't want to catch any infection,' Wolfgang revived and murmured, 'Süssmayer, was *The Magic Flute* crowded?'

" 'Full. As always. There were many encores. And *Bravo* Mozarts.'

"I thought he smiled then, but I couldn't be sure. Closset put a cold compress on Wolfgang's head, saying, 'It is burning, this will ease his fever,' and as the compress fell across Wolfgang's brow he was shocked into unconsciousness. Closset shrugged and said, 'There isn't anything more I can do,' and he walked out.

"Now I realized that Wolfgang was dying as I sat beside him—just the two of us; Constanze was prostrate in another room and Süssmayer was taking care of her. Hours passed silently and sombrely. I heard the bells of St. Stephen's strike midnight; and some time later, as I was thinking, His ordeal will never end, he mumbled, 'What the world does to its children.' Then with a convulsive effort of his mouth he sought to sound the drums in his Requiem. He lifted his head, as if to make certain that he heard them, and then turned his face to the wall and was quiet. I jumped to my feet, sought to revive him, but it was useless. His eyes were open and staring at me, and their fixity was terrifying. The bells of St. Stephen's were striking one, and I knew that it was Monday and that Wolfgang was dead."

Sophie sat as if she were still by his side, her eyes filled with tears. Jason was stunned by what he had heard, while Deborah, although she could hardly talk, had to ask, "Frau Haibel, what did he look like then?"

"Horrible. I've never forgotten it. Thirty-three years ago, almost to the day—he died on December 5, 1791—and his death is like it happened yesterday. His swollen body, fingers, his score on his bed that he couldn't hold because his hands had swollen so. His terrible boils, his protuberant belly, and hardest to bear, his staring, fixed eyes."

Deborah asked, "Who arranged the funeral?"

"I did, with van Swieten's help. It was the cheapest funeral there was—only a pauper's was worse—but I had no choice. There wasn't a kreutzer in the house. And nothing I could sell at the time—only Wolfgang's books, letters, scores, some still unfinished, clothes that had been valuable like waistcoats, a fur-lined fur coat, silk stockings, cravats, the matrimonial bed, and the usual household goods, but all worn out from use. And his musical things—a viola, pianoforte—oh, nothing you could get money for; no one was interested in his possessions then. And how could I bargain? When van Swieten handed me the eight gulden, fifty-six kreutzer, I remembered that Wolfgang had paid that much a few years before for the burial of a pet starling. But Constanze was still in bed, and I was very young for such a responsibility—I was just twenty-four—and I had to accept what I could get."

Jason asked, "Didn't you think of having the body examined since there were so many discrepancies in what was said about why he died?"

"Yes. But when I suggested doing that, Salieri said to me, 'Mozart is with God. He is at rest and you must not disturb him.'"

"When did this happen?"

"The next day. At the house. Salieri was one of those who came to pay his respects. And he went to the funeral at St. Stephen's, too. And afterward, I couldn't reach into the grave."

"If you could have found it," said Jason.

"That was another thing. I had to make the burial arrangements."

Jason asked gently, "Who was at the funeral?"

"Van Swieten, Albrechtsberger, Diener, Salieri, Gottlieb, Süssmayer. Whatever else they had done, or not done, I treasured them for that."

"Is Diener still alive?"

"He could be. He wasn't much older than I was at the time."

316 THE ASSASSINATION OF MOZART

"Did you know where his tavern was?"

"Yes. The Silver Serpent was on the Karnerstrasse. It may still be there. It used to do a thriving business, and Wolfgang went there often."

"Who was Gottlieb?"

"Anna Gottlieb sang in *The Magic Flute.*"

"Did she know Mozart well?"

"She was only seventeen. I'm sure Wolfgang regarded her as a child."

"Is she still alive?"

"I think so. She became a renowned performer in Vienna."

"Why didn't anyone go to the cemetery?"

"I heard that two people did that night. Albrechtsberger and Gottlieb. But by then it was too late. The body had vanished."

"Why didn't you go? Since you were so devoted to Mozart?"

"After the services at St. Stephen's some of us set out for the cemetery, but at the city gate the sky became cloudy, and Salieri said, 'It is going to storm. We would be foolish to go on, we will get soaked, and the road is terrible, muddy and rough.' And so we turned back."

"Did it storm?"

"No, Herr Otis. I should have gone. I didn't realize that since we were not paying the gravedigger, he wouldn't care."

"Do you think somebody else paid him to make the body vanish?"

"I don't know! There were rumors that Wolfgang had been poisoned, that Salieri didn't like him; but Salieri came to the house, to the funeral, and he even taught Wolfgang's sons music for a short time. You don't think he would have done all that if he was guilty?"

I do, indeed, thought Jason, but Sophie looked so upset, he said, "It must have been a nasty shock to the widow, being unable to visit the cemetery."

"It was. When I asked Constanze if she wouldn't like to put a cross over his body, at least somewhere in the cemetery, she replied, 'He'll get one, the parish will do it.' Then afterwards, when that didn't happen, I think she was too upset, she felt too guilty, as I did, to go."

"But you did go?" Jason persisted. "In the years after he died?"

"Several times. Until I moved away from Vienna. But you must understand that my sister had gone through a terrible time and if she had visited Wolfgang's grave, it would have reminded her of what she had gone through. I think she had been disturbed enough."

Constanze returned as if that was her signal to intervene, and she said, "Sophie must be very tired. It is always a great ordeal for her to remember the past."

Jason thought that Sophie looked disappointed at her sister's pronouncement, as if, for this day at least, she had been important, too.

Constanze continued, "I hope you appreciate what I've done. Now you can understand why I couldn't go to the cemetery. Why it became so painful afterward." Melancholy appeared on her face so that they would know how much she had suffered. Jason wanted to ask more questions, but she cut him short. "I've been most considerate of you. I'm very tired, too. All these questions are exhausting."

"But it's still snowing," said Deborah. "It will be difficult walking."

Constanze went to the window and said with obvious satisfaction, "It has stopped. You can go now. You are fortunate. When we get a heavy snow in Salzburg, you can be snowbound for weeks."

Jason and Deborah had put on their fur coats and were about to say goodbye when Aloysia swept in. But she never got a chance to speak, for Constanze said, "I trust you will have a pleasant trip back to Vienna."

"Won't we see you again, Frau von Nissen?" Jason asked.

"No. Sophie and I are joining our husbands in Munich, and we won't be back for some time. And I am closing the house, so Aloysia will have to go with us."

Jason was fascinated by the way the three sisters hurried to arrange themselves under the portrait of Mozart. Aloysia's husband had painted it, but each of the women placed herself as if she owned it. Three sisters, all resembling each other with the sharpness of their profiles—even Sophie's was severe now—as they stood frozen by time and memory.

Constanze had put herself in the center, insisting that she was the center; but Aloysia was smiling mysteriously, affirming that actually she was the center; while Sophie seemed content to be anywhere in this circle. Then suddenly they looked so different—Constanze in black and in mourning, Sophie in practical gray, and Aloysia in pink and still seeking to appear young. Yet they were destined to be tied for life, he reflected, three faces out of the past, bound by a common memory and love. Yes, he told himself, they had all loved Mozart in their own way. Each of them had known him dearly and would be remembered for that, if for nothing else. He wondered how Mozart would have painted them. He knew that he would remember them as long as he lived.

But Jason didn't express any of these feelings until they reached the inn; for the walking was exhausting, and they had to concentrate to keep from slipping and falling. Outside the inn, however, he said to Deborah, "They had one thing in common; they all loved him. In their own way."

"Perhaps."

"Don't you think so?"

"It doesn't matter. I'm convinced that he loved Constanze."

"Even though Sophie probably loved him best. And was the most devoted."

"He didn't want devotion. Constanze was the one he needed, so no one else really mattered as far as he was concerned. Isn't that clear, Jason?"

"I guess so." As he opened the door of the inn, he said, "You were very good with Constanze. You got her to tell me much that I needed to know."

34

My Cherished Nannerl

THE VISIT to Mozart's sister was simple and direct. Jason left word with her that he and his wife would be honored if they could pay their respects to her, she who exemplified Mozart's music best, and her response was immediate and cordial. Several days after they had seen the Weber women they stood in her music room and were greeted by a very old lady.

Madame Sonnenburg sat on a sofa to conserve her energy. They had been admitted by a friend who disappeared the moment they introduced themselves. She was like a withered flower, shriveled, bent, but with a skin that was still fair, and delicate hands. Her eyesight was failing, for she had to peer at them through spectacles to see them, yet the moment they were seated, she put her spectacles aside.

But Jason realized that the Nannerl of Mozart's childhood was five years older than Mozart, and thus, also older than any of the Webers.

Yet at seventy-three she was proud of her memory, that many things, particularly what had happened to her in childhood, she remembered as clearly as if they had taken place yesterday. When she spoke about her brother, it was as if he sat by her side at the harpsichord, where they had played memorable duets for the Empress Maria Theresa, Louis XV, George III, and others long dead but once powerful.

Jason was grateful that Madame Sonnenburg lived just around the corner from the Golden Goose Inn on the Sigmund-Haffnergasse.

"And just around the corner from the house on the Getreidegasse where Wolferl and I lived and were born," she reminded him. "This was as close as I could get."

He was grateful, too, that there had not been any more snow, and that walking had become easier and no one seemed to be spying on them. They had not seen Bosch anywhere, and Hans had kept out of their way, except at meals, where he had eaten with them as ordered. The house on the Nonnberg had been closed, shuttered, and bolted, and the Weber women had left Salzburg in the public diligence.

Like the Webers, however, Madame Sonnenburg had placed herself under a picture of Mozart, but which she was in, too. As she had intended, Jason was attracted by this painting and he stared at it intently. It depicted Wolfgang in a red dress coat and Nannerl in a lilac gown, playing a four-handed duet on the pianoforte. What was especially moving to Jason were two other presences. Their father was also in this picture, dressed in a black coat and a white wig and leaning on the pianoforte and holding his favorite violin. And above them hung an oval painting of their mother.

She said sadly, "Our mother was dead by then. The painter put her in the miniature so we would know that, yet so we would all be together. We were a very close family. Until Wolfgang went to Vienna by himself."

Deborah was surprised that there was a harpsichord in the music room instead of a pianoforte, and Madame Sonnenburg added, "I prefer it. It is the instrument Wolferl and I used when we made our grand tour of Europe."

"He was quite fond of you?" Jason suggested. "Wasn't he?"

"He loved me. Not like most brothers and sisters. He always wrote me affectionately, and he wrote me often. I was his 'cherished Nannerl.' "

"How did you feel about him?"

"We shared everything. Until he met the Webers. He was always 'my beloved Wolferl,' as I was, for him, 'my cherished Nannerl.' "

She fondled these words on her tongue so affectionately that Jason was thankful that his German had improved with constant use—he was almost as proficient in the language as Deborah now—and these days neither of them had trouble being understood or understanding. And he didn't want to lose a word that she was saying.

When they had been introduced, she had apologized, saying "I speak only German now. I knew some French when we traveled, but I haven't traveled for such a long time. Wolferl was the linguist in the family; he spoke French and Italian fluently, and some English—he loved England"; and she was relieved that both of them had been able to answer her in a clear German.

The little old lady in her neat brown dress had felt deserted for many years. Her husband had died a long time ago, her stepchildren ignored her, and the best loved of her two children had died and the other one seldom saw her. People who came to Salzburg because of Mozart usually visited his widow and avoided his sister. She rarely saw the Weber women, and never as friends. She had not even known when Constanze had wed again, and only Sophie, whom she saw on the street occasionally, was civil.

But these youthful, attractive American visitors were so attentive, so respectful, they gave her a feeling of importance she had not possessed for ages. It was remarkable; it was the same feeling she had had when she had played with Wolferl. She no longer felt dried up, a relic. As she spoke of Wolferl it was as if she were unlocking a treasure for them.

She said tenderly, "We were always Wolferl and Nannerl to each other, and to Papa and Mamma. We were a very close family. We did everything together, but especially music. Even when Wolferl and Papa were away, we felt together. We had such a sense of family."

Deborah was astonished at how much she welcomed Nannerl's gentler plunge into the past. The last hours with the Webers had left her drained; there had been too much malice and envy for her to feel comfortable, in spite of her sympathy for Constanze. And Jason, who had said that Sophie was the one sister whose memories they could trust—he felt that Aloysia and Constanze had made a few adjustments to the facts, but that Sophie had told him the truth as she remembered it—was more relaxed, too, listening to Mozart's sister with a kind of contentment.

But Deborah knew she couldn't allow Nannerl's nostalgia to neutralize reflection. Nannerl, too, must have been involved in some of his crises, and questions had to be directed. She interrupted, "Was he sick much?"

"Not as much as people think."

"What do you mean?" Jason asked, alert again.

"Wolferl was supposed to be frail because he was small and slight."

"Was he, Madame Sonnenburg?"

"He had several serious illnesses in childhood, as many children do, but once he recovered, he was fine. He could work as hard as anyone I have ever seen. When he was practising or performing or composing he was tireless, and no one and nothing could confine him. The two operas he composed in a few weeks, *The Magic Flute* and *La Clemenza di Tito*, proved that he was not a sickly person, even just before he died."

Jason asked, "What do you think it was that caused his sudden death?"

"I wasn't there. He had such a quick sense of humor. He adored making me laugh. We had such wonderful times together. He would dedicate his letters to my lung, my liver, my stomach. He would write four lines in four different languages. He would make up words like *schumpl*, and in the next breath a well-turned sentence. He gave everyone he liked pet names, like our precious fox terrier, Bimperl, whom he missed as much as anybody. Yet he said that without work he was like a dog with fleas. And he loved ridiculing names, particularly pompous ones, even his own. Such as the time in Italy he was being extravagantly praised by being called, *"Il Signor Cavalieri Filarmonica Wolfgango Amadeo Mozarto."* He wrote me, "It is one too many." The next time he was addressed that way, he signed himself, *"Johannes Chyrsostotomus Wolfgangus Amadeus Sigismundus Mozartus,"* and this time he wrote me, "that ought to cure them." The tragedy of my brother is that we remember how he died, and so we think he was a sad person, but he wasn't. And it wasn't that there was something wrong with him, but that there was something wrong with the world around him. He had great promise, he lived up to that promise, and that should have been his only concern. There was a great deal of happiness in his life, especially when he was with us. We accomplished so much together. All he needed was an audience and he created music. Even when some of them acted, as he said, "Like asses. If they are constipated, they ought to take an electuary." Or the time Wolferl wrote me that a castrato who was singing in one of his operas declared that if his duet didn't succeed he would let himself be castrated again, and after the duet Wolferl handed him a knife. But what I remember best is his music."

Jason asked, "When did you discover that he was so musical?"

"I think he had his ear from the moment they poured water on him."

Deborah said reflectively, "It must have been a wonderful time."

"We had no fear. We knew our father would take care of our problems and that he and our mother would give us love. But when his music was misunderstood, he would get annoyed, saying, "Why don't they hear what I hear! I'm always hearing." I couldn't answer him, for I didn't realize then what I know, that he wrote each note with his heart."

She paused, and Jason stood up, saying, "You must be tired."

"No, don't go. I don't like being alone any more than Wolferl did."

Deborah said, "But your memories are always with you."

"And the people, nearly always, dead. Stay, just a little longer."

Jason had avoided the subject, but now he asked, "Do you think that your brother was poisoned?"

"You suggested that earlier."

"No, I didn't."

"It is what you meant. I think he would have lived longer if he had listened to our father. Our father never trusted Salieri."

"But neither did your brother."

"Herr Otis, our father was more skilful at intrigue."

"You think your brother was naïve."

"Not naïve. Not interested. Our father had a favorite saying, with which he cautioned us constantly: 'Accept as inevitable that all men tell lies or manipulate the truth, insofar as it suits their own purposes.' Wolferl knew this. He was aware of duplicity as much as anyone. You see it in his operas. But he disliked intrigue. Our father could have been a brilliant diplomat; he was deeply interested in intrigue. But Wolferl was different. After Marie Antoinette was thrown into prison and there was talk that the Hapsburgs would intervene, he wrote me: 'There is much talk of war here, I think, to terrify us. One day we see many soldiers marching through Vienna, the next day there is much gossip about our Austrian Princess effecting a compromise and returning to Vienna. Then, soon after, there is word that no compromise can be reached. Meanwhile, one hears that secret negotiations are taking place but that it will harm the safety of the state if we are informed. Is it any wonder that I prefer to absorb myself composing my magic opera for Schikaneder.' "

"You've justified your brother, perhaps, but what about your father?"

"In 1785 he visited my brother in Vienna. It was the last time they saw each other. And while Wolferl was prospering, our father was pessimistic about his future."

Nannerl paused a moment to gather fresh strength, then resumed. "But some of our father's dreams came true. My brother arranged a gala concert for our father, at which the best musicians in Vienna were present—Vanhal, Dittersdorf, and Haydn. I've always remembered this, it made such an impression on our father. They played quartets Wolferl had dedicated to Haydn, and afterwards a greatly moved Haydn told our father, *Your son is the finest composer I know,*' and what pleased him most of all: *'Herr Mozart, I truly wonder if there would have been a Wolfgang without a Leopold.'* "

"Yet you said your father returned unhappy over his son's future."

"Herr Otis, my father was troubled because while my brother was earning two thousand gulden a year, he wasn't saving a kreutzer, and his wife was a poor manager, never knowing where the money was going. He felt that Wolferl didn't realize what could happen to him if his fortune changed."

Deborah asked, "Do you think your father was right?"

"In 1785, when Wolferl was the toast of Vienna, his list of subscribers to his concerts covered eight pages and included the leading aristocrats and music lovers in Vienna. A few years later when he tried to revive these subscription concerts, he could get only one name, van Swieten."

"What happened?" Jason was puzzled.

"My brother had alarmed the musicians of Vienna with his genius and had aroused their envy. So they intrigued against him at Court. And he was unable to intrigue back. He was too busy. Composing. Performing. Yet to survive in Vienna, a musician had to be a master of intrigue. But that was not his nature. That was where he needed our father. Only once he became involved with the Webers, our father was secondary in his life."

Jason said, "Are you implying that your brother would have lived longer if he hadn't married Constanze?"

Nannerl nodded.

Deborah felt that she was exaggerating, and she said so.

"Perhaps," Nannerl answered. "But she did hurt him." Nannerl was positive of this. "With her extravagances, selfishness, she didn't even go to the funeral, or to his grave for many years, while I went to my father's grave until she appropriated it for her family."

Nannerl was so bitter that Jason changed the subject and said, "We do have his music. Do you still play?"

"Rarely. But more like Wolferl than anyone else. We played together better than anybody I have heard. I have his clear, lucid tone. Listen."

But she had to be helped to the harpsichord, although she insisted that she was strong enough to perform. At the last moment however, she asked Jason to join her. "You do play, too, don't you?"

He nodded and sat beside her gently.

Her eyes had grown misty, but she refused to put on her spectacles. "I don't have to see to know what to play. But the music is here for you to read, Herr Otis." When he placed it on the stand, she smiled and added, "Wolferl adored blues, violets, and pinks. Did you know that?"

"I had heard."

"I'm glad you wear colors he favored."

Jason began the sonata with a studied tenderness, seeking a fusion with Mozart's sister, and for a little while they were in harmony. But then she hit a wrong note, several, and her playing became uncertain, shoddy.

Suddenly she halted and wailed, "My right hand can still execute the passages, but my left hand can no longer press down the keys. My strength on that side is gone. All gone. My hands are so heavy. So tired."

Jason asked, "Would you like me to finish? By myself?"

"I can't. My hands are no better than bones. Yet Wolferl said they were so finely shaped, so delicate, like his own. If I rest, perhaps I will feel better. My hands were like my brother's. He had such lovely hands. I took such pride in them. I still see them sometimes."

Jason and Deborah had to help her to the sofa, where she lay down, so pale and tired they were frightened.

"You are very thoughtful," she whispered. "But I'm not sick, just old. Will you call my friend upstairs, Herr Fogel? He will know what to do. He lives on the first floor. I reside on the ground floor so I won't have any steps. He looks in on me often to see how I am managing."

"You live alone?" Deborah was shocked.

"Herr Fogel keeps an eye on me, and several other neighbors."

While Jason went to fetch him, Nannerl asked Deborah to sit by her side and held her hand as if she would never let it go.

When she regained some strength, she said to Deborah, "Treasure him. He seems like such a nice young man. I didn't marry until I was almost a spinster and very lonely, and then I was never very happy. My husband was much older than I was, a widower with five children, and he didn't approve of Wolferl. I never saw my brother again after I married Sonnenburg."

Herr Fogel was back, a heavy-set, middle-aged, soft-spoken shop-keeper who knew just what to do. "You must rest, Madame Sonnen-burg. Talking about the past, particularly about your brother and your father, always exhausts you. You have the pride and enthusiasm of a young girl then."

She smiled wanly and said, "And each year I grow older. I wanted to prove that I could still play. But don't think, Frau Otis, that we Mozarts were weak. We weren't. My father and mother lost five of the seven children they had, but everybody did. The two of us that survived were strong and healthy. We worked all the time. Like our father."

"We are here because of our respect for you and your brother."

"And our father. Don't forget our father. And what Haydn said."

"We won't," Deborah assured her. "We won't forget any of this."

Nannerl smiled, then remembered in a burst of energy, "If you are truly interested in why Wolferl died so young, don't ignore the Colloredos."

"The Archbishop?" Jason was surprised. "But I thought that once your brother left his employ, he was free of him."

"In the Hapsburg dominions no one was free of the Colloredos. They were one of the most powerful families in the Empire. I'm sure the Archbishop hated Wolferl, although he pretended to be above that. And his family could never forgive a musician standing up to a Colloredo. She sighed, "Wolferl wrote such lovely music. He put his heart into each note. To come to such an end is unbelievable. We live in a dark time."

Jason bowed and said, "Madame Sonnenburg, it has been a great privilege to meet you."

"No, Herr Otis. No one likes old age. And certainly not young people. And least of all the person themselves. Now I cling to life instead of marching through it."

"You will be better, I'm sure. After you rest."

"Will you visit me again?"

"We would like to, but we have to return to Vienna as soon as possible. Our visas have expired and the authorities could be un-pleasant."

"To such a nice young couple as you? I wouldn't worry about that."

"Thank you." Little by little they had edged toward the door so parting wouldn't be too difficult, and now they were almost there.

She was not fooled. She said, "It is better to go swiftly, when one has to leave. Whenever Wolferl left us, he did it quickly."

Deborah suggested, "If you would like us to write you?"

"And who would answer you? I am just a remnant."

Deborah looked confused, and Herr Fogel whispered, "She can't see."

"He means I am nearly blind. I couldn't even see the keys of the harpsichord." As they said goodbye, she sat up to deny her own weakness and said, "Mozarts go back many generations. You will preserve my brother's memory, please."

"We will try," Jason said gently, and Deborah added, "We will do our very best. It has meant much to sit here with you."

35

Lest They Forget

IT BEGAN to snow the next day. Jason awoke early that morning, eager to arrange their departure from Salzburg, and as he gazed out the window to judge the weather, he was depressed. He had enjoyed a satisfactory sexual joining with Deborah the previous night, in their unity she had expressed her approval of the wisdom of what he had done in Salzburg, but now that appeared as ephemeral as the weather. The snow was falling steadily and growing stronger. He realized that unless it stopped soon they would be unable to leave Salzburg today. And by the time Hans met them in the dining room for breakfast, the snow was spreading over Salzburg so heavily it veiled the town and the mountains in a ghostly grayish-white blanket.

Hans announced pessimistically, "Herr Raab says it is a blizzard."

Deborah asked, "Does he have any idea when it will end?"

"He thinks it could last several days. That is why I thought we should have left earlier. When it snows in the mountains, it can last a long time."

Jason said, "I will make the decision about when we leave."

"What about our visas, sir?"

"I told you before that I would take care of them."

Hans was not soothed and neither was Deborah. In a few days it would be January, and even if they left today, they wouldn't be back in Vienna until after their visas expired. But at least they would only be a few days late, which might appease Huber. As she started to say that, Jason hushed her and told Hans to go outside to see if the weather had improved.

"Then I was right about him," she said. "You don't trust him either."

"I don't trust anybody. We musn't worry about the visas. A month later shouldn't be worse than a week. We have a good excuse, the weather."

She didn't agree, but she didn't argue—Hans had returned.

Hans said, "Herr Raab tells me that he sees no relief in sight."

The storm lasted a long time and when it stopped much snow lay upon Salzburg. But when the sky cleared the following day, Jason asked Raab about the possibility of leaving for Vienna. The innkeeper climbed on the roof of his inn, scanned the horizon, and returned with the news "There isn't a road to be seen. Salzburg is buried under several feet of snow. It is a calamity. Outside the Golden Goose there are snowdrifts higher than our door. Everything is blocked. Nothing can move."

"Is this unusual?"

"It is early for such a severe storm. But when we have a blizzard, we are cut off from the outside world for days, sometimes weeks."

The next few days there was no movement in and out of Salzburg. They were in the mountains, which made it even harder to clear the roads, for outside the town the drifts were many feet high.

Delay, delay, delay, Jason thought bitterly. He was appalled by the situation. Yet nothing could be done. He contemplated visiting Friedjung, and Raab said that the doctor had left for Vienna just before the storm. "On business, I presume. He is quite rich and he has investments there."

Jason wondered if this visit had anything to do with him. Bosch, too, had left Salzburg before the blizzard, and Jason had a vision that they were the two spies who would betray him. Then he told himself this was foolishness; he must have no more regrets or doubts.

Deborah suggested they visit Nannerl again, but he disagreed. "No, we will get too involved, and that will make it even harder to leave."

He found out from Raab, who knew much about the private life of many of the natives, that Madame Sonnenburg was ill in bed, after having exerted herself too much recently, and that she was in no condition to see visitors.

After it was possible to walk about Salzburg, Jason climbed up the Nonnberg, but Constanze's house was still closed. Most of the houses had cleared away the drifts from their doors by now, but her house stood like a dark gray shadow, the snow piled high above its door in a vast drift, and it looked isolated from everything in Salzburg, even Mozart.

And when Deborah's entreaty "What will we do?" couldn't be answered with just a simple "Wait!" he replied, "I'm going to put it in a book."

She asked, "Is that wise? If what we suspect is found on your person, you could be thrown into prison."

"I have to put it down or I will forget it."

"At least, then, if you write down your suppositions, keep them hidden."

"For your sake," he said. But he was annoyed that she still assumed they were only suppositions; and he was taciturn, concentrating on his growing stack of papers, which, however, he hid carefully in the lining of his green velvet waistcoat.

Three weeks after they had seen Nannerl, they left Salzburg in their coach. Raab had warned them to wait until spring, saying that the road to Linz might be blocked—no coaches had reached Salzburg from Linz since the blizzard—but Jason, like Deborah, had decided that any further delay would be even riskier than the road. They couldn't wait any longer.

A few miles east of Salzburg they came upon a mountain pass that was still clogged with snow; but as Hans hesitated, Jason cried "Go on!" remembering that the road was downhill after this pass and should be clear.

Deborah thought Jason was being optimistic to mollify and impress her, but as they descended into a valley and the snow vanished and the road improved, she felt better. They were almost a month late, but at least, if conditions got no worse, they wouldn't be much later. The sky was clear, and after the blizzard that seemed extraordinary. They rode through many valleys, and when they reached Linz there was no snow at all.

But, as on their previous journey, the road from Linz to Vienna was the worst of all. While there was no rain or snow, the road was muddy and rutted or frozen solid and as hard as rock. Jason felt this highway was cursed, and he resolved to avoid it hereafter.

When Deborah saw Vienna ahead, she sighed with relief. It was the third of February, 1825, and she bathed in the thought that once they established the reason for their delay, there would be a large, warm cozy bed in their rooms on the Petersplatz to rest in. Her fingers would no longer be numb, her damp feet would stop feeling like blocks of ice, and she would lose the dread of being forever chilled and she would be able to sit without aches and a constant soreness in her behind.

Her exhilaration vanished at the city gate, where the customs official, the instant he examined their visas at the black-and-yellow toll entrance, summoned the chief police inspector, who ordered everybody to stand back, stuck his head into their coach and forced them to get out. Then he stated, "Your coach is confiscated. Your visas are not in order."

Jason explained, "I was delayed by the weather."

"Over a month? That's no excuse! Why were you delayed?"

Jason repeated his reason and Hesser, the chief police inspector, a fat, florid-faced bully with a loud voice and a pompous manner, cut him short. "I don't believe you. Your visas are marked 'politically unreliable.'"

Deborah felt she would die of self-pity, for everyone was staring at them with undisguised suspicion and they were being searched again.

Nothing was found that was seditious. "And a good thing," Hesser grumbled—Jason had hidden his writings—but Hesser wasn't finished.

He called eight soldiers over, and they surrounded the coach. Deborah thought this was the most humiliating experience she had ever known. Her protests were ignored, while Jason stood in a silent impotent rage.

Hesser wasn't interested in any further explanations; it was enough that their visas were questionable and that they had violated them.

They were taken to a jail with four soldiers marching on each side of the coach. Hans sat in terror, barely able to drive, although they were only moving at a walk, and as they entered the Graben and then turned into a small street, Jason had a feeling that this jail was part of Huber's headquarters. No one, however, paid any attention to his questions.

And when Jason cried out, "I want my rights! I am an American citizen!" he was regarded with contempt by Hesser, who was sitting on the outside of the coach in triumph. As Jason repeated that, Hesser snarled, "One more word from you and I'll put you in chains."

At the jail Hans was taken elsewhere, while Jason and Deborah were thrust into a cell in the cellar of the building. The cell was just high enough for them to stand in, a few feet square, and without any windows, lit only by a flickering candle, which stood on a small table by a bench.

Deborah couldn't believe this was happening to them, but as the light of the candle faded until they were almost in total darkness, she had to struggle to keep from screaming. Jason had hidden some money on his person—all that he had carried openly had been confiscated by Hesser—and he grabbed the bars, shaking them and shouting, "Can't I get a hearing!"

A burly warder knocked his fingers off the bars of the cell.

Jason cried, "But this is a mistake!"

"Is that why you are here?"

Panic clawed at his throat. The candle was almost out, and to be in total darkness was inconceivable. He could hear Deborah sobbing, but he tried to be calm, "If I could speak to Herr Huber?"

"Who?" The guard had turned and was attentive now.

"Herr Huber. The internal security officer."

"What reason do I have to tell him that you are here?"

"Two gulden."

"You still have money on you?"

"Yes."

"I could take it from you myself."

"And I could yell so loud another guard will come."

"He won't stop me."

"He will want half."

The guard debated that a moment, then said, "I want more."

"Four gulden?"

"That's not enough."

"Huber says that is too much. And I haven't any more on me."

The guard wavered a moment, then said, "Be quick. Before anyone else comes."

Jason retreated to the rear of the cell where he couldn't be seen, found four gulden he had hidden, whispered to Deborah, "Don't worry, we'll be out soon," although he wasn't at all certain, and then gave the guard the money.

The guard sneered, "How do you know I'll tell him that you are here?"

"I will tell the other guard that you stretched out your hand without thinking of him."

"And I will say you lied."

"Somebody will come to see us eventually. You can see from our clothes and coach that we are important people."

"I can see that you are suspected of something."

"My name is Otis. Jason Otis. If you get our name to Huber, there will be four more gulden. I will leave it on the bench for you." Then he felt something run by him and he cried out, "What is that?"

"A rat, probably. They get hungry, too."

Thousands of moments seemed to pass as they sat there, in total darkness now, each of them wondering if there would be any salvation. Jason had walked up and down after the guard had left, but his legs had become very tired and he felt dizzy. Now they held each other's hand, and the acknowledgment that they needed each other helped a little.

Then she blurted out, "Imagine what they will say when we tell them about this when we get back to Boston!"

If they ever got back, he thought, but he said, "Yes."

"Do you think it is night yet?"

"I don't know."

"I wish I could tell."

"We must do something. Until the guard returns."

"You're sure he will, Jason?"

"Yes. Huber did say we could apply for a renewal of our visas."

Deborah didn't answer. She wanted to lie down, to shut out everything, but there was no place to do so. The bench was too short, and she didn't want to deprive Jason of his place, and the floor was heavily cobbled, wet, and cold, and she felt unclean as it was. Neither of them spoke now, lost in their own thoughts. Then she heard Jason breathing, which was a relief. She never thought that would sound so important. He had drawn away from her. She put her hand on his shoulder for comfort, and he took it off and said guiltily, "Look what I have led you into."

"Yet you won't stop—not for me, not for anyone, not even for Mozart."

"I would if I thought I was wrong."

They were silent again. Just as Deborah felt she couldn't endure the darkness any longer and Jason seemed unable to speak, as if stricken by their predicament, and perhaps they had been forgotten, she thought, there were footsteps in the corridor. The guard led two men to their cell, each of them carrying a candle. But before the guard handed them over to the men, he made sure there were four gulden waiting for him on the bench.

Then he said, "They will take you to Huber. He wants to talk to you."

Jason said, "Thank you."

The guard laughed. "He would have seen you anyhow. Eventually."

As they were led into Huber's office, Jason had the feeling that all of this had been prearranged: the arrest at the city gate, the cell, the nightmarish darkness, even the willingness of the guard to be bribed. Was this a warning, he wondered, or a threat, or a deliberate effort to frighten them?

Huber sat at his desk in the same posture he had assumed several months ago, but his sternness was mixed with self-satisfaction as he said, "I warned you that if your visas were not in order you would be thrown in jail. You should take my warnings more seriously."

"We were delayed by the weather," Jason hurried to say.

Huber had added more elegance to his office, as if to emphasize how he had grown in importance. His nude Venus had a companion, a marble Apollo. There was a new scarlet brocaded drape over his window, and his lamps were very bright, mocking the situation they had been in. Jason felt he had been surrounded by invisible eyes when Huber said, "Is the weather the reason you visited Mozart's widow and sister?"

Jason sensed that Huber expected him to lie, and he replied, "I beg your pardon, sir. What was wrong with that? Many people visit them."

"Many people consult doctors, too. But not about poisons."

Jason flushed, and Deborah said quickly, "My husband was ill."

"I am well aware of when people are sick and their kidneys are bad."

Jason felt that Huber was taking pleasure in this colloquy, spitefully.

"You are fortunate, Otis. If we had found seditious material on you, you would have stayed in jail."

Jason's hand went to his waistcoat where he had hidden his papers.

"Do you have a pain? Are you ill again?"

"It's my heart. From the excitement. The shock. Can we go now?"

"Just a moment."

"It has been a long day and we are very tired."

Huber said coldly, "You are not in a position to make conditions."

Deborah volunteered, fighting against a growing headache, "But we understood that we could stay until Beethoven finished the oratorio."

"Nothing is understood, except the date on your visas."

"You suggested they could be renewed if we were delayed by the weather."

"I suggested nothing."

"Sir," said Jason, "there was a blizzard in Salzburg, the worst in . . ."

"You are five weeks late. That is reason enough to imprison you."

"As my wife said, we wanted to give Beethoven time to finish his work."

Huber smiled cynically, indicating that he didn't believe him.

Jason said indignantly, "But to be thrown into a jail without a hearing!"

Deborah added, "And for simply being late."

Huber said, "There are many offences in the Empire where one can be punished with jail. Stealing, attacking a nobleman, criticising the Emperor are among the most conspicuous, but there are over two hundred offences if all are enforced. We will have no revolution here."

Deborah cried, "We're not revolutionaries, sir, we're . . ."

"Of course not. You are two young Americans from Boston. But criticism of the Royal family is not tolerated or taken lightly here."

"Criticism of the Royal family?" said Jason. "I don't understand."

"Each time you criticize Antonio Salieri, you criticize the Royal family. He has been a Hapsburg favorite for over fifty years."

Jason was silent.

"Did you think I didn't know what you were up to?"

Jason said, "Mozart was admired by the Emperor Joseph."

"That is a matter of opinion. And Joseph has been dead many years, and the present Emperor has different views. Lest you forget."

"Is that why you had us arrested?"

"Your dossier is getting full. Two visits to Frau von Nissen, one visit to Madame Sonnenburg, two visits to Doctor Friedjung."

"But, sir, our visits to Frau von Nissen and Madame Sonnenburg were merely to pay our respects, and I did see the doctor because I was sick."

Huber smiled sceptically and returned their belongings that had been confiscated at the gate: Deborah's handbag, Jason's watch and money. Jason looked surprised when he was given only two hundred gulden, for two hundred and forty had been seized. When Huber saw his expression, he said, "We are not thieves. New visas, even temporary ones, cost twenty gulden each. There is much work involved." He tore up their old ones, wrote out new ones and asked, "How long do you intend to stay now?"

Jason hesitated, not sure.

"April first ought to do. That should give Beethoven time to finish his oratorio. We will not renew them again."

"June first, please, sir, if you don't mind."

"Why?"

"Then we can travel in good weather. After what we have just gone through, I could never take the road west in bad weather again."

Huber wrote June first, then said, "You take risks, Otis."

"Waiting for Beethoven to compose an oratorio?" Jason asked innocently.

"Let us not be childish. If you were impoverished, you would still be waiting below. How much did you give the guard?"

"Four gulden."

Huber shook his head reprovingly. "I told you two was enough. You will spoil them. Americans don't know how to keep people in their place." Yet he felt satisfied again. He had had doubts about releasing them and giving them new visas, but now he was sure he had pursued the right course. Better to allow the weed to sprout a little, he reflected, so he could be certain it was a weed, then he could cut if off when it grew too high.

Jason's elation at being free lasted only until they reached their coach and a white-faced, waiting Hans. For then, in the daylight, he could see that Huber had written across their new visas, as before: *"Politically unreliable."*

36

And Then

 F RAU HERZOG had rented their rooms on the Petersplatz. Jason asked indignantly, "How could you have been so inconsiderate?" and she retorted more indignantly, "You said you would be back in a few weeks and you've been gone three months. I couldn't keep such choice rooms empty. And I have such a nice couple in them, I just couldn't ask them to leave."

"Where are our books and clothes?"

"In the attic. As you left them. Except they were inspected once."

Deborah, who ached painfully from the indignities and the discomforts of the past few hours and who had been concerned only with rest and quiet, came out of her self-pity and shouted, "Who inspected them?"

"He said he was a police inspector. But he was polite. He left everything as he found it. Do you have anything on your consciences?"

"Is that the real reason you rented our rooms?"

"I was losing money while they were empty, and you wouldn't have wanted them anyhow if you had known who lived in them before you."

"An old musician, wasn't it? Who died?"

"Violently. It is still not known whether it was murder or suicide."

"Did Ernst Muller know?"

"Certainly. He was his friend."

Jason interrupted, "Have you seen him lately?"

"He came once, a few weeks ago, to find out if you were back. But when I told him that the police had been here, he got very pale, and I haven't seen him since. I hope you are not in trouble with the police. I run a respectable house. You will be better off elsewhere."

Jason had taken such pride in these rooms he was unable to reply.

They moved back into their first quarters in Vienna, the White Ox Inn on the Platz Am Hof, and rented comfortable rooms on the top floor. Jason told Deborah, "It doesn't matter if we are spied on. We will be, wherever we live; and here at least we will be conscious of it. And maybe Huber will relax his watch, since this inn was his original recommendation."

She thought he was deceiving himself, but she was so grateful that he had found a place where she could rest she didn't object.

The clothes and books they retrieved from Frau Herzog's attic seemed as they had left them, but the awareness that they had been examined by alien hands made them unclean. Deborah couldn't wear the dresses, while Jason was unable to read the books without a feeling of uneasiness.

Jason knew he should dismiss Hans, for by now he believed that Hans had reported on their movements, but he had a passionate desire to trap him, to find out if he really was a spy. He wondered if this was the way Huber felt toward them. Was Huber getting a sadistic pleasure out of it? Or loved the process of the game even more than the end itself? He said to Deborah, "If Hans is an informer, we can use that to our own advantage."

She doubted he was right, but she was too tired to argue.

Jason left his new address at Police Headquarters, but he avoided Huber. He felt the cell had been a torture devised by the internal security officer, and he hated him for that. It was safer to stay away from Huber, he decided. It had been difficult as it was to control himself, and he sensed that Huber would enjoy driving him into exposing himself.

When they were settled, they visited Grob. The banker greeted them cordially, said that they looked well and he hoped that they had enjoyed Salzburg, although he was surprised that they had been away so long.

Jason said, "It was because of the bad weather."

"Yes," said Grob. "Winter can be very hard in the mountains."

"But Huber was unpleasant about our visas."

"Why?"

"They had expired."

"He must have had another reason. The visas are just an excuse."

"Could you have helped us if he hadn't released us?"

"That depends. I have some influence. What was his real reason?"

Jason hesitated—he didn't trust Grob either and yet it might be better to know where Grob stood. He said, "He implied it had to do with Salieri, that any criticism of him was criticism of the Royal family."

Grob exclaimed, "I warned you about that months ago!"

"You think I'm wrong, sir?"

"Indiscreet, at the best. You will solve nothing. No matter what you find out about Salieri, I must remind you, he is an object of reverence to the Royal family. They don't like such objects to be disturbed. Whatever contributions you wish to make to history, make them elsewhere."

"Have you heard from Beethoven recently?"

"Not directly. But I saw Schindler the other day."

"The oratorio is progressing, I hope. I will have to leave soon."

"I warned you there, too, that he would probably procrastinate."

"Beethoven is not pregnant?"

"It is not amusing. He has moved again, which always disturbs him, and he complains that he has so little time to compose."

"Six months isn't enough time?"

"I think he needs a new body. His real trouble is, he's ailing."

"Does Schindler think there will be an oratorio?"

"Schindler says, *'We can only pray.'* "

Deborah suggested, "Perhaps if we visited Beethoven again."

"He is not seeing anyone these days, even lovely young ladies like yourself. But there is some hope. Schindler says that Beethoven still wants to compose it. He fancies himself a Jeremiah these days."

Jason asked, "Could I speak to Schindler myself?"

"If you wish. Should I send him to your rooms on the Petersplatz?"

"We've moved. Back to the White Ox Inn on the Platz Am Hof."

"A good central location. I will inform Schindler."

Deborah asked, "Herr Grob, have you heard from my father recently?"

"No. Did you expect to hear from him?"

"He usually writes me every month or so."

Jason turned on her accusingly, "Did you write him without telling me?"

"Shouldn't I write my own father?"

Grob intervened, not wanting to lose good customers and family quarrels could be uncomfortable. "Herr Otis, do you need any money? There is five hundred gulden in the account. Salzburg must have been costly."

Jason didn't want to admit it, but he was in desperate need of money. The rent at the White Ox Inn had increased and was expensive, and even five hundred gulden might not be enough to return to America.

"How much do you wish? Don't look sad; that's what it is for!"

"A hundred gulden." Jason couldn't admit that he needed more.

"I'll give you two hundred. I'm sure there'll be more coming soon."

This time Deborah was surprised, asking, "What makes you think so?"

"You will need more to get back to Boston. Your father knows this."

Jason took the two hundred without another word, not bothering to count it, wishing to indicate it really wasn't important, when actually it was vital.

They were visited by Schindler the next day. They received him in their rooms. Beethoven's factotum said he had just a minute, but Grob had told him that they were anxious about the oratorio and he hoped they would not cancel the commission, but be patient. "I assure you, Beethoven wants to compose the oratorio, but the police have put a closer watch on him. We always knew they watched him, but now it is closer than ever."

Jason asked, "Do you think it has anything to do with us?"

"In what way?"

"Perhaps what we asked about Salieri got back to the police."

"It is possible. What Beethoven thinks, he says."

Deborah suggested, "We would love to see him again."

"Beethoven isn't seeing anyone at the moment. It has to do with his deafness. He has become increasingly self-conscious about it."

Jason asked directly, "What should we do about the oratorio?"

Schindler said portentously, "Wait."

"Is that why you came here?"

"To advise patience. The Master cannot be hurried, but once he accepts the increased police surveillance as a necessary evil, it could aid his composing, give his oratorio the proper note of righteous rage."

"How much time should I give him?"

"How much longer are you staying?"

"Two or three months, at the most."

"I will try to hurry him. But you must realize that between his anxieties and his inclination to procrastinate, this is a very hard time for him. Yet he hasn't forgotten you, and he sends his sincerest regards and begs you to be patient with an aging musician. That once his ailing belly, which has been ruined by bad medicine and careless doctors, is restored to reasonable health, he will return to the oratorio."

Jason ordered a bottle of the best wine for Beethoven. When it came, he handed it to Schindler as an expression of their admiration for the composer. The factotum said, "It is much too costly. You are generous indeed; I can't take it. But if you insist, Beethoven will be deeply pleased; it will help his digestion and spirits more than anything I can think of, and I will keep you informed about the progress of the oratorio."

Schindler departed, holding the bottle of Nessmuller passionately.

Several days later Jason visited Ernst. He went to great effort to avoid being followed, and Deborah was dizzy from turning up many devious alleys; and now, as they stood before his house, Ernst's landlady told them, "Muller isn't in Vienna. He has been gone some weeks. He didn't leave word when he would return. I think he is in Prague. I don't know why."

After they left their name and address and were back in their rooms, Deborah asked Jason, "Do you think Muller went to avoid the police?"

"I hope not. In a sense, he got us into this." Then he felt guilty that he had made such an admission, and he was silent.

"I feel that Huber is a spider weaving a web about us. Your illness in Salzburg, the trouble with the coach, his knowing where you have been, Frau Herzog's getting us out of her rooms. I'm sure the police were responsible, and now they are threatening us through Beethoven. Huber is preparing to feast on us." Deborah shivered, suddenly chilled.

How could he answer? The carpet in their reception room had a deep softness, and he stood in it with an abrupt feeling of weariness. He thought unhappily, Perhaps I should give up the whole affair. Too much is against me. It is too difficult. Yet he also knew that searching for Mozart—for it had become that as much as anything else—made him whole. Even if it were an addiction, without it he was lost. Only to be alone felt worse, and he never felt alone when he was with Mozart. But now, standing in the middle of Vienna, he felt frightfully alone, small and preposterous in the vast, shadowed immensity of the past, roving in a graveyard for a body he would never find, alone among the corpses, the worms and the maggots. What terrified him most was the feeling that he couldn't trust anyone, not Ernst, not even Deborah—he was sure now she had written her father without telling him, and that was a deception, too.

"You haven't answered, Jason? You're not going to tell me that all these things I spoke about just happened accidentally?"

"Perhaps they are not accidental. But you make too much of them."

Jason sat down at the writing desk in an effort to arrange a plan of action, but while he slashed at the paper with his pen, he came to no conclusions, only questions. How could he find Diener or Anna Gottlieb? If they were still alive? Who could he ask? Vienna was a city of over two hundred thousand people, and he couldn't even find the grave of Mozart. Then there were their shrinking funds. Even with the gulden that Grob still held, they would be unable to get back to Boston.

He fell into a depression that became an emotional paralysis.

Deborah got sick, but she refused to call a doctor, saying they hadn't helped him or Mozart, that it was just a chill she had caught from the travelling and that she would get better with rest. All she wanted to do was to lie in bed, while Jason brooded, unable to write, to plan, to do anything. Their money continued to dwindle. Days dragged by until it was the beginning of March. They had only three months left in Vienna, and there had not been a word from anyone, not from Beethoven or Muller or Grob or even her father.

Hans stopped in every day to offer his services, although he was no longer eating with them; and one day Jason couldn't resist asking, "Why do you hang on, Hans? I may not have any money soon. Why don't you quit?"

"Sir, I wouldn't think of doing that! You will be taking trips again, visiting people, and you will need me when you leave Vienna."

"Suppose I fire you?"

Hans was so disturbed it was pathetic. Suddenly Jason felt sorry for him. Yet he knew he musn't indulge in sentimentality: Hans was his enemy; he must be, why else was he hanging on? "You can't, sir."

"What do you mean, I can't?"

"I'm sorry, sir . . ." Hans was stuttering now. "I didn't mean it that way. But I feel like part of the family, and it would be a great blow."

"What about your own family?" Deborah asked. She had been lying on a chaise-longue by the window, looking out on the Platz Am Hof, but she didn't want Hans to fool Jason.

"I see them occasionally. But they are distant relatives, actually."

"And you feel closer to us?"

"In a way, Frau Otis. We have gone through much together."

Jason said, "You can go now." Hans left quickly, and when Deborah reproached him for being too indulgent, he retorted, "Can I trust you?"

"What do you mean?"

"I know you wrote your father."

He was so positive she made no attempt to deny that, but shrugged.

"Why didn't you tell me?"

"I was asking for money. I thought you might be offended, hurt."

He knew he should be furious, but he was relieved. More money was essential. Yet he grumbled, "You still should have told me."

"I would have, but I was afraid that you would stop me."

"You're right. I would have, if I hadn't been robbed."

"I still think the police were responsible, whatever Huber pretended."

"Possibly. How long do you think it will take your father to reply?"

"Soon. I wrote him months ago. By special post."

When Pickering's letter came a few days later there was one surprise. He wrote Deborah that he was sending her a thousand gulden, to be deposited in her name with Grob, but he added the following postscript:

> This is the last money I will send you in Vienna. Whatever your mother's will states. Your expedition has become frightfully extravagant, and I cannot allow you to deplete your funds any further. I know this will anger you, but on reflection you will realize that I am right.

After Deborah read it, she handed it to Jason without comment.

He knew he should still be angry at her, but he was so relieved by the arrival of the money it was difficult to be. Then whatever anger was left in him was dissipated by her father's words.

When she saw that Jason was sympathetic, she said, "He is using the money as a weapon to force me to return. He knows he can't keep my money from me, but that I can't fight him from here. Unless you have to stay?"

"You would stay if I insisted?" he asked. "Even without money?"

"If you wanted to. And if we could."

"Why should I want to stay?"

"To study music. To compose."

"Deborah, did you believe I thought I could be another Mozart?"

"One never knows what someone else thinks."

"If I ever had such illusions, they're gone. I'm a competent second-rate composer of hymns, a good craftsman who knows how to borrow. As da Ponte said, and Ernst, although I hated them when they said it."

"What about Vienna? You seemed to fall in love with it when we arrived."

"I was falling in love with Mozart. He was Vienna. Then. I can't endure the city any more. It gives me the shudders."

"Maybe we ought to go now. It is March. Traveling shouldn't be too bad."

"When I am so near to finding out about Mozart and Salieri?"

"The more you find out, the more dangerous it is. And you can't say anything here, whatever you discover."

"I can when I get back to Boston. If I could only find Diener. Let's walk on the Karntnerstrasse and look for his café, the Silver Snake."

" 'The Silver Serpent.' I think that is what Sophie said."

That afternoon they walked the length of the Karntnerstrasse, but they found no tavern called the Silver Serpent or the Silver Snake. She suggested that they ask passersby about the tavern, but he said they might be spies or informers, although she felt his real reason was his need to find Diener himself. And as they entered the White Ox Inn someone brushed against him. For an instant Jason recoiled, expecting to be attacked. Instead, the person—he couldn't tell who it was, the person passed him so swiftly—pushed a note into his hand and was gone. Jason held the note in his fist so no one could see it, and only when they were in their rooms and he was sure he could not be spied on did he look at it. Then he read:

Drop everything and meet me at the White Lamb Inn on the Schulerstrasse near its end, the part away from St. Stephen's. Make certain that you are not followed. I will expect you tomorrow afternoon at three.

Deborah wasn't sure they should go. It could be a police trap, she thought, since it was unsigned; but Jason was convinced that the note must be from Ernst—no one else would have assumed such a peremptory tone.

The next afternoon Jason sent Hans to Grob with a message that they would visit him tomorrow to arrange for the payment of the thousand gulden that had come from America. Then they slipped out of the back of the White Ox Inn, through an unused door he had found, and instead of walking down the Graben, which was the shortest way, they went by a roundabout route.

Deborah was annoyed, for now it was such a long walk. But Jason had allowed for that, which caused her to marvel, for at three that afternoon they entered a dark little tavern called the White Lamb. They saw no one they knew, but Jason sat down in a secluded corner and waited. And suddenly someone was next to him, saying, "Why were you in Salzburg so long?"

It was Ernst, as Jason had expected.

But he had changed. He was either sick, confused, or a very scared man, thought Deborah, he looked so awful. His hands trembled, his once-chubby face had become gaunt, he sat with a stoop, and he had lost his spryness. Yet his question had some of his old tartness; and when Jason didn't reply, he added," You were away much longer than I expected."

Jason said, "You don't look well. What's wrong?"

"It isn't me. It's Otto." Ernst couldn't go on, and broke down.

"When did it happen?" Jason asked more gently. But, as before, Otto Muller seemed so remote, so far away.

"A few months ago. They said it was old age, but he wasn't that old, only seventy-five. Ever since you came to Vienna his health has been bad."

"But he is responsible for my being here."

"I was, actually. The idea started with me."

"And now he will never know."

"Know what?" Ernst's tone sharpened. "Have you learned something I don't know?" His voice dropped to a whisper. "Is Salieri really guilty?"

"Why did you go to Prague?"

"I thought I might learn something. Mozart was in Prague in September, 1791, for *La Clemenza di Tito*, just a few months before he died."

"Did you learn anything?"

"Some people said he was sick. Others said he was fine. It was confusing. But everyone agreed that the Emperor didn't like the opera."

Deborah asked, "Is that the only reason you went, Herr Muller?"

"Why?" Ernst looked defensive, suspicious.

"You could have been avoiding the police."

"Why should I avoid the police?"

"Why should you see us so secretively?"

"We have to be careful these days, Frau Otis, as I warned you."

Jason asked, "Why did you tell me that you arranged for the Weber women to see me, when actually they were living with Constanze?"

"If I had told you that, you might not have gone. You might have thought that they wouldn't see you."

"Constanze didn't really want to, I suspect."

"But she did," Ernst said eagerly. "What did you learn?"

"I'm not sure Constanze trusted me, and I know she didn't trust you."

"And now you don't either, Otis?"

"I don't know."

"That's unfortunate. But what other choice have you?"

"I can stop searching and return to America now."

"After having come this far! What did Constanze tell you?"

Deborah cut in, "She said that she didn't like you."

"Many people don't like me, Frau Otis. Isn't that so?"

Jason said, "Sophie told us more than Constanze."

Deborah added, "Aloysia gave her version, too. Which was different."

"Who did you believe?"

"All of them, in part," said Jason. "But Sophie most of all."

"Did they convince you that I was wrong? That Mozart wasn't poisoned?"

"They convinced me that you could be right."

"What more do you need to know?"

"I must see Salieri."

"That will be arranged. His keeper is better, and I will be seeing him at a lodge meeting soon. I will talk to him about that then."

"You are a Freemason?" Jason was surprised.

Ernst said proudly, "The Three Eagles Lodge. Mozart was a brother, too."

Jason said, "But I thought they were forbidden."

"They have always been forbidden. But less so some years then others."

"What about this year?"

"We are careful. As long as we are not political, we should survive."

Jason said, "I've been warned that my inquiry is very political."

"Naturally!" Ernst smiled. "That is why you were enlisted. Whatever you find out, I cannot expose in Vienna, but once you are safely in Boston, you can say whatever you want. What evidence is still missing?"

"I'm still not satisfied about the burial and how it occurred."

"You must have learned who was at the funeral from the Webers!"

"Sophie told me who started out for the cemetery: Süssmayer, Salieri, van Swieten, Diener, Albrechtsberger, Gottlieb, and herself."

Ernst stated, "Albrechtsberger, van Swieten, and Süssmayer are dead."

"What about Anna Gottlieb? Do you know who she is?"

"Of course. She is one of the finest actresses in the Empire. Why didn't I think of her? It was said that she was in love with Mozart."

Deborah asked, "Do you know Anna Gottlieb?"

"Not personally. But I know people who do. I will find out if she is in Vienna. Her acting takes her to many cities; she is in great demand."

Jason said, "I still think Diener could be the most important of all. He was the first one to see Mozart after the dinner at Salieri's, the one who realized he was sick, who sent for the doctor, who should remember, if anyone does, what Salieri fed Mozart. Food was his business."

"Don't the Webers know whether Diener is alive?"

"No, but Sophie did say that he had a tavern on the Karntnerstrasse. I looked all over for it, but I haven't been able to find it. Yet she said it was well known, The Silver Serpent."

"No, no, no, it was The *Golden* Serpent! I remember now!" Ernst almost pounded the table in his excitement. "It was on the Karntnerstrasse, but downstairs, in the cellar. Mozart did go there, and I think it is still there—I don't go to taverns these days. It was very close to where Mozart lived; it was one of the reasons he went there often."

"The Golden Serpent," repeated Jason. "Near the Rauhenstein-gasse."

"Yes. Diener could be important. And Anna Gottlieb. I must go now. I will see you here in a week."

Deborah said, "You haven't mentioned the oratorio or the police?"

"Why should I? You know that they are there. The same time, Otis?"

Jason nodded.

"Sit here after I go, so if anyone is watching outside, they won't connect us. Remember, confide in no one, whatever they tell you."

Ernst was gone then, almost his old self again, spry and animated, and Jason was a different person, too, excited and eager to resume his quest.

37

Joseph Diener

THE NEXT day Jason visited Grob on the assumption the thousand gulden was his to use as he pleased. Grob replied, "I want to be helpful, but I'm not sure this is proper. Herr Pickering made a special point that this draft was to be paid to his daughter. . . ."

Deborah interrupted, reminding him, "I specified that all my funds were to be deposited in both our names. If you cannot comply, I will find another banker."

Grob was distressed then, and said he didn't want to offend anybody, that he prized their friendship and naturally he would do his best to please her. But Deborah wasn't satisfied until the thousand gulden was signed over to Jason, displaying a firmness that surprised even Jason.

Then she said to Jason, "Take whatever you want."

"I need the balance of the first draft. Three hundred gulden."

"In cash?" asked Grob. "Are you sure that is wise?"

"You never know what emergencies will arise. I don't intend to be robbed again. I will take the thousand gulden when we leave Vienna."

"Is it definite that you are departing on June first?"

"Huber said we can't stay any longer. He wrote that on our visas."

"I'm sure he is more agreeable now. I've told him about the thousand gulden and he seemed impressed. It has an important bearing on your situation. Police officials are impressed by wealth, too. If you stress the oratorio and leave the political matters to the police, you will have no further trouble. And Schindler was in, to make sure the money is still on deposit, and he told me that Beethoven has resumed work on the oratorio. Beethoven, like the rest of us, has no wish to be penniless."

That afternoon, refreshed by this victory and even more conscious that Diener could be vital to his inquiry, Jason was all the more eager to find him. He realized now he had a greater impulse for this pursuit than he had for his own mediocre composition. He was proud he had developed a way of avoiding the hotel servants, and Hans, and anyone else who might be spying on them, by slipping out the back alley.

Deborah followed him despite some doubts that this route was as safe as Jason claimed, and it was she who found the Golden Serpent. It was where Ernst had remembered it, near the Rauhensteingasse. But that wasn't easy. The sign was in an ancient German script that only she could read, and heavy dust, which had to be brushed away, blurred the letters, and then a small arrow, also blurred by time and dirt, pointed downward.

They descended a badly lit stairway and came, to their surprise, upon a well-lit, spacious tavern, which, however, was quite old. There were a few people sitting at the tables, none of whom they recognized, and Jason strolled over to a waiter and asked, "Is this Diener's tavern?"

"Who?"

Deborah used an expression she had heard Raab use, "Is Joseph Diener, the *Hausmeister,* in?"

"No. You're not Germans, are you? Your accent isn't."

"It is not his tavern?" Jason asked frantically. Was Diener dead after all? He wasn't sure he could go on after such a disappointment.

"Diener, the *Hausmeister!*" Deborah repeated loudly.

"Oh, him? He comes only at night. Who should I tell him called?"

Jason said relieved, "We don't know him."

"Except by reputation," said Deborah. "What time do you expect him?"

"About seven or eight. It depends on who he thinks is coming in. Many musicians still eat here, although not like the days of Mozart and Salieri."

Jason asked eagerly, "Did Salieri eat here, too?"

"He never ate much—he was a suspicious sort—but he liked our coffee."

"Thank you. What does Diener look like?"

"Like everybody else. He says he is a man of the people."

But when they met him that night they were startled by his appearance. In a world of short men he was even shorter than anyone they had met. Joseph Diener was less than five feet tall, the size of a boy, and he had a curvature of the spine that accentuated his smallness. He was like a fragile bird, thought Jason, except for his head, which was large, with a wide face, a fine, strong nose, a handsome high forehead, a striking face that nature had treated as generously as it had slighted his body.

Diener, however, regarded them suspiciously as they approached him, for he could tell that they were not customers by their dress and manner. He didn't look up from the counter where he had been counting the day's receipts, as if it was easier to avoid them. And he didn't relax when Jason said, hoping that would ease matters, "We're friends of Mozart."

Diener muttered, "Mozart is dead."

"That's why we're here, Herr Diener. You are Joseph Diener, aren't you?"

"Is this an official visit?"

"I don't understand." Jason was puzzled.

"The authorities express themselves in many ways."

"We're Americans," said Deborah, "Who are interested in Mozart."

"He is dead. Don't you know that? Thirty-three years last December." Suddenly, seeing someone complaining, he shuffled over to the customer to quiet him. After he succeeded, he didn't turn back to them but turned to the door as if to go.

Panic-stricken, Jason wondered, What can I say that will cause him to recognize the genuineness of my interest. But Deborah was ahead of him. Stepping in front of Diener at the door and smiling with all of her sweetness, she said, "We were told Mozart liked you. Very much."

While his coldness didn't change, he asked, "Who said that?"

"His widow."

"How would she know? She only cared that I did her errands."

Jason said, "His sister-in-law said so, too."

"Which one?"

Jason had a feeling that if he said the wrong one Diener would never talk to him again. He took a deep breath and said, " Sophie."

A slight smile appeared on Diener's face.

"Sophie told us how you paid for the doctor when she had no money."

"She remembered?"

"Yes." Jason sighed, relieved that he *had* remembered.

"That happened over thirty-three years ago. And she told you."

"Sophie never forgot it. She kept talking about how you responded when Mozart fell ill, how you called the doctor."

"Somebody had to. He was all alone."

"She said how much he depended on you. How much he liked you."

Suddenly, abruptly, Diener bit his lips to keep back the tears, but they came anyway, and he couldn't talk from emotion, turning from them, wiping the tears from his eyes and saying, as much to himself as to them, "He was such a kind person. So good-natured. He never mocked anybody. Even if I made a mistake in his order. Those last few weeks he ate here often, until something destroyed his appetite. Would you like a drink?"

"Whatever you suggest," said Deborah. "If you will join us."

Diener led them to a table in the corner and said, pointing proudly but sadly, "Mozart used to sit there. In that very chair."

Neither Jason nor Deborah could sit in Mozart's chair, placing themselves on each side of it while Diener faced it. He ordered wine, saying it was his treat, but none of them took more than a sip as he said, "You couldn't have known Mozart. You're much too young."

Jason said, "We know him through his music."

"But that's not a personal thing!"

"Isn't it, Herr Diener?"

Diener didn't seem to hear him. He sat with his hands folded in a kind of prayer, staring at the empty chair as if Mozart was there, and suddenly he said, "It was such an awful winter. So cold, dreary."

"The winter of 1791?" Jason asked.

Diener nodded, but his reverie didn't cease. "Many composers came here, some like peacocks, others morose like Salieri, but no one as pleasant as Mozart. We were his habitual haunt that year, especially when his wife was away. Salieri came in occasionally, but as much to keep an eye on Mozart, I felt, as for any other reason, for he rarely ate anything. Yet he was always asking me what the Kapellmeister was eating, which meant Mozart, while he sipped a little wine. We had several guest rooms, but Mozart, even when he was composing, preferred to sit here. Unlike any other composer I ever saw, he seemed to compose even better when people were around him. And we had a special feature, the permitted and authorized German, Italian, French, and English newspapers, and he liked to read them. He could read in each language, which made me marvel, for notes were like words to him also. And when the police came in, especially when Salieri was here, they were very polite. But as Mozart's appearance grew untidy and he didn't always wear his wig, the police began to eye him suspiciously. Yet he wasn't any different." He paused.

Deborah said tenderly, "You must have known Mozart very well."

"I knew him." Diener was suspicious once more.

"But in a way that no one else did. Like Sophie said."

"Why were you seeing her? And me, now? No one has wanted to see me for years. When he fell mortally ill, yes, and when he died. But after that, his wife never thanked me, his friends ignored me."

"They ignored him," Jason reminded Diener. "They let his body vanish."

"Did they?"

"Do you think it could have been deliberate?"

"I went to the city gate. Then it looked like rain. Salieri said, 'It is foolish to go on, Mozart is with God,' so we went home."

"Was that the right thing to do?" Jason asked.

"You still haven't told me why you are here. Why what I know should be important. I'm just a humble tavernkeeper with a few memories."

"Precious memories."

"Don't tell me what to say."

"Unless Sophie lied, you were the one person Mozart turned to when he fell mortally ill. That he felt he could turn to."

"So? I was here!"

Deborah said, "You could have run away. As my husband could have run away when he discovered that Mozart might have been poisoned, and instead seeks to find the truth, however difficult. As you nursed him, however difficult that was. But if you don't help us, we will never know."

Diener deliberated, then asked, "What do you want to know?"

Jason said, "If you could tell us what he ate when he got ill."

"He didn't get ill here!"

"I didn't say that, and neither did he."

"What did Mozart say?" Diener snapped.

"Mozart said he got sick after eating at Salieri's and that you were the first person to see him after that."

"That's true."

"And several weeks later he was dead."

Diener said sorrowfully, "It was the most melancholy time of my life."

"Did anything occur that made you suspicious of Salieri?"

"That is a very serious accusation."

"Mozart made it. Should we ignore him?" Diener was listening intently and Jason said passionately, "Mozart wouldn't have come to you first if he hadn't thought you could help him, would he?"

"It was too late," Diener said sombrely. "He was past helping."

"Do you know why?"

Diener pointed to the empty chair and said sadly, "It happened here, right in his favorite chair. It was a miserable November night, rainy and cold. There was hardly anyone in the tavern because of the weather, and suddenly I saw Mozart in the doorway. I was shocked by his pale, emaciated appearance. It was not a night to be out unless you had something vital to do, and I wanted him to sit by the fire. Instead, he insisted on sitting here, although he was so weak I had to help him to the chair.

"Then I asked, 'Do you want anything, Herr Kapellmeister?'

"He shook his head No, but I ordered some wine. Yet when it came, he couldn't touch it, his hands in front of his eyes as if to shut out what he was seeing; and I asked him what was wrong, and he whispered, 'I have that burning pain in my stomach again, Joseph, and I can hardly stand. And my head is on fire. As it was after Salieri's dinner.'

"I took him home then. He couldn't have done it alone, although he lived just around the corner. And by the time we got there we were drenched, and meanwhile I had also sent for his doctor.

"I kept remembering something else. Several weeks before, Mozart had gotten into the habit of dropping into the Golden Serpent for his meals, which had to be very carefully prepared—he had had some violent stomach attacks the past few months—and when he didn't appear at the tavern for several days, I was sure something was wrong.

"As I expected, I found him in bed. He hadn't eaten for several days, but he hadn't called anyone. I asked him what had happened, and he pointed to his stomach and said, 'It's ruined. It's hard to swallow the wrong things. Do you think I made a mistake, accepting Salieri's invitation to dinner? When I left his rooms I felt fine. *The Magic Flute* had gone beautifully, even Salieri seemed impressed, yet several hours later I was dizzy, nauseous, and my stomach cramps were violent. And still are.'

"I shrugged. How could I reproach him? But my flesh crawled, for Salieri was not his friend. Everybody knew that. Yet I said, 'You must have been hungry for a good meal. Especially with your wife away.'

" 'I was, Joseph!' he cried, 'Hungry and lonely!'

" 'What did you eat there?' I asked. 'Perhaps it was the food.'

" 'Oh, no! He served livers of geese that were remarkable!'

" 'But you are not supposed to eat them, Kapellmeister!' I exclaimed. 'They've upset you for a long time.'

" 'One time shouldn't have hurt me, and they're such a delicacy. Although I did think that they were on the fatty side.'

" 'Why didn't you have veal? That is all that Maestro Salieri ever eats here. Preserved veal, if possible, and he always insists on seeing the meat before we cook it. If the flesh isn't pink, firm, smooth, and fine-grained, he won't touch it. Let the meat have the slightest discoloration or blotchiness or fat, and he acts as if we're trying to poison him. Yet veal is his favorite dish. Salieri should have served you that.'

" 'He said he wanted to serve a German dinner in honor of *The Magic Flute*, that he had gone to great pains to find out what I liked.'

"And what could make Mozart ill, I thought, but he was agitated enough without my adding to his suspicions. Then I recalled that Salieri had even gone into my kitchen several times when he had been eating in the Golden Serpent the same nights that Mozart was. To make sure, he said, that his veal was properly spiced. Salieri claimed that too much spice or the wrong one could be as harmful as acqua toffana."

Jason interrupted, "Are you certain about this, Herr Diener?"

"Some things are vague, but not this. Salieri's behavior used to puzzle me, for he always ignored me otherwise, but it shouldn't have surprised me. Salieri always liked to have his own way."

Diener seemed to shrink within himself with grief as he said, "When I told Salieri no self-respecting tavernkeeper like myself would make such mistakes, he replied—I always remembered this, for I resented his implication—'One man's food can be another man's poison.'

"Oh, I've tried to shut that out of my heart! But then I see Mozart clutching the bedpost in his anguish even as we were talking, yet saying to me, 'I had such a need for a good dinner.'

" 'After the way Salieri has acted to you, Kapellmeister?' I asked.

" 'It's a large world. I thought there was room in it for both of us. And Salieri said at dinner, 'I've gone to such pains, Mozart, to have something you like.' He was proud of his table. But later I had the strangest metallic taste in my mouth and a terrible thirst.' "

Diener paused, then said thoughtfully, "Mozart grew faint, and when he recovered some strength, he didn't want to talk about that dinner—I think because it disturbed him so much. Instead, he tried to compose and teach, although he had only one pupil, a young medical student, and one day this pupil came when I was there. I had to let him in, Mozart was too weak, I had just brought Mozart his daily soup and wine, and Mozart insisted on seeing him, then begged him to keep studying. And while the medical student said he would and left two gulden, I knew he would never return, and Mozart must have known it, too, for he sat staring after him as if his music room was filled with ghosts. And soon after, Mozart was gone."

Jason said, "You've been very helpful. We will always be grateful."

"You won't be able to prove it. They won't allow that in Vienna."

"I don't intend to prove it in Vienna. Was there anything else?"

"Mozart said that there had been an unusual amount of garlic in the food, but he didn't question it, since Salieri, as an Italian, would favor it for seasoning, although he thought that, too, was hard on his stomach."

"Now do you think he was poisoned by Salieri?"

"How can you be sure without the body? It was strange. The weather wasn't that bad, and he wasn't unknown. If it had been somebody like myself, a humble tavernkeeper who died impoverished, such a burial would have been expected. But Mozart had been famous all his life, from the age of six, and his latest opera was the toast of Vienna."

Jason said, "That is one of the reasons we embarked on this search."

"Persist," Diener blurted out suddenly. "But be careful."

"You be careful, too," Deborah said, and took his hand warmly. "We don't want you to be harmed on our account."

"That's what Mozart said when I brought him his meals. He said I was neglecting my business. I don't think the authorities will bother me. I'm too insignificant to be considered dangerous." Yet as he escorted them to the door, he appeared to have grown in stature. He held his fine head high, as if his shrunken body didn't matter, although his eyes were red with emotion. And suddenly he said, "I should be grateful to you, too. You've reminded me of things I forgot. I wished that I could have turned Mozart inside out to learn what had damaged his insides. And strange, but after Mozart died, I don't recall Salieri ever coming here again, and certainly never again into our kitchen. I've wondered often why Salieri ate here at all. It surely wasn't his kind of food."

A week after they had seen Ernst at the White Lamb, they met him there again. But Ernst, instead of being excited by what they had learned from Diener, said it was what he had expected and was just another link in the chain that was almost complete. "Two more links, probably," he whispered to them. "I've arranged for you to see Gottlieb and Salieri. Gottlieb is eager to see you, I think almost too eager; and I met Salieri's keeper at our lodge meeting, and he is trying to arrange a time when it will be safe. Is there anything new with Beethoven?"

"Not a word," said Jason. He had seen Beethoven one day in a café on the Graben and had been tempted to talk to him, but Deborah had said it was not the place to approach him, and he had heeded her advice.

"It is just as well," said Ernst. "The important thing is that the authorities still believe that the oratorio is your reason for being here."

He gave Jason the address where they could visit Anna Gottlieb and the time she would be available to see them.

38

Anna Gottlieb

ROYAL red curtains draped the tiers of boxes. Gold-brocaded chairs were everywhere. Huge crystal chandeliers hung from the ceiling. Many high silver mirrors adorned the walls. Purple tapestries covered the windows and bore the Hapsburg Imperial Eagles. But the Burg-theater was empty except for the vocalist rehearsing on stage with the accompanist.

It was midday, the time arranged by Anna Gottlieb to meet her. The front door had been open, and Jason and Deborah had walked in without seeing anyone, only to halt at the rear at the sound of her singing.

Yet this was the address Ernst had given them, and Jason had had Hans drive them here, for a visit to the Burgtheater shouldn't arouse any suspicions. Jason thought it was wise to arrange their meeting with her here, and some of his confidence in the old musician returned.

But he hadn't expected such indifferent singing. Her voice was small and cold, and she looked insignificant upon the stage as he and Deborah stood listening in the rear of the theater. And the Burgtheater had such an empty, barren feeling. The music sounded like Mozart, but for once his music didn't seem worth this expenditure of energy.

When she saw them she indicated they should join her on the stage. She didn't introduce them to her accompanist, an elderly, wispy man, but told him to return in a few minutes. Jason apologized for interrupting her rehearsal, and she said, "It was my idea for you to come now."

Anna Gottlieb hadn't said why, however, thought Deborah, and she sought to observe her without staring. Her hair was a natural brown, and she must have been quite pretty when she had been younger, Deborah decided; but now she was fifty with heavily shadowed eyes and wrinkles on her neck. She was short, yet she stood with authority. She didn't ask them to sit down, but addressed them as if she were doing the questioning.

Jason asked, "You are singing his music, Madame Gottlieb?"—he had learned by now that all female performers were addressed as Madame—and she replied, "Yes. Do you think he was poisoned?"

Jason was startled, while Deborah said cautiously, "We are trying to find the truth," even as she felt that Anna Gottlieb was hiding something.

"It is the music that matters," Anna Gottlieb said abruptly.

They were interrupted by a young man who said, "I'm sorry to interrupt you, Madame Gottlieb, but I'm from Count Sedlnitzky's office."

"What is it now?" She looked resigned and not pleased.

"The censorship office wants to know the nature of your program."

"Songs. By Mozart. Utterly harmless music."

"I'm sure you're right," the tall, lean young man said quietly, "but the Emperor has said we must be fastidious about anything with words, and you are singing music with words."

She handed him her program and said, "I hope you find it is diverting."

He read it quickly and said, "I'm sure it will be a beautiful program."

"When will I know if the program will be permitted?"

"In a few days."

"You won't wait until the performance? As you did with Beethoven?"

"I don't think so. This music should be, say . . . *gemütlich*."

She frowned, then said, "All the arias are devoted to love."

"I'm sure that Count Sedlnitsky will be delighted. As soon as the words can be read, you will be given an answer." He retired.

Deborah expressed alarm that there might not be a concert, and Anna Gottlieb said, "Money works wonders. If I make the proper donation to whatever charity the Count has organized, the concert should go on."

Jason asked, "Has it always been that way?"

"Yes. But worse since Metternich. I haven't anything else to say."

Jason was so disappointed he couldn't speak, and Deborah, sensing that, said, "You agreed to meet us."

"I said I would see you. I didn't say I would talk to you."

"Isn't it the same thing?" But she felt almost as helpless as Jason.

"No."

Deborah was silent too now, wondering if this was a nightmare.

Then Anna Gottlieb smiled slyly and said, "However, if you would like to attend my concert, something might be arranged."

Jason was too angry to say yes, but Deborah managed to mutter politely, "We would be honored, if it wouldn't be too much trouble."

"Trouble to sing Mozart? Difficult, yes, but not trouble. I was told you are at the White Ox Inn on the Platz Am Hof. Is that correct?"

Deborah nodded, hoping that she was doing what Jason desired.

When he was still reluctant, Anna Gottlieb said, "The music is Mozart."

It sounded almost like a concession, and he asked, "Why did you agree to see us here if you didn't want to talk to us?"

"I wanted to find out if you were cannibals or missionaries." Her accompanist had returned, as if on cue, and she dismissed them.

Jason thought her remark too enigmatic to mean anything, and he said, "She is probably afraid of the police, or she has been warned off since Ernst spoke to her. She will not send us the tickets, it is just a gesture." But Deborah replied, "I think it is something else. Whatever her reasons for being so curt, she hasn't told us and I doubt that she will."

"Then you do think that she will send us the tickets?"

"Yes. She just doesn't want it to appear too easy."

Two tickets arrived several days later with a brief note: "If you enjoy the concert and would like to stop backstage afterward I will be in my dressing room." Jason was angry enough to refuse, until Deborah reminded him that Mozart had liked her voice enough to cast her as the original Pamina and Ernst had said that it was rumored that she had been in love with Mozart. But he went expecting very little.

The Burgtheater glowed with life and color. Every seat was taken, and they were in a box on the first tier and next to the stage, the best box in the theater for hearing. Jason saw Schindler in another box, Schubert standing in the pit and gazing up at the stage with eager anticipation, the young police official in the wings, and Ernst sitting in the rear of the pit where little could be seen but where the acoustics were good.

Anna Gottlieb began with one of Susanna's arias from *Le Nozze di Figaro*; then she sang an aria by Despina from *Così fan tutte* and an aria by Zerlina from *Don Giovanni*, music he had never heard. She concluded the first half of the program—after the accompanist played a Mozart sonata—with another aria from *Le Nozze di Figaro* and one from *Die Zauberflöte*.

The first of the final pair was Cherubino's *"Voi che sapete."* The small, cold voice of the rehearsal had become strong and warm, but what attracted Jason was not this tremendous improvement or her superb style or her authoritative technique, but her emotion. She was singing with such love it was as if Mozart were standing before her.

Deborah was as absorbed as he was, he noticed with delight, when Anna Gottlieb began *"Ach, ich fuhl's"* from *Die Zauberflöte*. She sang with so much tenderness he felt Mozart must have written this aria for her. Every note came from her heart. Every note sang. The words didn't matter. The notes were the words. They were indestructible.

Jason longed to apologize to her. This aria was irresistible, and he could only listen and be grateful that his search had brought him to this.

And as she came to the last part of the aria she had introduced to the world so many years ago at the age of seventeen, she stood in front of the intent audience and it was as if a gentle prayer was rising out of her. Then Jason felt she was calling Mozart and Mozart was calling her, and gradually desolation crept into her voice. Now she was singing that she couldn't find him and never would, and in her grief Jason felt stricken. The notes died away with the utmost delicacy, and his eyes were wet.

During the intermission he had no desire to talk to anybody. He was grateful Deborah sensed that, for she sat by his side silently and seemed content to stay there. He couldn't tell whether the recital had penetrated her the way it had him, but she kept staring where Anna Gottlieb had stood.

The second half of the program was different in tone, two concert arias, a soprano solo from one of Mozart's unfinished masses, and a miniature concerto for a soprano in three movements, his *Exsultate, Jubilate*.

By now he knew he shouldn't be amazed. Yet he feared the intrusion of anything that could come between him and the music, and he shut his eyes and listened for the moments of melodic peace and beauty. But he thought, too, of the long journey that had brought him here. This music pierced his heart and offered a dream of happiness which was disapproved by so many human acts. Was the beauty of Mozart's music an illusion? Yet long after the concert ended, the echo of the music remained.

He went backstage reluctantly. He had told Hans to wait outside of the Burgtheater with their coach, that he wouldn't be long. Madame Gottlieb's maid expected them and led them into her dressing room. There were a dozen people paying their respects, and Jason saw Schubert and Schindler and the young police official among them, but before he could talk to any of them, they were gone. Deborah was more sure than ever, however, that Anna Gottlieb was hiding something, for when she saw them she looked pleased and asked them to sit down.

Jason muttered, still self-conscious, "We haven't much time."

More to protect himself than anything else, Deborah thought, for when Anna Gottlieb took his hand and drew him to a chair, he sat down.

But he said, "We can only stay a minute."

"Of course," she answered. "What did you think of the concert?"

"It was beautiful. I wondered why you were giving it here, the Burgtheater seemed too vast, too . . ."

"Cold and barren," she added. "It always is when there is no

audience. But more of his music was played here than anywhere else."
Deborah was surprised that Anna Gottlieb was ignoring her other
callers, although they seemed important in their formal clothing and
jewelry. "This is where four of his operas had their Vienna performance, where three of them were world premieres. He played many
concerts here. These walls have heard his concertos, symphonies, music
of his of all kinds. Think of what they could tell us if they could speak.
No other place in Vienna was so appropriate for his music. I had to use
the Burgtheater. It belonged to him. It was his theater."

Jason bit his lip, not sure he should say it; then he had to. "They
should have buried him here."

"How fitting!" There were tears in her eyes, and she turned to the
others and said impulsively, "I hope you will excuse me, but my young
friends"—indicating Jason and Deborah—"have come all the way
from America to talk about Amadeus, and they will be leaving soon."

The dressing room emptied quickly, but when they went to follow,
she stopped them, saying, "I meant that."

Jason said, "But what you said at the rehearsal."

"That was a rehearsal."

Deborah asked, "Were you testing us?"

"I had to find out how you felt about Amadeus."

Deborah said, determined to be as candid as she was, "And you
loved him, didn't you?"

"I was seventeen and he was thirty-five. And when I first sang for
Amadeus for the original *Figaro*, I was only twelve. As he said, a
child."

Deborah said, "A child's love is sometimes the most enduring."

She changed the subject. "Herr Otis, what did you want to know?"

Jason repeated, "Madame Gottlieb, were you testing us?"

"I was testing your regard for Amadeus. Why you were here."

"I've asked myself that many times. Actually, as I see it now, I never
could have any contentment with my mediocre talent. I was compelled
toward a great talent, the greatest, and when I heard Mozart's music, I
felt something I had never felt about myself. It was as though I could
no longer remain at peace within my own body. And perhaps this is
why I've searched for his body. This pursuit has become more natural
to me than anything I've ever done. I've even made a martyr out of my
wife."

"Not a martyr," Deborah interrupted, deeply touched by what he
was saying, "but impatient sometimes."

"Yet I've had to go on. Just as Salieri had to destroy the greater
talent, I have to revive and return life to it."

"What surprises me is that someone didn't make this inquiry
before."

Deborah said, "Perhaps they were afraid. We've been threatened."

"So was I. When I was cast for *The Magic Flute* I was warned that I would never sing again in the Royal Opera Company if I took the role."

Jason asked, "And what happened, Madame Gottlieb?"

"I never sang a Royal opera again. But, fortunately, I didn't have to. I became an actress. After Amadeus died, I had no taste for opera."

"Then why did you give this concert?"

"I sing his music in concert whenever I have the chance."

"How was Mozart's health when *The Magic Flute* opened?"

"Fine. He told me, *'I must be temperate, eat plain food, nothing spiced, nothing fat, but if I am careful, I should have no trouble.'* "

"Yet he ate differently at Salieri's?"

"He may not have realized what he was eating until it was too late."

"Did he ever rehearse with you?"

"Often for interpretation, Herr Otis."

"Did he have pain when he sat at the pianoforte? If one has kidney disease, it is impossible to sit there for any length of time."

"He rehearsed me shortly before he fell ill, and he had no such pain. But we had other concerns. It was believed that *The Magic Flute* was based on Freemasonry and that the Queen of the Night was a harsh portrait of Maria Theresa. I heard that made the Hapsburgs angry at Amadeus."

Jason asked, puzzled, "Then why did Josepha sing it?"

"A Weber could never resist anything musical. They were a very musical family, and it was a striking role, with two brilliant arias."

"Did you know Josepha or Aloysia Weber?"

"They ignored me. They were prima donnas. But fine singers. Pamina was my first major role, but Aloysia looked down on it. To her *The Magic Flute* wasn't opera, and she was critical of Josepha for singing in it."

Deborah said, "Da Ponte believed that *Figaro* was held against Mozart and that the Hapsburgs never forgave him for that."

"It is possible. The character of Figaro is rebellious, and the music justifies that. I know that it irritated the Court. And by the time *The Magic Flute* was done, Amadeus was in such bad repute with the Hapsburgs, I'm sure they would have supported Salieri in anything he did to Amadeus. But the situation was a paradox. Once Amadeus left the Burgtheater for the Freihaus Theater auf der Wieden, his career was over as far as the Hapsburgs were concerned. Yet *The Magic Flute* was such a popular success it scared the life out of Salieri and must have made him murderous. Then Amadeus, in composing *The Magic Flute,* was liberating himself from the Hapsburgs and their establishment, something they could not forgive or tolerate. Salieri knew this, and it must have given him the courage to follow his impulses and prompted him to act, knowing that whatever he did to Amadeus, he would not have to pay the consequences."

Jason asked, "You think the Hapsburgs actually encouraged Salieri to harm Mozart? To poison him?"

"Not directly. Not by telling him to do so. But by implication. By looking the other way and supporting Salieri in whatever he did."

"Is there anything else that happened that makes you wonder now?"

Anna Gottlieb grew reflective. She had been very young when she had fallen in love with him, and she had loved him a long time, ever since she could remember. She hadn't wanted to talk to them before because they were intruding on her privacy, her secret love, and she had kept it a secret. Yet one thing she had experienced had baffled her; and perhaps if they heard about it, they might help her understand it. She said slowly, "There was someone at the cemetery the night of his funeral. Myself."

They looked astonished as she expected, and she continued. "I didn't believe Salieri when he said that it was going to storm. After the others turned back, I decided to follow the coffin. But it was too far to walk, and by the time I was able to find a carriage, the funeral cart was out of sight. I never did catch up with it, although I urged my driver to hurry. But his horses were old, slow; and while I felt I was going faster than the funeral cart, I wasn't going as fast as I wanted to go. Yet I knew I should reach St. Marx's before the burial was finished; I should have time to pay my respects and mark the spot. But it was December, the days were very short, and when I arrived at the cemetery night had fallen and everything was dark. There were no gravediggers or funeral-cart drivers about; indeed there was no one about except the caretaker.

"He told me there had been some burials earlier, but he didn't know anything about Amadeus' body; he had no recollection of any funeral cart having arrived recently. I sensed, however, that the caretaker felt sorry for me. I was young, pretty, and he must have thought from my grief that the missing body was my lover. So, to console me, I suspect, he pointed to a pile of freshly spaded dirt and said, 'He must have been put there, in the common grave.' I walked to where he pointed. The ground was newly dug, and as I stood there I made a silent prayer for Amadeus.

"But I have always wondered about the swiftness of the burial. Not much time could have elapsed between the moment the funeral cart could have come and my own arrival. Had the caretaker taken the path of least resistance and sent me to the common grave to avoid complaints?"

Jason asked sadly, "Why didn't you think of that then?"

"I was grief-stricken, in a state of shock. All I could think of was that he couldn't have disappeared; his music would always be a part of me."

"And now?" asked Deborah.

"Now I think it is possible Amadeus' body never reached St. Marx's."

They sat in stunned silence until Anna Gottlieb said, "That is another reason I sing his music every chance I get."

Deborah said intensely, "Then you did love him. And still do."

"I am proud and grateful that I knew him." Anna Gottlieb hesitated, and then impulsively took a locket off her neck and handed it to them, saying, "This is the most precious thing I own."

On one side was a miniature of Mozart, on the other a withered flower.

"Amadeus gave me this carnation at the opening of *The Magic Flute*. He said, *'You must always be charming and admirable.'* I will treasure that as long as I live. I think at that moment he did love me."

They regarded the flower so reverently it prompted her to continue.

"It will be buried with me, in St. Marx's. I have arranged to be buried there."

Then she was emotionally exhausted, but even as she was saying goodbye and Jason and Deborah were thanking her for a beautiful concert, she had to add, "If you see Salieri, be careful. I don't think that even now you can be sure whether he is sane or insane. But there was one thing he could not take away from Amadeus. His music. That is his triumph. Amadeus remained true to his music to the very end, and for that we must be eternally grateful."

39

Salieri

JASON was still thinking of Anna Gottlieb's parting words when Deborah discovered that their coach was gone. At first he couldn't believe it. He had given Hans orders to wait, but there wasn't a coach in sight. St. Michael's Platz was deserted, and even the cafés on the Kohlmarkt were closed. He knew they were within walking distance of their inn, and he had memorized the route—straight down the Kohlmarkt to the Bognerstrasse and then left and on to the Platz Am Hof—but he had a bitter taste in his mouth. He felt that Hans had betrayed him after all. Then he thought of Anna Gottlieb, she could drive them home, but when he turned to the Burgtheater the doors were locked and she was gone.

He took a silent, oppressed Deborah by the arm and said that since they had to walk, there was no reason to wait. They went arm in arm through the shadowy Kohlmarkt. It was after midnight and the streetlights were dim. They heard only the sound of their own footsteps and saw no one else. He felt better when they turned into the Bognerstrasse without incident, although this was a narrower, darker thoroughfare, for while they still hadn't seen anyone else, they were almost at their inn.

Jason sighed with relief as the Bognerstrasse curved into the Platz Am Hof. It had been an effort to keep his composure, for the walk had been terrifyingly dark and quiet. He had expected to be ambushed at any moment, and he hadn't even a sword for protection. He almost felt safe now, even when he heard the clop clop of horses' hoofs. For a moment he was glad—there was someone else about. Then a monstrous black object careened out of the narrow mouth of the Bognerstrasse and hurtled down upon them. In that instant he realized that it was a massive coach. Instinctively he pulled Deborah into a doorway as she screamed, "They've lost control!" The coach missed them by inches and then it was gone, but Jason wasn't sure that the driver had lost control.

Even after they stood in the inn, he was filled with horror at how close they had come to being run down and possibly killed. But he said, "It must have been an accident. A runaway."

"Or a warning," she replied, white-faced and shocked. "But I don't think there will be any more warnings. The next time it will be the real thing. We ought to pay heed to it, and leave. I can't stand much more."

"I've come too far to turn back. If I don't see Salieri now, I'll never forgive myself. But we'll go," he promised, "as soon as we see him."

Yet the next day when Jason returned from the stable, where he had gone to find out why Hans had left him to walk home last night, he was having a new struggle to retain his composure. Deborah was waiting for him in their reception room, and he said in a torrent of emotion, "He wasn't there. I always treated him like a human being. I never thought he would do that to me. I left word that he come here as soon as he returns."

"Do what? What did he do?" Deborah asked. Jason was quite shaken.

"Maybe I shouldn't have done it, but his coat was hanging on a hook, and after what happened last night I had to look, even if it meant spying."

"What did you find?"

"He had a list of all the places he had taken us to in his pocket."

Hans was at the door, saying, "Someone came out of the Burgtheater, sir, and said not to wait, that Madame Gottlieb was taking you home."

Jason asked, "Do you know who it was?"

"A man I had never seen before. He said he worked in the theater."

Hans stated that with such conviction Jason believed him. But when Jason confronted him with his list and he insisted that he was innocent, Jason was sceptical, pointing out, "It is a list of everywhere we've been."

"Sir, somebody must have put it in my pocket."

"In your handwriting? No wonder Huber knew where we had been."

"Not because of me. Herr Otis, I am devoted to your interests."

"I should have dismissed you months ago," Jason said suddenly. "But I will pay you in full. Then I expect you to be gone at once."

"You can't, sir!"

Deborah asked harshly, "What do you mean, we can't?"

"If you dismiss me, I'm lost."

Deborah said coldly, "You'll get another job. Betray someone else."

"I won't be able to get another job. I know you've never liked me, Frau Otis, but if I lose this post I don't know what will happen to me."

"You are an informer," she said. "As I assumed."

"You musn't assume anything." He knelt at her feet, kissing the hem of her skirt in an agony of pleading. "If they hear I've been dismissed, they'll kill me. I've already been warned about that. A long time ago."

Jason had been counting out Hans's wages, but he looked up. "When?"

"When we first came to Vienna. I wanted to quit then, but they wouldn't let me. It was either drive you, or jail. I had no choice."

Jason said, "After what happened last night, even if I hadn't found this list, I would have had to dismiss you."

"What did happen last night, sir?"

Deborah said, "We were almost run over."

"That's why I was told to go home," Hans said somberly. "Couldn't you keep me in your service? Just don't take me with you when you have certain places to visit. As you have been doing anyway."

Jason was startled, "What are you referring to?"

"It is known that you slip out the back way."

"And I am being followed?"

"I'm not sure. But it is known that you try to avoid it."

Deborah asked, "How do you know?"

"I've told you too much already." But Hans's terror was real. "They won't find out anything from me that will hurt you."

"Who will find out?" Jason asked. "Huber?"

Hans was so afraid he couldn't speak. With trembling hands he reached out entreatingly to Jason. If they knew his heart, they would not blame him. He didn't want to violate anybody's trust, but he didn't want to die either, he thought plaintively, and until they started back for America he had to be sure he was working for them.

Hans was holding on to him so tenaciously Jason couldn't endure it. He thrust Hans's pay into his icy-cold fingers and said, "If you are not off these premises in an hour I will report to the police that you confessed you were in their employ and betrayed them."

"What will you do with your coach?"

"I will hire another driver, if necessary."

"They will make him a spy, you see."

Jason pushed Hans out the door, although his trembling didn't cease.

They met Ernst each week while they waited for him to arrange the meeting with Salieri. But Jason resolved to go as soon as that was done, whatever happened with the oratorio. He hadn't heard from Beethoven or Grob, and he was relieved by their absence; he was in no mood for pretence.

Ernst was pleased with the way the mission was going. He said that the near coach accident had been very likely a drunken driver—they were common in Vienna, and many people were injured and killed in such idiotic accidents—they must just be more careful. He didn't think they should be upset about Hans; if Hans hadn't spied on them, someone else would have. The vital thing, Ernst declared, was not to be caught.

And even while Jason was almost as anxious as Deborah now, he was delighted with the April weather. Spring had come to Vienna, and most of the days were mild and soothing, and as they strolled about the city no one bothered them. There was no sign of Hans or anybody else who might be watching them, and if they were trailed, there was no trace of it.

Jason felt that his view of Mozart and Salieri was almost complete. He used this interval to store in his memory what he had learned, so that he could avoid carrying any incriminating papers, and Deborah joined him in this memorizing. In gratitude he was romantic to her, and she felt that perhaps he did love her, although he still hadn't said so.

Many nights, while they waited for the meeting with Salieri, they were able to indulge their sexual satisfactions with a passionate ardor. There seemed no limit on how much they could enjoy each other. Jason felt that she had become gentler, warmer, lovable. Deborah thought he was almost knowable, and now he seldom looked for vicarious gratification in Mozart. And yet she, too, felt Mozart in the labyrinth of her memory, and she had a new view of their journey. It had become a necessary venture that would come to fulfilment in America when Jason published what they had learned. She was determined that if no one would publish his revelations, she would furnish the money for that herself.

Jason didn't replace Hans, but Ernst wasn't worried about their lack of a driver. He said, "I'll hire the driver myself. My friend is waiting for the best time to see Salieri. Some weeks he is very ill, other weeks he is better."

But when the date was settled, it was hard to believe. It was arranged for the second of May, in the evening when it would be dark, yet Jason was very careful when they slipped out of the inn. He had developed the habit of going out the front door to lure whoever might be watching them into apathy or carelessness, and so when he went out the rear for the first time in several weeks, he was gratified that no one saw them. Around the corner they entered a coach that Ernst had hired. The driver was being well paid, and Ernst had advised Jason to bring twenty-five gulden for the keeper—Ernst said the keepers were paid very poorly—and so Jason carried an extra hundred gulden for any emergencies that might arise.

Neither Jason nor Deborah spoke as they rode to the hospital, each of them contemplating the questions they wanted to ask Salieri. Jason longed to hurry, while Deborah wished it was over with; and Ernst was in no mood to indulge in pleasantries, as if, finally, in this act, he had become a personage, and anything else would be superficial.

Ernst halted the coach within walking distance of the hospital, but out of sight, and told the driver to wait, unless he saw any officials, and then to drive away. He took Jason and Deborah to the rear of the hospital, and there, as planned, the keeper was waiting for them.

Ernst didn't introduce anybody by name, but simply referred to the three of them as "my friends," which was safer, and left them at the gate.

The keeper was tall, gaunt, elderly, with a shuffling walk and a morose manner. He unbolted the high iron gate with a large key, said grimly, "If we are careful and lucky, you should have no trouble getting in and out unobserved. No one uses this part of the grounds except to bring in the food and to take out the garbage. None of our inmates are allowed out of the hospital, and our rare visitors enter and leave by the front door."

"Can't we be seen from the windows?" Deborah asked. As they approached the flat, shabby gray building, it looked more like a prison than a hospital, and she noticed that there were bars on all the windows.

"If anyone sees you in the dark, which is unlikely, they will think you are members of the Vienna council that donates money to our upkeep. Your clothes will indicate your wealth. Don't worry, everything has been prepared carefully. I was a member of the same lodge as Mozart and Muller. But remember, if anyone comes in, nobody knows that except us."

At the door to Salieri's quarters the keeper hesitated until Jason handed him twenty-five gulden and said, "For getting us in. There will be twenty-five more when we are safely outside."

The keeper nodded and unlocked a heavy steel door which opened on a spacious room. There was a bed in one corner, a pianoforte in another, a mirror near the entrance, thick bars on all the windows, and as the steel door closed with a clank, a reminder that this was also a prison.

Salieri sat at the pianoforte, staring vacantly into nothingness, his back to them. He didn't turn when they entered, as if he hadn't heard them, and Jason whispered, "Can't he hear?"

"His hearing is satisfactory. It is his attention. It wanders."

Salieri shifted his position as they stood there, and now Jason could see him better. Time had wrought havoc with him, thought Jason; he had become very old and frail. Salieri's small body had shrunk, and the cosmetics he had daubed on his face gave his skin a grotesque, painted look. The flesh on his face had eroded, and by contrast his bulbous nose and pointed chin had become too large for the rest of his features. Yet his eyes were dark, bright orbs in two cavernous sockets. They lit up as he saw them, and then, not recognizing them, lapsed into sullenness.

The keeper whispered, "Don't offer him any food or talk about it. It makes him suspicious. He eats very little, and then only after we taste it first. He is always talking about his cats who were poisoned. He says that people are always trying out poisons on cats."

Deborah asked, "Why is he here?" Ever since she had heard about his confinement in this hospital, she had wondered if he was really insane, although Jason from the beginning had assumed that, or whether he was being kept in protective custody by the Court as a way of silencing him? The keeper gave her a strange look, and she added, "Medically?"

"His nature keeps dividing. Often he acts as if he is being persecuted; other times he has a strong need to talk about his conquests. It is like a war going on inside him. It is so fierce sometimes, I think it is going to wear him out. I doubt he will live much longer."

Deborah said, "Yet he is not in bed."

"He says that if he goes to bed he will never get out. He dresses every day, as if that will keep death away. Yet there are moments I think he would welcome it."

"Has he tried to commit suicide?" Jason asked.

"Not here. Maybe now that he is seventy-five, he has to hold on to whatever life he has left. Even when he wants to die."

"Yet you say that he doesn't know we are here."

"I'm not sure. He may be pretending, to find out who you are. He is very suspicious, he doesn't trust anybody. That is one of the ways he is ill."

Jason asked, "How much time do we have?"

"About half an hour. I made sure the other keeper would be absent before I arranged this meeting, so no one else will know you were here."

"Suppose Salieri talks about it?"

"Nobody will believe him. He talks to himself, he says he hears voices, he has many delusions. But you will be lucky if you can get him to talk at all, he is so suspicious."

Deborah impulsively yet fearfully walked toward Salieri, who recoiled and retreated into a corner as if to hide, mumbling, "I am Antonio Salieri, born Legnano, Italy, 1750, died Vienna, 1791, a pupil of Gassmann, and composer and First Court Kapellmeister after Bonno. Born 1750, died . . ."

His voice faded into an unintelligible monotone, and Jason said excitedly, "Died 1791! Does he say that often?"

"It's a date that fascinates him. He is always talking about it."

But when Jason spoke to Salieri, he turned his back. To have come so far and then fail was too much to endure, and as Jason desperately tried to think of what to do, Deborah suddenly reached out for Salieri's hand, which was limp and cold, and said, "We are friends from America."

Salieri repeated "America" as though it were an unknown place.

Deborah persisted. "America is the New World. On this side of the ocean it is the Old World. Columbus discovered the New World."

Suddenly Salieri seemed to grasp something and he said,

"Columbus, my countryman. The most famous Italian explorer in the world. I am Italian."

"Yes, we know. You are right to feel such pride in your countryman."

Salieri smiled wanly, then became distracted.

Jason said, "We've never been to Europe. This is our first visit."

Salieri pulled his hand out of hers and ignored both of them.

She said, pronouncing each syllable carefully, recalling that Salieri disliked German and seldom spoke it, "Our parents in America, since we were coming to Europe for our honeymoon, asked us to see an old friend they had lost track of. We were told you would know where we could find him."

Salieri's attention had returned to her, and he was listening again.

She added, "Our parents haven't seen our friend for a long time. Do you know where we can locate Mozart, the composer?"

Salieri was terribly jarred, and he gazed fearfully behind him and at the door, and whispered breathlessly and secretively, "He's not here."

She asked, "Do you know where he is, Maestro?"

"They won't allow me to say that name. All these years, how many years. Shhh . . ." Yet he seemed relieved as he cried, "I'm an old man, I'm sorry I was ever a young man. They won't allow a priest to come to me and hear my confession. Oh, my soul will burn in hell if I can't confess!"

Jason said gently, "You can say Mozart to us as much as you like."

"Will you get me a priest since you knew my countryman?"

"I will try to be your priest. Say Mozart. There's nothing wrong in that."

Salieri groaned, appeared about to utter something he had yearned to say for a long time, and then he halted and glared at them suspiciously again. He was hearing voices again, they were talking to him, but it wasn't these Americans, but a voice that should have been dead for many years. Then he heard another voice, arguing with the first voice, and it sounded like his own, angry, disturbed, terrified. The first voice was Mozart's. But it couldn't be, he shouted back inside, it was not 1791. Yet it persisted, saying, "You committed murder four times." And he was denying that, even as he remembered that three of his cats had died. But he had loved his cats. Every chance he got he had taken them on his lap and had stroked them, and if they had died suddenly and mysteriously, there had been no other way to test acqua toffana on a living organism and he had felt very sad. Were these Americans snooping? Were they here to denounce him? If he could only exorcise that first voice! Wasn't Mozart ever going to give him any peace! He had gone to the funeral, personally.

Deborah said, "We are fond of the pianoforte, Maestro. Would you mind playing for us? One of your own sonatas?"

He thought, Perhaps that will shut out these voices, and he said,

"This is a favorite of mine. I composed it for the Emperor himself."

Salieri played with such concentration, care, and devotion that Jason sensed that music was his God, what mattered to him more than anything else. His eyes glowed, and the music which was dull at first became gay and sparkling. Jason cried out, "You are playing Mozart!"

Salieri halted and shouted furiously, "It's mine! It's Salieri!"

But when he resumed, the sonata was even more Mozartian.

"I'm sorry," Jason said, "but it is Mozart, Maestro."

Salieri became hysterical, banging on the keys loudly and discordantly and declaring, "It isn't! We're not allowed to mention that name here! Did I tell you what I did to him?" He waited avidly for their response.

There was an intense silence. Even the keeper was listening carefully.

Salieri announced, "In a hundred years they will not play his music at Court. I was the First Court Kapellmeister. I didn't imitate him. I was better than him. I was older. Six years older. I taught Beethoven, Schubert. Without me, Beethoven would be nothing. I could have taught him, too, only he wouldn't listen. Even as a child he considered himself my superior, I, the richest and most important and powerful musician in the Empire."

"What happened then?" Jason asked.

"I conquered him! What is this nonsense about his music? I put it in its place." He picked up a sheet of music as if it were a document and said, "This is what I told the Emperor to write him when an opera of his was submitted to the Imperial and Royal National Court Theater."

Salieri read as if he had memorized the following many times:

Thank you for submitting to us the score of your latest opera, Le Nozze di Figaro. We on the committee have considered your work and we are forced to inform you that there is no possibility of giving this work at the present time. There are no interesting or new things in your score, and you have repeated many things that have been already more eloquently expressed in Paisiello and Gluck's work, which we feel renders your present work superfluous and unsuitable. The committee also believes that your libretto would not be received favorably at Court, with many personages of high rank taking offence at certain passages. We feel your opera has neither the distinction nor the merit to be considered favorably. We will send you ten gulden for your recent performance of your dinner music, and in calling, you are requested to use the rear entrance. The Hofburg is the Emperor's favorite residence, and His Majesty is disturbed by the boot marks you left on the grand entrance.

Jason asked, "Maestro, did you really tell the Emperor to write this?"

"Yes. My own words. I had more influence than anybody else."

"But *Le Nozze di Figaro* was done. Even if this letter was written."

"Emperor Joseph overruled me. He wouldn't allow it to be sent. But I'll send it now. Joseph's brother, the new Emperor, listens to me."

"He's dead. His son Franz rules now. And has for many years."

"The Royal family are my dear friends. At the Congress of Vienna I directed a concert of one hundred pianofortes. I knew they disapproved of him. *Figaro* has vanished like his body. Can you find his body?"

Jason was shocked. Was Salieri sane after all and defying them?

Salieri paced up and down, looking triumphant.

Deborah asked, "Did the Royal family agree with you about Mozart?"

"Of course!"

"Did they tell you?"

"Madame, I am not a crank, a madman. They didn't have to tell me. I understood their feelings. I was a *virtuoso*. Prince Metternich said that I was such a master of intrigue that if I had been his opponent he would truly have had to worry. Do you think I am here because I am sick?"

"Why are you here?" Deborah asked.

"Shhh." Salieri became very conspiratorial. "I'm here to be protected. There are people who wish to see me dead."

"Who?"

"If I told you, you would tell them. But I got rid of da Ponte."

"He is still alive," Jason reminded him.

"He will never write opera without me. His partner is dead."

"Did you feed Mozart livers of geese the last time he had dinner with you?" Jason asked.

"That barbaric German garbage! Who said that?"

"Several people. Did you use the livers to poison him, Maestro?"

Salieri said authoritatively, "Many foods can kill one, not just poison."

"Then why did you give Mozart such food? If you didn't like it?"

"It was not poison. There are many ways to poison one, a packet of powder dropped in wine, an infected glove, a poisoned water closet."

"And then the body vanished," Jason said thoughtfully.

"The ashes were strewn to the wind. There was nothing left to tell anything. When a body cannot be found, no one can be brought to trial."

"Did you go to the cemetery?"

"There was a terrible storm. It drove me away."

"Do you know why the body vanished?"

Salieri started to laugh and he couldn't stop and his laughter became hysteria, then tears, and suddenly he was afflicted with an attack of coughing and he looked as if he was going to choke. The keeper handed him some water, but he refused to take it until the keeper sipped it first, then he gulped it furtively and his coughing ceased. But now he lapsed into a sullen silence, shunning them, thinking, They are closing in on me, dragging me back, if I poisoned the cats it was my own business, they were my cats, and they will never find the apothecary, I gave him a false name and he didn't know me, he was very old even then and he must be dead by now, and no apothecary could detain a casual customer asking for a poison, even arsenic, and they can't touch me, I have connections at Court, that is why I am here, if I could only find a priest, then I wouldn't care, I wouldn't burn in hell through all eternity.

Then he heard the keeper saying to his visitors, "You had better go. I wouldn't want him to die while you're here. It could be most embarrassing, and dangerous. His health is very bad. It could happen any time now."

And there were other voices, too, shouting in his head, "No more time to lose, Antonio, no more time to lose, Antonio, you are dying, all your days are done and distributed and you have no more time, they are closing in on you." And as he turned toward his visitors he saw himself in the mirror in the wall. But that was not him, he exclaimed to himself. That was a stranger. The man in the mirror was old, ugly, shrunken, broken.

Torn between his need to boast and his need for repentance and weighted down by the burden of the past, Salieri stared frantically into the mirror until that image was the only reality, and the voices mounted again in his head—Mozart's, but he was dead, da Ponte's, Joseph's, and then Mozart's again. Wasn't Mozart ever going to allow him any peace? Couldn't he ever be rid of him? Mozart was creeping up on him, out of the grave, but there was no grave. If Mozart would only go away!

Salieri went to smash the face in the mirror, that ought to stop the shrieking voice in his head, what a crescendo that would be! and then he paused, did they hear what he heard—such beautiful music! And he was filled with despair and envy and hate, for he knew he could never write such music, and he could never forgive Mozart for that.

Jason and Deborah started toward Salieri, for he looked as if he were going to walk straight into the mirror. But at the last instant he halted inches away from his reflection in the glass, put his hand to that face to blot it out, and shrieked, "Assassin! Assassin!"

When the figure in the mirror didn't answer, he evaded their grasp and fell upon the floor, begging for release from his tortured body and screaming, "What I did to Mozart!"

40

The Final Solution

ERNST was waiting impatiently for them outside the gate, and before they could speak he was asking, "Did he confess? You were so long.

Jason was too shaken by Salieri's behavior to answer quickly, while Deborah was silent so that he could manage the situation. He gave the keeper twenty-five gulden for seeing them out safely, and the keeper wished them bon voyage and shuffled back to his patient.

Ernst was too emotional to wait any longer, and he whispered, "What did Salieri say? He didn't convince you that he was innocent, did he?"

Jason said, "He said many things. Some of which I believe."

"Do you think he is guilty? Now that you've spoken to him directly?"

"I am convinced."

"You will expose him when you return to America?"

"I will tell what I've learned." Deborah had walked on while they were talking, eager to get away from the hospital. Jason hurried after her, and as he helped her into the coach, he asked the driver to be careful.

Deborah, who was still wondering about Salieri's behavior, said, "He had to assume guilt, because even if he didn't do it, he wanted to."

"No," said Jason. "Salieri did more than just want to. Ernst, it was ugly, shocking, terrifying. I believe Salieri knew very well what he was doing, that he was causing Mozart terrible pain and suffering, that he was not mad then, but malevolent, assassinating Mozart in many ways."

He was relieved that nothing happened the next few days, and he told Deborah, "Apparently we did succeed in remaining undetected, and there will be no painful consequences." On her urging he was deciding to make the final arrangements about the oratorio and their departure, whatever the state of the commission, when they received an unsigned note from Ernst:

Salieri has died. Yesterday, May 7. There is a brief announcement in the newspapers but no cause of death is stated. I think it

advisable that you leave Vienna as soon as possible, oratorio or no
oratorio. If it gets out that you saw him a few days before he died,
you could be blamed.

Jason visited Grob at once and said that since their visas were
expiring soon, it would be better if they left now, before there would be
any complications, and that he would like the oratorio to be delivered
now.

Grob didn't seem surprised by Jason's decision, but relieved, thought
Deborah, who had accompanied Jason. The banker said that he was
sorry to see them go, but May was an ideal time for traveling. He would
have their funds ready for them in a few days, and he would send
Schindler to them as soon as he reached him.

Jason asked, "Couldn't I see Beethoven himself?" He wanted very
much to say goodbye to the composer in person, whatever the fate of
the oratorio.

"Not unless you wish to go to Baden. He is there because of poor
health, and he has left Schindler in Vienna to do his business."

"You think he hasn't finished the oratorio?"

"Yes. As I warned you. I hope you are not too disappointed."

"It would have been a great honor for Boston. When will I get back
the money I left with you if the oratorio is not forthcoming?"

Grob affectionately put his arm around Jason as he escorted them to
the door. "You know I have always held your interests in the highest
esteem. We'll settle the account after you hear from Beethoven."

The possibility that there would be a further delay caused Deborah
to be restless and anxious again, but Jason assured her that this was
normal with bankers. She didn't agree. She felt that their affairs were
going too smoothly to be trusted, and she had no faith in Grob either,
but she tried to be patient, and she hid her apprehensions.

To her relief, Schindler appeared promptly at the inn the next day,
in obvious distress, and said sorrowfully, "It causes me great pain, but
it is impossible for the Master to complete the oratorio."

Jason asked, "Is this official?"

"Indeed! I'm his agent, although Grob acts as if he is."

"What's wrong with Herr Beethoven?"

"He's upset by the food he has been fed. He feels he's been
poisoned."

"Poisoned?" Jason was startled and Deborah was shaken.

"Not like you think, but by bad food and worse cooking. But
perhaps Schubert could compose your oratorio for you. You remember
him?"

"Yes, yes," said Jason, "But he is a composer of songs."

"Essentially. But he needs a commission desperately. He's had very
bad luck lately. He was at Gottlieb's concert, the one you attended, in

the hope she would sing his music; but she said she sings only Mozart now. Then he has written a new opera, but the subject has been prohibited by the censor. He is very depressed. The oratorio would be useful to him."

Jason had thought from the moment he had met Schubert that the composer could use twenty-five gulden better than Constanze and some of the others he had given money to, and suddenly he said, "I could give him some money."

"For the oratorio?"

"No, no, we've stayed in Vienna too long as it is. As a present."

"Schubert would never take it," Schindler said mournfully. At the door he said abruptly, "Of course, you heard about Salieri?"

"Heard what?" Jason sought to look blank, unknowing.

"He died. Suddenly. Unexpectedly."

"Indeed!"

"You don't sound as surprised as I thought you would be, Herr Otis."

"I had been told he was quite ill. What was the cause of death?"

"Strange, but there's been no official reason given in the newspapers. The announcement was shockingly terse. There's no mention even of where Salieri is to be buried. Were you able to see him before he died?"

For a moment Jason was tempted to tell him, but then he said, "I'm afraid not. Would you excuse me, Herr Schindler, we have to pack."

"Too bad. It would have been interesting to talk to him. I trust you have a safe journey." He bowed like an envoy from an imperial power and handed him a letter. "It is from Beethoven. A farewell note."

The instant Schindler was gone they read:

My Dear Honorable and Cherished Friends:
I write you to tell you of my regret that I have been unable to deliver the oratorio as I promised. It has caused me much embarrassment and suffering. I have started it many times but it has been impossible for me to sit at my writing desk without difficulty or pain, and so, sadly, I have been unable to continue to compose as I used to. This is something I would have preferred to have told you in person, but I am sure you will understand my position when I say my health has deteriorated so badly I have had to seek recuperation amid the unspoiled nature of Baden. But I will always remember the generosity with which you paid your respects. It has made me think much about Mozart and Salieri since I spoke to you, and I have come to the conclusion that Salieri will be remembered only because of Mozart, and that Mozart will be remembered forever. So be it.
I wish you a happy and healthy journey home and I embrace you and your lovely wife in heart and in spirit. Your friend. Beethoven.

Grob refused to give Jason the four hundred gulden the Society had mailed him for the oratorio, saying, "It belongs to them. I have to send it back as they sent it to me," and when it came time to return the other hundred gulden, he handed Jason fifty.

Jason expostulated, and Grob looked deeply hurt and said, "Dear Herr Otis, I would give you my heart if you needed it, but as your agent in this matter I must have ten per cent of the total as my fee for the difficulties I have endured. The letters I wrote, the appointments I made, the abuse I ʳook from Beethoven. How are you going? The voyage up the Danube from Vienna to Linz is beautiful at this time of the year."

Jason had not given this matter much thought, but the idea of taking the coach road that had caused them so much discomfort was an unpleasant prospect.

"I will give you drafts on banks in Munich and Mannheim so that you won't have to carry much cash. I'm sorry about the oratorio, but Vienna is an education in itself. Did you hear about Salieri?"

Jason and Deborah nodded, not wanting to commit themselves.

"Sad. Such a distinguished career. To come to such an end. Most distressing. I hope you are not too disappointed about the oratorio."

Jason sighed, then shrugged.

"Yes, the more I think about it, the more I would go by boat to Linz if I were you. Besides, since you dismissed your driver, it will be easier than hiring one." Grob sounded like he was inspired now. "You could use the money from the sale of your coach for the water ordinary, then go by public diligence all the way to Paris and the Channel."

I am terrified of the water, Jason wanted to shout. I can't swim, not a stroke, the trip across the Channel was one of the worst moments of my life. But he was ashamed to admit that and he was silent.

Deborah liked the idea of going to Linz by boat. She had worried about the coach trip, it was so easy to have an accident, and she said, "It would be more relaxing, Jason. Especially at this time of the year."

Grob said, "The Danube is calm at this time of the year."

"How long will it take?" Jason asked.

"Two or three days. And it is the way Mozart first came to Vienna."

"Let's take the boat, dear," Deborah said. "It would be a change."

She was so eager he agreed, although hesitantly and reluctantly.

It was the visit to Huber that worried Jason the most. He had destroyed all his papers; he had not heard from Ernst since the note about Salieri; he saw no reason why they should be detained, since they had enough money to take them to America. Yet there was the constant fear that Huber would find an excuse to detain them or throw them into prison. But he couldn't put it off forever, and finally, when all the business arrangements had been concluded and he still hadn't heard from Ernst, he and Deborah went to Police Headquarters to ask for their passports.

To their surprise they were admitted to Huber's office quickly. Huber didn't rise to greet them or ask them to sit, but he did say, "Grob notified me that you are leaving. You are lucky to have such a worthy banker as your agent. He tells me that you are taking the water ordinary to Linz, Otis."

"Probably," Jason answered.

"We will find out in any case. You wouldn't want any more delays?"

"No."

"How much did you get for your coach?"

"Fifty gulden."

"I told you that the man who sold you the coach in Mannheim overcharged you. You paid two hundred gulden for it, didn't you?"

Deborah said, "You have a good memory, Herr Huber."

"It is serviceable. As yours is, I'm sure." For a moment she felt he was saying something to them beyond the meaning of his words. "Did you think I would believe that Beethoven would compose your oratorio?"

Jason said, "It was a genuine offer."

"We are not that easily deceived. And we are not toothless either."

Neither Jason nor Deborah replied. Both had the same fear: Huber was going to detain them after all. And Jason had a feeling that Huber knew about all their visits, even the one to Salieri, and wanted them to know that; that whatever views Huber had to express officially, his vanity was so vital to him that he had to remain in a position of superiority to them, had to let them be aware that they had not fooled him.

"But it would be pointless to detain you. We don't want any scandal."

Jason said, "May we have our passports, Herr Huber?"

Huber took them out of his drawer in exchange for the temporary visas and said, "You are wise to go now. When the weather is good." He wrote across their passports in a large, bold script, *"approved,"* added, "That will simplify the customs' procedures," and handed them to Jason.

This was difficult to believe. Jason felt, somehow, that his sudden feeling of optimism was treacherous, yet Huber was smiling as he spoke.

"We don't want to discourage visitors from America. As long as they are not dangerous to the Throne."

"Thank you, sir. We appreciate your cooperation."

"As we will appreciate yours. Did you hear about Salieri?"

"We heard that he died. We saw that in a newspaper."

"And now we must let him rest in peace. Correct?"

"Yes, Herr Huber."

"The guard will show you out."

With the same motion, Huber called the guard and turned back to his desk without even a gesture of dismissal. The guard appeared instantly, as if this had been timed carefully, and his appearance shocked Jason. It was the guard who had insisted on being bribed to get them out of the cell. But now, as he led them out, it was as if they had never seen each other.

On the street Jason said to Deborah, "That should be the end of Huber."

"I hope so." She walked away, to be rid of the Vienna she hated.

Two days later Jason and Deborah were about to board the boat for Linz. They had gone through the customs and police examination without any difficulty; Huber's *"approved"* had eliminated the previous difficulties. Jason was hurt that there had been no word from Ernst, although Deborah secretly was relieved, when suddenly, abruptly, Ernst appeared.

Ernst was dressed in his best clothes, and when Jason got over his surprise, he exclaimed, "Why so late? And wouldn't it have been safer to have seen us privately? So they didn't know about our connection?"

Ernst said, "I don't think there is any danger now." Deborah was frowning. "What's wrong, Frau Otis, aren't you glad to see me?"

"It's unexpected," she said. "Like so many things you've done."

"My sources of information indicate that the authorities, with Salieri dead, hope the situation will be forgotten. And I couldn't allow you to go without saying goodbye. After all, I brought you here."

She was surprised to see tears in his eyes.

He put his arms in theirs, and placing himself between them emotionally, he walked them to where no one else could hear him and said passionately, "If I have hurried you, if I have been hasty or curt or rude, please forgive me. I am an old man and I haven't much longer to live. So I prodded you, to keep you going. Perhaps more than I should have."

Deborah asked, "You didn't think we would go through with this?"

"I never could be sure. You were strangers. Americans. How could I be sure that Mozart would mean much to you?"

Jason said, "He gave my life meaning."

"I couldn't be sure until you saw Salieri and proved what I suspected."

Deborah said, "You are sure now, aren't you, Herr Muller?"

"As sure as it is possible to be. As your husband said, Mozart was assassinated by Salieri, by the Hapsburgs, the nobles, indifferent friends, carelessness, inefficient doctors. But I think the actual physical culprit was Salieri with poison and poisoned food."

"I agree," said Jason, "It was an assassination and assassinations."

"You two, you strangers, have justified my life. I felt that my life would not be in vain if I could cleanse Mozart's memory, take away the stigma that he died because he was foolish, stupid, improvident. I never could have rested in life or in death until this was proven wrong. I could never have written about it here."

Deborah said, "We will do our best. When we get back to Boston."

"I'm sure you will. But be careful, please. The boat trip is lovely and the public coach from Linz should be comfortable, the highways are good at this time of the year, but an accident could still occur."

Deborah asked, "What did happen to the musician who died in our rooms?"

"That has always troubled you, hasn't it."

"Yes."

"I'm not sure. He was found hanging from a rafter. It was known that he was in disfavor. And there was no reason he would commit suicide. But I didn't want to worry you, and it was the only way that I could get you such good rooms. You should be safe now. We musn't think of death now. You have many years ahead of you. Goodbye."

Deborah was embracing him and Jason was shaking his hand and Ernst was crying and saying, "It is hard to stay in one piece."

The last they saw of Ernst was an old man walking away from them, his head down, determined not to look back. It was too painful to look back, for he knew, as they did, that they would never see each other again. They would not return to Vienna and he was too old to go to America.

None of them saw the big coach and the four horses that bore down on Ernst after he went through the gate and out of their sight. There were many conveyances near the docks, and Ernst was thinking of Jason and Deborah and staring at the ground in front of him, the cobbles were rough here and he didn't want to slip. Then he heard the sound of heavy hoofs on the cobbles and he turned to see where it was coming from. It couldn't be a drunken driver, he thought, in the middle of the day. He felt a stunning blow on the back of his head, another smashing blow in the neck, and then there was only blackness. As the wheels of the coach finished the work the hoofs of the horses had begun, the driver whipped them on and increased their speed and was around the corner and out of sight before anyone could identify him. Ernst Muller was dead. His body, its neck broken, lay silently just out of sight of the boat to Linz.

The first day Jason and Deborah rested. But as the weather remained clear and the Danube calm, they spent most of the second day on deck. The boat was comfortable, filled with middle-aged peasants and small-town folk going home after visiting relatives in Vienna, and they saw no one they knew. They didn't mind; they wanted to be alone. They liked the deck, and after dinner the second day Jason wanted to spend more time on it.

Deborah didn't want to go on deck, they had been on it most of the day, and she said, "I'm tired. And you did promise to go to bed early tonight."

Jason smiled. Last night had been their best night together. When they had made love, he had felt that finally, now that they were going home, they were united in spirit as well as in the flesh. And he had convinced her that he had been right to take this journey, he thought, that he had not been a fool. Even if she didn't admit that, her passionate response did. It had been easier to give to her, for he was starting to understand himself better, particularly some of the reasons that had driven him on this quest. But he couldn't tell her that by standing out by the rail he was fighting his terror of the water and that was vital, too.

When she said, "Please, Jason, it is getting chilly, and dark, and soon there will be nothing to see," he said, "In a few minutes. I don't want to go to sleep yet, and the twilight is beautiful. Look!"

The boat had swung south suddenly with a curve of the river, and the setting sun was in their eyes and over the far shore.

He was thinking, Mozart has been an effort to fight against my own insignificance as much as to find out the truth. But that didn't upset him now, for he felt now that greatness was for only the rare moments, that one had to go on with the day-by-day affairs, that constant excitement, even at best, was exhausting. And he was homesick, although he couldn't admit it.

Yet when Deborah took his hand, he said, "I'm glad we're going home."

"And no regrets?" she asked.

"There are always regrets. But we did the best we could. I learned a little more about the world, Mozart, myself."

"I think you learned most of all about yourself."

"It is possible this journey was an exploration of myself, too. As composing must have been for Mozart. Until his life was cut short."

"You are sure he was assassinated?"

"Yes. The more I put the pieces together, the more I am convinced that his body, weakened by neglect, poverty, and poor medical attention, was an easy victim for Salieri's poison and tainted food. I believe that Salieri gave him arsenic in the form of acqua toffana over a period of months until Mozart's body was vulnerable, and then he finished the job with tainted food so that he wouldn't be discovered. And then saw to it that the body disappeared to prevent any further investigation."

"I wonder how many assassinations are unknown?"

"We'll write about it. Isn't the country beautiful?"

"But so desolate. I thought when we approached Linz the country would become more settled. Instead, there isn't a sign of life on either bank. And it is so rough! The mountains come right down to the shore. It would be almost impossible to climb onto it, even if one reached it.

And as it is, if one fell overboard it would be a very long swim." She shivered.

"I wouldn't worry," he said. "The boat is stable, and the water calm. We must stop being afraid, Deborah. We can't live with constant fear."

"Yes, with Salieri dead, we should be safe. Let's go to bed."

"Just one moment. When the sun goes down. It'll be only a few seconds."

She thought she felt somebody behind them, but when she turned no one was there.

"We'll take the express coach from Linz, so we can get home as quickly as possible. I must improve myself as a musician, despite my mediocrity."

Deborah replied strongly, "You are not mediocre. You comprehend music very well, and you have helped me to comprehend it better also."

Jason was listening intently. It had grown totally dark, and it was time to go below. There was nothing to see at all now, nightfall had blotted out the shore, but he wanted to hear what else Deborah had to say, she was in such an understanding mood. He thought he heard footsteps nearby as she spoke, but he was so involved in what she was saying that he ignored them as she declared, "You have made Mozart live for me, too. You have convinced me that . . ."

Jason didn't hear the finish of her sentence. He was falling, somebody had pushed him. They had been ambushed after all, and he couldn't swim! As he hit the water, the air in his lungs brought him to the surface. He saw Deborah swimming toward him. They had pushed her, too, he thought in a rage, and he must help her. He gasped, "I got you into this, I must get you out. . . ." But the boat was pulling away, and the shore was so far from them, and he heard her cry, "Hold onto me, I'll try to make land." She slipped an arm under his shoulder to keep him up. He felt her cheek against his, and he wanted to protest, she could swim to safety if she would only let him go. Instead, she was trying to propel him toward shore, and he was filled with a terrible weariness, and he couldn't move, and as they went under he felt a deep sadness that they could have done this to Deborah. Then it was cold and dark, and his body went down with her vainly fighting to overcome the pull of the water, until just a few air bubbles and ripples remained and the dark was everywhere.

Several days later it was reported in the Vienna newspapers that Mr. and Mrs. Jason Otis of Boston, travelling on the Danube water ordinary from Vienna to Linz on their way back to America, had been swept overboard by a storm and drowned and their bodies had not been found.

When Grob recovered from his shock, he wrote her father a letter of condolence. Quincy Pickering must not think that he was a barbarian.

It is with deep regret that I must inform you of the death and disappearance of your daughter and your son-in-law on their way from Vienna to Linz by boat. Sadly, their bodies were not recovered after they fell overboard, the Danube is very wide and deep near Linz, but everyone in Vienna is convinced that it was an accident.

Meanwhile, I am sending you the money you deposited with me for the oratorio, and since I gave your son-in-law drafts for most of the money you sent recently for banks in Munich and Mannheim, I am pleased to inform you that not everything was lost.

I trust that when you recover from this terrible loss you will be able to keep in touch with me and that we will continue to do business.

Rest assured, I will always remember your daughter with affection. I am sure, too, that you will be relieved to know, as I was, that there will be no need of an investigation. The authorities are convinced it was death by accidental drowning, as I am, and that is the official verdict.

Yours respectfully. Anton Grob.

But one thing nagged him. Had he told Huber too much? Then he decided that he had behaved quite honorably. It had been his duty to keep the authorities informed, even about his friends.

Huber was promoted soon afterward. Before he left his old office, however, for his new quarters as assistant to the chief of police, he cleaned out his desk. He lingered with considerable satisfaction over his file on Ernst Muller, and then wrote on it: *"Closed."*

Then he examined his dossier on Hans Denke. The driver had kept him informed, but eventually, like most frightened servants, he had failed to fulfil his obligations. And he had learned too much. Denke had left him no choice, and it had become necessary to dispose of him too. That had been the only solution. No one in the Empire would question the death of an itinerant coach driver. That happened frequently, and it would be assumed that it had been an accident. And nobody would know whether the horses had kicked him or not.

It was with even more satisfaction that he came to his file on Jason and Deborah Otis. When he wrote *"Closed"* upon it, he had a special feeling of accomplishment. Only one thing irritated him. The official account had stated that there had been a storm, when that could easily be disproved. And then he decided that this inconsistency didn't matter much, once the bodies had disappeared, nothing vital could be proven.

He burned all the files.

The bodies of Jason and Deborah were never found.

Sources

Anderson, Emily, *Letters of Mozart and His Family*, 2 v. 1966.
Anthony, Katherine, *Marie Antoinette*. 1933.
Artz, F. B., *Reaction and Revolution*. 1934.
Ayles, H. N., and Brookes, V. J., *Poisons, Their Properties*.
Baedeker, Karl, *Austria*. 1900.
                    Austria. 1923.
                    Eastern Alps. 1911.
                    Southern Germany. 1923.
Barea, Ilse, *Vienna*. 1966.
Barrington, Daines, *Account of a Very Remarkable Young Musician*. 1770.
Barzini, Luigi, *The Italians*. 1964.
Bayr, Rudolf, *Salzburg—City and Province*.
                    Beethoven—Impressions of Contemporaries. 1927.
Belloc, Hilaire, *Marie Antoinette*. 1909.
Berlioz, Hector, *Evenings with an Orchestra*. 1956.
Biancolli, Louis, *The Mozart Handbook*. 1954.
Blom, Eric, *Mozart*. 1963.
Bonavia, F., *Musicians on Music*. 1957.
Bond, Raymond T., *Handbook for Poisoners*.
Boos, Dr. William F., *The Poison Trail*.
Bourne, C. E., *The Great Composers*.
Breakspeare, Eustace, *Mozart*. 1902.
Brion, Marcel, *Daily Life in the Vienna of Mozart and Schubert*. 1962.
Brockway, Wallace, and Weinstock, Herbert, *The World of Opera*. 1962.
Broder, Nathan, *What Was Mozart's Playing Like?* 1959.
Brown, M. E. J., *Schubert*. 1958.
                    Essays on Schubert. 1966.
Browne, C. A., *The Story of Our National Ballads*. 1960.
Browne, G. L., *Reports of Trials for Murder by Poisoning*.
Burk, John N., *Mozart and His Music*. 1959.
                    Life and Works of Beethoven. 1943.
Burney, Charles, *A General History of Music*, 4 v. 1789.
                    Dr. Burney's Musical Tours in Europe. 1959.
Castelto, André, *Queen of France*. 1957.
Castiglioni, Arturo, *A History of Medicine*. 1941.
Chase, Gilbert, *America's Music*. 1955.
Cooper, Martin, *Gluck*. 1935.

Cox, Cynthia, *The Real Figaro*. 1962.

Creed, Virginia, *All About Austria*. 1950.

da Ponte, Lorenzo, *Memoirs*. 1929.

Demuth, Norman, *French Opera—Its Development to the Revolution.*

Dent, Edward J., *Mozart's Operas*. 1947.

Deutsch, Otto Erich, *Mozart—A Documentary Biography*. 1954.
　　　　　　　　　　　　Mozart—His World in Contemporary Pictures. 1961.
　　　　　　　　　　　　Schubert—A Documentary Biography. 1946.
　　　　　　　　　　　　Schubert—Memories by His Friends. 1938.

Dolge, Alfred, *Pianos and Their Makers*. 1911.

Durant, Will and Ariel, *The Age of Voltaire*. 1965.
　　　　　　　　　　　　Rousseau and Revolution. 1967.

Eaton, Harold, *Famous Poison Trials*.

Einstein, Alfred, *Essays on Music*. 1956.
　　　　　　　　Gluck. 1962.
　　　　　　　　Greatness in Music. 1941.
　　　　　　　　Mozart, His Character, His Work. 1945.

Ellinwood, Leonard, *The History of American Church Music*. 1953.

Elson, Arthur, *The Book of Musical Knowledge*. 1927.

Erang, Robert, *Europe from the Renaissance to Waterloo*. 1939.

Ewen, David and Frederic, *Musical Vienna*. 1939.

Fitzlyon, April, *The Libertine Librettist*. 1957.

Friedell, Egon, *Cultural History of the Modern Age*, v. I, II. 1954.

Frischauer, Paul, *The Imperial Crown*. 1939.

Funk, Addie, *Vienna's Musical Sites and Landmarks*. 1927.

Garvie, Peter, *Music and Western Man*. 1958.

Gay, Peter, *The Age of Enlightenment*. 1966.

Geiringer, Karl, *Haydn*. 1946.

Gheon, Henri, *In Search of Mozart*. 1934.

Glazer, Josef and Heinz, *A Guide to Schönbrunn*. 1965.

Gloag, John, *Georgian Grace*. 1956.

Gooch, G. P., *Maria Theresa and Other Studies*. 1951.
　　　　　　Catherine the Great and Other Studies. 1954.
　　　　　　Germany and the French Revolution. 1920.

Goodwin, A., *The European Nobility in the Eighteenth Century*. 1953.

Gotch, J. A., *The Growth of the English House*. 1889.

Graf, Max, *Legend of a Musical City*. 1945.
　　Great Styles of Furniture.
　　Grove's Dictionary of Music. 1927.

Hadow, W. H., *Oxford History of Music—The Viennese Period*, v. V. 1931.

Hamburger, Michael, *Beethoven—Letters, Journals and Conversations*. 1960.

Hamlyn, Paul, *The Life and Times of Beethoven*. 1967.

Harding, Rosamund, *The Piano-Forte*. 1933.

Harding, T. S., *Fads, Frauds and Physicians*. 1930.
Herman, Arthur, *Metternich*. 1923.
Herriot, Edouard, *The Life and Times of Beethoven*. 1935.
Holmes, Edward, *The Life of Mozart*. 1845.
Houts, Marshall, *Where Death Delights*.
Howard, John Tasker, *Our American Music*. 1929.
Hunt, Leigh, *Dramatic Criticism*. 1949.
Hussey, Dyneley, *Wolfgang Amadeus Mozart*. 1928.
Hutchinson, Ernst, *The Literature of the Piano*. 1964.
Jahn, Otto, *The Life of Mozart*. 1882.
Johnson, W. B., *The Age of Arsenic*.
Josephson, Matthew, *Stendhal*. 1946.
Kelly, Michael, *Reminiscences*, 2 v., 1826.
Kenyon, Max, *Harpsichord Music*. 1949.
        Mozart in Salzburg. 1953.
        Mozart's Letter Book. 1956.
Kerst, Friedrich, *Mozart*. 1905.
        Mozart—The Man and the Artist Revealed in His Own Words.
King, A. Hyatt, *Mozart in Retrospect*.
Knock, W. J. G., *Austria and the Hapsburgs*. 1960.
Kochel, Ludwig von, *Chronological and Classified Listing of W. A. Mozart's Works*. 1965.
Kohn, Hans, *The Hapsburg Empire*. 1961.
Leverus, A. S., *Imperial Vienna*. 1925.
Loesser, Arthur, *Men, Women and Pianos*. 1954.
London Detection Club, *Anatomy of Murder*.
Lowenberg, Alfred, *Annals of Opera (1597–1940)*. 1943.
Marek, George R., *Opera as Theater*. 1962.
Mattfield, Julius, *Variety—Music Cavalcade (1620–1950)*. 1952.
Morris, Constanze Lily, *Maria Theresa*. 1937.
McGuigan, D. G., *The Hapsburgs*. 1966.
Nettl, Paul, *Mozart and Masonry*. 1957.
Neumann, Paul, *A Guide through the Imperial Palace (Hofburg) of Vienna*.
Nicolson, Harold, The Age of Reason. 1960.
        The Congress of Vienna (1815–1822). 1946.
Novello, Vincent, *A Mozart Pilgrimage*. 1855.
Padover, S. K., *The Revolutionary Emperor, Joseph the Second*. 1934.
Perkins, C. G., *History of the Handel and Haydn Society of Boston*.
Pick, Robert, *Empress Maria Theresa*. 1966.
Plumb, J. H., *The First Four Georges*. 1957.
Praz, Mario, *An Illustrated History of Furnishings from the Renaissance to the Twentieth Century*. 1964.
Prezzoline, Giuseppe, *Machiavelli*. 1960.
Pushkin, Alexander, *Mozart and Salieri*. 1830.

Quennel, Marjorie and Peter, *History of Everyday Things in England (1733–1851)*. 1934.

Rickett, Richard, *St. Stephen's Cathedral in Vienna*.

Roberts, Henry D., *The Royal Pavilion—Brighton*. 1959.

Rolland, Romain, *Beethoven the Creator*. 1929.

        A Musical Tour Through the Lands of the Past. 1922.

Roughhead, William, *Trial of Dr. Pritchard, Poison in the Pantry*.

Rude, George, *Revolutionary Europe, (1783–1815)*. 1964.

Russell, Raymond, *The Harpsichord and Clavichord*. 1959.

Schenk, Erich, *Mozart and His Times*. 1959.

Scherr, Marie, *Poison At Court*.

Schindler, Anton, *Beethoven as I Knew Him*. 1960.

Schlegel, Richard, *The Castle of Hohensalzburg*. 1962.

Schlink, F. J., *Eat, Drink and Be Wary*.

Schmiedbauer, Alois, *Salzburg*. 1956.

Schonberg, Harold C., *The Great Pianists*. 1963.

Sedgwick, H. D., *Vienna*. 1939.

Shaw, Bernard, *How to Become a Musical Critic*. 1961.

        Selection from the Musical Criticism of Bernard Shaw. 1955.

Sigerist, Henry E., *The Great Doctors*. 1958.

Sitwell, Sacheverell, *Baroque Art*. 1928.

        Great Palaces of Europe. 1964.

Smith, E. H., *Famous Poisonous Mysteries*.

Spaeth, Sigmund, *The History of Popular Music*. 1948.

Sullivan, J. W. N., *Beethoven*. 1927.

Summerson, John, *Georgian London*. 1946.

Thayer, A. W., *The Life of Ludwig van Beethoven*. 1960.

Thackery, W. A., *Miscellanies (The Four Georges)*. 1873.

Thompson, C. J. S., *Poison and Poisoners*.

Thomson, R. H., *Liberalism, Nationalism, and The German Intellectuals: (1822–1847)*. 1952.

Thomson, Virgil, *Music Reviewed—(1940–1954)*. 1967.

Towson, Robert, *Travels in Hungary and Vienna*. 1797.

Turner, W. J., *Mozart, The Man and His Work*. 1938.

Valentin, Erich, *Beethoven—A Pictorial Biography*. 1958.

        Mozart—A Pictorial Biography. 1959.

Vaughan, Warren T., *Strange Malady*.

Wandruszka, Adam, *The House of Hapsburg*. 1964.

Wangermann, Ernst, *Joseph II to the Jacobin Trials*. 1959.

Watson, E. B., *Sheridan to Robertson*. 1926.

Weiss, David, *Sacred and Profane*. 1968.

Wickenburg, Erick G., *Salzburg*. 1961.

White, E. W., *The Rise of English Opera*. 1951.

Wyndham, S. H., *Annals of Covent Garden Theatre*. 1906.

Zweig, Stefan, *Marie Antoinette*. 1933.